EDEN

Dean Crawford

Copyright © 2013 Fictum Ltd

All rights reserved.

ISBN: 1494939479
ISBN-13: 978-1494939472

Also by Dean Crawford:

The Ethan Warner Series
Covenant
Immortal
Apocalypse
The Chimera Secret
The Eternity Project

Eden Saga
Eden
Eden: Redemption

Holo Sapiens Saga
Holo Sapiens

Soul Seekers Saga
Soul Seekers

Individual novels
Revolution

Want to receive notification of new releases? Just sign up via: http://eepurl.com/KoP8T

"We men are wretched things."

Homer, the Iliad

It wasn't supposed to happen this way.

For all of us a new era had begun, an age for which none of us could have been prepared. Some said that mankind's fall had been written in our bloodline throughout eternity, nature's gifted yet volatile child doomed to destroy itself. Scribes wrote of it and film-makers imagined it, of our collapse amid the wrath of our own hellish devices. Yet when it happened there were no explosive impacts, no pandemic diseases turning humanity into flesh-eating monsters, no nuclear disasters or conflicts of nations fought through blood and bullets upon smouldering plains of ash. Instead it fell upon us as gentle as starlight, our only warning the very skies above us. We call it now the Great Darkness.

Once thriving cities awoke to absolute stillness; once vibrant citizens to utter despair. They fled for their lives as others slept or worked or watched television or tended fields across the globe, unaware of the disaster rushing toward them, of horrors not known since our ancient ancestors huddled around meagre flames in lonely caves, fearing the darkness and the beasts of the night as they long awaited the coming of dawn.

The collapse was swifter than any of us could have imagined possible. What we had believed might take months or even years occurred within weeks. Man turned against man, woman against woman, child against child in a world starved of all but the weapons of war. Most were driven by the insatiable lust for food and water, the rest for power in the violently shifting world around them. We became the animals that we had always been, some grovelling on our knees in terror, others rampaging with dark hearts bared. Amid panic and conflict the spectre of disease decimated entire regions. Untended and crumbling power stations imploded and spilled their toxic wastes into the atmosphere to scour the land with a seething hail of acid rain and radiation. Cities burned, and amid their smouldering remains the poisoned, starving survivors haunted the streets in the wake of the four horsemen. No human endeavour prevailed: no hope, no technology and no religion. The time of man had come to an end.

It was the silence that killed us: the silence that followed the calamity which brought our species to its knees in a single night and our own inexcusable silence beforehand. It pains me to admit that we could have defended against it. That we should have defended against it. But long before the Great Darkness we had already abandoned the compassion that generations of our forbearers had laboured so hard to culture, and thus had we lost our humanity in every sense of the word.

Senator Larry Dennis, formerly Boston, USA

ALERT FIVE

National Aeronautics and Space Administration Directive: NPD/3765.11/CR

Study: Psychological stress via sustained social deprivation.

Purpose: Initial terrestrial assessment of human capacity for long-duration mission to Mars.

Your name, age and qualifications: *Jake McDermott, 54, climatologist.*

Mission duration: *6 months*

Location: *Alert, Nunavut, Arctic*

Write a brief narrative to justify your funding request from NASA:

I am the leader of a six-strong team of scientists due to spend several months in complete isolation in the northern-most inhabited location in the world, on behalf of the United Nations Global Atmospheric Watch program. Our Air Chemistry Observatory, Alert Five, is located just five hundred nautical miles from the North Pole and is some fifteen hundred nautical miles from the nearest permanent settlement. We will be stationed there for the duration of the Arctic winter, a period during which the sun never rises. I believe that the conditions, terrain and isolation make Alert as hostile an environment as the surface of Mars. Our assignment will closely mirror the kind of experience that astronauts may encounter upon arriving upon another planet.

Please list the names of your team members and a brief description of their role.

Charlotte Dennis, 28, is a solar scientist specialising in atmospheric studies. Robert Leary, 22, is the youngest member of the team and recently majored in meteorology. Bethany Rogers, 26, is a geologist and is responsible for the extraction and preservation of ice-cores. She is also a qualified medic. Reece Cain, 38, is a microbiologist researching bacterial presence in ancient ice-cores. Cody Ryan, 32, is a biologist who has recently joined our expedition.

Please list any further relevant details to your application:

My team represents a microcosm of personalities, some of which may clash in our confined living spaces. How we resolve those disputes, and how we conduct ourselves during our prolonged assignment away from family and loved ones, may provide valuable data for NASA in its proposed missions to other planets.

This study must be conducted without the knowledge of the participants. Please sign below that you understand the reasons for this, and that you will comply with the directive:

I understand the reasons for secrecy regarding this study, and will comply with all stated directives. Dr Jake McDermott.

FORTITUDE

Dean Crawford

1

Alert, Nunavut

North-West Territories

'Say goodbye to the sun, guys. Once we've descended you won't be seeing it again for six months.'

The voice sounded disembodied to Cody Ryan's ears as he sat in an uncomfortable seat in the shuddering belly of a giant CC-130 Hercules aircraft, the loadmaster speaking into a microphone that connected to the headphones Cody wore to protect his ears from the tremendous roar of the engines.

Through a small window beside his shoulder, Cody twisted his aching body and peered at the frigid atmosphere outside the aircraft. The wing stretched away above him, huge turboprop engines trailing turbulent vapour that glowed in the light of a sun blazing down into a stream of molten metal searing the distant horizon behind them.

Far below a featureless canvas of ice fields stretched away into infinity, cast into dark and frosty shadows as the sun slowly faded from sight beneath the horizon. Cody found himself transfixed by the scene, unable to tear his gaze away as though the sun were leaving him behind for good. He could have chosen to join any number of expeditions, any number of projects. That he had chosen this one said much about himself that he did not wish to confront right now.

'We'll make our final approach to Alert in the next few minutes,' the loadmaster said as he walked between them and tugged on their harnesses. 'This is a military field so don't get up until you're told to. Understood?'

Cody saw his five companions jab their thumbs in their air in unison. He nodded to the loadmaster, who took a seat opposite and strapped himself in as though he had not a care in the world.

Cody glanced outside as the Hercules dipped its wing and began a gentle turn. The beams of pale sunlight glowing through the windows into the aircraft's cavernous interior vanished as they were plunged into darkness. The engine roar subsided enough for Cody to hear the flaps and undercarriage deploy to the sound of whining hydraulics, the huge aircraft dipping and bouncing in the wintry gales blustering across the vast ice plains. Cody clenched his harness as a tight knot of anxiety in his guts threatened to eject his breakfast over his boots. He noticed Jake McDermott watching him with an expression of vague amusement. The old man winked once and gave him an encouraging thumbs-up but said nothing as Cody looked away.

Through the open hatchway to the cockpit far to his left, Cody spotted the green glow of cockpit instruments and a glimpse of twinkling runway lights stretching out into the dark void ahead. The Hercules bumped and gyrated as it descended, and then a thump reverberated through the fuselage as the aircraft touched down on the ice and the pilots deployed the spoilers and threw the huge engines into reverse. The aircraft thundered and vibrated as though it were coming apart at the seams, and then finally slowed as it turned off the runway and taxied toward a parking spot.

Cody breathed a sigh of relief and closed his eyes. He heard the engines shut down as he watched the loadmaster get out of his seat and hit a large red button inside the fuselage. The rear of the Hercules yawned slowly open as a ramp dropped down onto the ice. Half a dozen soldiers, wrapped up in thick Arctic camouflage and armed with rifles, strode up the ramp. The loadmaster pointed at Cody's group and waved them over.

Cody unstrapped himself from his seat and hefted a large holdall onto his back. He then pulled on thick gloves, tightened his thickly padded jacket and pulled the hood tight over his features.

'Jake McDermott?' one of the soldiers, an officer, shouted above the buffeting wind blustering in from outside.

'Yeah, plus five.'

The officer waved them all to follow and moments later they walked down the ramp onto the darkened ice fields. The remaining five soldiers formed a loose guard around them as they walked toward a large tracked vehicle nearby, its exhaust bellowing plumes of hot vapour that glowed in the vehicle's tail lights. Cody got his first good look at Alert as a frigid blast of Arctic air snatched the breath from his lungs.

A single road ran through the snow away from the runway toward a series of low buildings crouched against the rumbling winds. Beyond, Cody could see the lights of the Canadian Forces Station, a military listening post built during the Cold War to monitor the Soviet Union for any hint of an impending pre-emptive nuclear strike. Beyond lay the endless ice sheets shrouded in darkness, the mountainous skyline illuminated only by a faint glow from the sun somewhere far below the horizon.

'Get in the BV,' ordered the officer. 'My men will load your gear.'

The Bandvagn 206, or BV, was an articulated all-terrain vehicle with four powered tracks capable of carrying up to seventeen people. The bright yellow, fully amphibious machine could move at some five kilometres per hour in water and nearly twice that over rough terrain, and Cody knew from his expedition briefing that there were six of them based at Alert.

Cody and his companions obediently clambered aboard the vehicle, the officer following them up and pulling the main door shut once their equipment had been loaded aboard from the Hercules. The officer pulled his hood back to reveal a surprisingly young face as the vehicle's diesel engine roared and it pulled away across the bumpy ice. He looked directly at Jake.

'The rules are simple. You remain a minimum distance of one hundred metres from the military station and under no circumstances do your breach the perimeter without prior permission. My men have orders to shoot unidentified intruders. Is that clear?'

Jake nodded as the officer went on.

'The station receives supply flights about once per week, weather permitting. Your own supplies will be included in these flights and will be transferred to you directly. Fuel for the weather station comes from our own supply, obviously. Two of my men will be posted alongside you as both protectors and observers. They do not answer to you but can be asked to assist you in your work if required, understood?'

From beneath is thick hood Bobby Leary looked up at the officer. 'How often do dancing girls visit?'

The officer glanced at Leary, his eyes as glacial as the ice fields outside. 'I'm assuming you've all been made aware of the dangers of frostbite, snow blindness and local predators?'

Cody's team all nodded inside their hoods. Each of them had attended a two day course to prepare them for the extreme environment, including the dangers presented by polar bears, which were more than willing to hunt humans.

'We're as well prepared as we can be,' Jake said, his breath puffing in thick clouds as the vehicle rattled along.

'Any of you worked up here before?' the officer asked them.

'Kind of,' Jake responded. 'I spent two years down at McMurdo Station in the Antarctic.'

'Good,' the officer replied, 'you'll be site liaison and can contact me with any issues you might have.'

The journey across the ice fields took half an hour, most of which was passed in silence. Cody stole glances at his new colleagues and tried to recall their names. There had been little time back in Boston for him to get up to speed with their studies before the departure, so hurried had his application been.

The BV pulled up and the officer turned, opening the door once more to reveal the Air Chemistry Observatory building, Alert Five. Bathed in the glow of a series of lights reinforced against the polar weather, it consisted of a square two-storey building with a multi-tier metallic tower and steps attached to one side where atmospheric measurement equipment was attached along with a communications dish and an antenna that quivered in the gusting wind.

Cody jumped off the vehicle and with his companions hauled their gear onto the snow. The officer checked that the rear of the vehicle was empty, then turned to Jake McDermott and handed him a chunky set of keys.

'Only set you'll get, so don't lose them and as you know never, ever leave any doors open.'

As Jake took the keys, two soldiers clambered from the vehicle's cab and marched over, each cradling an assault rifle. Cody glimpsed within their hoods and behind eye shields the faces of a Canadian and somebody who looked like they might be an Arctic native, an Inuit.

'Your escort,' the officer introduced the two soldiers. 'They'll be your guard for the duration of your stay.'

Without another word the officer turned away and climbed into the BV's cab. With a belch of diesel fumes the truck rumbled its way past the observatory and turned about before growling away into the inky darkness. Within seconds the glow of its tail lights vanished into the gusting snow.

'Nice to meet you too,' Cody heard Jake utter as he turned to the door of the observatory.

It took a few moments of fumbling with the keys in his thick gloves before Jake got the door open and the group hustled inside. Cody helped drag their kit in through the door as Jake turned on the interior lights, the two soldiers ambling inside behind them without interest. Cody hauled the last bag through and then leaned on the door until it slammed shut, abruptly cutting off the wind.

The observatory building was large enough to house six scientists and was equipped with living quarters, small bedrooms, a bathroom and a kitchen. The laboratories were down the far end of the main hall. Cody looked around at the Spartan layout of the living quarters and wondered what the hell he'd gotten himself into.

'Home sweet home,' Charlotte Dennis uttered as she pulled back the hood of her jacket and revealed thick tresses of auburn hair that reached half way down her back.

Cody yanked his own hood off, and in the blackened square of a triple-glazed window he saw his reflection. Just like the barren wilderness outside, there was little of interest. A plain face, nose a little too large, hair that kind of did its own thing no matter what he tried. Only thing in his favour was that he'd never smoked and drank only socially, a lifestyle that shaved a few years off his appearance. He looked like he was just out of college and ready to take on the world but for the shadows haunting his eyes.

Cody turned away from his reflection as he pulled his gloves and stole a covert glance at his colleagues. Jake McDermott, with his salt and pepper goatee beard, was checking the fuse box on the wall to make sure nothing had blown out since the summer team had left a few days previously. Charlotte Dennis was checking her reflection in the darkened window nearby, pushing her thick hair back further on her head and fussing with her collar. Bobby Leary was shaking off his jacket and whipping snow from his head with one hand, bright young eyes hunting for something to do. Bethany Rogers, her dark hair in a neat pony-tail, was struggling to haul her kit up onto a table as Jake stepped in to help her. And at the back of the room, Reece Cain quietly unpacked his belongings and avoided eye contact, hiding behind a long black fringe that belonged more to a teenage Goth than a middle-aged scientist.

The two soldiers introduced themselves to Jake as Bradley Trent and Sauri, shaking hands briefly. Bradley was a tall, muscular soldier with a flat-topped buzz-cut. His companion was short, stocky and apparently the silent type.

'Jesus, this one's heavy!'

Cody turned to see Bobby Leary heft a steel storage box onto the table in the centre of the room. It was marked C. Ryan.

'It's okay,' Cody said. 'I've got it.'

'What you got in there?' Bobby laughed, 'a cannon ball?'

'Near enough,' Cody replied with a grin. 'I bought just about everything I could fit inside.'

'You guys must all be totally insane.'

Cody turned to see Bradley Trent watching them with a disapproving gaze.

'Why?' Jake asked.

Bradley gestured with a wave of his gloved hand across the room. 'Me and Sauri, we were posted here on orders. You guys have got the whole world to do your experiments in and yet you come here, to the boil on the ass of the world.'

Cody glanced at Sauri, the Inuit soldier who stood alongside his companion and watched the activity in silence. His face was carved with the same sharp angles as the glaciers that enveloped the bleak landscape that was his home, his eyes as black and dark as the night outside.

'You agree with that, Sauri?' Jake asked him.

The Inuit's only response was to raise one eyebrow a fraction. Bradley laughed out loud and clapped his hand across Sauri's back.

'Old *Sorry* here doesn't say much,' he reported, 'nothing wrong with his English, mind. He's just not sociable.'

'Great,' Charlotte uttered. 'Six months with a mute Eskimo and a gobby Canadian. You owe us all a drink Jake, come the summer.'

Bradley looked at Charlotte as though he'd been slapped. Cody thought he saw a glimmer of amusement in Sauri's eyes.

'Who's the wench?' Bradley asked Cody as he jabbed a thumb in Charlotte's general direction.

'Who's the goon?' Charlotte snapped back before Cody could reply.

'Great start guys,' Jake uttered. 'We'll have time for happy-clappy introductions later. Right now let's just get our gear unpacked and get our heads down. We've got a lot of ground to cover in the morning.'

'We?' Bradley uttered as he turned away. 'Sauri and I are done here. Don't wake us up too early, 'kay?'

Cody watched the two soldiers make their way out of the entrance hall, dragging their kit bags behind them.

'Please don't put me next door to either of them,' Bethany muttered to Jake. 'Trent gives me the creeps already.'

'Same here,' Charlotte agreed.

Jake sighed. 'Fine, you girls go pick your rooms. We'll follow you in.'

'Looks like you're too late,' Bobby said as he gestured across the living quarters.

Cody looked up just in time to see Reece Cain vanish down a corridor toward the rooms and turn into the nearest one.

'He always that friendly?' Jake asked.

'I have no idea,' Charlotte said. 'He's barely said a word to me since we met.' She turned and looked over her shoulder at Cody. 'Nor have you, for that matter.'

Cody managed a grin and stuck his hand out. 'Sorry. Cody Ryan.'

Charlotte took it as Cody introduced himself to the others.

'Cody was late to the party,' Jake said. 'Jeff Dawkins was supposed to be up here with us, but he got sick. Cody here jumped in to replace him.'

'Mighty brave of you,' Bethany smiled. 'And what possessed you to come up here?'

Cody looked at her for a long moment before he replied. 'Once in a lifetime opportunity, I guess.'

'Well, you sure as hell got yourself that,' Charlotte uttered as she hauled her gear onto her shoulder and headed for the rooms. 'See y'all in the morning.'

Cody watched her leave with Bethany close behind. Only Jake remained as Cody hefted his bag onto his shoulder.

'You going to be okay up here?' Jake asked.

Cody looked at the old man. 'Sure, why?'

'You're the only team member with a young family,' Jake said. 'Kind of odd that you'd sign up for something like this.'

Cody twisted his lips into a grin again. 'The things we do for science, eh?'

Cody turned away and walked out of the living quarters without looking back.

2

Week 1
Dear Maria,

The crew have settled in and we've started work on both the atmospheric sampling and the extraction of ice cores. Jake has already proven himself an effective leader and is using our acoustic suite to measure ice density changes since the last team made their measurements in the fall. Workload is relatively high and we're spending a lot of time out on the ice getting our experiments set up. Jake is keeping all of us busy and so far the lack of sunlight doesn't seem to be creating any issues for me.

Our guards, Bradley and Sauri, remain aloof and disinterested in our work. In addition, Reece Cain prefers to sleep in the small ice camp that's been set up five kilometres out from the observatory. This is causing some friction with Bradley, who resents having to send Sauri out each night to accompany Cain due to the threat from polar bears investigating the camp.

Charlotte hit it on the head though: Sauri and Reece both shun contact. They're probably perfectly happy out there.

I miss you very much, and I hope that you're behaving for your mother. Overall, I have no issues here so far and everybody is working well together.

*

'You idiot!'

The shout rang out across the sheets of shadowy ice as though it had cracked the frigid air. Cody looked up from his work placing a sensor to see Charlotte Dennis storming across the darkened plain, one arm pointed across to where Bobby Leary was standing near an excavation.

Although Charlotte was almost entirely encased in her thick Arctic clothing, Cody could tell it was her just by her strident gait against the pale sky on the horizon.

Bobby stood rooted to the spot as Charlotte raged up to him.

'You drill an ice hole while I'm trying to calibrate acoustic sensors a hundred yards away?!'

Bobby raised his arms. 'Do I look clairvoyant?'

'It's on the goddamned duty roster in the hall,' Charlotte raged. 'Calibration diagnostics from two until three! You can read English, right?'

'Oh me, oh my,' Bobby snapped, 'I didn't realise that Queen Charlotte's experiments trumped everybody else's! Maybe you should let us all get set up before you start dictating who's doing what and when!'

'You've had all week to drill your goddamned holes!' Charlotte raged. 'What the hell have you been doing all of this time?'

Cody watched as Jake set his sensor packages down nearby and began walking toward the pair as their voices echoed out across the lonely ice sheets. The horizon was awash with a faint glow of orange that drifted slowly from east to west during what passed for daytime at Alert. The sky above was a deep blue reflected by the ice, but for once there was no wind whatsoever. A pillar of steam from the observatory's generator rose vertically up into the sky to touch a glittering veil of stars twinkling high above their heads.

Cody checked his watch. 14.32pm.

'How about I drill a hole in that goddamned head of yours?' Charlotte snapped and wafted her gloved hand across Bobby's hood.

'Take it easy,' Jake said as he approached the pair and put himself between them. 'Bobby, how many more sink holes are you planning on?'

'Just one,' Bobby replied, 'right under Princess Pouty here.'

Charlotte's eyes narrowed but she said nothing as Jake ushered Bobby aside. 'Let's just get this done, okay? You got a timetable for finishing?'

Bobby sighed. 'Another hour I guess. It's hard finding places where the ice is old enough. With the winter setting in it's changing all the time.'

'Fine,' Jake said, 'an hour. Get to it.'

Bobby stomped away through the snow as Charlotte snapped at Jake.

'Couldn't you have hired somebody who's not just out of Kindergarten?'

'Bobby's doing fine,' Jake said. 'We're not yet ready to begin measuring, Charlotte.'

'I'm ready,' she uttered. 'I can't help it if everybody else is dragging their heels.'

'This is a team,' Jake insisted. 'A team requires compromise.'

'I don't have to compromise. One call and I'm on a plane out of here.'

Cody managed to swallow down the resentment that swilled like hot coals in his belly as he heard Charlotte's words. Jake replied to her.

'I know, but the rest of us can't. Our careers depend on us being here, so if you're not one of us then you'd better make that call right now, okay?'

Charlotte's eyes flew wide. 'Are you trying to tell me what to do?'

'I'm not trying,' Jake replied. 'You're either part of our team or you're part of its history. Decide.'

Jake turned away from her and walked back across the ice toward his sensors. As he did so he drifted toward Cody and inclined his head as he looked at him. Cody fell into place alongside Jake, the old man's beard laced with ice crystals. Their footfalls crunched in unison as they walked.

'First crack in the eggshell?' Jake asked.

'You're asking me?' Cody replied.

'You're the oldest on the team except Reece and I,' Jake explained, 'and Reece is not exactly a social soul. I need somebody to rely on.'

Cody stared down at the ice for a moment as he walked.

'I don't think there's anything to worry about,' he replied finally. 'We need more time to get into a routine. It's only been a few days.'

'A few days is all it takes for people to get pissed at each other up here,' Jake pointed out. 'They don't realise it, it just happens.'

'You think we're already cracking up?'

'Sure we are,' Jake insisted. 'We just pretend we're okay but it's happening already, little by little. There's no way to adapt to this place, we just get dumped here and have to acclimatise to it while on the job. Permanent darkness, crippling cold, storms that last for days and leave everybody cooped up inside to get on each other's nerves? You name it, it's going to happen. Hell of a location.'

Cody nodded as they walked. 'How come you keep coming back up here then?'

Jake chuckled.

'I guess I just figure that this is a unique place to be. There are not many places on Earth this remote and pristine with a permanent presence. We're lucky to be able to witness it, and if the military were not here nobody would see this place.'

Cody looked up at the distant twinkling lights of the Canadian base. 'What are they doing up here anyway?'

'It's a listening station,' Jake explained. 'They built it during the Cold War to keep an eye on the Soviet Union and China.'

'Security seems pretty tight,' Cody observed, 'seeing as the Cold War is over.'

'Probably something to do with equipment, classified stuff I'd imagine. On rare occasions they let civilian companies fly supplies into Alert. The crew of the aircraft are not allowed more than three metres away from their airplanes.'

Cody nodded and then scanned the horizon beyond the base. Although geographically he was looking south, the magnetic North Pole was in fact somewhere out to his right. But the glow of the distant, hidden sun told him that he was looking in about the right direction as they came to a halt on a low ridge of snow.

'Boston, eh son?'

'Sorry?'

'You're from Boston, like the rest?' Jake asked.

'Yeah,' Cody confirmed and looked back at the sun's distant glow, 'Massachusetts Institute of Technology. You?'

'Cali,' Jake replied.

'Jesus, that's an environment change.'

'Your file said you've got a daughter?' Jake asked as they stared at the distant glow.

'Three years old,' Cody replied, and felt a smile tug at the corner of his lips despite the cold. 'Maria.'

Jake nodded slowly as they stood together. 'And you came here?'

'This was a once in a lifetime opportunity, to get to Alert and do this research.'

'Ice is getting thinner,' Jake replied. 'Ice breakers are getting through easier. There's no reason to believe that the science is urgent.'

'Climate change isn't urgent?' Cody almost laughed.

'Your presence isn't,' Jake replied.

Cody turned to look at the older man, letting his hood conceal his expression a little. 'Why are you giving me a hard time about being here?'

Jake smiled. 'I just like to know who I'm working with is all.'

'You're working with a bunch of people who like being stuck a couple of thousand miles away from pretty much everybody else. That should tell you something.'

'It only tells me the how, not the why,' Jake countered. 'I've worked in places like this plenty of times before and believe me it can be hard on folk. Sooner or later there'll be a bust-up of some kind. Just make sure it's not you, okay?'

Cody looked at Jake for a long moment before replying. 'Sure.'

Jake gave Cody a thick gloved pat on the back, then turned and trudged away toward the observatory.

Cody let out an irritated breath onto the frozen air and watched the cloud of vapour spiral away from him. The last thing he wanted was to babysit everybody else. Christ, escaping company was half the reason he'd travelled all the way out here. The vast, empty expanses of the Arctic plains seemed to draw away from him as his brain began to calculate just how far away civilisation was. How much he had done. Why he had done it. Whether or not he should have.

'Yo', Cody!'

The voice rolled across the ice from far behind him and Cody turned to see Bethany standing in a pool of light on the observatory steps with her thumb and forefinger pressed to the side of her head as she pointed at him. Then she tapped her wrist and gestured to the observatory.

Cody gave her a thumbs-up and started off through the snow.

Dean Crawford

3

'She's beautiful.'

Bethany walked past Cody as she left the observatory's communications room, smiling broadly.

The heat in the interior of the building felt almost tropical as Cody pulled off one of his three sweaters and walked into the room. He glanced up at the clock on the wall, which read just after three in the afternoon as he sat down in front of a monitor and looked straight into his daughter's big, brown eyes.

Maria Ryan was the cutest bundle of perfection that Cody had ever laid eyes on, and now the sight of her after just a couple of weeks away caused sharp needles of pain to pierce the corners of his eyes as his throat twisted upon itself.

'Hi honey,' he managed to rasp as he reached out and touched Maria's face on the screen.

'Daddy!'

She was sitting in her mother's lap, writhing and giggling as she saw her father's face. A satellite relay-connection to a base called Eureka, several hundred nautical miles to the south, allowed researchers stationed at Alert to make video-calls to their families once a week, provided adverse weather didn't scramble the transmissions. Now, with clear skies outside he could hear Maria's laughter and excitement as she scrutinised his image on the screen in their Boston home. They spoke for a few moments until he heard his wife's voice.

'C'mon Maria, wave goodbye to daddy now.'

Maria shook one hand at the screen in a gesture that could as easily have been a threat as a wave but for the broad smile between her bright red cheeks. 'Bye daddy!'

'Bye honey,' Cody waved back, his own features aching with the smile plastered across his face.

His wife, Danielle, lifted Maria out of shot and then reached out to the camera, tilting it back slightly so that he could see her face.

'Hi,' Cody said as the ache faded away.

'Hi.'

There was no passion in the response, as if she were reading from a script. Cody waited for more words to come forth but Danielle stared at the monitor as though she were looking at a painting.

'How's Maria been?' he asked.

'She's good,' Danielle replied, 'been to her Gran's this morning. She says hello.'

The sound of Maria running up and down and singing to herself out of shot stretched another smile across Cody's features. On the monitor he saw Danielle's expression soften as she glanced at their daughter.

'She asks after you every day.'

Cody nodded and ducked his head as fresh waves of pain stabbed at his eyes. He dragged a hand across his face and took a breath that shuddered through his chest. Words spilled from within him as though escaping of their own accord.

'I'm sorry. I shouldn't have come out here.'

Danielle glanced down into her lap but said nothing. Her long brown hair fell over her face and she swiped it aside.

'You'll miss her birthday.'

Cody felt a surge of anger seethe through his belly but somehow he managed to beat it back down.

'I know I'll miss her birthday. If I could change things, I would.'

Danielle glared out of the monitor at him and bit her lip but said nothing. Cody took another deep breath of cold air.

'Pack ice is building up and the winter storms are starting here. Communication might get difficult. Can you do me a favour?'

Danielle stared at the screen. No movement or words.

'Can you video Maria, maybe just a few minutes a week, and e-mail it to me? I know I can't be there but I don't want to miss too much.'

Danielle nodded once. 'Maybe you should have thought of that?'

Cody felt his fists ball in his lap and felt his jaw aching again, this time for all the wrong reasons.

'The military flights are rare and civilian aircraft even more so. Chances of me hitching a ride out of here early are zero. Besides, it wouldn't do us much good, would it?'

Danielle gave a dismissive flick of her eyebrows as she looked away from the camera. Cody's anger finally spilled over.

'You think that I chose this? You think that what happened was somehow my fault? You think I want to be stuck up here freezing my ass off?'

'I don't know what I think.'

'Then how can you judge me?'

'I'm not goddamned judging anybody!'

Danielle's voice was a harsh whisper as she tried to prevent their daughter from hearing the anger in their exchange. Cody reined himself in.

'Five months,' he said finally. 'Five months and this will all be over, okay?'

Danielle looked at him for a long moment.

'This will be with us forever, no matter what we do or where we go. We'll never escape it, Cody.'

Cody lost patience. 'Better that, than the alternative.'

Cody reached out and terminated the connection on the computer. He dragged a hand down his face as though trying to wipe the slate of his life clean and then got up and walked out of the room.

The lights in the living quarters were on, the windows black as though it were midnight. Cody mentally reminded himself that it was barely past three in the afternoon. This far north the pale twilight that passed for day lasted only a few hours, the pink and gold glow on the horizon swiftly fading.

Bethany Rogers sat at a dining table with a series of charts in her hands, and tapped one with a pencil.

'Best place for the new CO_2 monitors is definitely out at the ice camp,' she said. 'There's a slim chance that aircraft activity at the airbase could contaminate our measurements here.'

Cody nodded vacantly as he peered out into the darkness. 'Sure. Reece will do it.'

Bethany snorted in amusement. 'Be quicker for us to take them out. Reece hasn't set foot back in the observatory since we set the camp up.'

Cody nodded.

'You okay?' Bethany asked.

Cody blinked out of his glum reverie and turned to her. 'Yeah, sure. Sorry. Just spoke to my wife and daughter, kind of brings it home how far away they are.'

Bethany smiled. 'You should have got this assignment out of the way before playing happy families, Cody.'

'You got a boyfriend?' Cody asked.

'Are you hitting on me?'

'No, not at all, I meant that… '

Bethany giggled. Cody picked up a pair of winter gloves and tossed them at her.

'I'm not attached,' she replied as she ducked the missiles. 'I was, but we split up a couple of months back.'

'Sorry to hear that.'

'It wasn't serious.'

'What about the others? They got families, partners?'

'Why do you ask?'

Cody shrugged. 'Jake seems interested in getting a feel for everybody's status, for want of a better word. Says it helps figure out how well people will cope up here.'

'You think they'd tell me?'

'Maybe,' Cody replied.

Bethany shrugged.

'Well as far as I know Bobby Leary is either single or a serial adulterer because I can hardly hold a conversation without him checking me out. Reece seems like the kind of guy who has only ever had a relationship with a petri dish, and Charlotte probably only mixes with other senator's children.' Bethany thought for a moment. 'She'll suffer the most.'

'What makes you say that?'

'Bobby will chase me around the whole time here, Reece will stay on his own, you're married, I'm happily single and Jake's too professional to play kiss-chase with anybody. Charlotte's the fish out of water. It can't be easy spending your life mixing with politicians and movie stars and then getting dumped out here on your own.'

'I thought she said she wanted to do her research while she was young enough.'

'Bull crap,' Bethany snorted. 'She's only at home with caviar, champagne and chauffeurs. This is probably something her father arranged to bring her back down to

Earth. You can tell she doesn't want to be here and doesn't like any of us.'

'What about the two soldiers, Brad and Sauri?'

'What about them?'

'I figured they're on some kind of punishment detail, getting stuck with us here instead of with their team over at the base.'

'Makes sense I guess,' Bethany agreed. 'None of the military seem interested in us.'

Cody nodded and looked out of the darkened windows at the distant lights of the base.

'Not exactly a comforting thought,' he said.

4

Crystallised.

That was the only word that described the Arctic for Cody as he guided one of four heavy duty snowmobiles across the bleak terrain. It felt as though he were in a vast dome of glass, the icy plains frozen in time and glistening as they reflected the starlight in the soaring vault of the heavens above. A thin sword of light glowed across the horizon ahead, keeping distant hills in silhouette. A few thousand miles away, down in Boston, it was midday and people were bustling out of their offices for lunch.

Here, it seemed like they were traversing the surface of the moon.

The snowmobile's engine growled as Cody guided it toward a series of small prefabricated buildings erected out on the lonely plains, the headlights reflecting off sparkling particles of ice whipped up by the powerful belts of Jake's snowmobile a few yards ahead.

Behind Cody followed Bradley Trent and Charlotte Dennis on two more vehicles. Jake guided them in to the camp and slowed. Ahead, Cody could see Reece Cain about a hundred yards away out on the ice erecting a tower of aluminium tubing some ten feet tall. Nearby, Sauri stood guard with a rifle cradled in his grip.

Cody shut off the snowmobile's engine and revelled in a deep and frigid silence broken only by the sound of boots crunching on the ice as they dismounted.

'He's still building that?' Charlotte asked, her voice muffled by the thick mask and goggles she wore.

'Been too windy to finish it until now,' Jake pointed out as they began walking toward the skeletal tower. 'It's too dangerous to risk a fall up here.'

Cody hauled from the back of his snowmobile a plastic container some four feet long with a large disc at the end, as though the case contained a giant banjo. He hefted the container onto his shoulder and followed his companions out toward the tower.

They were half way there when Bradley Trent slowed and crouched on the ice.

'Wind wasn't the only reason,' the soldier said and gestured them to join him.

Cody felt a ripple of consternation as he looked down at a series of huge paw prints tracking their way across the snow field. He glanced up at the pre-fabs a couple of dozen yards behind.

'Size?' Jake asked.

Bradley looked up and down the tracks. 'Big enough and it passed pretty close to the camp. Polar bears can smell a seal from a kilometre away even when it's hiding under the snow. Reece and Sauri would have stunk like a madras curry.' Bradley stood up. 'It knows they're here.'

Charlotte looked down at the tracks and placed her boot down over one. The large, ragged print completely surrounded her boot.

'Jesus,' she uttered. 'And Cain wants to stay out here?'

Jake started walking again. 'He hasn't come screaming back yet.'

They reached the tower, a rigid contraption of poles caked in frost and icicles. Reece Cain stood up on a narrow platform of aluminium plates coated in thick rubber as he yanked on a wrench, fastening the last of a series of bolts into the frame.

'Afternoon,' Jake said, raising a thickly gloved hand.

Reece finished tightening the bolt and looked down at them. He nodded once and then glanced at Cody's burden.

'Just set them down there, thanks,' he said, and pointed at the base of the tower.

Cody slid the plastic container down onto the ice, then jabbed his thumb over his shoulder.

'You guys have had visitors out here.'

'They're not a problem.'

'They will be,' Jake replied as Reece clambered down onto the ice. 'Polar bears are fearless and inquisitive. Sooner or later it'll be sniffing around the doors. Once these are set up you should probably come back to the base.'

Reece slipped the wrench into a nearby hold-all. 'No thanks.'

Jake glanced at Cody. Despite the mask and the goggles, Cody could see that Jake was looking for support. Cody sighed behind his mask. Thousands of miles from anywhere and yet Reece Cain was still not quite as far from human beings as he clearly wanted to be.

'You're missing out,' Cody tried. 'Super Bowl's on, spread bets are being made, still good odds available if you're in.'

Reece looked at him, albeit with his head and face entirely in silhouette against the glow of the horizon.

'I'm good.'

Reece started unpacking the container that Cody had carried out to the tower. A series of disc shaped detectors on four-foot poles, designed to be fixed to the top of the tower that Reece had erected.

Cody turned to Sauri, who was watching the exchange with his gloved hands clasped patiently before him, the rifle now slung across his shoulder.

'What about you?' Cody asked. 'Feel lucky?'

Sauri gazed at him and shrugged. 'No money,' came the muffled, shy response.

'Jesus,' Bradley Trent uttered with a laugh, his mask caked with droplets of pearlescent ice frozen from his breath. 'If these guys are happy out here with the bears, why worry?'

Charlotte Dennis turned her head to look at the soldier. 'I'm worried for them. Perhaps you should stay out here too, just in case that bear comes back?'

'Like hell,' Bradley shot back. 'I'm not going anywhere without... '

Bradley fell silent as a faint humming noise broke the otherwise endless silence of the Arctic around them. Cody looked around them in confusion, unprepared for the deep rumbling that suddenly seemed to reverberate through the ice.

'What the hell is that?'

The rumbling intensified into a deafening roar and Cody almost stumbled backwards as from out of the sky to the south a series of bright lights suddenly flared into view and bore down upon them. From behind the brilliant lights appeared wings and engines as a giant Hercules aircraft thundered overhead, streams of vapour trailing from its engines onto the brittle air.

Cody instinctively ducked as the aircraft passed over their heads and thundered away toward Alert.

Three more Hercules roared overhead in pursuit of the first. Cody and the team watched the aircraft fly away toward the tiny sprinkling of lights against the inky blackness of the Arctic to their north as the engine noise faded away.

'What the hell do you suppose that's all about?' Charlotte asked.

'Supply flights?' Reece suggested.

'Had one two days ago,' Jake pointed out.

Cody looked across at Bradley. 'What's going on then?'

Bradley looked across at Sauri. 'You ever see that many planes fly in at once?'

Sauri shook his head.

'They were in a damned hurry too,' Jake pointed out, 'straight in approaches, one after the other.'

Jake looked at the instruments Reece was holding.

'You sure you don't want to leave that until tomorrow?'

Reece shook his head. 'Sooner they're up, the sooner we're recording data.'

Jake turned to Bradley. 'Stay with them until it's done. We'll head back to base and find out what's going on.'

'I don't want to stay out here with these two goddamned mutes.'

Jake took two paces across the ice and got into Bradley's face.

'There are polar bears in the area. You're here to protect our people, so get to it. You don't, I'll bring Sauri back with us and leave you out here on your own with Cain. Your call.'

Bradley scowled behind his mask and goggles and then stormed away across the ice to nowhere in particular.

Cody followed Jake and Charlotte back to the snowmobiles. The engines shattered the silence as they were gunned, powerful lights flaring into life as they turned and aimed for the distant lights of Alert.

The half-hour ride across the rough ice plains was every bit as hard as it had been coming out, the bitter cold seeping through even multiple layers of dense Arctic clothing. Cody dimly recalled how Alert got its name: from a British vessel named HMS Alert that wintered in nearby Cape Sheridan in 1875. How the crew of a wooden sloop, using technology over a century old, had survived this bleakest of places stunned him. Much of the surrounding terrain was named after members of HMS Alert's crew as testimony to their hardiness.

Cody glimpsed a couple of Arctic hares bound away from the snowmobiles and the glowing eyes of an Arctic fox glimmer briefly from out of the darkness as they passed by. The lights of Alert grew brighter as Cody's hands grew colder. He could see floodlights out near the end of the runway and the huge Hercules aircraft parked beneath them.

Jake led the way into a small compound outside the base and pulled up as Cody swung in alongside him and killed the engine on his snowmobile.

'You see the aircraft?' Jake called above the noise of Charlotte's snowmobile. 'Their engines were still running.'

'Why would they do that? Some kind of exercise?' Cody asked.

Jake didn't reply as he walked out of the compound. Cody hurried alongside him with Charlotte behind as they walked across the icy surface of the road outside and scrambled up the snow bank opposite.

Cody reached the top first and looked out across the plains to the distant airfield.

The four Hercules were sitting on a parking area on the far side of the airstrip, the huge ramps at the rear of the aircraft lowered onto the ice as vehicles drove up into their enormous interiors. The sound of the sixteen aircraft engines turning was a deep hum muted by distance.

'They're loading up,' Charlotte said. 'Why?'

Cody had no answer for her, and any that he might have concocted was drowned out as a Bandvagen thundered toward them down the road, its headlights slicing through the darkness. They turned as the vehicle suddenly shuddered to a halt and four soldiers got out. Three of them were armed, their rifles held at port arms but their eyes watching Cody, Jake and Charlotte as an officer clambered from the cab and gestured to them.

'What are you doing here?' the officer demanded.

'We saw the planes come in,' Jake replied. 'We wondered what was going on.'

'Bradley Trent, Sauri. Where are they?'

'At the field station, just south of the observatory,' Jake answered.

'How far away?'

'Five clicks south of here. Why?'

The officer looked past the compound toward the fading horizon, clenched his jaw for a few moments, and then turned to the three armed soldiers behind him. He shook his head and waved a level hand across his throat. The soldiers whirled and leapt back into the transporter.

The officer clambered up into the BV's cab.

'Hey,' Jake shouted as he scrambled down the bank. 'What the hell's going on?'

Jake's last words were drowned out as the BV's engine was gunned and the vehicle thundered past in a cloud of snow and fumes. Cody watched as the vehicle's tail lights wound their way toward the airfield. Minutes later, it was driven carefully into the back of the last Hercules in the line.

Jake joined him again at the top of the bank and they watched in amazement as the four aircraft withdrew their boarding ramps and lined up on the runway.

'They're leaving,' Charlotte gasped in disbelief. 'They're leaving us.'

'Can't be,' Jake said. 'It must be some kind of exercise.'

The roar of the Hercules' engines increased and one after the other they thundered away down the ice strip amid clouds of ice spray until their winking navigation lights climbed into the night sky and turned south. As the last aircraft faded away into the darkness, Cody felt a twinge of concern twist in his guts.

'They wanted to take Bradley and Sauri with them,' he said to Jake.

Jake looked at the distant aircraft as they vanished from sight.

'Get back to Alert Five and get on the radio,' he said, 'Find out what the hell is going on.'

5

Cody hurried into the observatory compound, yanking his Arctic gloves and jacket off as he stumbled into the communications room.

The computer was still on from when he had spoken to Danielle, and next to it was a bank of radios that linked to both terrestrial and satellite detectors. He glanced at his watch. A little after six in the evening. The time in Boston was almost the same as Alert and there would no doubt be somebody available back at MIT — the place never slept.

Cody dropped into the chair and grabbed the microphone.

'Boscombe Base, this is Alert Five, repeat, Alert Five, do you copy?'

A long hiss of static was followed by a cheerful voice that crackled as it was distorted by atmospheric turbulence and the extreme range.

'Well a very good evening to you Alert Five, how fares thee in thine icy…'

'Guys, something's going on up here and we need some help,' Cody cut across the jovial reply. 'The Canadian Forces Station just cleared out and abandoned us.'

A long hiss of static. *'You're kidding.'*

'Would I joke about something like this?' Cody snapped. 'They've cleared out, flown south. You want to find out why?'

'Yeah, sure. I'll call back. Give me a minute.'

'Great, make it fast okay?'

Cody sat back in his chair and glanced at the monitor. The Internet Homepage of the Massachusetts's Institute of Technology glowed back at him. Cody leaned forward and typed in the URL of a world news service and watched as the homepage opened. Maybe something major had happened in Canada and they were pulling in their service personnel for some reason?

The page showed news reports from a fatal police chase near Seattle; the American President's speech to the Senate on immigration reform before departing for a foreign affairs conference; New York getting its first dusting of snow; orange harvest failures after California's drought. There was nothing untoward happening anywhere in North America, Canada or Alaska. In fact Canada was so quiet its Prime Minister was also departing for a conference overseas.

Cody glanced over his shoulder and then typed in another search. A tingle of alarm pulsed through his body as the Boston Globe's main pager flashed up a major headline:

POLICE SEEK IDENTITY OF MALE HOMICIDE VICTIM FOUND NEAR LOCAL RESERVOIR

Cody stared at the headline for what felt like an eternity as prickly heat irritated his back and shoulders and his heart thumped against the wall of his chest.

'Alert Five, Boscombe Base, do you copy?'

Cody grabbed the microphone. 'Alert Five, go ahead.'

'I called the expedition manager. He's on the phone now to Yellowknife but as far as I can tell there's absolutely no word on why they've cleared out of Alert. It might be some kind of exercise or something.'

'They deploy infantry to exercises,' Cody pointed out. 'They don't evacuate high security listening posts.'

'Well, there's not much we can do here except wait and see but don't panic. If for some reason they've pulled out permanently I'll

arrange to have the nearest ice-breaker detour to Cambridge Bay to pick you guys up. It'll mean abandoning the study though.'

'To hell with the study,' Cody replied. 'I'm not having us marooned up here through an Arctic winter.' Cody saw an image of Maria in his mind and made his decision. 'If you don't get an explanation by morning, send the ship anyway. The pack ice is solidifying fast up here — another week or two and nobody will be coming out this way. Call me first thing in the morning, okay?'

'Will do, Boscombe out.'

Cody relinquished the microphone and stared at the news feed on the monitor.

'What's that?'

Cody jumped as though a live current had pulsed through his body. He whirled to see Bethany pointing at the Internet news report.

'Nothing,' he uttered in reply. 'I was looking for news that might explain why the base has cleared out.'

'Because of a homicide in Boston?' she smiled.

Cody grinned. 'No. I was just looking at the Boston Globe. There's nothing in the news about Alert or anything untoward happening in Canada. It doesn't make much sense for them to clear out without explanation or apparent reason.'

'All the more likely that it's just an exercise then,' Bethany pointed out.

Cody shrugged. He wanted to believe her but something jangled in his nerves, a sense of foreboding that he couldn't shake off. He glanced at the computer monitor and then berated himself as he leaned over and clicked the web page off. He had enough on his mind without worrying about events several thousand miles away.

The phone in the communications room rang and Cody felt himself jolt a little at the noise. He hoped that

Bethany hadn't seen his reaction as he leaned over and picked up the phone.

'Alert Five?'

'*Doctor Jake McDermott please,*' answered a gruff voice.

'Sure, who's calling?'

There was a pause on the line. '*Boston.*'

Cody shrugged. 'Wait one.'

He walked out of the office with Bethany in tow, and hollered out for Jake.

The old man passed Cody in the corridor. 'Who is it?'

'Just said Boston.'

Cody walked back to his quarters, and pulled out his diary.

Week 2

As I write, there has been something of a crisis.

The forces at the Canadian station have pulled out, and within an hour of them going Reece, Bradley and Sauri were back at the observatory, having shared a snowmobile ride. Bradley was shouting at anybody he could see, demanding to know what's been going on. Even Sauri, who says little, seemed concerned and spent a lot of time looking out of the windows of the compound toward the south.

It makes no sense. Alert is one of the most sensitive listening posts in the world, a deeply secure base. We were ordered to go nowhere within one hundred metres of its perimeter. Now, it's been completely abandoned with us still camped a few kilometres away.

Home base will be in contact in the morning with news. Right now, Charlotte appears unperturbed: she says that her father, the senator, would have informed her of anything important. The fact that the military base is Canadian, not American, has apparently escaped her attention. Bethany remains watchful and avoids Bradley. Jake is assuring everybody that things are just fine. I wish I shared his sentiments but I'm not so confident. It feels as though we're being kept in the dark both literally and metaphorically.

The only person who is apparently not concerned by all of this is Reece Cain. In fact, when he saw the departing aircraft he apparently told Sauri that he hoped they didn't come back soon.

*

'Jake McDermott.'

The voice on the other end of the line was neither threatening nor friendly.

'Doctor McDermott, this is Detective Allen Griffiths, Boston Police Department. Are you able to speak confidentially?'

Jake turned in the small communications room and kicked the door shut with the heel of his boot. 'Sure, how can I help?'

'Sir, do you have a contingent of scientists from MIT present with you at your base at this time?'

'I do.'

'How well do you know them?'

'We only met a couple of weeks ago,' Jake replied. 'What's this about?'

'Can I confirm that you have not been present yourself in Boston between five and six weeks ago?'

'Like I said, I only met the team two weeks ago,' Jake confirmed. 'I flew in from Los Angeles.'

'Had you met any of your team members before this time, sir?'

'No,' Jake answered. 'Seriously, what's this about?'

'I'm afraid I cannot tell you over the phone, sir, until we have obtained the necessary warrants. We cannot take the risk that the suspect may take flight if they learn of our investigation.'

Jake held the phone close to his ear for a long moment.

'We're isolated,' he replied. 'I doubt anybody will be taking flight. We're a thousand miles from the nearest settlement.'

'That's probably why they're there,' Griffiths replied. *'Let me put it another way: we don't want to cause any awkward situations for you or your team.'*

'What, you mean like a hostage situation or something?'

'I'm sure it won't come to that, Doctor McDermott. We'll be in touch with instructions as soon as we've contacted the Canadian forces at Alert.'

The line clicked off before Jake could reply. He looked at the phone for a long time before he set it back in its cradle.

*

Bethany Rogers was not afraid of the Arctic Circle.

Despite being stationed several thousand miles from home in one of the most inhospitable places on the planet, she knew that man had survived here for thousands of years: the native Inuit populations had made a living across the Yukon and North West Territories for generations. However, she did allow herself the cautioning thought that few humans made it this far north of the Taiga, the Boreal Forest that marked the northern limits of the tree line. Arctic tundra was an unforgiving environment for even the resourceful few who made its glacial wastes their home.

About the only thing she missed was her little brother, Ben, who lived with her uncle and aunt in Boston. Bethany's parents weren't the best, both addled by methamphetamine habits that had cost them their home years before. Both had spent much of the preceding decades in jail or prison, enduring an endless cycle of abuse and recovery that seemed to have vacuumed the very life from their bodies until she could barely recognise them at all. Bethany hadn't seen them for several years and had no great yearning to. She was used to going it alone.

Thus, the departure of the Canadian forces stationed at Alert a few hours before didn't bother her much. It was almost certainly a temporary measure and she supposed the arrogance of youth prevented her from becoming too worried. After all, an aircraft could be sent to extract them pretty much any time they asked, weather dependent. Medical emergencies, compassionate leave, even criminal prosecutions would all see the persons concerned hurried back to America without as much fuss as Jake and Cody were making.

Cody intrigued her. Quiet and yet persistently interested in the comings and goings of the rest of the group on Jake's behalf, he was a curious mixture of youthful enthusiasm and world-weariness. She had no idea what his beef was, but that something plagued him was as clear to her as the Arctic chill that surrounded them.

Bethany shrugged to herself as she closed a small flask and used a vacuum pump to extract the air from within it.

The Air Chemistry Observatory's chief role, to measure the levels of gas in the Arctic atmosphere, required that containers be checked either hourly or week depending on the nature of the gas being collected. Carbon Dioxide, Methane, CFCs, Carbon Monoxide, Hydrogen, Nitrous Oxide and others were painstakingly measured and recorded to provide a detailed record of both natural and anthropogenic influences on the atmosphere.

Bethany hauled on her thick coat and zipped it up as she prepared to head outside. She checked her watch: 19.52pm. Right on, for the hourly CO2 flask switch. She wrapped a thickly gloved hand around the flask and headed for the main door, glancing out of a window as she did so.

Bethany froze.

With the lights on in the station she had not initially noticed anything wrong. But as she stood and looked out of the window she realised that despite the eternal night she could see everything. The ice plains, the distant ridge of mountains, the snowmobiles parked nearby. Everything was illuminated in a weird green glow that shimmered across the heavens.

A pulse of alarm raced through her as she hurried to the main door and flung it open. Bitterly cold air caressed her face as she stepped out into a world that was entirely different from the one she had left just twenty minutes before.

All around her, the sky was on fire.

*

Cody lay on his bed, his hands behind his head as he stared blankly at the ceiling and thought of his little daughter, Maria. She would be in bed by now, probably sleeping soundly after another busy day of creating havoc.

He had never really understood how somebody so small could create such utter devastation in such a short amount of time. If it was loose, discarded, forgotten or forbidden, she would find it and either hide or destroy it. Cody had lost three cell phones in as many months due to tiny hands and very large tantrums.

He turned his head. On the floor nearby lay the heavy steel storage box he had brought with him.

He should never have left. He knew it now. Hell, he had known it then but just hadn't been able to admit it to himself. Running away never solved anything. All lies led to the truth. He should have stood up and been counted, the better to…

'Cody!'

Cody's train of thought derailed and he cursed inwardly. He wasn't unaware of the irony of his mission to escape the rigours of his life, only to become equally irritated by the intrusion of others into what he had believed might be a peaceful isolation.

'Cody, get out here!'

He slid off his bed as Charlotte Dennis burst into his room, her hair flying in a wild halo as she struggled to get into her coat.

'Jesus, Charlie, take it easy,' he said. 'Where's the fire?'

Charlotte jabbed a thumb over her shoulder. 'Everywhere. Come on!'

Cody sensed panic in her voice and in an instant he was hauling his own coat on as he followed her out to the main doors. As he walked through the darkened galley he felt a sudden supernatural twinge as he saw the world outside glowing green and orange, the galley illuminated in the weird light.

He felt his panic subside as he walked. 'It's just the Aurora Borealis,' he replied, 'the Northern Lights. There's nothing to worry about.'

'Yes there is,' Charlotte insisted as she threw open the main doors.

Bright green light shimmered through the doorways as though the sun was rising across the horizon. Cody's breath caught in his throat and he slowed as he moved out into the open air, instinctively pushing the doors shut behind him as he stared in disbelief at the sky.

'Jesus.'

Cody knew the Aurora Borealis well enough, having seen it on several occasions in the past. The result of solar material colliding with the Earth's atmosphere and stripping electrons from particles high above the planet's surface, the energy released by the process followed the shimmering veil of the Earth's magnetic field as light, glowing in beautiful colours that represented the different gases being ionised miles above their heads. But he had never seen one even vaguely as powerful as this.

On a clear night in the high Arctic the sky was filled with a billion blazing stars that peppered the dusty band of the Milky Way like jewels encrusted into a silken banner. Cody had first realised that the stars were different colours when he had travelled to the Arctic six years previously to a research station down in Labrador. In cities, streetlights and pollution blinded the human eye to the faint reds, blue-whites and yellows of the great nuclear Leviathans blazing in the heavens.

But now across the entire sky was a gigantic arc of green light, a shimmering veil that glowed brightly enough both to bathe the entire Arctic in light and to obscure the glittering panorama of stars beyond it. It was like looking out across the ice fields using night-vision goggles, but brighter.

'Is it usually like this?' Bethany asked Jake, who had joined them.

Jake shook his head. 'It's never like this.'

Cody could see the slowly rippling banners of light glowing far down on the horizon, probably right out over Quebec and Canada, maybe even further down across the United States.

'Remote station to Alert Five, you copy?'

Reece Cain's voice was distorted on Jake's radio, the transmission crackling. Jake unclipped it from his belt.

'Go, remote.'

'You guys seeing all of this? It's amazing!'

Cody had never heard Reece say so many words in one go.

'Kind of hard to miss,' Jake replied.

'No shit.'

Charlotte stepped further out onto the ice, her head tilted back in wonder at the tremendous aurora, and spoke in a concerned tone.

'We've got shut everything down,' she said as she began backing away from the blazing skies.

'What?' Cody asked.

'Shut everything down,' Charlotte said, turning for the station door. 'Shut the power down, right now!'

'What the hell are you talking about?' Jake uttered. 'We'll freeze!'

Charlotte ignored him as she dashed inside the station.

Moments later Cody flinched as a bright flash and a loud bang like a gunshot shocked him. He whirled to see one of the observatory's lights scatter sparks as its bulb blew. Another bulb blew out further along the station, plunging the northern section into darkness.

'What the hell is happening?' Bethany shouted.

Cody dashed inside and saw Charlotte running through the building, shutting off lights and computers as she went.

'Help me or we'll lose everything!' she yelled.

Cody and the team spent the next few minutes shutting everything down inside the observatory. Jake shut off the main power under Charlotte's command and the observatory fell silent. With the generators out, the building became bitterly cold within minutes and a deep blackness filled the interior.

'Are you sure about this?' Cody asked in the darkness.

'I just hope I'm wrong,' Charlotte replied.

The team gathered inside the living quarters and Cody was about to ask her what was happening when, slowly, as though alive, the lights in the room began to glow again.

'I thought you shut the power off,' Bradley uttered to Jake.

'I did.'

Charlotte stared up at the ceiling as the lights grew in brightness until they hummed with the current surging through them. Then, one by one, they silently blinked out as their fuses and bulbs blew in quick succession and the building was plunged into absolute blackness once more.

'What was that?' Bethany asked her.

'We won't know until tomorrow,' Charlotte whispered in response. 'Best thing that we can do now is get our heads under our duvets and keep warm.'

The team dispersed silently to their rooms, Cody climbing into his sleeping bag and laying down to look out of the window at the brilliant aurora shimmering across the heavens outside and illuminating the distant mountains to the south.

He hoped that Maria could see the same spectacular display from where she was, thousands of miles away.

6

Cody was running.

Running hard, trying to flee.

He could feel them behind him, knew that they would catch him. Everything had become a lie. Everything was coming down on him and he knew that he would never, ever escape it. He cried out at the top of his lungs that it wasn't his fault and that it wasn't meant to happen as the whole world plunged down onto him and crushed him beneath an unbearable burden of shame, guilt and regret.

Cody's eyes flicked open, and for a moment he believed that he was blind such was the absolute blackness. His mind began reconnecting itself as his dream faded away, memories replacing the phantoms of sleep. He glanced at the faint outline of his window but behind the curtains he could see that the green glow was gone, darkness having resumed sometime during the night. Cody hauled his duvet off and clambered out of bed.

The cold hit him first as he saw his breath condense on thick clouds. The floor was like ice beneath his feet. He looked down in surprise and then threw his clothes on as quickly as he could. If the generators were still down they were in deep trouble.

He made his way into the living quarters.

Empty.

He turned and leaned out into the corridor down to the main doors. Empty and black but for a faint, flickering light.

Cody turned and walked to the communications room, briefly remembering that Boston were supposed to call him back this morning. As he turned into the room he was surprised to find Jake, Charlotte, Bethany and Bobby all crammed around the radios and the computer with Sauri and Bradley, Jake in the seat.

A lone candle burned on a table nearby.

'Morning folks,' he said as he walked in. 'Any news about how far south the aurora got last night, and what's happened to the heating?'

Jake dialled a frequency into the radio banks. 'Any station, this is Alert Five, please respond, over?'

Cody blinked, patted his own chest with one hand. 'Have I passed away? Can anybody hear me?'

Charlotte turned to him, her features stricken. 'We've got a problem, Cody.'

Jake turned in his seat as if realising for the first time that Cody had joined them.

'I can't raise anybody on the radio, on any frequency,' he said.

Cody stared at Jake for a long moment. 'Communications antenna is probably iced up, I'll take a look.'

'I already did that,' Bethany said. 'It's fine.'

Cody looked at the computer monitor. The screen was dead.

'It's down,' Jake confirmed as he saw the direction of Cody's gaze. 'Everything's down.'

Cody struggled to digest what Jake was telling him.

'Our signals must be disrupted or something,' he said. 'Maybe we can use the satellite phone to…'

'Dead,' Charlotte cut him off. 'So are the cell signals.'

'It must be our equipment then,' Cody replied.

'I checked out our own radios using our static detectors, to see if they picked up the signals. Everything's dead.'

Cody stared at the computer monitor as if willing it to suddenly spring back into life.

'You try calling Boston?' he asked Jake.

'Repeatedly,' Jake nodded. 'We've got nothing, no phones and no power.'

Cody forced his mind into action, drove the confusion away.

'Maybe the power lines got hit,' he suggested and turned to Charlotte. 'That aurora from last night. They've been known to trip satellites and transformers out, right, overload circuitry and such like?'

She nodded.

'Sure, but they shut the satellites down when solar storms hit to protect them, then turn them back on afterward. Same for the lines, except that the forces station cleared out yesterday so there was nobody to shut them down.'

'So we start up the oil-burners and hunker down until they come back,' Cody suggested. 'Most of our communications go through a satellite so it explains everything.'

'Not everything,' Bobby said. 'I've tried every radio frequency we've got on a standard analogue dish, from short to long wave, ultra, you name it. There's not a sound coming in from anywhere.'

Cody felt a new chill shudder up his spine. 'Nothing at all?'

'Nobody is broadcasting on any wavelength that I can detect. No music, no forecasts, no news channels. Nothing.'

Cody looked at Jake. 'You ever had this happen before?'

Jake shook his head. 'Never, and if any station up here ever did lose contact with the outside world a rescue package would be dispatched within hours.'

'And the weather's been okay the last twelve hours,' Bobby said. 'They could have sent an airplane to pull us out at any time.'

Cody watched as Jake wracked his brains.

'We've got to assume the fault's at our end,' Jake said finally. 'Maybe we just need the power back to gain a signal. Even the dishes down at Eureka have to be positioned horizontally to detect a satellite. Up here, we can't even see them.'

'What do you have in mind?' Bethany asked.

Jake rubbed his head for a long moment. 'Nothing. I don't know how best to deal with this. Our main concern should be survival first, then re-establishing contact.'

Cody looked at the other members of the team, finally sensing the unease infecting the cold air in the room.

'I've got an idea,' Bradley said. 'I think we should try the base. If anywhere is going to have equipment tough enough to still work, it'll be there.'

'They said they'd shoot to kill if anybody trespassed,' Bethany pointed out.

'Hard to do that if there's nobody there,' Jake said in Bradley's defence as he got out of his seat. 'And besides, I'd define this as a goddamned emergency.'

'But if we've got no power what makes you think the base does?' Charlotte asked the soldier.

'Alert is protected against pretty much everything,' Bradley replied, 'even things like electro-magnetic pulses produced by nuclear attacks, and its power transformers and lines have extra shielding. They might be holding up.'

Jake stood up and began buttoning his thick jacket. 'That's good enough for me. We pack up and move north, because if we stay here we'll be frozen solid by this afternoon.'

Jake pushed his way out of the communications room and past Cody, then tugged at his arm.

'Cody, you give me a hand with something?'

Cody nodded and followed Jake out of the block. The darkness was complete but for a row of emergency glow-sticks that Bradley was cracking to illuminate the corridors with a chemical glow. Cody followed Jake through the pools of light and outside, zipping up his jacket as he did so. The air outside seemed frozen solid in the darkness, the glittering stars across the heaves above even brighter now without the station's external lamps on.

Jake walked across to the parked snowmobiles and then turned to face Cody.

'Have you done this?'

Cody stared at Jake in surprise. 'Come again?'

'Have you shut the station down, sabotaged it in some way?'

Cody gaped in disbelief. 'Why the hell would I do that?'

Jake yanked a piece of paper from his pocket and handed it to Cody. Printed upon it was a screen grab taken from the computer in the communications room, the cover of the newspaper and the hunt for a killer.

'I went through the search history last night,' Jake said, 'after that phone call I got from Boston.'

Cody shook his head. 'I looked at the Boston Globe's main page when I called home yesterday. What's this got to do with me?'

'Nothing,' Jake replied, 'except that the call I got was from a police detective in Boston.'

The air around Cody seemed to get suddenly colder as he stood and stared at Jake. 'What did they want?'

Jake took a pace closer. 'You tell me?'

Cody struggled to keep his features even as he spoke. 'You think I'm responsible for all of this? Jesus, the Canadians cleared out Jake. What the hell could I have to do with that?'

'Any of the others know about this, Cody?' Jake asked, then pointed at the print out.

'Not that I know of,' Cody replied. He took a deep breath as he looked at the image in his gloved hand.

Jake watched him for a moment. 'Somebody here is wanted for something serious in Boston, and I can only assume that means either large scale fraud or homicide.'

Cody was about to reply when the door beside them banged open and Bradley Trent stormed down the metal steps, pulling his hood up against the frigid air.

'Maybe we should send a message ahead of some kind, to warn anybody who might still be at the base?' Charlotte said as she followed Bradley out into the darkness.

'They didn't inform us of why they cleared out,' Jake replied for the soldier. 'Why the hell should we inform them that we're going in?'

'Maybe they left guards behind?' Charlotte suggested.

'Doubt it,' Jake said, gesturing to Bradley Trent. 'They wouldn't have bothered to come looking for this loser if they were leaving people behind.'

'Up yours,' Bradley muttered. 'I've got the lead out there. You don't pass me unless I tell you to, understood?'

'Fine by me,' Jake replied. 'If there are any guards remaining, they'll probably shoot you first.'

Jake shot Cody a concerned look as he turned for his snowmobile. Bradley mounted his and tried to start it. Nothing happened.

'Damn, battery's gone,' he uttered.

Cody tried his key, turned it in the ignition, but nothing happened.

'Christ, even the snowmobiles are dead!' Jake said in disbelief.

'We'll have to walk,' Bradley said. 'If I'm right, we can use the snowmobiles from Alert instead.'

'It's five kilometres,' Cody pointed out.

'Then the exercise will do you good,' Bradley snapped. 'Got a problem with that?'

'Start packing up some of our gear,' Jake called back to Charlotte. 'We might need to move into the base.'

Cody followed Bradley out into the bitter darkness, the soldier leading the way along the twisting road that led to the airbase. The darkness seemed to close around him as though he himself was being pursued. He tried to shrug off the sense that thousands of miles away his life was falling apart and there was nothing that he could do to prevent it.

The walk across the lonely ice road took over an hour, the only sound the crunching of their boots on the ice. Nobody spoke, and Cody guessed that was because nobody really knew what to say.

The first thing that Cody noticed as they approached was that the runway lights were off and the base itself was enshrouded in total darkness. Only a tiny building near the edge of the base showed any signs of life, a single window illuminated from inside that he glimpsed as they walked. The remainder of the base was so inky black that if he hadn't known it was there he would never have seen it.

The base consisted of a series of large hangar like buildings, surrounded by accommodation blocks all served by eight large fuel silos beside the airfield road on the far side of the base.

Bradley strode alongside the nearest of the hangars as Jake, Cody and Sauri joined him.

Cody looked at the large buildings, most of the accommodation blocks prefabricated out of aluminium and standing on legs that elevated them above the ice. The larger service hangars stood on the ice itself.

'How come this place is so big?' he asked Bradley. 'I thought it was just a listening post?'

'It is,' Bradley replied. 'But normally there are about seventy people based here on rotation, plus vehicles to haul goods, refuelling bowsers, am-tracks, snow clearers, you name it. We need enough gear to keep the place running through the winter for long periods when supply flights can't get through.'

Jake walked alongside Bradley as they strode between the huge buildings.

'What about ships?' he asked. 'Can't they run stuff through?'

Bradley shook his head.

'Not in the winter. The Lincoln Sea is covered in ice thick enough to stop any vessel, although in summer it's navigable. Most captains don't venture up here though as the ocean's still full of icebergs. One wrong move and *wham*!'

Bradley punched a gloved fist into a palm with a thump that echoed between the buildings. He reached out to doors as they passed them, yanking on them to no avail.

'Everything's locked up,' he said as they searched the complex.

'Why would they do this?' Cody asked. 'Surely they must intend to come back at some point?'

'You'd think so,' Bradley muttered. 'Not like my unit to abandon their own, especially not in a hell hole like this.'

'There was a light on in one of the buildings,' Cody said. 'I saw it on the way in.'

'Motion sensor,' Bradley replied. 'Probably a fox set it off.'

'Looked like it was an interior light,' Cody insisted.

'Where?'

Cody led them in a direction he felt was about right for where he saw the light. They walked out of the complex of large buildings and found a series of smaller blocks, one of which glowed from within.

'I'll be damned,' Bradley said with a bright smile that glowed in the starlight.

Bradley jogged across the ice as Jake, Cody and Sauri followed. He reached the door to the small block and burst in, a bright rectangle of light spilling out into the eternal darkness. Cody climbed the block steps and walked inside to see Bradley holding a piece of paper, his eyes scanning from left to right and his features collapsing as he did so.

'What is it?' Jake asked.

Bradley dropped the piece of paper. Cody could see it contained a hand-written note.

'We're screwed, is what it is,' Bradley uttered.

Cody looked down at the paper as Jake read from it out loud.

'Brad, Sauri. Evacuation order given at one hour notice. No details. Forced to pull out regardless of situation. All personnel accounted for except yourselves and the American team. Asked for time to find you. Denied. Advised that the scientists would need protecting until our return. No date given for this. Sit tight buddy, whatever the hell's happened I'm sure we'll be back before long. Keys on the table for Polaris Hall to let us know you're okay. Light left on so you'd find them. Probably get my ass kicked for it but hell, I don't like seeing men get left behind. Best of luck, Tyrone and the guys.'

Cody looked at the keys Bradley held. The soldier hefted them thoughtfully for a moment and then shrugged as though he wasn't bothered.

'Let's go and see what we can find.'

Bradley led them across the base to Polaris Hall, the communication centre, a blocky building festooned with satellite dishes and aerials. Bradley unlocked the door and they walked in to find the interior silent but warm: the departing soldiers had left the heating on to protect the computer stations and sensitive devices within.

'Bingo,' Bradley said as he pointed at a series of computer terminals. 'We've got power here.'

A series of small blinking lights winked at them from what looked to Cody like a bank of supercomputers humming in a room next door. Bradley hit the lights, fluorescent tubes clicking as they flickering into life.

A large map of Russia and Alaska dominated one wall of the room, marked with pins and lines drawn on a protective acrylic sheet covering the map. Clocks above the map tracked time zones across the region.

'Missile silos in the former Soviet Union,' Jake guessed as he looked at the map. 'They must still listen in on them.'

'All the time,' Bradley replied as he moved from one computer to another, switching them back on.

The room began to fill with the hum of hard drives as the screens lit up one by one. Cody watched as Bradley finished his sweep of the room and stood back.

'All of these computers will have access pass codes which I don't possess,' he said as he looked at Jake.

'So what's the point in starting them up?'

Bradley gestured to a pair of large monitors mounted upon the rear wall of the room.

'Those two monitors relay electro-magnetic signals from the listening station. The signals are crunched by the supercomputers and run through these stations before reaching those screens. Even though we can't access the stations themselves, the information being detected by the satellite dishes will still automatically pass through and reach the monitors.'

'Good enough,' Jake replied as he turned to look at the two screens.

As the computers hummed so the screens both blinked and a graph appeared on each, a time line and a frequency scale a little like a heart monitor in a hospital. Running along the graph was a line that hovered around a mark on the graph calibrated as "zero / background".

Cody, Jake, Bradley and Sauri waited for the line to pick up as the dishes outside relayed their information.

And waited.

Bradley shook his head. 'That's not possible, man.'

'Where's the signals?' Jake asked the soldier.

Bradley shook his head. 'I've been up here on rotation for four months. That screen has always recorded something. There's always a signal, even if it's just a bunch of asshole truck-drivers talking over the airwaves. The damned thing's always alive.'

'What does background and zero mean?' Cody asked, already suspecting the answer but unwilling to admit it to himself.

For the first time, Sauri spoke in a clear accent touched with a slight Canadian drawl.

'Background radiation, from natural processes.'

Jake stared at the screen for a few moments longer and then he turned to Cody.

'You realise what this means?'

Cody tried to think of something to say but no words came forth. He felt a quiver of apprehension as he looked into Jake McDermott's eyes and saw a glimmer of something he'd never expected to witness there: fear.

'There's nobody out there,' Jake said. 'The whole world's gone silent.'

Dean Crawford

7

The team reconvened in the Alert Five building.

Cody had spent the entire journey back from the base in a stupor, unable to grasp the magnitude of what had happened. First and foremost in his mind was Maria, and close beside her, Danielle. He had not yet been able to find in himself the frantic fear for their safety that must surely come upon him soon, and he realised that it was because he simply could not allow himself to believe what the instruments at Alert were telling him.

The world had fallen silent.

The rest of the team took the news in a similar kind of stupefied silence.

Bethany, Charlotte, Reece and Bobby were sat in a row across a bench at the rear of the communal room. Bradley and Sauri leaned against the wall nearby, their rifles slung across their backs. Jake stood in front of the darkened windows as Cody leaned against the closed door and listened to Jake.

'Okay, it's now eleven fifty three in the morning. Our connection to the outside world was lost approximately eight hours ago. We've lost our transmitters, receivers and electrical power here, but there is nothing wrong with those at Canadian Forces Station Alert. That means that for reasons I can't even begin to fathom there are no signals being broadcast from anywhere in the world within range of this station.' He sighed. 'Given CFS Alert's sensitivity, that may well mean the world in its entirety. Opinions, people.'

Nobody spoke for a long time. The room felt sombre, filled with an unspoken dread frozen in place by the Arctic chill.

'Could be atmospheric,' Cody finally forced himself to break the silence. 'Maybe some kind of temperature anomaly that's blocking signals?'

Jake looked across at Reece, who shook his head, his black fringe swaying across his eyes.

'It's possible, but unlikely. Temperature inversions in water can create channels of silence where submarines like to operate, and similar things can happen in the atmosphere but not with enough variation to block all signals. Something would always get through.'

'What about fossil fuels running out?' Bethany asked. 'Oil runs everything, right?'

'Wouldn't stop the broadcasts so fast,' Jake said. 'There'd be generators running, nuclear power stations would still supply fuel to cities and so on. We wouldn't be cut off so quickly.'

Bobby Leary raised a hand, his face pinched with concern.

'What about a nuclear war?' he said in a voice that seemed hushed, as though he were afraid to raise the possibility.

Jake looked across at Bradley.

'I don't think so,' the soldier said. 'CFS Alert's monitoring equipment would have recorded the blasts, and there would have to have been hundreds of them to silence literally everything. Every city would have needed a direct hit. If that had happened we'd see it in the atmosphere even out here, the smog and debris and from so many cities burning.'

'I suppose,' Bobby said, 'although I've heard that nuclear weapons emit an electro-magnetic pulse that can fry electronics, shutting them down for good. Maybe that could have....'

'It wasn't a bomb,' Charlotte said simply.

Everybody fell silent as Charlotte kicked off the bench and landed with a thump, staring into space.

'How can you be sure?' Jake asked.

'The aurora, last night,' she replied. 'It coincided with the loss of signals from outside?'

'Roughly,' Cody agreed.

'We lost satellite communication at the same time that the aurora started,' Jake added.

Charlotte ran a hand through the thick tresses of her hair then turned to face them.

'I know what happened,' she said finally. 'It's why I tried to shut the power down here, and why it came back on all on its own. It was caused by something known as a Coronal Mass Ejection.'

'A what?' Bradley uttered.

'A solar storm,' Charlotte explained. 'Giant blasts of solar material a thousand times larger than our planet normally held in loops of the sun's magnetic field. Some of these loops become large enough that they break free of the solar surface and blast across the solar system. They occur every day, but most times we don't know anything about them as the Earth's magnetic field deflects any that head directly for us, causing the *aurora borealis* and *aurora australis* as waves of charged particles batter our atmosphere.'

'Okay,' Bobbie said. 'So far, so normal, right?'

'Yeah,' Charlotte agreed, 'but just a few years ago NASA took the unprecedented step of making a global warning about the possibility of solar super-storms over the next decade or so. The sun works in eleven year cycles, pulsing up and down in its level of activity. If a major super-storm coincided with a weakened magnetic field here on Earth, which is what we're experiencing right now, then there would be nothing to deflect the storm itself.' She looked across at Jake. 'It would strike the Earth's surface, perhaps for hours.'

'In English, for Christ's sake,' Bradley shot at her. 'What the hell's happened?'

'It's like the electromagnetic pulse from a nuclear weapon,' she said, 'but many orders of magnitude greater and across the entire planet.'

Bradley stared at her. Beside him, Sauri spoke. 'The whole planet?'

Charlotte nodded, her brow furrowed.

'The huge power of the blast bathes the atmosphere with charged particles. They in turn hit ground level and strike power grids, navigation devices, computers, cell phones — anything with a current running through it. The extra power overheats the circuit, whatever it is, and either melts it or blows it up. Silicon chips run virtually everything, and without them… '

'There's no power, no electricity,' Reece finished the sentence for her.

'Instantly?' Bethany asked, and was rewarded with a nod from Charlotte.

'How could it happen across the whole planet?' Cody asked.

Charlotte glanced out of the window into the darkness.

'The storm lasted for hours, and the Earth revolves as it moves through space in orbit around the sun. That storm could have hit pretty much the entire planet, enough to take out every single industrialised nation. '

Cody felt a new and nauseating pulse of alarm thread its way through his body.

'But the authorities must have known about this. They must have had some kind of contingency plan?'

Charlotte scoffed in disgust.

'NASA and the European Space Agency have been shouting about the dangers of a major solar storm for years. Every administration has simply ignored them. Governments across Europe ignored them. In 2008, the National Academy of Sciences published a report detailing the potential collapse of the United States technological base and the subsequent fall of civilisation as we know it.' She shook her head. 'Nobody took any notice.'

'This is ridiculous,' Jake said. 'The population isn't going to disappear because of this. They'll rebuild the infrastructure. They'll get the power back on, get things moving again, right?'

Reece shook his head.

'It's not a problem of technical repair. It's an issue of scale. We're not talking about a few transformers popping or a couple of GPS satellites going off line. It's every single electricity-reliant system on the planet. Power grids and stations, financial systems, water plants, air travel, transport, farming, communications, computers — everything. There's no way the whole thing could be repaired in time to prevent a collapse. With no power there will be no heat, no light, no fresh water from taps, no hospitals, no military, no nothing. Within days people will be suffering from starvation and dehydration. They'll eat mouldy food, drink contaminated water. Sickness will emerge, and from that, pandemics. Make no mistake about it: if Charlotte's right about this storm then everything's about to go to hell.'

'How would you know all of that?' Bradley snapped.

'I'm a *prepper*,' Reece replied. 'My folks lived out in Montana, spent their entire lives waiting for some goddamned apocalypse that never came. Oil running out, new Ice Age, super volcanoes — you name it, they worried about it. Didn't worry about smoking though, which was what got them both in the end. I learned a lot from them over the years and kept a little emergency stash just in case.

Trouble is all my damned survival gear is back in Great Falls.'

'Jesus,' Bradley uttered. 'That's why you're so damned sociable.'

'How come this hasn't happened before?' Bethany asked Charlotte.

'It has,' Charlotte said. 'In 1859 the Carrington Event, a major geomagnetic solar storm, hit the Earth. The aurora was visible even over the Caribbean. They were so bright during the night over the Rocky Mountains that miners began preparing breakfast, believing the sun to be rising behind the clouds. Telegraph systems across the United States were totally blown, often shocking the operators and settling paper alight, and the telegraphs often carried messages even after they'd been unplugged, such was the charge.'

Cody's mind focused on Danielle and Maria as Charlotte went on.

'It happened again in 1989, when a minor storm took out the Hydro-Quebec power grid for nine hours. This isn't a rare occurrence. It's just that in recent decades we've become so reliant on electrical energy that we've become vulnerable to these storms.'

'Couldn't they have sent a warning?' Bobby asked her. 'The government I mean, or people watching the sun? That's your speciality, right?'

'Yeah, it is,' she agreed. 'But it depends on the energy of the blast. Normally they take three or four days to reach the Earth, plenty of warning time. But the storm in 1859 got to us in seventeen hours because a previous, smaller event had cleared the path between the sun and the Earth of solar debris and particles. The sun is currently at its solar maximum, at its most ferocious. If this recent storm was also ejected after a smaller outburst then it could have travelled here in twelve hours or less. There would be no time. The best that governments could do is attempt a shut down of the global power system to mitigate the damage, but even that might not work if the storm was powerful enough.'

Bradley Trent slapped his own head with his hand. 'I thought you damned people were supposed to be geniuses? You're telling me that overnight the entire planet's gone to hell and we're stuck up here on our own?'

Jake looked at the team around him and his gaze fell on Cody.

Cody rubbed his head with thumb and forefinger as a dull ache spread between his eyes.

'Without power and infrastructure, food will run out in a matter of a few days,' he said, hating the sound of his own words as images of Maria filled his mind. 'Fresh water will disappear from cities as the pressure in the system is lost. No central heating and as it is winter most of North America will freeze. People will try to flee the cities, searching for food and water. Federal and State government will be totally overwhelmed. They'll try martial law but it won't work. There are nearly four hundred million people in the United States and without modern farming and transport they'll be facing mass starvation in just a few days.' He hesitated as the enormity of what was happening struck him. 'The same things will happen across the globe, in every country, to billions of people.'

An image of Maria's face, smiling and laughing on the computer monitor, swelled in his mind as pain pinched at the corners of his eyes.

Cody looked up at Jake. 'Jesus, we've got to get out of here, right now.'

Cody turned and burst out of the accommodation block and across the ice, scrambled up a bank near the edge of the compound until he looked out across the dark and barren plains toward the south where sheer cliffs and mountains maintained a lonely vigil against the Arctic storms.

Across the horizon, a faint glow of pink light shone like the distant star that it was.

The bitter chill bit deeply through his three sweaters as a fine hail of snow swept across the ridge before the wind, but he felt nothing but a horrified numbness that encapsulated his body in a rigor of despair. Cody's legs failed and buckled beneath him as he crumpled to his knees in the snow, his gaze fixed upon the feeble rays of sunlight sweeping the heavens a world away.

The thought of his little girl trapped in a world collapsing into anarchy and despair filled him with an acidic horror that scalded through his veins.

'Oh God, what have I done?' he gasped.

Tears spilled from his eyes, running as far as his cheeks before they froze into globules of ice.

Foot falls crunched through the snow behind him, and Cody swiped a sleeve across his face as Jake joined him on the ridge. Cody did not look at Jake, his eyes glued to the distant sun as though its light were the only thing keeping him alive.

A heavy Arctic Jacket fell gently across his shoulders as Jake laid it there, ice crystals pattering against the fabric as they skimmed through the frigid air. Cody reluctantly pushed his arms into the sleeves as he heard other footfalls joining them on the ridge.

Jake slowly squatted down on the ice beside Cody and stared out toward the distant sunlight.

'You know that we can't leave here, Cody,' he said. 'It's much too far. We'd never make it.'

'The snowmobiles,' Cody snapped. 'We'll tow supplies.'

Jake shook his head. 'We couldn't take enough fuel and food with us. It's more than a thousand miles to the nearest settlement. We'd die long before finding anybody.'

Cody felt the rage of a lifetime swell inside him, as powerless to escape as he was. It seethed and seared and then imploded into helplessness.

'I can't leave them,' he managed to rasp. 'I can't.'

'You already did,' Jake said. 'But right now all you can do is stand up.'

Cody looked at Jake, who stuck out a thickly gloved hand.

A thousand conflicting thoughts and memories passed in utter silence through Cody's mind. He wanted to leap off the ridge and start running south. He wanted to punch Jake in the face for not understanding. He wanted to find a gun and turn it on himself for his stupidity and his selfishness. He wanted to die. And he wanted to live.

Cody took Jake's hand and got to his feet.

'We need a plan,' Jake said.

Dean Crawford

8

Week 7
My dearest Maria,
I don't know where to begin.

It is hard to write these words. Something inside of me wants to destroy everything, to burn and break in fury at the cruel blow that fate has delivered us all. My every thought is with you. I cannot sleep for the fear that infects me, of what you may be going through and for rage at my inability to help you. Nothing in my imagination could have prepared me for such terrible suffering, yet I know that it pales into insignificance compared to what you must be facing right now.

Despite our shared horror at what has befallen mankind, we have managed over the past few days since the solar event to formulate a plan of action. Jake has become the rock of our team almost overnight. He has, I suspect, the least of concerns as he has no family to worry about. Bobby, an orphan, appears also to have risen to the challenge. The rest of us labour through our duties like robots, unable to free our thoughts from family and loved ones. For all we know, as we work our cities burn and citizens are dying in countless numbers.

Like all of them, I can only hope and pray that somehow the spirit of human cooperation and companionship that allowed us to rise above our fellow species on this planet will shine through once again, and save those dearest to us from the unimaginable fate of succumbing to the disaster that hangs over us all.

*

'We're on our own.'

Jake's voice had sounded small in the immense darkness outside the observatory.

Cody had stood alongside Bethany, the rest of the team beside them. Hoods raised, puffs of their breath billowing out into the cold air. The entire group had been overwhelmed with a sombre resignation that had reminded Cody of the soldiers who had fought in the trenches of the First World War or stormed the beaches of the Cotentin on D-Day: still alive and yet doomed. The futility of their situation had hit hard but they had remained silent as Jake spoke.

'We'll shift the rest our gear to the Alert base and live there permanently. There are more resources, the fuel tanks are larger and we'll be able to monitor the airwaves using their equipment. We can only hope that somebody's still out there that can make some kind of rescue attempt.'

Nobody had argued.

'We'll re-route all power to the smallest accommodation block to conserve fuel. Everything but the snowmobiles can freeze to hell for all I care. Brad? How much fuel does the base hold?'

Bradley had shrugged. 'Two or three month's when full, about half that right now.'

'Good,' Jake said. 'That's for the whole base. We might last a year or more if we conserve it down to a single building. We'll need to create an inventory of the remaining food and then take a good look at some of the snowmobiles they've got there. It's a long shot but maybe, somehow, we can figure out a way to drive them far enough south to get us out of here once the winter breaks.'

'I thought you said that was impossible?' Charlotte had asked. 'That we couldn't carry enough fuel?'

'It is,' Jake had admitted, 'at the moment. But staying here indefinitely is what's really impossible. Maybe we can jury rig one of the vehicles to carry enough fuel to get us down to Eureka.'

Cody had mentally pictured the outpost of Eureka, hundreds of miles away on the southern tip of Ellesmere

Island. No longer permanently occupied, it would likely hold stores and supplies, perhaps even fuel.

'Let's get to it,' Jake had clapped his gloved hands in the darkness, the sound echoing out into an icy oblivion, and in that one motion had condemned the team to a winter north of the Arctic Circle.

*

The interior of the storage facility at CFS Alert was utterly black as Bradley Trent unlocked a side door and slipped inside, Sauri close behind. The door slammed shut with an echo that chased around the big metal building.

Bradley flicked on a flashlight and the beam sliced through the darkness, illuminating ghostly tendrils of diaphanous mist that swirled on the freezing air and glistening ice clinging to the interior walls like galaxies of tiny stars. Crates and boxes were stacked high on pallets, marked with labels that denoted the contents: jackets, boots, snow chains, bathroom necessities.

'Where's the food stored?' Bradley asked.

Sauri gestured toward the far side of the building, where ranks of empty metal racks stood near a wall that faced the accommodation block. Bradley hurried over, his flashlight sweeping the empty racking.

'Jesus, they cleared us out.'

Sauri said nothing as Bradley hunted up and down the racks and rifled through nearby cardboard boxes. The soldier lifted a tin from one of the boxes and stared at it in disbelief. In the darkness and in the harsh beam of the flashlight, his sudden laughter seemed almost demonic.

'They left us the biscuits!' he roared.

Sauri said nothing as Bradley turned and hurled the tin against the wall of the building with a crash of cold metal against cold metal. The tin rattled to the floor as Bradley hammered a gloved hand against his head.

'Why didn't they come and get us?' he shouted. 'Why leave us here to rot?'

Sauri looked at his companion for a few moments. 'We won't rot. Much too cold.'

Bradley stared at Sauri for a long beat. 'Well thanks genius, glad to see your cup's still half goddamned full.'

Sauri looked at the boxes of biscuits. 'How many tins?'

Bradley glanced down at the pallet of five cardboard boxes.

'Twenty five,' he uttered.

'Between eight people,' Sauri replied. 'Three boxes each. We can have raffle for last one.'

Bradley shook his head and began chuckling to himself. Sauri said nothing. Bradley's chuckle faded away as he looked at the biscuits.

'We'll keep the biscuits.' He looked across at Sauri. 'Just you and me.'

'But the others will need… '

'They're not our responsibility,' Bradley snapped, his head down as he rummaged through the rest of the boxes. 'We'll stash these out back somewhere.'

A long silence as Sauri digested what he had heard. 'We are here to protect Jake and his team.'

'We were,' Bradley corrected him as he hefted a stack of tins across the building toward a distant rack. 'That was before everything went to hell.'

'It is our duty.'

'It's our damned duty to get home,' Bradley shot back as he slid the tins out of sight behind boxes of Arctic clothing. 'Where are you from, Sauri?'

'Inuvik.'

'Great. I'm from Yellowknife. You think that Jake and his little crew will want to head our way if we get out of here? You heard them.'

'They need us. We have the weapons.'

'We'll give them a rifle and wish them the best of luck,' Bradley retorted.

'If there's no power, everybody in Yellowknife will have left or died,' Sauri pointed out. 'Too cold without power.'

'That's up to us to find out, right?' Bradley challenged. 'You're either with me or you're with them. Decide.'

Sauri looked at Bradley for a long time, and then shouldered his rifle and began carrying the tins across the building.

*

It took several hours to shuttle their belongings across the rutted and rolling ice valleys of the plain, the headlights of the snowmobiles flickering in the eternal night like lonely stars wandering an empty universe.

Cody drove back and forth between the two camps, one eye always cast toward the faintly glowing horizon as he worked, unable to break his thoughts away from his wife and daughter. They could see that same glow, brighter where they were. The pain of separation was a dull ache that infected his chest, throbbing with each beat of his heart as though he were already bleeding out.

The base at Alert was shrouded in darkness but for a pair of lights that illuminated the accommodation block on the south west corner. Cody guided his snowmobile through the snow blustering across the beams of his headlights and turned in alongside the main block.

Bethany and Charlotte appeared at the door to the block and began hefting boxes and crates from the sledge behind him as Cody watched Jake's heavily laden snowmobile follow him in. Jake killed the engine on his snowmobile and joined Cody as they walked up into the block.

'You guys done yet?' Jake demanded as he yanked his hood back.

Charlotte hauled the block door shut as Bethany joined them and dumped a crate on top of a pile near the window.

'We'll get this lot logged,' Bethany said, 'but it's not looking good.'

'What isn't?' Cody asked.

Charlotte jabbed a thumb out toward the main buildings. 'Brad's just gone through the stores and there's no food. Looks like the soldiers took everything with them.'

Cody felt a new fear twist his stomach as he realised the depth of their situation.

'They cleared out everything?' Jake uttered in disbelief.

'The whole damned lot,' Bobby Leary confirmed. 'All we've got is supplies for maybe a month at most.'

'That's all?' Cody asked. 'There's no way we can stretch that out until the spring.'

Jake dragged his hand down across his beard. 'Jesus Christ, did they *want* us all to die out here?'

Reece Cain walked into the block from the rest room and gave a bleak laugh.

'May as well have done,' he muttered. 'Ration packs, water bottles, sterilisation packs — you name it, it's gone.'

Cody's mind raced as he tried to hold back thoughts of his daughter and think for a moment.

'Survival,' he said. 'They were thinking about their own survival.'

Jake nodded as he sank back against a tower of boxes. 'They knew what was coming. Maybe their listening devices picked up the coming storm?'

'But then who sent the airplanes?' Bethany asked.

'It doesn't matter,' Jake said. 'They cut us loose and now we're on our own. We either live or die, understood? There's nothing to gain by us hating whoever decided to leave us out here.'

'Got to be worse for Brad and Sauri,' Charlotte said. 'Their own comrades abandoned them. Their own countrymen.'

Cody thought for a moment and then made a decision. 'I'm heading back out.'

'Back out where?' Bethany asked. 'It's late and there's a storm building up.'

Cody fastened his jacket. 'We've got to assume that they didn't abandon us out of spite — there are only eight of us. We were five clicks away across the ice, an hour's snowmobile trip for them to fetch us. My guess is that there just wasn't time for them to come and get us and clear out before the storm stranded them too. They had to cut and run, or die out here themselves.'

'So?' Charlotte demanded.

'So there's a chance they had a plan and may have ridden out the solar storm,' Jake guessed Cody's train of thought, 'and may come back.'

'Hell of a long shot,' Cody admitted. 'But if there's a chance that they've survived this, we've got to try to let them know we're alive.'

'How?' Bethany asked.

'I'll set up a distress beacon at Alert Five,' Cody explained, 'and start using Alert's radios to search for signals from the outside world. If somebody hears us, especially our absent military friends, it may be reason enough for them to come back and get us.'

Charlotte frowned.

'If satellites are down surely there's no way for people to hear the beacon at a ground station? They might not hear us.'

Cody smiled grimly as he pulled his hood up. 'What if we don't bother to send a signal at all?'

'We should do it all from here,' Jake cautioned him. 'No sense in risking an accident out at the observatory.'

'It's just a few clicks to Alert Five,' Cody said. 'But that might be the difference between a signal being picked up and being missed. It's not a chance I want to take.'

He yanked open the block door and strode down the gantry onto the solid ice. Jake's hand rested heavily on his shoulder as he climbed onto his snowmobile.

'I'll back you up.'

Cody shook his head. 'We need to conserve fuel. If I get caught out by the weather, I can still overnight at Alert Five.'

'That's not good procedure, Cody,' Jake replied.

'I know it's not good goddamned procedure,' Cody shot back, and then reigned himself in. 'I just need some time to myself, okay?'

Jake's gloved hand remained on Cody's shoulder for what felt like an age, then it slipped away.

Cody gunned the snowmobile's engine and the headlights blazed strips of white fire through the falling snow.

'If I don't see you back here within twenty-four hours, we'll all be coming out to find you, understood?' Jake shouted.

Cody turned away and accelerated out of the compound. He took the road at full throttle with his hands gripping the throttle as tightly as he could, his teeth grinding in his jaw as he rode at a pace that he would once have never dared to attempt.

The blizzard swept across the ice plains, obscuring everything but the reflective markers placed every ten feet to guide him toward Alert Five. Thick snow caked his jacket and hood and tumbled endlessly around him, encrusting his goggles in delicate geometric patterns as he rode until he could no longer feel his hands or feet.

Alert Five loomed almost without warning ahead of him, its radio masts quivering in the tremendous winds as Cody slowed the snowmobile down and turned it to park in the shelter of the station's leeward wall. He left the engine running as he got out of the saddle and looked out toward the south. The temptation to keep going was almost unbearable, but somehow his rational mind prevented him from racing hell for leather toward the sun that he knew was out there somewhere beyond the blinding veils of snow and endless night.

Cody turned to the observatory and struggled up the steps. He unlocked the door and hurried inside. Already the walls were dusted with sparkling ice crystals and the windows thick with frost.

Cody grabbed a box from a wall cabinet and cracked it open. A yellow Personal Locator Beacon lay inside, designed to transmit on the 406Mhz global satellite signal and on a 121.5Mhz homing signal. It was able to operate in temperatures of minus 20 degrees Celsius, but only for around forty-eight hours. He would have to replace it regularly to maintain a permanent signal. Although Alert was too far north for its transmission dishes to detect communications satellites, a six station repeater chain between Alert and Eureka provided a terrestrial link to the satellite receivers in Ottawa. Even at Eureka, to detect a geosynchronous satellite to the south would require dishes to be set horizontally, so far north was the station. A satellite not directly due south would be invisible beneath the horizon.

Cody hurried to his bedroom. Ice glittered on the walls as he stepped inside and reached down for the heavy steel storage box. He dragged it backwards through the station and burst out of the accommodation block and back onto the ice. He left the storage box for a moment and fought against the blizzard as he clambered his way up the radio tower steps and onto the multi-tiered roof platform. His gloved hands made work difficult, but he was able to attach the beacon to the main aerial extending up into the inky black sky above.

Cody fastened the beacon in place and then activated it.

A bright red light flashed at him, making the falling snow speeding past look like glowing globules of blood. A smaller green light confirmed that the beacon was transmitting.

Cody clambered back down the steps and turned. He hefted the storage box toward a deep snow drift a few dozen yards away from the station, the kind that stayed throughout most of the year, rising up against shallow north-facing hills near the station and sheltered from what little sunlight reached this far north.

Cody spent several minutes excavating a deep hole in the drift. Then he opened the lid of the box and dumped the contents deep inside the hole before filling it in again. He then hurried back to his quarters and placed the box back where he had stored it.

Exhausted, he trudged back to the snowmobile and looked toward the south as he got into the saddle. Through the blizzard and the blackness he could see nothing, his only tenuous link with home obliterated by the uncaring storms.

He sat for several long minutes, immobile with indecision, before finally turning the snowmobile north and accelerating away into the bleak darkness.

9

'You think he's coming back?'

Jake McDermott did not look up from the large map he was scrutinizing, a creased image of the North West Territories and Greenland unfolded across a table top.

His breath still clouded on the air, but with the station's generators running blessed warmth was evaporating the ice on the walls of the accommodation block. Compared to the frigid night outside, it felt almost tropical.

'He's coming back,' Jake replied as he drew a finger down the east coast of Ellesmere Island toward Baffin Bay, almost a thousand kilometres south.

'No chance,' Bradley Trent uttered from nearby as he sipped from a flask of coffee.

'Cody Ryan isn't dumb enough to try to make it home alone,' Charlotte Dennis snapped at him.

'Wasn't talking about him,' Bradley shot back as he gestured at the map. 'The Lincoln Sea is frozen all year round but its surface is pack ice, like a glacier. You try to move down south on that it'll take you a year.'

Jake glanced up at Bradley. 'You got a point?'

The soldier shrugged over his flask. 'Just sayin'.'

'He's right,' Bethany sighed. 'The winter ice extends only about as far as the abandoned Etah station in Greenland anyway. We'd need a boat after that.'

'That's what I was hoping,' Jake murmured as he pored over the map.

'You want to trek five hundred clicks south and then jump on a boat?' Bradley chortled and shook his head. 'You don't think that anybody with a working boat hasn't already high-tailed it south?'

Jake did not reply to Bradley and instead look over at Charlotte.

'What's the chances of us running the current south of Etah?'

Charlotte raised her eyebrows in surprise as she moved closer to Jake and looked down at the map.

'The current is strong beneath the ice in the Nares Strait, pretty much a steady southerly flow once it breaks free. If we could make Baffin Bay then we'd be clear all the way down to the Davis Strait and into the Labrador Sea. Full of icebergs obviously so treacherous all the way, but it's a possibility.'

Bethany joined them at the map. 'Then what? Overland?'

Jake shook his head.

'Too slow. If we can ride the natural currents we could cover distance ten times faster than staying on land, and without using fuel. We'd have to stay out of Hudson Bay, hug the coast as much as possible, get to Newfoundland.'

Bethany brightened. 'A lot of native communities all the way down through there, people used to living off the land who might be able to get by without electricity.'

Jake's eyes were fixed on the map, but he watched from the periphery of his vision as Bradley Trent and Sauri exchanged a long glance. Jake rapped his knuckles down on Labrador.

'From there, we can go wherever we want to.' He drew a short breath. 'If there's anything left to see.'

Bradley screwed the lid back on his flask and smiled at Jake.

'Easy as that, huh? Two thousand miles across freezing terrain in the middle of winter with no fuel for warmth and unable to carry enough food. Sure, we could shoot stuff along the way but then how the hell do you cook it?'

'You ever do anything but complain, Brad?' Charlotte asked.

'I keep it real,' Bradley snapped back. 'Sauri and I have had Arctic warfare training. We're used to operating up here and I can tell you that your little plan won't work. You already said it yourself: we can't carry the resources we need to move that far.'

'Staying here's not an option,' Charlotte pointed out. 'We said that, too.'

'Agreed,' Bradley flashed her a grin, 'but setting out in the hopes that we'll find a boat that's just right, that the owner decided to leave up here instead of taking it south, is tantamount to suicide.'

'So is staying here,' Bethany retorted. 'Jesus, Brad, the moment the ice clears enough for me to see the ground I want to be out of here.'

'How far could we make it per day using the snowmobiles?' Charlotte asked Bradley.

'Not far enough,' the soldier replied. 'Nowhere near.'

'And the BV's were taken away when the military left?' Bethany asked.

'We saw them loaded up,' Jake replied for Bradley.

Charlotte stared into space for a few moments and then her eyes met Bradley's.

'There were only four airplanes that came in,' she said.

'And the BV's are too big to get more than one aboard each plane,' Bradley replied.

Bradley turned and grabbed his jacket. As one, the entire team tumbled out into the bitter darkness and marched across the solid ice to one of the big warehouses.

It took Bradley a few moments to find the right key and get it into the lock of a side door.

Bradley turned the lock and tried the door. Nothing. He stood back and slammed hit boot against the door and it cracked open with a spray of ice chips. The team followed him inside, and as his flashlight sliced into the deep darkness it reflected off the yellow metal bodies of two large Bandvagns parked inside the building.

'I'll be damned,' Jake said as they all stared at the tracked vehicles.

'Could we get one of them to Eureka?' Charlotte asked. 'How far could they travel in a day?'

Bradley looked at her for a moment. Any retort on his lips evaporated as he sighed and thought for a moment. 'In good weather, maybe fifty miles.'

'That would make it a couple of weeks to get to Eureka,' Jake mused out loud.

'Which is empty in the winter,' Bradley pointed out.

'But which probably has fuel and maybe even food,' Bethany countered. 'We use it as a staging post, head south east from there down to Grise Ford.'

Jake glanced across at Sauri. 'You know anything about the population down there?'

'Inuit,' Sauri replied. 'No more than a hundred permanent residents, but there's a harbour.'

'A thousand kilometres,' Charlotte Dennis murmured. 'Best we could hope for out of the BVs is about a hundred fifty kilometres across the ice per tank.'

'If we used them both,' Jake said, 'one for carrying the fuel with us in the other, it would be tight but we could make it.'

Bradley shook his head. 'Too dangerous.'

'Didn't know you cared,' Charlotte uttered.

'You're assuming a free run with no setbacks,' Bradley explained. 'Engines could freeze overnight or blow gaskets, we could lose our way, be forced to backtrack. Anything could happen that could run us out of gas.'

'If we stay here we'll run out of fuel eventually,' Charlotte replied. 'So it's either certain death or a slim chance of survival. Which do you want, Brad?'

Jake looked at her for a moment and then across at Bradley. This time, the soldier shrugged.

'It's probably our best shot,' he agreed.

Jake was about to reply when the door to the building opened again with a blast of snow and Cody staggered inside. He heaved the door shut behind him and stared at the vehicles in surprise.

'Christ, do they still work?'

'No reason why they shouldn't,' Bradley said. 'They were both switched off and in here when the storm hit. If any cables have fried we should be able to find replacements from the communications building.'

'You set the beacon?' Jake asked Cody.

Cody nodded. Even wrapped up against the bitter cold with the best Arctic clothing available his skin was still mottled red and seemed raw to look at.

'It's done,' he gasped. 'But I barely made it back. Storm's too big.'

Jake looked across at Bradley, whose shoulders fell.

'And there's the catch,' he said. 'No GPS because the satellites are down. One wrong turn and even with all that fuel we could be stranded. Not to mention the danger of getting stuck in those damned crevasses. Some of them are a hundred feet deep and even a BV won't get back out, plus they're probably half filled with snow drifts by now.'

'We wouldn't see them,' Bethany sighed.

'Maybe we could use maps to track our progress, you know, like people used to do before GPS,' Bobby suggested. 'If we set up a beacon at Alert Five, we could home in on that, then away from it heading south. We get a few miles under our belt using that as a reference, we might have enough trajectory to maintain accuracy all the way south.'

'What's going on?' Cody asked.

Jake filled him in on the discussion. Cody digested it slowly.

'So we're done,' he said finally. 'Even with these things we're not getting out of here.'

'Not until the spring,' Jake said. 'Whichever way we look at it, we'll stand more chance of dying than living if we go now. We're just too far north and the conditions too dangerous to even attempt the journey.'

Cody felt numb and not just from the cold. He could no longer find the strength to say anything and simply stared into space as though he were a machine that had ground to a halt like all the others.

'There's nothing more we can do, Cody,' Bethany said.

Jake turned away from Cody. 'We'd best get our heads down,' he said. 'We can talk again in the morning.'

Jake turned for the warehouse door. Bethany looked at Cody for a long moment and briefly squeezed his forearm as she passed by. Bradley, Sauri, Reece and Bobby all moved off in silence. Charlotte hesitated as she left the room, and looked back at Cody.

'We'll think of something,' she said. 'We all want out of here.'

Cody managed a barely perceptible nod as Charlotte disappeared.

He didn't know for how long he stood in silence in the warehouse, staring into space and abhorring the vacuum of despair that seemed to have sucked all emotion from his body and left a crippled, empty shell.

He turned finally and walked out of the warehouse, slamming the door shut behind him. A set of keys jangled in the lock, their metallic tinkle just audible above the howling wind. Cody looked down at them for a long moment, and then yanked them from the lock and set off across the compound.

He walked with his head down, his Arctic hood battered by the howling wind as he fought his way to Polaris Hall. He fumbled with keys in the locks for several minutes before he found the right one and heaved the door open. He locked it behind him before fumbling through the darkened building by flashlight until he found the operations room.

It was dark but warm inside, and the darkness was speckled with hundreds of multi-coloured blinking lights as the satellite receivers continued to record the eerie silence in the world beyond the Arctic Circle.

Cody slid out of his cumbersome jacket and tossed his journal onto a nearby work station.

He hit the lights, illuminating the room, and then sat down in a lightly padded chair in front of a monitor. He spent a few minutes merely examining the room around him: the various stations, computers, screens, immense banks of radios and transponders.

Finally, he got up and moved his journal and coat to another station that faced a series of radios.

Cody had never worked in a military installation in his life, and knew that had he ventured into this building under ordinary circumstances he would have been shot on sight. But now that he was here it was fairly clear how the layout of the room betrayed the general role of the different stations.

The majority of the room was concerned with receiving and analysing signals intelligence. On one wall, a large map of the world was tagged with thousands of frequencies, probably bands used by military forces around the world.

The corner in which he now sat was a listening post, fitted with headphones and various frequency dials. Cody reached out and picked up a set of discarded headphones, then slipped them over his head. A featureless, empty hiss filled his lonely world.

Cody reached out and turned a dial. The dial altered a digital display that read the frequency being listened to. Cody hit a button marked AMPLIFY. The hiss in his ears changed tone and became sharper.

Cody leaned back in the chair and used the instruments before him to set the radios on a band-sweep from the lowest frequency signal to the highest. Then, he set them to sweep both for range and for emergency distress beacons.

Almost instantly the earphones yelped in his ear and he nearly fell out of the chair as a loud, rhythmic claxon rang through his skull.

Cody stared at the banks of radios as the insistent beeping filled his world, and then sank back into his seat in disappointment at his own stupidity. The system was detecting the distress beacon at Alert Five that he had placed himself.

A useful test, he reminded himself.

Cody settled back into his seat and reset the sweep.

SAVIOUR

Week 21

My dearest Maria,

I struggle now to write to you, so bleak is our predicament. Though I know we are probably doomed, I cannot bring myself to abandon the hope to which we all cling so desperately.

The winter has been appalling. Storms blast the ice without surcease for days on end, entrapping us within the accommodation block. We are prisoners here, Mother Nature our merciless gaoler. All is darkness, briefly illuminated by aurora that seem meek compared to the tremendous conflagration that consumed the skies months ago.

Our food supplies are perilously low although water is still being pumped from Dumbell Lake without issue. The diesel fuel stocks remain plentiful, but the bitter winter has taken its toll on us all. We are exhausted and suffering from bouts of depression brought on by our hunger and the permanent darkness that enshrouds Alert. Even the arrival of periods of twilight where the ice and sky glow a peculiar blue-grey has not alleviated our symptoms. The lack of contact with the outside world weighs heavily upon our shoulders.

Jake remains in command and his leadership has been unquestioned, but he is tiring physically. I have no desire to take over from him but am offering what support I can. Reece Cain has withdrawn into himself even further. Charlotte is depressed and almost unapproachable, Bethany even more quiet than usual. Bobby remains active and, frankly, is pulling the load for us when it comes to hard work in the storms outside.

Bradley and Sauri remain thick as thieves, but they hunt for us and bring back a variety of Arctic hares, even wolves on occasion. Such food is infinitely appreciated, but sometimes I feel as though we are surviving as much on our hopes of rescue as anything.

The air quality measurements we have continued to take from the Air Observatory have shown a puzzling and ominous trend. Atmospheric pollutants of all kinds are declining over time. Bethany assures us that this can only be caused by one thing. Pollutants have risen consistently for decades during mankind's tenure on our planet. Now, only humanity's complete absence of industrial activity can account for the reversal of the trend. Few of us are willing to dwell at length on the consequences of this most damning piece of evidence.

To support it, the rest of the world remains utterly, brutally silent.

I cannot express in words how much I miss you, Maria. I wish I could.

10

The ice glowed a strange, luminous blue, glistening and sparkling as though encrusted with a billion diamonds. Shadows cast by ripples in the surface sliced the ice like stripes on a white tiger.

Cody Ryan stood on a low ridge and looked toward Crystal Mountain and Mount Pullen, about nine miles due south of Alert. The saddle between the two mountains was glowing as though aflame, distant bands of cloud ripped and torn by buffeting winds as rays of sunlight soared across the heavens like the outspread fingers of a god.

Cody watched as for the first time in months the sun rose with a sudden flare of bright light that hurt his eyes, brilliant in the clear Arctic air. Though a cold wind fussed its way across the plains he barely felt it, his skin hardened to the polar chill by the harsh caress of a hundred winter blizzards.

Bethany Rogers stood alongside Cody, her arm looped through his. Cody's other arm was draped across Bobby Leary's shoulders as they watched the glorious sunrise. Jake McDermott stood with Reece and Sauri, Charlotte Dennis alongside Bradley, whose arm was draped around her waist. Nobody spoke. All simply stood and let the wondrous light wash over them. There was no warmth, even the sun's immense power humbled so far north.

But that mattered little.

'Thought we'd never see it again,' Bobby murmured.

Cody stared at the sun rising agonisingly slowly between the two mountains, a fearsome halo of nuclear fire that had stripped the planet of mankind's presence and yet now washed over them like the first sip of water after months of drought.

Jake McDermott's reply was laden with caution.

'Baby steps,' he replied. 'We'll have to let the ice melt before we can make a move.'

Cody swallowed thickly but said nothing. Bradley hawked up a globule of phlegm and spat it out onto the pristine ice at their feet.

'Like hell. We're out of here.'

The soldier turned to walk away but was arrested by Jake's voice.

'Nothing's changed,' the old man insisted. 'Just because the sun's up doesn't mean that ravines are passable. We need to give ourselves every advantage before we set off because we'll only get one shot at this. Screw it up and we'll be pinned down for another winter.'

Cody saw Charlotte's head fall within her hood, a puff of breath clouding in disillusionment as she turned away from the sunrise and began trudging back toward the base.

'This isn't about our chances,' Bradley snapped back at Jake, his voice loud on the silent air. 'This is about morale, which in case you hadn't noticed is about as low as the goddamned temperature right now.'

Jake glanced at Cody for support. From somewhere deep inside Cody dredged up the will to speak.

'We've been up here five months,' he said to Bradley. 'A couple more weeks isn't going to make much difference.'

'How the hell would you know?!' The soldier pointed toward the rising sun. 'A couple of *hours* could make all the difference. I thought you had family down Boston way? You not worried about seeing them again?'

Cody glared at Bradley from within his hood as a spark of defiance flared through him.

'We'll only get a couple of hours of light per day right now,' he pointed out. 'At ten miles a day it'll take us two months to make Eureka. You want to spend all that time cooped up in a Bandvagn, you just go ahead right now! We'll follow you in a few weeks and probably pass the wreckage of your BV down a crevasse somewhere. Your call.'

Bradley blustered and fumed, but did not reply. Instead he stormed back toward the base, muttering under his breath.

'He's losing it,' Bobby observed. 'Becoming more of a hinderance than an asset.'

Jake looked at Sauri, who was watching them in silence.

'Keep an eye on him,' Jake suggested. 'He decides to steal a BV, let us know, okay?'

Sauri said nothing in reply.

'We need to leave,' Bethany said, 'as soon as it's safe.'

'We will,' Jake promised her. 'But right now we've got supplies to last us another few weeks and…'

'It's not about supplies,' Bethany cut across him. 'Brad is right. We can't survive much longer up here alone. Even if we had food and supplies and everything that we wanted, we're not supposed to be here Jake. It's not our place. If we stay too long it will kill us all long before we run out of food.'

Jake watched Bethany as she turned away, her hands shoved in her pockets as she walked through the snow toward the base. He glanced across at Cody.

'We can't leave yet,' he said. 'Not yet.'

Cody struggled to control his own desperate desire to set off for home, as though he were keeping a lid on top of a boiling cauldron of fury.

'The inactivity is driving us all crazy,' Cody replied. 'Just making some kind of progress might help.'

Jake nodded thoughtfully and made a decision.

'Okay, get Brad to start up the BVs. We may as well begin training to drive the damned things, just around the base. It'll set us up for when we leave.'

Cody turned and walked off the ridge, waving for Sauri to join him.

'Now that we've got a little more light,' Cody said to the Inuit, 'how about you take that rifle of yours and see if you can find us something to eat that will last longer than hares?'

Sauri nodded and looked up at the horizon.

'I'll need Brad with me,' he said. 'Polar bears and their pups come out of dens with the spring, and the wolves are hungry.'

'Sure,' Cody agreed. 'I'll get Brad to instruct me on the BVs. Then he can go with you.'

Sauri was silent for a few moments as they walked.

'Bethany is a vegetarian,' Sauri said. 'She doesn't eat much of the meat.'

Cody looked down at the Inuit in surprise. 'I didn't know. When did she tell you?'

Sauri spoke quietly. 'She gives me her meat. I give her my biscuits.'

'What biscuits?'

Sauri said nothing for a long moment, looking down at his feet as he walked.

'Brad found biscuits in the storage hangar when we moved here. He hid them in case we run out of food and reckoned he and I would take them with us if we decided to try for Ottawa.'

Cody digested this for a moment. 'Why didn't you tell somebody?'

'I told Jake,' Sauri replied, 'right after. He said to say nothing to anybody. I think he wanted Brad to leave.'

Cody nodded. 'How come you got stuck with him? Before, I mean, when we arrived?'

'The camp commander asked me to keep an eye on Bradley,' Sauri explained. 'He said that Bradley was a rotten apple.'

'No shit.'

'You say nothing, okay?' Sauri asked.

'Nothing.'

Cody walked to the accommodation block and told Brad about the training. For the next hour Cody drove the BV up and down the snow covered runway, avoiding the larger drifts as he practiced. The sun set behind the Winchester Mountains, and the BV's headlights cut through the darkness as he drove back into the main compound and into the storage hangar where the other BV sat waiting.

'Nothing to it,' Bradley clapped him on the shoulder as he sat alongside Cody in the cab. 'We'll try rougher terrain later, but as long as you plan ahead you'll be fine.'

Cody shut off the BV's batteries and clambered from the cab.

'First thing in the morning, you and Sauri need to go hunt something tasty, okay?'

'Fine by me.'

Cody slammed the cab door shut as they walked to the hangar's main doors and began hauling them closed. As he watched Bradley drive his shoulder into the metal doors he wondered what motivated the man to make plans to deceive his companions within just days of their problems starting. Cowardice? Selfishness? Stupidity? Nothing quite fit.

The doors crashed shut and Bradley dropped two heavy latches into place to secure them against the storms. Cody decided to take a chance as the soldier worked.

'Brad, I need you to do me a favour.'

'What's that?'

'I think that Jake is tiring. He's burning the candle at both ends trying to keep everybody motivated and it's wearing him down.'

Bradley secured the latches and stood up. He was a couple of inches taller than Cody and probably twenty pounds heavier, all of it muscle.

'So?'

'So I want somebody to help him lead the group.'

Bradley looked down at him for a long beat. 'You think I'm some kind of asshole?'

'What?'

Bradley's wide jaw fractured into a grin. 'You don't like me. Nobody here much does because I speak my mind and don't give a damn about what you all think. You don't want me to help you lead this little group, and who says you're taking charge anyway?'

'It's not about taking charge,' Cody replied. 'It's about having some kind of hierarchy, no matter how subtle. Jake's the most experienced of us all but he's too damned cautious. We need to get out of here.'

Bradley's grin did not slip. 'Are you thinking of a mutiny, Doctor Ryan?'

'A vote,' Cody said. 'We pull out in a couple of weeks, not a couple of months.'

'You think that your girlfriend will go for that?'

'Bethany wants out, so does Charlotte.'

'I know what Charlotte wants,' Bradley replied. 'What about Cain?'

'Who the hell knows?' Cody uttered. 'But if you, Sauri, Bethany, Charlotte and myself all stand together, we'll win the vote.'

'Can't speak for Sauri,' Bradley muttered. 'Hell, he can hardly speak for himself. I can test the water though.'

'Do it,' Cody said. 'Or we'll be half and half and that won't achieve a damn thing.'

Bradley mulled it over for a moment longer as Cody turned for the accommodation block.

'Leave it with me.'

*

Bethany walked across the ice toward the accommodation block with a series of hand-written notes clutched in her hand and an anxious expression on her face. Cody looked up at her as he crossed from the hangar.

'You okay?' he asked.

'More bad news,' she replied as she climbed the steps to the block and opened the door for him. 'You and Jake both need to see this.'

They walked inside together to see Jake pulling on his jacket. Bethany set the paper down before them on the table.

'What's this?' Jake asked.

Bethany sighed. 'These are air samples taken over the last four months. I've collated them by hand using the sampling kits we've got left. Thankfully, they don't need electricity.'

'And? Cody asked.

'Clearest data I've ever seen yet,' Bethany replied. 'All major pollutants have receded by as much as fifty per cent. That now includes some heavy metals as well as the usual suspects like Carbon Dioxide and Monoxide.'

Jake looked at Cody. 'Industry's definitely gone, then.'

'Manufacturing, vehicles, everything,' Cody nodded, a fresh pulse of fear inside as he considered this latest confirmation of their isolation. 'A complete shutdown of the global economy, the end of fossil fuels, maybe even farming.'

'Methane's down too,' Bethany confirmed. 'A loss of cattle on a global scale could cause that kind of dip.'

Cody sighed in resignation. 'It's been months since the storm.'

'And winter in the northern hemisphere,' Jake added.

The conclusion was brutal in its simplicity.

'The world's never coming back,' Bethany whispered. 'It's really over.'

Jake zipped up his jacket. 'There's no way they could rebuild infrastructure on that scale after so long. It's likely most power stations have been abandoned, millions of miles of power lines fallen or corroded, essential drainage and waste disposal collapsed.'

'That's the other bad news,' Bethany said, and pointed to one of the hand-written notes. 'There have been faint pulses of some radioactive elements. Not sufficient for an exchange of nuclear weapons but… '

Cody finished her sentence for her.

' …enough for the collapse of nuclear cooling systems, spent rods radiating energy out into the atmosphere across the world.'

'Any danger to us here?' Jake asked her. 'From the fallout?'

'No,' Bethany replied. 'The readings are not far above background.'

Jake looked at Cody, who shrugged his jacket back on.

'I'm going to the radios again,' he said. 'It's about all we've got left.'

*

Cody sat at the Signals Development Position inside Polaris Hall's communications room, one hand on the digital frequency shift modulator.

The room had become his home from home over the past few months. Inside the building, with no windows in his direct line of sight, he had found himself encapsulated in a fantasy world where he could pretend that he was back at MIT, fiddling with computer analysis of chemicals or calculating gas spectrometry experiments.

The white-noise hiss in the earphones he wore for two hours at a time had metamorphosed from the flat-lining death knell of humanity into a blank canvas onto which he could place any sound he desired. Cody had sat for hours, slowly changing the frequencies by unthinking reflex as he imagined sudden contact from the outside world. The loss of communications had been temporary, an atmospheric aberration. Law and order had been restored. The airplanes were returning. He had imagined the joy their fractious group would share as the landing lights of the big Hercules aircraft appeared again in the sky. The journey home. Holding his beloved Maria for the first time in so long.

The news reports.

The novels and the movies.

The calling all stations please rece*ive signal… Break… Alert Five*….

Cody sat bolt upright in his seat as his warm, cosy daydream was shattered by the signal crackling through his headphones. He grabbed one of them instinctively in his hand and pressed it hard to his ear as he struggled to listen.

'…… *receive… any station, Aler… hear… cannot reach…*'

Cody scrambled for the microphone transmit button and punched it down as he shouted down the line.

'Unknown call sign, this is Alert Five, do you copy?'

A hiss of undulating static roared in Cody's ears, then the crackling noise again.

'... Alert Five... mess... ken... Prepare to... coordin... ver...'

'Alert Five, say again! Repeat transmission!'

The featureless hiss returned, humming with emptiness. Cody sat in silence for what felt like an eternity, staring at the banks of instruments in front of him and wondering if he had imagined the voice he had heard. Surely he could not have gone insane?

The static in his ears burst with noise once more.

'... sendin... range parameters... digi...orse Code.... Receive...'

Cody was about to reply when a sudden series of beeps and pops of noise filled the airwaves. Cody grabbed a pen and a piece of paper as he scrambled to write down the broadcast of what could only be Morse Code.

The broadcast lasted less than twenty seconds, repeated once, and then the band fell entirely silent.

Cody sat back in his chair and stared at the paper in his hand, filled with a line of mysterious dots and dashes that he had no idea how to translate.

11

'We go now, damn it!'

Cody burst into the accommodation block and froze as Reece Cain swung a rifle to point directly at him.

Reece was standing with the rifle pulled into his shoulder and another slung across his back, tears streaming from his eyes as he held the entire team at bay. His thick black hair was plastered across his face as though he were looking out from between the bars of a cell. Cody slowly pushed the door shut behind him, cutting off the blast of frigid air as he looked at Bradley and Sauri and realised that neither of them were armed.

Cody looked at Jake. 'What's going on?'

Bradley answered, his fists clenched.

'We went to the stores to draw our weapons to hunt, found this asshole there loading them up. Says it's time to leave. I think he's lost his marbles, you know what I mean?'

'Shut up!' Reece screamed and swung the weapon to point at Bradley.

'Shove it, creep,' Bradley snapped back.

Jake stared at Reece, seemingly unsure of what to do next. Cody stepped forward, put his hands out in front of him.

'Easy Reece, what's happened?'

Reece kept his eyes fixed on Bradley, glaring as though he could shoot the soldier with merely a look.

'I'm going home. Give me the keys to the BV.'

Cody kept his hands up. 'You can't take the BV Reece. We need both vehicles because we won't have enough fuel in one of them to reach…'

'To hell with the fuel!' Reece bellowed and swung the weapon to face Cody. 'There's no point! There's nothing left out there. We're all dead already!'

Cody felt a shiver of apprehension as he realised that Reece was making no sense. He was armed and beyond reason.

'Then why leave at all?' Cody asked, as gently as he could.

Reece shivered as he cried in short, sharp gasps. 'I want to go home. I don't want to die here.'

'We don't want to die here either,' Cody pointed out. 'And we might not have to.'

Cody kept his eyes on Reece as the rest of the team's heads turned to look at him.

Cody spoke slowly. 'I picked up a signal, a man's voice, broadcasting.'

Jake was about to speak but Reece cut across him. 'Bullshit! I'm not falling for it, Cody. I'm leaving and if you stop me I'll shoot, you understand?'

Cody looked at Reece for a moment longer, then reached into his pocket and pulled out the keys to the BV. He tossed them down onto the table between them.

'Fine. You go ahead. Save yourself.'

Reece stared at the keys through his bleary, tear stained eyes, and the rifle dropped briefly as he did so.

Bradley lunged forward, one solid forearm smashing the rifle's barrel down to point at the ground as his right fist flashed through the air. It connected with Reece's temple with a dull crack that made Cody wince. Reece's head flicked sideways and the light in his eyes blinked out as quickly as the power had done months before.

Reece crashed onto the floor as Bradley yanked the rifle from his grasp and span it to point at his head.

'No!'

Jake leaped forward and put himself between Bradley and Reece, shielding the scientist with his body.

'He's a liability!' Bradley raged. 'Let's just finish him!'

Cody rushed forward and stood in front of Bradley.

'He's not a liability,' he insisted. 'He needs our help. You're no good to us if you're going to shoot anybody who cracks up.'

Bradley scowled and yanked the rifle up and away from Reece.

Cody stepped back as he looked down at Reece, who was slumped in Jake's arms and weeping softly to himself, his face buried in his own shoulder.

'Jesus, what set him off?' Cody asked.

Jake shrugged helplessly.

'The sunrise,' Bethany guessed from behind Cody. 'It's got all of us riled.'

'The hell with that,' Bradley snapped. 'What's this about a broadcast? Were you just saying that to get this asshole to drop the rifle?'

Cody looked at them all.

'No. I picked up a transmission, ultra high frequency. No idea what it was saying or where it came from.'

'You didn't talk to them?!' Bradley demanded.

'I could barely hear them,' Cody shot back. 'But they were there.'

'Could have been from anywhere,' Charlotte pointed out. 'Maybe even some kind of artefact, bouncing around in the atmosphere from before the silence.'

'No,' Cody shook his head. 'They tried to respond, I could tell. Couldn't understand what they were saying though, it was such a weak transmission. I'm guessing it may have been direct, not through a satellite?'

'Unlikely,' Bradley pointed out. 'It would take a hell of a powerful transmitter to get a signal all the way up here. What frequency were you on?'

'Two five zero, decimal eight,' Cody replied.

Bradley and Sauri exchanged a glance. 'That's a military waveband,' Bradley said.

'Doesn't much matter,' Jake said. 'Somebody, somewhere, is alive.'

'Damned right,' Bradley said, 'which means we've now got a good reason to get the hell out of here. You can argue all you want, old man, but I'm not spending another minute sitting on my ass waiting for the perfect spring day to pull out. I say we call a vote and put this to rest right now.'

'You just threatened to shoot Reece because he wanted to leave!' Bethany pointed out. 'Now you want to go?'

'I threatened him because he was aiming a rifle at me,' Bradley snapped at her. 'We all want out of here, right? It's time.'

Jake stared at Bradley for a long beat and then looked across at the rest of the team.

'You all feel this way?'

Cody saw Bethany and Charlotte both nod in rare agreement with Bradley. Bobby and Sauri both said nothing. Cody took his chance.

'Fine, let's just do it then. Who wants to leave within the next couple of days?' he asked.

It felt like a betrayal, as though he were about to commit a crime, but Cody had no choice but to put his own arm in the air first. He saw Jake's cragged features sag slightly, crestfallen, but did not make eye contact with the old man.

Bradley's hand shot up into the air. Charlotte and Bethany looked at Jake, stricken with indecision. Bobby hesitated, uncertain.

Sauri slowly raised his arm in the air.

Then Charlotte followed suit.

'Half and half,' Jake said. 'That's not helping anybody.'

Cody felt a pulse of consternation as he realised that the group was in danger of fracturing into two camps. He was about to speak when from behind the table where Reece was slumped down against the wall a pale hand rose up to be counted.

'Five to three,' Bradley grinned without warmth. 'We're done here.'

The balance of power had shifted from Jake to Bradley, and Cody knew that he was the cause. The soldier turned to him.

'That signal you heard. You get a location on it, anything at all?'

A thousand thoughts flashed through Cody's mind as he considered the man before him, and of what Sauri had told him. Bradley couldn't be trusted. He shook his head.

'I got nothing.'

Bradley glared at Cody. 'You get the first contact we've had for five months and you don't think to triangulate the source?'

'I didn't see you sitting up there at that station for hundreds of hours,' Cody shot back, 'might have been useful if you'd told us you knew how to work the equipment.'

Bradley ground his teeth in his jaw and he gripped his rifle tighter. 'You record it?'

'No.'

'So it's useless then,' Bradley said. 'Even if we get away from here we don't have a clue where to go.'

'We've got some idea,' Cody replied. 'Think about it. It's been winter in the northern hemisphere. There's no power. People who have survived long enough will have tried to migrate south, toward the equator. There's no point in us heading for Canada or Quebec.'

'So you're saying that we just bypass them and head south, for America?' Sauri asked.

'I'm saying that we get clear of the snowline as quickly as possible,' Cody replied. 'The most likely place that electrical equipment might have survived is probably equatorial regions where the impact of the solar storm was at its weakest. It's also where we'll most likely find any survivors as their winter will have been less harsh than elsewhere.'

'We can't know that for sure,' Jake cautioned. 'I'm not saying you're wrong, but it's a big gamble to bypass the nearest settlements.'

'There'll be nothing at Eureka that we don't already have, except fuel and maybe discarded equipment. The place wasn't manned any more anyway. By running directly south we'll save a hundred kilometres of travel. We should head for Grise Fjord.'

Bradley slung his rifle over his shoulder.

'We can argue the toss about this on the way,' he snapped. 'Right now we're wasting time. Who wants to help me load up the BV and get the hell out of here?'

Bradley didn't wait for an answer. He turned and strode out of the block, pulling his hood up against the cold as he shoved the door open and disappeared.

Charlotte and Bethany followed him, Sauri and Bobby close behind. Cody waited until they had left before he looked across at Jake.

'You sure you know what you're doing?' Jake challenged. 'This could get us killed. It's too soon.'

Cody didn't answer as he left the block.

*

Bradley led the team at a breakneck pace in loading the BV, packing as many supplies and barrels of diesel fuel as they could fit into the trailer section. They worked in the hangar until late at night, and as the team slipped away to rest Cody offered to lock the hangar behind them.

'I'm going to head to Polaris Hall before we leave,' he explained. 'See if I can pick up that signal again.'

Cody trudged alone to the building and upstairs to the Signals Development Position. He switched on the radios and slipped the headphones on. The gentle hiss of static filled his ears again, strangely comforting now.

Cody kicked his chair back slightly from the desk and began rifling through a series of drawers. It took him only a couple of minutes to find what he was looking for.

He placed the small book on the table before him, and then from his pocket he fished the scribbled dots and dashes. Carefully, he began translating the coded message until he had a series of figures written before him.

42N70W

Cody looked at them for a long time before he finally folded the coordinates into the book. Then, he had a better idea. He sat back and read the numbers over and over again until he could recite them from memory.

Then he tore the paper into tiny shreds and stuffed them into his pocket. He shut down the radios and put his jacket back on before heading for the exit.

As he locked the door behind him and left Polaris Hall, he lifted the shredded paper from his pocket and let the pieces be taken by the buffeting wind whistling between the blocks. The sound of an engine roared above the gale and he whirled as a snowmobile rattled up alongside him.

'What was that you just tossed?'

Bobby sat in the snowmobile's saddle, his face in shadow within his thick hood.

'Junk,' Cody replied. 'Where are you going?'

'To Alert Five,' Bobby replied. 'Reece is out of commission, so I figured I can replace the distress beacons for him and then recharge the old one using the snowmobile's battery. Once we get moving we can carry them with us, give people a way of tracking our position. If there's somebody out there like you said, they might hear it.'

'We don't know that for sure, Bobby,' Cody cautioned. 'The signal was weak and…'

'All the more reason to do it now,' Bobby interrupted, 'while they're still maybe searching for us. We get it done, we're golden. You want to risk leaving it until tomorrow?'

Cody looked out to the south, the horizon long lost to the darkness and the snowfall.

'You sure you'll be okay out there? Sauri said the polar bears will be hunting by now.'

'I'll overnight at the observatory if I have to. I can set up an arc light so you can home in on the station tomorrow, and we go from there. It's worth it, Cody.'

Before Cody could say anything further, Bobby gunned the engine and the snowmobile's glowing tail lights vanished into the bitter darkness.

12

'I can't see a damned thing!'

The cab of the BV was filled with warm air blasting from vents in the dashboard as the vehicle rattled and thumped along the ice. Cody held on to his harness as Jake guided the BV in pursuit of the lead vehicle, its tail lights glowing through the horizontal snowfall sweeping across the plains now aglow with the pale light of dawn.

'Just keep an eye open for Bobby's snowmobile!' Charlotte said. 'He's got to be out here somewhere!'

The world outside the vehicle was a featureless grey and white mass of thick snow, solid ice and sixty knot winds. The interior of the cab smelled of grease and diesel-tainted air and was illuminated by the glow from the instruments and the glare from the headlights. The windscreen wipers hissed rhythmically as they struggled to keep the glass free of ice and snow as the engine noise hummed through the cab to where Charlotte and Bethany sat in the rear seats.

'I knew I shouldn't have let him go,' Cody uttered.

'Patience,' Jake soothed. 'The storm was bad last night. He obviously decided to stay put.'

Bradley drove the lead vehicle. Cody assumed it was because the soldier was impatient to leave, but it was just as likely that if Brad's vehicle went down a crevasse, Jake's would have time to stop.

'Just follow Brad,' Cody replied. 'He knows where he's going.'

Jake hung grimly on to the wheel as he chuckled bitterly.

'Sure, as far as the observatory. After that, it's anybody's guess.'

Cody glanced at the tachometer, which they had reset before leaving Alert an hour previously. Five kilometres. They might make forty clicks a day if they could find a path south, which meant a minimum of twenty days to reach Grise Fjord.

'Alert Five should be up ahead,' Bethany said from the rear seat, holding a map in her lap as she searched for landmarks and guide posts through the swirling snowfall.

The guide posts were almost obscured by thick snow drifts, making it hard to pick out the reflective caps. Without constant use and clearing work, the road to the station was already disappearing beneath the ever changing Arctic.

'We're on track,' Jake confirmed and gestured to the vehicle ahead in the gloom. 'But this is just the beginning and we're struggling already. What does Brad think it's going to be like in a hundred miles' time?'

Cody couldn't think of anything useful to say, so he sat in silence and watched the eerily featureless landscape shudder slowly by.

*

Bobby Leary pushed hard against the station door as he struggled out against the gale. He held in his hand a pair of locator beacons and an arc-light, which he kept huddled beneath his arm as he shut the door behind him and trudged against the wind toward the side of the building and the communications tower.

His boots clanged loudly on the metal steps as he clambered wearily up them, thick snow swirling into his face and the wind howling like wolves through the structure as he reached the upper level. The severity of the storm had prevented him from leaving the previous night, and he had spent the long hours of darkness curled up in his sleeping bag in the observatory.

The aerials were quivering in the gale, ice coating their surfaces with horizontal icicles. Bobby pulled one of the beacons from its cradle under his arm and attached it to the largest of the aerials. Nearby the previous beacon was shrouded in ice and frost, its battery long dead.

Bobby ensured that the beacon was secure and then activated it. A bright red light flashed and a steady green light signalled that it was emitting. Bobby turned and took the arc-light out and affixed it to the mast, then turned it on. The brilliant disc of light flared into life, illuminating a shaft of snowfall out into the gloom. Bobby turned it until it pointed north. Satisfied, Bobby turned for the steps and then froze solid as though he had died mid-step.

A low, muffled rumble reverberated through the wind. Like a growl.

A huge white head appeared at the top of the steps, black eyes squinting against the wind and a thick black nose sniffing the air. Even in that terrible instant Bobby noticed how the wind ruffled the enormous bear's fur in beautiful parallel ripples.

The head, as big as Bobby's entire torso, swivelled around until the two black eyes were fixed upon his.

There was no uproar. No noise. No fuss. The polar bear blinked once and then clambered up onto the platform. Its huge bulk, the size of a small horse, dwarfed Bobby even in his thick Arctic clothing. Four foot high at the shoulder, five at the top of its head and weighing maybe a thousand pounds, Bobby was both stunned and terrified by its sheer size.

The bear padded toward him across the platform, filling his vision.

Bobby turned and hurled himself over the platform railing and down toward the snow some thirty feet below.

His stomach flipped as he plummeted and thumped down into the thick drifts. Even as he landed he felt his right leg slam into something hard, felt a crack shudder through his bones as liquid pain seared his thigh. His cry of agony was snatched away by the fearsome gale as he lay stranded on his back in the snow, looking up at the huge animal that was peering down at him through the cold metal bars of the communications tower.

The polar bear sniffed the rails, turned, and began padding back toward the steps.

Bobby heard his own cry of despair as he tried to haul himself out of the snow. Raw, deep pain surged through his leg and he felt bone grating against bone inside it. He flicked his head to one side and a globule of vomit stung his throat and splattered across the snow beside him. His arms felt weak with fear and cold as he swiped at the snow for purchase and dragged himself out, his broken leg trailing behind him.

The station door was barely thirty feet away but it seemed like thirty miles as he reached out and hauled himself across the ice. He made six feet before he heard a rhythmic, throaty breathing and turned to see the polar bear watching him from ten feet away.

Bobby stared in a rictus of horror at the immense predator. The bear loped forwards a single pace and sniffed at the vomit staining the snow. A big, thick tongue licked the mess briefly, and then the polar bear turned and lumbered across to Bobby.

Bobby grabbed a handful of snow in his fist and hurled it at the bear's face. The animal did not even blink as it bent down and crunched its huge jaws around Bobby's bloodied thigh.

*

'I can see the light! Look, out there!'

Cody ducked to avoid Charlotte's arm as it pointed at a faint blue-white light flickering through the dense snowfall as they followed Bradley's BV toward the observatory, the buildings almost completely obscured by deep drifts.

Jake closed up behind Bradley's vehicle and was about to say something when the brake lights on the BV ahead suddenly flared into life and the tracked vehicle slid to a halt on the thick snow.

Cody braced himself against the dashboard as Jake slammed on the brakes and their vehicle shuddered to a halt mere inches from the vehicle ahead. Cody saw the cab door flung open as Bradley leaped from the vehicle with his rifle in one hand and a serrated combat knife in the other.

'What the hell's he doing?' Jake uttered.

Cody saw the bear a moment later. The huge animal loomed over something in the snow and peered up at Bradley as he charged toward it. Bradley drop onto one knee and aimed his rifle. A gunshot cracked out above the howl of the gale and the bear's flanks quivered as the shot hit it. The animal roared and turned to face Bradley.

The soldier stood up and waved his arms, shouted at the top of his lungs as he suddenly charged at the animal. The polar bear roared again and bounded through the thick drifts like a giant white whale plunging through icy waves. Bradley kept going, his arms outstretched and his knife flashing in the weak light as the enormous beast loomed before him.

For a moment Cody thought that Bradley was going to take the immense beast on single-handed. Then he saw Sauri, on one knee, taking careful aim.

A second gunshot, snatched away by the brutal winds, and the polar bear's head flicked sideways as its legs gave way beneath it as it plunged down into the snow barely six feet from where Bradley stood.

Jake opened the cab door and leaped out. Cody followed, fighting to open his door against the wind. The snow was deep and tugged at his boots as he ran off the track toward the observatory. Cody's guts convulsed as he saw Bobby sprawled motionless on blood stained snow.

Sauri put another round into the bear's skull for good measure as Cody ran past.

Cody dashed to Bobby's side and slid down into the snow alongside him. He fought down a glob of vomit as he saw the terrible damage to the kid's thigh. The clothing had been torn free and the flesh stripped away in a ragged, bloody mess. Tendons and skin flapped and quivered in the wind, caked in snow.

Cody turned, saw the team approaching. 'Beth, get over here, now!'

Beth stumbled across the Cody's side.

'Oh Jesus,' she uttered. 'Help me get him into the BV.'

Cody managed to get his arm under Bobby's back and together they lifted him from the snow and carried him across the ice to the nearest of the vehicles. Jake helped as they hefted Bobby aboard and lay him across the rear seats of the cab.

Beth squeezed in alongside him and snatched a medical kit from her bag as Cody knelt alongside her and yanked the cab door shut.

'Cody,' Bethany said, tears streaking down her face, 'he's in a bad way.'

Bobby's face was pale with the cold and he was mumbling a feeble and incoherent stream of nonsense, his eyes closed.

'You got morphine?' Cody asked.

Bethany struggled to get hold of arterial clamps as she handed Cody a vial of morphine.

'Wait until I've stemmed the blood loss,' she managed to say as she fought back her tears. 'Or it'll be wasted.'

Cody watched, trying to ignore his squeamishness as Bethany used the clamps on the frayed arteries spilling blood across the seats and onto the cold metal floor beneath them.

'The cold's helping him,' he managed to observe.

The arteries should have been firing high pressure blood like water cannons, but instead it was pulsing in lethargic spurts.

'He's lost a lot of blood,' Bethany said, her speech quivering with cold and grief. 'He's fading fast.'

'Stick with it,' Cody encouraged her, closing his eyes and turning away from the bloody mess.

'Okay,' Bethany snapped. 'Get it in him.'

Cody yanked Bobby's right glove off and pushed the capsule's needle into the back of his hand. The seal broke automatically and the morphine drained into Bobby's body. Within minutes his ramblings had ceased and he lay in silence, breathing softly.

Bethany sat back and stared at Bobby's shattered leg in dismay. Her hand flew to her mouth as she averted her head and choked on her sobs.

'Can you do anything?' Cody asked as he slipped an arm across her shoulders.

'Jesus no,' Bethany gasped, looking at Bobby's shattered leg once more. 'It's too far gone. He'll lose the leg. But we can't do it here.'

Cody sat back in the cab and wiped a hand angrily across his face as he looked down at Bobby.

The door to the cab swung open with a blast of frigid air and snow as Bradley ducked his head inside.

'What's the verdict?'

Cody sighed. 'He needs surgery. We'll have to go back.'

Bradley stared at Cody from inside his hood for a brief moment, surveying the wounds.

'He won't make it,' he said clairvoyantly. 'Best we keep movin'.'

Cody turned and leaped out of the cab, forcing Bradley to stand back. 'You think?'

'He's a liability now!' Bradley insisted. 'We can't drag him around with us. It was his choice to stay out here all alone and now he's paid the price.'

'He came out here to prepare the beacons,' Cody shouted above the gale. 'He was taking a risk on our behalf! Are we going to leave him now to die for it?'

'Better him than the rest of us!' Bradley bellowed back. 'We're not going back!'

Jake's voice cut above the gusting wind.

'Then good luck, Brad. You're on your own.' Jake turned to Cody. 'Get Bobby back to Alert. We'll follow, with or without Brad, after we've loaded the bear on board for food.'

Jake turned and trudged toward the second BV without giving Bradley a chance to respond. Cody turned and slammed the BV's door shut before heading for the cab. Reece and Sauri started off toward the dead polar bear.

'Where the hell are you going?' Cody heard Bradley shouted at Sauri.

The Inuit did not respond. Cody saw Bradley curse and shout as he stormed away.

The team was Jake's again.

*

Jake reached up for the lead BV's cab door when something stopped him in his tracks.

The blustering snow whipped across the ice fields almost horizontally, obscuring details in the snow and constantly reshaping the land around them. Jake could see the gruesome bloodstains where Bobby had been attacked, Reece, Sauri and a reluctant Bradley now hauling the huge corpse of the polar bear toward their BV.

A trail of blood in the snow marked where Bobby had been carried to the other BV, but from where Jake stood a second, fainter trail of blood led away from the station through the snow.

It was possible that the bear had eaten nearby and that Bobby had inadvertently disturbed the animal, which may have attacked if it felt that its food source was threatened or that it was being challenged. Jake turned and trudged across the snow field in the hopes of finding an uneaten seal or similar.

The trail was feint, pink splotches in the ice, but it led to a deep drift to the south of the station. Amid the snow, Jake could see patches of blood and fragments of clothing.

Panic flushed through him as he ran to the drift and saw a deep hole in the snow stained with ugly patches of black-brown blood. Strips of filthy fabric fluttered in the bitter wind, and as Jake reached the edge of the hole and squatted down a waft of putrid air hit him, stained with rotting meat and putrefaction.

Jake gagged, one gloved hand over his mouth as he peered down into the hole and saw the head of a man peering lifelessly out at him, thin hair fluttering on the wind, bloated purple tongue poking from between yellowing teeth and the whole macabre sight surrounded by a pair of severed hands, one of which had been shredded by the bear's teeth.

Overcoming his revulsion and hoping that he had discovered the remains of an Inuit or polar explorer, Jake reached down and lifted the undamaged hand from the snow. It took him only a moment to realise that the hand was neither petrified nor fully decayed.

The body could not have been in the ice for long.

13

Week 24

My beloved Maria,

Our situation has not improved since I last wrote to you. Tragically, it is even worse.

Bobby Leary's injuries were such that Bethany was forced to remove his leg. The base at Alert has a small operating theatre, but without professional staff we were forced to amputate using only morphine. Bobby recovered well for a few days, but then suddenly began a decline. He is now very sick and we have no means of treating him. Bethany suspects some kind of blood poisoning, perhaps from the bear that attacked him or from the broken femur he sustained when he leapt from the tower at Alert Five.

With Bobby so ill we are unable to travel. Bradley is threatening us all with physical violence if we do not depart soon. We have placed a permanent watch on Bobby in case Brad attempts to intervene and "put an end to his suffering", as he so casually puts it, but we all think it's just bluster and arrogance: it was Brad who charged the bear without thought for himself. Had he not done so, Bobby might not have survived at all.

I don't know what we will do, Maria. The sun is permanently above the horizon now and daylight reigns. The ice in the Lincoln Sea cracks and thunders as it breaks up and the tundra is becoming visible all around us as the snow melts away into the sea. It would be truly beautiful and something that I would love for you one day to see were it not so brutally lethal to us now.

Our food runs low and the meat from the polar bear is almost gone.

We all know that we cannot remain here much longer.

*

Bobby lay on a bed in the accommodation block, a room to himself. Cody leaned on the wall outside and saw Charlotte Dennis sitting in a chair beside his bed, quietly reading a novel that he was fairly certain she had read twice already over the winter.

'He said much lately?'

Charlotte looked up from her book and glanced at Bobby. She shook her head.

Bobby's skin was pallid and sheened with a thin film of sweat. He lay beneath a duvet, a saline drip in his arm that Bethany had rigged for him. Although nobody really believed that Bradley Trent would wander in and throttle Bobby as he slept, the watch also prevented Bobby from thrashing in his delirium and ripping the line from his arm.

The idea of the kid dying of both blood poisoning and dehydration was too awful to bear.

'How are you holding up?' Cody asked her.

Charlotte smiled weakly but said nothing. She closed the book in her lap and stared at the floor.

'We'll get out of here soon enough,' Cody said, just to break the silence.

'Do you think they're waiting for us?' she asked.

Cody figured he knew exactly what she meant, but for reasons he could not explain he asked: 'Who?'

'Our families,' Charlotte replied, seemingly immune to Cody's apparent ignorance.

Cody looked at his boots for a moment, wondering what the hell he could say that wouldn't sound trite.

'We've got to hope that they are. What have we got, if we don't have that?'

Charlotte stared at Cody for a moment and he feared that he had uttered something ridiculous.

'My father,' she said, 'was a senator…, *is* a senator. I never heard a word from him about what was happening out there. There was no warning call, nothing to let me know what was going on. Nothing.'

'You said that it would have happened fast,' Cody replied. 'And the storm came during the night for the folks back home. Maybe he was asleep, didn't have chance to do anything before the lights went out and it was all over.'

She smiled faintly but Cody could see that he had not convinced her.

'There would have been some warning,' she said, 'even if only a few hours. NASA would have known about the coming storm. They had a satellite called SOHO that did nothing but observe the sun's activity. The loss of power across the country, perhaps across the world, would have had immense defence significance. The military and the government would all have been informed.' She shook her head. 'Yet, he said nothing to me.'

Cody watched her for a few moments.

'You think that they knew this was going to happen and they didn't tell anybody?'

Charlotte shrugged. He had never before realised how small she looked, her shoulders narrow and her frame light. Maybe it was the near starvation rations that they were being forced to endure since the wildlife had fled the area when Bradley and Sauri had started hunting in earnest.

'Maybe,' she said finally. 'Sure would have solved a lot of problems, I guess.'

Cody looked at Bobby, aware of the sudden metaphor their conversation had created. Bobby was holding them back. Without him, they could escape Alert and make a break for Grise Fjord. They could be down there in as little as….

Cody struck the thought from his mind. To do so would be barbaric, cruel.

'We're not animals,' he whispered.

'What?'

'How long do you think he'll last?'

Charlotte looked again at Bobby and sighed. 'Bethany would know better, but he's been getting steadily worse. A few days, maybe?'

They had already used up half of their meagre supply of antibiotics on Bobby, trying to fight the infection that was raging through his body to no avail. Now, the kid had no choice but to fight it on his own.

Charlotte's eyes flicked up past Cody's, and he turned to see Reece watching them from the doorway, his face stricken and his eyes big and black in the dim light.

'I did this,' he uttered. 'I should have been there.'

'It wasn't your fault,' Cody said. 'Don't put this on yourself, okay?'

Reece stared at Bobby and then turned and rushed away down the corridor outside.

'Cody?'

Jake McDermott's voice carried down the corridor as Reece vanished, laden with urgency. Cody turned and hurried down the end of the corridor where Jake stood holding the door ajar.

'What's up?'

'All sorts of things,' Jake murmured. He kept his voice low as he spoke, to avoid alerting Charlotte to their conversation. 'I don't know how to tell you this, but I found a dead body in the ice near the observatory.'

'A body?'

'The human kind,' Jake whispered, 'the sort that hasn't been long dead.'

Cody swallowed thickly. 'Have you told anybody else about this?'

'No,' Jake whispered. 'I figured that I'd keep it to myself, but now it looks like Bobby isn't going to make it and I can't help but think that we shouldn't care if he does or not.'

Cody felt a tremor of unease ripple through him. 'You think that *he* killed the man you found?'

Jake stared at Cody. 'I didn't say it was a man.'

Cody winced. 'For Christ's sake, there are far more men than women up here, Jake.'

Jake shrugged. 'I guess.'

Cody rubbed his temples. 'Jesus, it never rains.'

'That police detective who called from Boston, before the storm,' Jake said, 'they must have suspected somebody here of murder. All of you guys came from Boston, right? And that news report you were viewing, about the homicide? Maybe that was the crime.'

Cody looked Jake straight in the eye. 'You still think I had something to do with this?'

Jake held his gaze for a long beat and then sighed. 'No. If I was looking for a murderer in our group I wouldn't look at the only family man here, and I wouldn't really pick Bobby either. I'd pick a recluse, somebody who looked like they wanted to get away from a crime.'

Cody felt a chill ripple down his spine. 'Reece?'

'He's the odd man out,' Jake whispered, 'the odd ball. If he buried somebody's remains out here, he'd have been indirectly responsible for the attack on Bobby. The bear must have sniffed out the body.'

Cody's vision blurred as he glanced back toward Bobby's room. 'Christ, I hadn't even thought of that.'

'And Reece was the one who had the meltdown,' Jake pointed out. 'What if he wasn't just cracking up from isolation and fear? What if he really did kill somebody?'

'What do you want to do about it?'

'How the hell should I know?' Jake uttered. 'Maybe we should tell Bradley about this, get him on side?'

Cody shook his head. 'Bradley could just as easily be a killer, Jake, we just don't know.'

Jake was about to answer him when Reece stuck his head through a door at the end of the corridor.

'Brad's leaving!' he yelled.

Cody exchanged a glance with Jake as they rushed outside, shrugging on his Arctic coat as he walked. He heard the chugging of a BV's diesel engine even before they got outside.

Bradley was fussing around the vehicle's engine, closing an access door and checking the tyres and lights. The sky above was a vivid twilight cast by the low sun setting behind the Winchester Mountains, ribbons of tattered cloud drifting before a strong wind that spat brief snow squalls across the plains. The asphalt around the compound was now visible, the snow reduced to drifts piled up against the block walls.

Cody walked across to Bethany and Sauri.

'What's he doing now?' Cody asked.

'Says he fed up with waiting for Bobby to die,' Bethany explained. 'So he's off whether we like it or not.'

Cody looked at Sauri. 'You goin' with him?'

Sauri shrugged but said nothing.

Bradley saw Cody and clapped his hands, a tight grin on his face.

'You coming with me Doc?' he asked. 'Or are you just going to whine about how it's not the right thing to do?'

'We've been here before, Brad,' Cody said. 'You leave us, you're killing everybody.'

'We don't leave,' Brad shot back, 'then Bobby has killed us all.'

'Would you want us to leave if it was you lying sick in there?' Bethany challenged.

Bradley walked right over and jabbed a finger at her. 'Yes, I would.'

'That's bullshit,' Bethany uttered. 'You'd be crying like a baby for us to…'

'You don't talk down to me!' Bradley yelled at her.

Cody stepped between them, his face inches from Bradley's. 'Nor you her, understand?'

Bradley laughed in Cody's face and shoved him backwards with one big hand. 'And what are you going to do about it?'

Cody staggered off balance. Anger flooded his synapses and surged like fire through his body, but somehow it failed to break the surface. He steadied himself. Bradley chuckled and shook his head.

'That's what I thought,' the soldier uttered, 'nothing.'

'That's right,' Cody replied. 'Because we're nothing if we don't stick together. A few weeks ago all you could do was whine about how we'd never make it out there. Now you're threatening to run away like a scared schoolboy. The biggest problem we've got right now isn't Bobby, it's you.'

Bradley chuckled again and turned his back on Cody, his voice mocking him as he walked away.

'Like I said, there's nothing you're going to do to stop me.'

Cody heard a clicking sound from somewhere off to his right. He turned and saw Jake lift a shotgun from the back of the BV and aim it at Bradley.

The soldier stopped in his tracks as he heard the weapon being cocked. Any humour that his features might have harboured vanished as he glared at Jake.

'You point that at me, old man, you'd better be prepared to use it.'

'I am,' Jake replied. 'That vehicle isn't yours to use, Brad. It's a ticket out of here for all of us. You either wait or we'll be travelling one person lighter.'

'You won't shoot Bobby to put him out of his misery but you'll shoot me?' Bradley sneered. 'I should have left that snivelling little shit to get eaten. Might have fattened the bear up before we shot it.'

'Not your choice to make, Brad,' Jake snapped.

'And it's not your place to stop me from leaving!' Bradley shot back. 'We've been here for weeks now sitting on our asses waiting for the sun to come up, for the ice to melt, for Bobby to stand upright for more than thirty goddamned seconds. We don't leave soon we'll be stuck here for another winter. Any of you fancy that?'

Bradley was pacing toward Jake, who kept the shotgun levelled firmly at the soldier.

'If we have to stay, we have to stay,' Jake uttered. 'But we're not going anywhere without Bobby.'

Bradley stopped walking just short of the end of the shotgun, shook his head and turned away from Jake with a chuckle of despair.

'You guys are all off your…'

Bradley span, one gloved hand flicking out to push the tip of the shotgun to one side as he stepped in toward Jake. Before Cody could even register what had happened Bradley had pushed Jake up against the wall of the accommodation block, the shotgun pinned between them and had a thick-bladed serrated knife shoved against Jake's neck.

'…rockers,' Brad growled. 'I'm taking the BV, and if you even think about trying to stop me I'll fill your ass full of buckshot. Clear?'

Cody swallowed thickly as he waited to see what Jake would do.

But Jake did nothing. There was nothing that he could do. He relinquished his grip on the shotgun. Bradley yanked it from his hands and stepped back as he slid his knife back into its sheath on his belt.

'You can all stay right where you goddamned well like,' Bradley informed them. 'But I'm out of here. Anybody wants to come along, now would be a good time to decide.'

Charlotte appeared from the block and looked at Bradley, her features drained and saddened. 'Is this who you really are Brad?'

'This is what it is,' he replied, 'and I've made my decision. You coming with me?'

Charlotte did not move.

Bradley looked at her for a long moment and then turned away.

Cody watched as Bradley strolled around to the driver's side of the cab and clambered aboard. Nobody followed. The BV's engine bellowed and it pulled out of the compound in a cloud of diesel fumes that swirled with the gusting snow. The vehicle's tail lights turned away into the darkening twilight and slowly crawled away toward the south until they vanished behind a hill.

*

The dawn came crisp and clear, the sky above a perfect blue. Cody stood out on the north ridge, the nearby fuel silos glistening in the sunlight as the last of the ice and frost melted and spilled out onto the scattered patches of snow flecking the barren tundra. Beyond the airfield the Lincoln Sea crunched and cracked as it drifted slowly past the shore, jagged islands of ice floating in dark, frigid water.

He spotted a school of Beluga a few hundred yards off the coast, fountains of white water blasted from their breathing holes, the sounds reaching him seconds later.

'We shouldn't be able to see water this far north.'

Bethany stood alongside him on the ridge, her hands shoved in her pockets but her hood down. Her hair was bound tightly around her head, her face scoured of make-up. Clear and clean like the Arctic itself, her eyes as green as the aurora.

'Climate change for you,' Cody said. 'The Lincoln Sea never used to melt this far up so early. It used to be solid until the Nares Channel at least.'

Bethany remained silent for a few moments before she sighed.

'What are we going to do?' she asked.

Cody shrugged. 'We wait for Bobby to recover then I guess we use the remaining BV.'

'We can't carry enough fuel with seven of us on board,' she replied.

'Bradley didn't leave us much choice, did he?'

Bethany shook her head and turned to climb off the ridge. 'I hope he rots in hell, or wherever he ends up.'

Cody stared at his boots for a long time but could think of nothing to say. It was as if his mind had removed from him the ability to feel despair. He knew somewhere deep down that he was never going to leave this place, that he would never again hold his daughter or see her pretty little face. The thought provoked a spasm of grief that swelled inside him, threatening to break free and fly screaming up into the cold and uncaring sky above.

It was only Bethany's voice that prevented Cody from falling to his knees.

'I've figured out how we're going to get out of here,' she said simply.

Cody's despair faltered somewhere in his chest as he looked over his shoulder at her. 'How?'

Bethany looked up at him, a smile as bright as the sunlight plastered across her face. She pointed out to the south.

'We're going to sail out of here.'

Cody looked toward the south and in a moment of sheer amazement he believed that his eyes were deceiving him.

In the far distance, in the midst of the thick chunks of ice floating slowly through the Robeson Channel, a towering set of sails billowed like giant white flags as though somebody had erected an enormous tent in the middle of the bitter waters.

As he focused on the tent, it resolved itself as if by magic in his mind.

'It's a ship,' he gasped.

'It's a ship!' Bethany echoed. 'It's a ship!'

Bethany hurled her arms around him and shrieked like a small girl on a Christmas morning, then whirled and ran down the slope toward the camp, shouting her last sentence over and over again.

Cody stood on the ridge and watched the vessel's glorious sails ripple as she eased her way north past lethal chunks of ice as large as tanks, and shook his head in wonder.

Dean Crawford

14

Jake drove the BV, squinting in the bright sunlight blazing through the vehicle's scratched windscreen as it bounced and juddered its way across the tundra. Giant white snowdrifts contrasted sharply with expanses of barren rock and tufts of hardy grasses that clung to a meagre existence in the cold soil.

Cody, like everybody else in the BV, stared at the ship before them.

'It's like she sailed out of a time warp,' Jake uttered in amazement.

The vessel was a tall-ship, a three-masted schooner of some kind. Her hull had once been a glorious white but was now stained with the grime of untold ages at sea, her sails dulled by the cruel blast of a thousand Arctic gales. Even as they closed on the beautiful ship at full throttle Cody saw the dark arrow of a huge anchor crash down into the dark water, sending chunks of ice spinning away on the undulating waves. A wash of relief and joy flooded his body.

'Oh God, they're heaving to,' he said. 'They've seen us.'

The schooner settled in the water, the wind spilled from her sails. Cody could see men hauling on rigging lines on the deck, dragging the heavy sails in to reduce the load on the anchor.

'We're going home,' Bethany said, hugging Charlotte.

Even Sauri seemed to have a smile on his face, but that might just have been a squint as the low sun blazed across the distant horizon. Only Reece remained silent, watching from behind the ragged veils of his black hair.

Jake pulled the BV up close to the edge of the channel and as one they all leaped from the cab and onto the rocky tundra, waving their arms and shouting as they looked up at the vessel and the heads of several men pointing at them from the decks.

A puff of smoke burst from one of the men's arms, and a chunk of stony earth was blasted upward in a fountain as Cody realised that they were pointing weapons at them.

'Cover!'

Jake's voice echoed across the tundra as Cody staggered to a halt and threw his arms in the air, his joy withering. Two more gunshots shattered the air, Charlotte and Bethany crouching down together and covering their heads as Reece tried vainly to shield them.

Cody stared up at the armed men in horror as a voice called out from the ship.

'You come any closer, the next shot will hurt!'

Cody glanced instinctively at Jake, who was slightly further back. As the closest to the ship Cody inadvertently found himself compelled to reply.

'We're unarmed!' Cody shouted back, his arms still stuck in the air.

'All the better for us! Don't move!'

Cody stood silent and still as several of the men vanished from sight. He heard a banging noise, and Cody watched as the men hauled canvas covers off a small launch and attached a winch before raising and swinging the launch over the side of the ship and down into the water.

Two men, both armed, clambered down a rope ladder into the launch. One rowed as the other aimed a rifle at Cody as they traversed the twenty or so yards between the ship and the shoreline.

The armed figure raised his head at Cody with a quick jerking motion.

'You, alone, now.'

Cody hesitated. He had no idea who the people aboard the ship were and all thoughts of a benevolent rescue mission sent valiantly from Boston vanished from his mind. He edged forward and reached out for the launch.

'No sudden moves,' the man snapped.

Cody climbed carefully aboard and was rowed across to the ship on the silent water. More men aimed weapons and suspicious gazes down at him as the launch bumped alongside the long, graceful hull.

'Up the ladder,' snapped the armed man.

Cody reached out and managed to grasp hold of the rope ladder. He dragged himself up the ship's hull and clambered over the bulwarks onto the deck.

Several men watched him in silence, but one was taller and more robust than the others as he stood forward to tower over Cody. He was dressed in a thick Arctic coat which was unzipped to reveal a barrel chest beneath layers of thick pullovers. A dense brown beard nestled beneath a hooked nose and cold blue eyes, his skin burnished to a leathery brown by the harsh caress of a thousand suns, and a gold crucifix dangled from a heavy chain at the base of his throat.

The armed boatman leaped onto the deck behind Cody.

'Stand over there,' the man growled, and pointed with the rifle to the ship's main mast.

Cody obeyed as the tall, bearded man leaned over the bulwarks and shouted down to Cody's companions in a booming voice that seemed to shudder through the ship's hull.

'Any of you make a move we don't like you'll get your friend here back in small pieces!'

Cody stood near the mainmast, acutely aware of the men watching him with sullen and suspicious eyes. All of them appeared haggard. Cody realised that any voyage this far north into the pack ice would have taken its toll on even the hardiest souls. He counted seven men, all armed with a weapon of some kind.

'What's your name?'

The question was fired at him as though from a shotgun as the bearded man turned away from the bulwarks and looked at him.

'Cody.'

'How many are you, Cody?'

'Eight,' Cody replied. 'One injured, another missing right now.'

'Eight?' the big man snapped, 'there's only *eight* of you?'

Cody nodded.

A ripple of murmured *Christ's sakes* drifted through the crew like a breeze. The big man looked down at Cody as though studying a small insect.

'What about Alert, the airbase?'

'Abandoned,' Cody replied, 'just before the storm.'

'You know about the storm?' the big man uttered.

'We're scientists,' Cody replied, and made a play for sympathy. 'The military pulled out in a real hurry, left us here.'

The big man peered at him with interest for a moment but his scrutiny was interrupted by a curse from one of the crew behind him.

'It's a bust, Hank. This whole damned thing was pointless, I tol' you so.'

Hank straightened and turned to face his crew. 'I didn't hear any better ideas from you, Seth.'

Seth was a short, wiry man with a straggly beard and a buzz cut who looked as though he'd just walked out of a maximum security prison wing. Purple tattoos stained his neck, the sinister tags of street gangs, and beneath one eye were two tattooed teardrops. Cody knew that they represented slayings, perhaps in prison.

'I didn't have one,' Seth muttered. 'But of all the places we could have gone, you dragged us into this hell hole.'

Hank turned to look over his shoulder at Cody. 'Have you been emitting any signals, anything at all?'

'Distress beacons,' Cody replied, 'a few miles south of Alert.'

Hank turned away and looked out over the barren, snow flecked tundra to the Winchester Mountains. Cody saw the crew glancing around them at the barren Arctic wilderness as though they already hated it with all their hearts. He realised that they looked gaunt, stricken with the same eternal hunger that plagued Cody's companions on the ice below.

'We didn't think that anybody would come,' Cody said. 'That there was anybody left.'

Hank nodded slowly but did not turn back to Cody as he replied.

'There isn't.'

Cody felt a chill run down his spine and fear poisoned his guts as he stepped away from the mainmast.

'I have a daughter,' he said. 'She's three years old. Boston.'

Hank's big head slowly turned to look at Cody. The rest of the crew all appeared to avert their eyes from Cody's as the captain responded.

'I'm sorry for your loss,' Hank uttered.

'No,' Cody whispered. 'They're not gone.'

Hank did not respond as he glanced down to the ice and the bedraggled group of survivors huddled together below them.

'Saunders?'

An older man with short grey hair and broad shoulders moved forward. 'We can't take them,' he said.

Cody gaze flicked across to Saunders. 'You'd leave us here?'

'We can barely feed ourselves,' Saunders replied without rancour. 'Another eight and we'll all starve.'

Hank remained silent, surveying the wilderness.

'I said we shouldn't have come out this far,' Saunders informed his captain. 'If there's anybody left alive who can help us they're not going to be broadcasting their presence, Hank.'

Cody glanced at the crew and at the weather beaten ship. 'You're looking for somebody?'

Saunders did not reply or even acknowledge that Cody had spoken, his eyes fixed upon the captain. Another crewman, a younger man with spiky hair and a deep scar across his left cheek, approached Hank's side.

'It's time to finish this Hank,' the man said. 'There's nothing left out there and chasing rainbows across the world is getting us nowhere. We need to….'

Cody barely saw the blur of motion as Hank's right arm flicked out and a big fist cracked across the spiky haired man's face. The crewman staggered backwards and crashed onto the deck, holding his injured nose as he glared up at Hank.

The glare melted away as the captain turned. 'How about I leave you here, Denton, and take Cody with us instead?'

Denton's eyes snapped briefly to look at Cody. 'He'd be useless aboard ship.'

'Just like you once were,' Hank growled. 'Don't forget where you came from boy, where I pulled you from. Question me again and I'll put you right back there.'

Hank turned to face Cody again. 'Does the base have supplies and equipment?'

'They cleared out all the food,' Cody replied, 'got a few working vehicles, plenty of diesel fuel, some medical supplies and a radio set.'

Hank nodded thoughtfully. His crew watched in sullen silence and Cody realised that the captain could only control such men with an iron hand: most looked like they would cut their own mother's throat for the right price. Denton dragged himself to his feet, blood dripping from his nose and a hateful gaze cast in Cody's direction.

Saunders stepped forward, unafraid of the big captain.

'What are you thinking? Clear them out and turn back?'

Hank turned and looked at Cody but he replied to Saunders.

'The spring thaw is under way,' he said. 'We can break free of the ice within a week or two at the most.'

'You know it's never going to be that easy,' Seth almost laughed from behind. 'We don't have room for these clowns. Cut them loose and let's get the hell out of here.'

'I agree,' said another of the crew, a tall and muscular black man, 'head for goddamned Hawaii.'

'Nobody would have come up here to hide,' said another. 'They'll have gone somewhere warm for Christ's sake.'

Hank stared at Cody throughout the exchange as though sizing him up. It was all Cody could do to meet the big man's gaze. The crew watched as Hank paced forward until he towered over Cody.

'I take you with us you'll work your place aboard the ship, understood?'

'We will,' Cody assured him.

'There is no *we*,' Hank uttered. 'You just got lucky. You got the balls to walk up here with a gun in your face you've got a berth aboard my ship. But we've got no room for your friends.'

Images of Cody's daughter flashed through his mind and he felt a painful tugging at his stomach. Cody held the captain's gaze and shook his head.

'I can't do that.'

'What do you mean you *can't* do that?' Hank growled.

'They wouldn't leave me behind,' Cody replied. 'I won't leave them.'

Hank scrutinised Cody further as Denton's wounded voice reached them.

'We don't need 'em.'

The captain turned away from Cody as he looked at his crew. 'I've got one man here who has a family in Boston yet who won't abandon his friends, and a crew who would cut them loose without even giving them a chance. You tell me: who are the people who would serve me best aboard this ship?'

Saunders' harsh whisper cut through the cold air.

'It's not about who stays or who goes, Hank. It's about how we damned well feed ourselves. We don't have room for eight passengers.'

Cody took a chance and stepped up.

'You wouldn't need to accommodate us for long,' he said. 'We only need to get out of the Arctic to somewhere we actually have a chance of surviving. Up here, we won't make it through another winter.'

Hank looked at Cody. 'You said one of your group is missing and another sick?'

Cody nodded.

'Then it's decided,' Hank shot back at Saunders. 'It's seven people, and one of them might not make it. We get extra supplies from the base and in return these people sail with us.'

Saunders looked away from his captain in despair. The crew stared down at their boots. Cody watched as Hank's voice boomed orders across the deck.

'Open the deck hatches!'

As the crew scattered miserably to perform their duties Hank turned to Cody.

'Get your people to load up anything of use aboard that vehicle of yours and get it here. We leave at first light tomorrow morning.'

Dean Crawford

15

Week 25
My dearest Maria,

I can scarcely contain my excitement: our saviours have arrived! A private vessel, the Phoenix, arrived this morning at Alert and we have negotiated, for want of a better word, a passage south. We have just finished loading our stores aboard the ship and I write this now in Polaris Hall. It is the last time I shall sit here.

The Phoenix's captain is Hank Mears. He appears an uncompromising man commanding an unsavoury crew but they represent our only hope of escape. Everybody is overjoyed at our sudden good fortune, but that joy is tempered by Bobby's deteriorating condition and Bradley's ill-timed decision to strike out on his own. If he fails to return by sunrise he will surely perish alone.

Hank Mears and his crew cannot be drawn on what has happened to the outside world. They seem intent only on loading supplies and escaping from the Arctic, for which I cannot blame them. I will pack the radios from Alert to take with us along with the distress beacons, and hope against hope that somehow you have survived these long months and that you and your mother remain well.

No matter what happens, I will never forgive myself for running away from you both. It brings me more pain than I can describe to know that had I remained I might even now be holding you both in my arms.

Hopefully, I will now travel closer to you both with each passing day.

*

A hefty, rhythmic thud jerked Cody awake. Several moments passed as he tried to remember where he was. He blinked, struggled out of his bunk and opened the door to his tiny cabin aboard the Phoenix.

Saunders stood before him in the passage outside. A small battery powered lantern in his hand illuminated the Phoenix's darkened 'tween deck corridors.

'First light,' Saunders snapped. 'Be on deck in ten minutes, understood?'

Saunders turned away and strode down the corridor to the next berth before Cody could respond. Cody hauled on his clothes in the cold darkness, wondering whether the crew had any coffee aboard. He fumbled his way down the shadowy corridor and clambered up a ladder, seeing weak light filtering ahead through from the skylights in the 'tween decks.

The schooner was some forty metres long and according to Jake a replica of a nineteenth century Baltimore vessel, with fore and aft deck houses that stood proud of the main deck. Her three masts were raked back slightly toward the stern, and Cody figured that in full flight they carried a tremendous volume of canvas that would give the Phoenix a swift turn of speed on the open ocean.

Below the main deck was the 'tween decks, as Saunders had referred to them in a manner that befitted the Napoleonic atmosphere their new life aboard the ship had taken. A crew room in the centre, with its skylights, was just aft of a galley, which in turn led on to the ship's bow and the 'heads, as the latrines were known. To the stern were the berths, then the dining room, and at the very rear of the ship were the mate's and captain's quarters. Wooden steps led down below the 'tween decks to the ship's hold, which was also accessible through the main deck's skylights and a large hatch in the crew room when loading stores from ashore.

The sky was a deep blue outside the crew room as Cody passed through, the panes of the skylight encrusted with geometric spirals and stars of frost. Cody climbed the steps at the stern of the room and walked out onto the main deck into the bitter cold, shut the hatch behind him and hurried aft toward the wheelhouse. Behind him, forward of the main mast, was the fore deckhouse, which held stores and a workbench to repair the ship's enormous canvas sails.

A warm yellow glow permeated the aft deckhouse, which was enclosed against the bitter cold. Cody hurried inside and closed the door behind him.

Heat billowed from vents in the deck, powered by a generator that Cody could hear rumbling somewhere below. Captain Mears stood at a table near the wheel, pouring over a map of the Lincoln Sea that was illuminated by a lamp. Cody glanced at the heaters and lights curiously.

'How come all your systems weren't shorted out by the storm?' he asked.

Hank Mears did not look up from the map as he worked.

'Sheer luck,' he said. 'We were trailing a sonar buoy at the time, listening to whale-song of all things, which effectively earthed the ship. We lost a few systems, lights and so on but managed to shut others down when we realised what was happening. You don't often see aurora off San Diego.'

Jake McDermott stood on the opposite side of the bridge, a steaming cup of coffee in one hand and another held out toward Cody.

'A quarter-spoon and no sugar or milk,' Jake said, 'house rules.'

Cody grabbed the cup and gratefully down the hot coffee as he spoke to Hank.

'How's Bobby doing?'

'Alive,' Hank replied without looking up. 'But he's in a bad way and we don't have any medicines aboard. There's nothing that we can do for him.'

Cody nodded, suspecting already that Bobby could not possibly now defeat the infection raging through his bloodstream.

'How did you sleep?' Hank asked.

Cody blinked, surprised at the captain's apparent interest in his comfort. 'Well, thanks.'

'Good, because it's the last decent night's sleep you'll be getting for a while,' Hank uttered as he stood up from the map. 'It gets rough down through Baffin Bay and we'll be dodging icebergs all the way there. The Phoenix is no ice-breaker. It's only her manoeuvrability that got us this far north.'

'And the ice melt,' Jake agreed. 'I never thought I'd be grateful for climate change.'

'It's still a hard voyage,' Hank said. 'We'll be moving with the current instead of against it, which will help, but there'll be a twenty-four hour watch throughout the trip until we're well clear of the ice. One wrong step and the hull could be crushed like an egg shell.'

Jake looked at Hank for a moment.

'What brought you all the way up here?' he asked. 'Surely not just our distress beacons?'

Hank did not reply. Instead, he folded the map and gestured to the bridge door.

'You're both up for duty,' he said. 'Saunders will assign you your tasks.'

Cody set his mug down alongside Jake's and they both ventured out onto the deck.

The Phoenix still lay at anchor in the clear water channel that hugged the coast of Ellesmere Island. Nearby, the pack ice crunched and rumbled as it drifted past, chunks the size of boulders floating in the frigid sea. Stars twinkled above in the dawn sky and Cody could see that the ship's bulwarks and rigging were encrusted with frost and thick icicles, like transparent bayonets hanging from the thick ropes.

'Ryan, over here.'

Cody looked up to see Saunders waving him over. Cody joined him at the foredeck. Saunders handed Cody a small hand axe.

'Ice,' he uttered. 'Remove it.'

'From the whole Arctic?'

'I'll do the gags,' Saunders replied with a brittle grin. 'Clear it from the rigging and sweep it from the decks wherever you find it. I don't want anybody breaking a leg.'

Cody got to work as Jake was detailed to perform the same tasks on the port side of the deck. The menial work did nothing to dampen Cody's mounting excitement at the prospect of finally leaving this awful place. He hacked away at chunks of ice on the bulwarks and watched them tumble into the black water below as though he were cleansing himself of the grinding helplessness that had burdened him for so many long months.

Captain Hank Mears had assigned Charlotte and Bethany to cookhouse duties, a sexist decision but not one that either of the women opposed. Cody wondered if the captain had more than just his own prejudices in mind when he had ordered them below decks. More than once Cody noticed members of the crew cast lingering glances at the two women, and it quickly crossed his mind that they were tough men who had been at sea for months with nothing but their own company.

Reece Cain found himself being trained to handle the rigging along with Sauri in preparation for their departure, the Inuit taking to his assignment with customary silent zeal. Cody noticed Jake keeping a close eye on Reece as he worked, no doubt suspicious of his every move. By the time the sun had cast its first brilliant rays across the flawless blue sky the captain bellowed his orders.

'Stern anchor, away!'

Saunders seconded the order, and as Cody looked up from his work he saw Denton alongside a hugely muscular crewman named Taylor. The two men heaved on a locking lever and released a small anchor that crashed into the water behind the ship, the chain rattling out for several seconds before it fell silent.

Cody watched in confusion, wondering why they would drop another anchor when they were about to depart.

'Rudder, hard to starboard!' Hank roared.

Saunders spun the ship's wheel. As the rudder turned, Denton and Taylor hurried to the bow deckhouse, rushing through the doors to man a capstan inside.

'Weigh anchor!'

The two men heaved into the capstan's bars and moments later the thick chain of the main anchor began rattling up through the hull. Almost immediately Cody felt the ship move as the bow began to swing out and away from the shore. He realised that the captain was letting the current turn the ship around while holding her in place with the smaller stern anchor.

'Stand by the stern!'

Two more crewmen, the tattooed killer Seth and an African American who apparently and appropriately in their current situation called himself Ice, waited by a capstan at the stern and as the ship turned to face directly away from the shore the captain gave the order to haul the stern anchor up. The two men shouldered their way into the capstan and the anchor quickly relinquished its grip on the seabed below.

With a stately glide the Phoenix moved away from the shore and began to drift with the current in the clear water channel as she turned slowly to face south. Cody looked up at the towering masts, the sails still furled against the yard arms. With the permanently flowing current the captain had decided not to use canvas and below decks the diesel generator was providing only heat, conserving precious fuel. The crew had loaded as much diesel fuel into the hold from Alert's copious supplies as they could. Cody figured that the Phoenix would likely have an engine too, something to help them if becalmed or mooring into a tight quay.

Cody moved across to the starboard bulwarks and watched the coast of Ellesmere Island drift away. Bethany and Charlotte, called up for the departure, stood alongside him with Jake, Bobby, Reece and Sauri.

'Thank God,' Bethany said softly.

'And not a moment too soon,' Jake agreed.

'What about Bradley?' Charlotte asked.

Jake looked at her in surprise. 'He took off, Charlie. It's not our fault.'

'He saved Bobby's life,' she replied. 'We owe him something, surely?'

'Could we raise him on a radio?' Cody suggested. 'Warn him somehow?'

Jake shook his head. 'He was heading for Eureka, much too far to reach him now.'

They stood in silence for a long time until one by one they returned to their stations.

The Phoenix drifted beside the endless ocean of broken pack ice, hemmed in close to the barren, rocky shore as though sailing down a narrow river. Saunders and the captain kept a close eye on the angular slabs of white surrounding the ship. It seemed obvious that they feared the ice building up around the ship and closing her in. Cody had read about and seen many pictures of vessels caught up in Arctic ice, their steel hulls crushed by the immense pressure. Although the melt was well underway the Nares Strait was still an immense ice bucket fed by Greenland's Petermann and Humboldt glaciers on the far side of the channel. Both glaciers regularly calved off icebergs hundreds of square kilometres across that broke up into equally lethal city-sized chunks further down the strait.

Cody worked all day, chipping away the chunks of ice that seemed welded to the ship. His only break, like the rest of the crew, was for a single cup of coffee and a hunk of dried bread and meat of questionable origin soaked in gravy. Cody guessed that the gravy probably hid the worst of the taste, although neither Charlotte nor Bethany could be drawn on what it was made from.

The days' meagre light began to fade within just a few hours as the sun sank to roll along the jagged blue horizon, but now it never got truly dark, the horizon awash with fearsome yellow and red banners of glowing watercolour hues. Cody overheard Seth report to the captain that the Phoenix had made some thirty nautical miles at an average of six knots. He could not help but compare that with the struggles Bradley might face in achieving the same distance alone in his BV and wondered if the soldier would even make Eureka.

'Alone, we're nothing.'

Cody did not realise he had spoken out loud as he looked out to the glowing horizon. The Phoenix had anchored in a natural cove, out of the path of any marauding icebergs large enough to do her damage.

'What's that?'

Saunders looked up from tying off a canvas cover on the deck skylights nearby. The covers protected the glass but also kept the ship's interior dark from the sky now glowing without surcease in the land of the midnight sun.

'Nothing,' Cody uttered, 'just thinking out loud.'

There was a moment's silence as Saunders finished his work.

'Sounds like some deep thinking,' the mate said finally, 'best not to dwell on things that can't be changed.'

Saunders joined him at the bulwarks, pulled back his hood and ran a rough hand through his stiff buzz cut.

'Your missing man?' Saunders asked. 'Is he any good?'

'He's an arrogant asshole,' Cody replied. 'But his heart's in the right place.'

'They're usually my kind of asshole.'

Cody managed a small smile. 'You got a deck light? Something we could leave on, like a homing beacon in case he shows up?'

Saunders scanned the wintry horizon for a few moments.

'We've got lanterns to avoid collisions at sea,' he replied, then turned away. 'I'll have one rigged to the maintop. If he's close, he'll see it.'

Cody watched Saunders walk away.

'Thanks.'

The first mate did not reply as he descended into the 'tween decks.

Dean Crawford

16

'How's he doing?'

The sick bay aboard the Phoenix held just two beds, the cramped conditions seeming to exacerbate Bobby's illness. He lay on the sheets of the bed with an intravenous line in his arm and a sickly sheen of sweat on his pale skin that glistened in the light from a lamp illuminating the bay.

Bethany sat on a chair beside Bobby, her expression scoured of emotion.

'He's sinking fast, Cody. This is the only saline bag that the crew can spare.'

Cody could detect a faint, offensive odour on the air and somehow he knew it came from beneath the bloody bandages wrapped around the stump of Bobby's leg. The infection from whatever had been trapped inside his body, perhaps a fragment of the bear's teeth or even dead flesh from the animal's previous kills, had already spread into Bobby's body before Bethany had amputated.

Cody knew that it was only a matter of time. He moved to Bethany's side and squatted down alongside her. Placed a hand on her shoulder. She did not look at him but instead spoke as she stared at the floor.

'When the bag's empty,' she said, 'maybe we should let him be. There's nothing that we can do to save him.'

'He might pull through,' Cody said. 'He might.'

Bethany looked at Cody and smiled in the soft light but there was no happiness in her eyes as she replied. 'We can't let him starve to death laying here. We have to release him.'

Cody swallowed. 'Morphine?'

'That would be the most humane way.'

'Hank won't give up the supplies. His crew comes first.'

Bethany kept her gaze on him for what felt like an age. Cody sighed and cast a long glance at Bobby's sickened body.

'Jesus,' he uttered. 'You're asking me to kill him.'

Bethany pinched her top lip between her teeth. 'He's doomed, Cody. The infection has already beaten him.'

Cody stood, his hand still on her shoulder. 'We're all invited for dinner, in the captain's cabin no less. I'm hoping to draw him on what's happened back home. I'll mention it.'

Cody turned to leave, but Bethany's hand pressed down onto his and held it to her shoulder.

'I'm sorry,' she whispered. 'I did everything I could for him.'

Her eyes were wide and yearning for some sign that she had done her best. Cody felt a hefty chunk of responsibility weigh down on him as he glanced at Bobby. Maybe it was right that he should make the decision and not Bethany. If somebody else became injured, it would do them no good if Bethany's confidence was so battered that she feared her every decision.

'Least we can do is keep him comfortable to the end, okay?' Cody put his other hand on top of hers and squeezed. 'Bobby was a busy kind of guy. He'll just get annoyed if we keep him hanging around.'

Bethany managed a faint smile. 'Okay.' She hesitated. 'When?'

Cody sucked in a lungful of air.

'Tonight, after dinner,' he said with a heavy sigh. 'Let's put him out of his misery.'

Cody turned to leave as Bethany released his hand.

'Bradley was right,' she said. 'We should have done this sooner.'

Cody realised that his choice of words matched those that had spilled from the soldier's mouth on numerous occasions.

'Bradley was an asshole,' Cody corrected her as he pointed at Bobby's body, speaking more for himself than for her. 'Enough people have died across the world already. Trying to save Bobby is what any human being would have done. I'm not about to let you, me or anybody else turn into some cynical survivalist who puts their own life above somebody else's, okay?'

Bethany blinked. 'I didn't know you felt so strongly about it.'

Cody glanced at Bobby one more time. 'Neither did I.'

Cody turned and walked from the sick bay. The shadows in the corridor seemed to follow him as though he were already haunted by the ghost of Bobby Leary.

*

The eerie glow of the sky was punctuated by a small number of glowing windows in the aft deckhouse as Cody climbed up onto the main deck. The air felt so cold it seemed he could crack it in his hands, the permanent dawn light haunting the ship as he walked.

Denton and Seth stood watch for marauding icebergs at the port bulwarks, Denton casting a silent, lingering glance at Cody as he passed by. Cody ignored both him and his tattooed friend and tilted his head back to look at the towering masts, rigid against a faint dusting of stars that spanned the heavens along the wispy lanes of the Milky Way.

There, atop the mainmast, a powerful lamp beamed a bright white shaft of light out to the west across the ice sheets and tundra. Satisfied both that he had done enough on Bradley's part and that the Phoenix's first mate, Saunders, was not entirely without heart, Cody hurried across to the wheelhouse and went inside.

Billowing warmth from the heaters filled the wheelhouse, chased by the sound of conversation. The wheelhouse led down to the dining room via a small staircase, which in turn led to the Captain's dining room and cabin at the very stern of the ship, thus bypassing the crew's quarters.

Cody made his way past the wheel, which was lashed to prevent the ship from turning against its anchor. He climbed down the staircase to the open dining room door. Captain Mears was seated at the head of the table, with Jake on one side of him and Charlotte on the other. Reece and Sauri occupied seats down each side, leaving two spare and a third at the opposite end facing the captain.

Plates lined the table and glasses of wine sparkled in the glow from the ceiling lights. A series of chromed serving dishes lined the centre of the table.

The captain raised his glass as Cody walked in. 'Ah, welcome Doctor Ryan.'

Cody shut the door behind him and stared at the captain's glass. 'You have wine?'

'Not the finest,' Mears admitted. 'But it's better than drinking our own piss.'

Reece chuckled, his cheeks flushed red and his eyes wide and glazed.

'Please,' the captain gestured to a seat, 'sit down. We've been waiting for you.'

Cody slid into the seat at the opposite end of the table, facing the captain. 'Bethany's on her way. She's just making Bobby comfortable.'

'What's his condition?' Jake asked.

Cody shook his head briefly. Jake looked at his wine glass but said nothing.

'There is nothing more you can do for him,' the captain said. 'If we could help, we would.'

Cody stared at the bubbles in his glass of wine. 'He needs morphine.'

'How bad is his pain?'

'He's not in pain.'

A silence descended around the table. Cody felt the eyes of the team upon him. Captain Mears studied Cody again for what seemed like hours before he spoke.

'We can spare two vials,' he said. 'Make sure they count.'

Cody noticed above and to one side of the door to the captain's cabin a ghostly shape haunted the wall. The wooden panels had probably faded over the years as sunlight beamed through the windows, but the crucifix that had once hung there was gone, only the darker wood betraying where it had hung for years. Cody looked at the captain anew and wondered what long held beliefs had collapsed when the world had fallen apart around him.

Bethany climbed down the steps from the wheelhouse into the dining room. She shrugged off her Arctic coat, surveyed the table and slid into the nearest seat to Cody. The captain raised his glass to her too.

'Miss Rogers,' he greeted her.

Bethany smiled briefly at the oddly jovial captain, and then her green eyes settled on Cody's and remained there. Cody offered her a brief nod and she sighed as though a great weight had been lifted from her shoulders.

'Shall we eat?' Hank suggested, making an effort to break the sombre mood as he stood from his seat. 'I must apologise for the nature of our meal as it is hardly gourmet dining. However, I understand that the ladies have done great things in the galley and made a great improvement on Denton's cooking, which was like eating your own feet.'

Reece chuckled again, the wine clearly going to his head. The captain lifted the lids on the serving dishes, revealing thick slabs of meat and what looked like roast potatoes. Steam billowed up from the thick gravy soaking the food.

'Christ,' Reece uttered. 'It looks like gourmet to me.'

'The finest polar bear,' Hank announced, 'shot just days ago. They're too inquisitive for their own good. Allow me.'

Charlotte watched as the captain began serving them.

'You know that the polar bear is an endangered species?' she uttered.

'So are we,' Hank replied. 'But with most of us now gone, the polar bears of this world will recover just fine I'm sure.'

The wine and the food tasted as though it had been served from Heaven itself. No doubt the potatoes were roasted because they were well past their best and the gravy helped to disguise the tough meat of the bear, but it mattered little.

Cody waited until they had all eaten a few mouthfuls before he spoke.

'You say that with all of us gone, the bears will do just fine?' he said to the captain. 'Just how many of us are gone?'

Hank focused on his meal. 'Perhaps we should dwell on more light hearted conversation?'

'No,' Charlotte replied for Cody. 'We've been up here for months with no knowledge of what's happened to the world outside, just hints and speculation. We need to know.'

The captain chewed on a thick piece of meat as he surveyed the group. He swallowed and washed the food down with a prodigious gulp of wine.

'You all feel this way?'

Nobody spoke, but all eyes settled expectantly on the captain's. Hank set his cutlery down and mopped his beard with a napkin as he spoke.

'Well, the best way that I can explain it is that your team has probably been in the safest place on Earth for the last six months. If you've been hoping to go home forget it. Forget all of it, because home no longer exists.'

Cody leaned forward on the table. 'Things can't have fallen apart so quickly.'

Captain Mears stared at Cody down the table as though he were a small, naïve child.

'Things fell apart within *weeks*,' he replied, and then exhaled noisily as he seemed to recall the calamity that had befallen mankind. 'Nobody thought that it could happen so fast.'

'Tell us,' Charlotte said, 'everything, from the beginning.'

The captain took another gulp of his wine and gestured to the vessel around them.

'The Phoenix was a training vessel,' he began. 'I'm a former captain in the United States Navy, retired now obviously. Myself and a few other veterans formed a company and bought the Phoenix with financial help from a local church. We spent years sailing the high seas teaching maritime skills to former convicts, trying to turn them away from crime by showing them that there were other things they could be doing with their time. We were doing okay, too. We were out a few miles off the coast of California with a group of recruits aboard when the Great Darkness came.'

'Great Darkness?' Bethany asked.

'It's what people call it,' Hank explained. 'After the storm there was no electricity, no power, so no lights. People living in the cities didn't realise how dark it gets at night without streetlights, so they started calling it the Great Darkness.'

'We saw the same storm,' Jake said, 'never witnessed an aurora like it.'

'Neither had we,' Hank pointed out. 'They're called the *Northern* Lights for a reason. We sat watching the show for a while until some of us realised what we were looking at. About that time we noticed fuses blowing in the wheelhouse and cell phones being fried. We managed to get some of the electrical equipment aboard ship shut off, like I told you.'

'Then what?' Reece asked.

'Then,' Hank echoed his question, 'nothing. The Phoenix is a blue-water vessel that can cross oceans and has a good communications suite. We tuned in to stations around the world and listened to them go off the air one by one as the storm swept across the planet.'

Hank looked at his glass for a moment before he went on.

'At first I kind of hoped it was just the satellites being taken out, losing the ability to relay signals. But then we saw all the lights in San Diego blink out, just like that.' He clicked his fingers loudly. 'You ever notice that orange glow you get against clouds on the horizon at night? You don't see it at sea. It's the light from cities and towns reflecting off the water vapour in the air. As we stood up there on the deck we watched that glow vanish as every city on America's west coast went completely dark.'

'There was no warning?' Jake asked. 'Nothing at all?'

'Toward the end some people got wise to it,' Hank replied. 'We heard some radio stations trying to warn people about the storm but I guess most people were standing outside looking up at the sky, not listening to radios. Countries on the other side of the world, in daylight, probably didn't see a damned thing. The power went out and that was it.'

'It doesn't make sense,' Reece said, slurring slightly. 'How the hell could something like this tear the world apart so quickly?'

Hank set his glass down.

'That, my young friend, is due to there being too many people being too damned stupid, including my business partners. We docked the following morning and they all tore off for their homes and families. At that point things weren't too bad. People just figured that the power would come back on and hey, we'd all be okay again. But as time wore on without information because there was no television, no news, no communication, people instinctively wanted to run to their families.'

Cody saw an image of Maria and Danielle, struggling to contact friends, family, anybody they could for help.

'Doesn't sound so stupid,' he said out loud.

'It is,' Hank smiled coldly, 'if you're prone to thinking. Tens of thousands of people rushing into and out of cities, crossing states and burning fuel that can't be replaced because the pumps in gas stations don't work without power. Before you know it people are scattered everywhere, running about like headless chickens. While they're doing that, the criminals are having a field day looting whatever they can find.'

'That fast?' Charlotte uttered.

'Within an hour of the power going down,' Hank nodded. 'The police had no ability to coordinate or communicate. They were powerless to prevent it. Once the looting had started and people realised that there was something seriously wrong they started hitting the convenience stores. Markets ran out of everything within a day or so. Nobody paid for anything of course, they just took it. Then other people wanted what had already been taken, and that's when the riots and the violence really got started.'

Cody leaned back in his chair, his belly full for the first time in three months, and stared at the plate before him. Finding food for a small group, even up here in the Arctic, was a feasible proposition. But in a major city of ten million or more, once the supermarkets emptied there was simply no way that the people could feed themselves and no natural resource for them to fall back on.

'What about water?' Reece asked. 'I thought that people could survive for weeks as long as they had water.'

'No water pressure,' Jake answered for the captain. 'With no power stations there's no energy to get the water to everyone. It was probably the first thing to go after the lights went out.'

Hank nodded.

'Water first, then the food, then the gas,' he confirmed. 'Within a week people were starting to fall sick with dehydration and starvation. They started forming groups, mostly young hoods who would raid people's homes for what little they had left. Home owners would shoot back in defence of their kids. Before the end of the second week there were dead bodies everywhere and cities started to burn as those with supplies were deliberately smoked out by those who had none.'

'Then the population fled for the countryside,' Jake guessed. 'Looking for food and water?'

'Exactly,' Hank nodded. 'Forget what you've seen on television dramas and at the movies: once the power was gone on such a large scale there was no way for it to ever be repaired, for the power stations and drainage systems to ever recover. The collapse was brutal in ways I can't even begin to describe, and even as millions of people streamed in an exodus from San Diego with gangs of armed thugs cutting them down for food, the Diablo Canyon and San Onofre nuclear plants imploded. Both used pumped sea water to cool the reactors, but with no power to do so the pumps underwent an automatic shutdown as soon as the back-up diesel generators ran out of fuel. A few days later the cooling tanks overheated and blasted radioactive waste all over the damned place and straight into the water table. You don't want to think about what that did to people in a state where water was already scarce.'

A momentary silence descended once more as Cody imagined the horror of an orderly, stable society crumbling and breaking down in a matter of days only to be poisoned by its own devices.

'What about the military?' he asked. 'Where the hell were they?'

'That,' Hank replied, 'is what we were asking ourselves.'

Dean Crawford

17

'Didn't the government instigate martial law?' Charlotte asked. 'Deploy the National Guard or something?'

The cabin creaked as the Phoenix rocked gently on the water in the cove, probably on swells created by an iceberg passing silently by outside.

'The military collapsed within days of the storm,' Hank replied. 'Most bases held out for a few days without power, but as the chain of command fell apart rations dwindled and staff began to worry about their own families, so they dispersed into the population. I can only imagine that senior officers, cut off from communications and unable to get orders from on high, realised that the game was up and abandoned their posts. I can't speak for other countries but in America there was no apparent military response to the disaster.'

Hank drained his glass as Charlotte shook her head.

'But the military forces at Alert abandoned the base *before* the solar storm,' she said.

Captain Mears froze in motion as his cold eyes locked onto Charlotte's. He set his glass down.

'So I heard.'

'They left us here,' Reece uttered, 'even their own like Sauri.'

Hank looked at Sauri, who said nothing but nodded once in confirmation.

'How long before the storm did they leave?' Hank asked Jake. 'Could they have been doing something else perhaps?'

Jake shrugged.

'Possibly, but Alert is a highly sensitive listening post with all kinds of classified equipment and they just abandoned it in a real hurry. My guess is that they either got some kind of warning of the storm or they independently realised what was coming and got the hell out while they could. The fact they just left us here I don't think was malice on their part — they just didn't have enough time to come out and gather us all.'

Hank appeared to consider this for a moment.

'What about the people back home?' Bethany asked him. 'What happened after the military collapsed?'

Hank shrugged as though the future had been a forgone conclusion.

'The winter set in real harsh, especially on the east coast. Without maintenance to major infrastructure most of the bigger cities began to flood during storm swells as the drainage failed. Those that didn't burned as stale gas burst from pipes or was deliberately ignited by people seeking warmth and shelter. Disease hit pretty fast too, things like cholera and typhoid, while pneumonia and influenza became overnight killers without antibiotics to treat them.'

Hank twirled his empty wine glass in one big hand as he spoke.

'Most of the hospitals got cleaned out when people really began to understand just how bad things were. There were riots for medicine just like there had been for food and water. It was about then that most people abandoned the cities for the countryside. Even those that survived the initial collapse and made it into the countryside died soon after.'

'How come?' Charlotte asked.

Hank shrugged.

'Hard to tell, but most people who own a gun can't shoot for shit,' he said. 'And animals have a habit of wanting to survive, just like humans. Plus a lot of city folk don't have a clue about how to gut animals, skin them, cook them and so on, or about how to clean water. Most just drink from rivers and streams thinking it's somehow natural and clean. God knows how many died from diseases brought on by eating uncooked food or swallowing who-knows-what horrible parasite from an unseen corpse lying in the water upstream, but I can tell you this: it's as quiet now in the hills as it is in the cities.'

Cody leaned forward on the table. 'You've been ashore? Where?'

'Baltimore,' Hank replied, 'where I'm from. When my colleagues split in San Diego I had nobody to run the ship but the damned convicts. Most split to their families but several had nobody to run to. Fortunately they also had enough brains to realise that the biggest threat to their safety was the people around them in the cities. They stayed aboard, and we made foraging runs into the city for supplies before it got too dangerous. We pulled out into deeper water. Some people were trying to board us as we left.'

'What happened to them?' Bethany asked.

Hank's cold blue eyes burrowed into hers. 'They failed the interview. I got out of San Diego with the skeleton crew we have now. Sailed down through Cape Horn because we couldn't pass the Panama Canal and then up through the Caribbean and along the east coast to Baltimore. A long voyage and we passed every major city along the way: Miami, Charleston, Norfolk, DC. All the same, smouldering and empty by the time we reached them. '

'Boston?' Cody asked.

Hank shook his head. 'We didn't stop there but you could see the smoke from the city from twenty miles off the coast.'

Cody felt his shoulders slump as he stared down at the table before him, a mental image of the smouldering remains of Boston hovering in his mind's eye, strewn with the rotting bodies of countless emaciated or murdered citizens. Danielle and Maria among them.

His fists clenched painfully as his fingernails dug deep into his palms and a scalding ball of acid lodged in his throat. Cody closed his eyes and tried to exterminate the vision from his mind, to replace it with Boston's busy streets bathed in sunshine, sandy beaches and the blue waters of Cape Cod Bay. Maria's cheerful giggling as he walked her along the shore, pointing at gulls and calling them *birdies*.

He felt a hand resting on his fist. He opened his eyes to see Bethany watching him as Hank's voice returned to his awareness.

'… nothing much there and Baltimore was empty too. The few people left were wandering around like escapees from an asylum, driven mad by hunger, thirst and disease. We grabbed what little supplies we could and made a plan.'

Jake looked up at the captain. 'What kind of plan?'

'The kind,' Hank said, 'that keeps people alive, keeps us from losing hope.' He looked at all of them as he spoke. 'You said it yourselves: the military pulled out of dodge *before* the storm, not because of it. Our space agency had satellites put up into orbit to do nothing other than look at the sun. Are any of you able to sit here and tell me that they didn't know what was about to happen?'

Cody stared at the captain for a long beat.

'What the hell are you saying?'

'What I'm saying,' Hank replied, 'is that they let this happen. They knew it was coming and they stood back and watched it.'

'Who is *they*?' Bethany asked.

'Government,' Hank shrugged, 'people of power.'

Jake's jaw dropped. 'Jesus, that's a hell of a stretch.'

'Is it?' Hank's eyes were fixed, probing each and every one of them in turn as he spoke. 'In the hours before the storm it seems that every major politician in the western world was hurrying off to what was described as a foreign meeting. Every newspaper we found littering the streets spoke of their departure, but not one actually said where they were going.'

The group sat in silence, but Cody was suddenly jolted by a vague memory that infiltrated his thoughts. Looking at the Internet in Alert, at the news of the President's departure for a foreign affairs conference, joined by Canada's Prime Minister who was heading overseas.

'Why the hell would they do that?' Reece wondered out loud. 'What's the good of being a leader if there's nobody left to lead?'

'What's the good of leading a dying world?' Hank challenged. 'Population was growing out of control and resources were dwindling. Gas costs were hitting record highs as were those for oil which was fast running out. The whole of civilisation was heading toward a tipping point that could well have seen us collapse anyway. What if they saw a disaster coming and decided that a natural cull was preferable to any other alternatives on the table?'

Jake frowned as he stared at his glass of wine. 'That's a risk I'm not sure that politicians would have the cojones to take.'

Hank chuckled and leaned back in his chair.

'Risk can be viewed from any number of perspectives. You and I see it as a matter of courage. A politician would see it as a matter of self-preservation. It would be an act of cowardice.'

Cody saw Charlotte's jaw clench as she looked at Jake and Hank.

'Not all politicians are cowards,' she hissed. 'Some work hard for their people.'

'I can't think of any,' Hank uttered.

'My father,' Charlotte snapped.

Hank's blue eyes swivelled to look at her. 'Your father?'

'Senator Larry Dennis, Ohio democrat,' she snapped back. 'He's spent thirty years on the floor of the Capitol busting his *cojones*, as Jake describes them, for the benefit of people he will never meet so that you two can sit here and insult him.'

Hank did not react to her tone, his voice level and calm.

'When did you last hear from your father?'

'Two days before the storm, via satellite link at Alert. He never mentioned a thing, and I know damned well that he would never have left me up there without trying to let me know what was happening.' Charlotte kicked her chair away from the table and stood to leave. 'You two can enjoy your little conspiracy theory as much as you like, but you forget that politicians are human beings with families too and no more likely to abandon them than you or I.'

She whirled away and had taken two paces when the captain's voice rumbled after her.

'Miss Dennis.'

There was something both commanding and conciliatory in his tone that brought Charlotte up short. She did not look back as the captain spoke.

'I apologise,' Hank said. 'We've all witnessed a lot and sometimes our anger clouds our judgement. I merely find it hard to believe that nobody, anywhere on Earth, knew anything of the solar storm. Please, stay with us for a little longer.'

Cody glanced at Charlotte. She sighed and turned back to her chair, the captain speaking as she retook it.

'When we realised that even the biggest cities were lost, the crew and I decided that it was likely that people of power would have escaped, fled before the carnage and sought a refuge. It was our hope to find that same refuge and join them.'

The possibility that men had indeed somehow managed to shelter from the fall of mankind in some nameless, distant but safe place appealed to Cody's hopes as much as the next man's. The fact that he had detected a distant, coherent radio signal from some far flung corner of the globe bolstered that thought. He looked at Captain Hank Mears and decided that now was not the right time to reveal the existence of the Morse Code message he had deciphered. He could not trust the captain or his crew, and if things turned ugly they would need a bargaining chip to survive.

'We picked up a signal,' Reece slurred. 'Cody heard it.'

Hank stared down the table at Cody. The rest of the team looked at him expectantly and for a moment Cody felt as though he were about to be interrogated.

'At Alert,' Cody said, 'a faint signal. I couldn't get a location on it and we could barely communicate the signal was so weak, but they heard me and I heard them.'

He looked at Charlotte and wondered, briefly, if the signal might have been from her father.

Hank leaned forward on the table. 'Are you sure it was a communication and not an emergency broadcast of some kind?'

'It was a communication,' Cody confirmed. 'Somebody's out there.'

Hank leaned back again. 'Yes they are,' he said, 'and with equipment powerful enough to transmit without the aid of orbiting satellites.'

'And where,' Jake asked, 'do you think that this mysterious refuge of theirs is located?'

Hank smiled ruefully beneath his beard.

'That's the catch, isn't it? We thought it was up here when we detected your beacons. It was in a location that might just be distant enough that other people wouldn't reach it, the kind of place politicians might choose to hide. The base at Alert was on our charts so we triangulated the beacon's source and set off from Baltimore in late winter hoping to catch the spring thaw north of the Arctic Circle. We anchored near Grise Fjord to wait out the worst of the weather before moving north again.'

Charlotte shook her head in amazement.

'You came all the way up here chasing a pipe dream?'

'What else is there to do?' Hank tossed her question back to her. 'Mankind just became virtually extinct. There isn't anything else for us now. All we can do is hope that people elsewhere had the same presence of mind to escape the disaster and that we can find them. The rest?' Hank shrugged and down the rest of his wine. 'That's evolution for you, the survival of the fittest.'

Cody spoke softly.

'Darwin never said that. But you're right that the only people who will make it out of this are those who are best adapted to survive.'

'The toughest,' Hank agreed, 'those unwilling to compromise their survival by dragging the weak along with them.'

Cody shook his head.

'The opposite. What made humanity great was our ability to cooperate and support each other. If what you say about the politicians is true then what killed humanity is the same selfishness that you refer to. Evolution isn't about dominating every other species, it's about passing on the traits that keep us all alive. If only a lack of compromise remains then you'll die out fast captain, because your ruthless allies will eventually eliminate you, or you'll eliminate them and end up alone.'

Hank watched Cody for a long time. 'How would you know so much about it, Doctor?'

'I'm a biologist.'

The table remained silent for a few moments.

'You got a name for this new haven of yours?' Jake asked the captain, 'if you find it?'

Hank nodded and refilled his glass.

'We'll find it', he said. 'If there are people already there then it'll have a name. If not, we'll christen it ourselves. But for now we're just calling it Eden.'

The captain raised his wine glass as he spoke.

'We might be the last people alive on earth who are not right now in imminent danger of dying. But whatever happens we need to find a safe place to live, somewhere with the resources we need to survive and the defences we need to keep it our own.' He paused. 'To Eden, ours or theirs.'

Cody slowly lifted his glass. Jake, Bethany, Charlotte, Reece and Sauri followed suit in chorus.

*

Cody pushed the cabin door closed behind him and stood in silence, the alcohol warming his veins and blurring his thoughts. Time seemed to spill past but he could not tell how fast or how slow it moved, just like the bitter waters flowing by outside in the channel.

Fatigue pushed him on and he sat quietly down beside the bed. He thought of his daughter, of his wife, of his parents and of all the people he had ever known who might have since passed on from this life into a great unknown that all feared and yet all must one day face.

Cody reached out and pushed his index finger into the crook of Bobby's neck.

He searched for several moments before he felt a feeble, erratic pulse threading its way past his touch.

Cody sat for a few moments more and then said a silent prayer that echoed through the empty vaults of his mind. He watched his own hands break the seals on the morphine vials and invert them before punching them into Bobby's chest and letting them empty into his body, close to his weakening heart.

'I'm so sorry, Bobby,' he whispered. 'I wish this could have turned out differently.'

Cody sat for a long time, hovering somewhere on the abyss of sleep as he felt life slip silently away from the room and leave him with anything but peace.

18

'Put your back into it, Ryan!'

Cody heaved, his hands slipping on the frosted beam as he pushed his chest into it and the capstan turned agonisingly slowly. He heard the lethargic rattle of the thick chains through their mounts and then the anchor broke free from the seabed and the capstan loosened.

'Easy now,' Denton wheezed beside him, 'bring her up steady so we don't foul the chain or hit the hull with the anchor.'

Cody kept a steady pace around the capstan opposite Denton, matching him stride for stride until the huge anchor reached the limit of its travel and clanged against the hull mounts.

'Stowed!' Denton yelled, and then grabbed a belaying pin from a nearby rack and used a hammer to drive it through a link in the anchor chain into a hole in the capstan. With the anchor secured, Cody released pressure on the capstan.

'Out on deck,' Denton snapped. 'Saunders will want you.'

Cody did not bridle at Denton's tone. He had decided that he and the team were passengers aboard the Phoenix, visitors who needed to earn their keep. Besides, Denton was a scrawny little shit not worthy of the attention. Cody turned his back on the capstan and walked out onto the main deck. He looked up and saw the beacon still glowing in the dawn light atop the mainmast. Saunders had kept the thing burning up there all night.

The Arctic tundra was striped with shadows and bright beams of sunlight as the distant sun blazed low across the horizon. Cody squinted into the light, shielding his eyes with his gloved hands as he scanned the barren wilderness for some sign of Bradley Trent and the BV.

'He ain't coming back.' Jake patted Cody on the back.

Cody sighed. 'Idiot, if he'd only waited another day.'

'Yeah,' Jake replied, 'but if we'd given in and joined him we'd have missed our ride. We did the right thing, staying with Bobby. I got what you said last night to Hank, loud and clear. We stick together.'

Cody stared out across the wilderness.

'Cody?' Jake asked.

Cody turned to face the old man, who gripped his shoulder tightly. 'We stick together.'

Cody looked into Jake's eyes, more than half a century of experience looking back into his own. He nodded.

'Then let's get to it,' Jake said. 'We've got ice to clear.'

*

Week 26

My beloved Maria,

Our passage south is laborious but consistent. The current that flows down through the Nares Strait maintains a steady five knots and is supported by northerly winds. However, the captain is reluctant to use canvas because of the icebergs that litter the surface of the channel. Some are far larger than the ship itself, leviathans of ice that tower over us and calve chunks the size of houses into the brutal water.

EDEN

This place is of such beauty that I cannot describe in words how it feels to witness it, a world unstained by mankind but for our silent passage. Beluga whales sail with us, diving beneath and around the 'bergs. Polar bears track our progress and Arctic seals watch from the shores. We are forced to shoot them from time to time for food but we only take that which we need to survive. Bethany and Charlotte maintain five days' emergency stock of meat, never more. The captain has urged them to accept more as we will soon leave the channel and it will become harder to find food, but they have both refused as there is no room in the ship's only working ice-box for further supplies.

Our one great hope is that the ship's radio suite is now broadcasting the signal of the distress beacon we took from Alert. If there is somebody out there with the ability to track us, they will know we have left the Arctic and are sailing south.

Bobby passed away two days ago. His body is stored below decks in what I'm told was a gunpowder store in the original vessel from which the Phoenix derives. Lined with tin and bitterly cold, it preserves his remains until we reach Baffin Bay. Everybody agreed that the last place he would have wanted to be interred was the unforgiving permafrost of Ellesmere Island.

The weather is improving steadily although sudden fogs impede our progress from time to time. The captain intends to avoid deep water sailing because of the treacherous conditions through Baffin Bay and the Davis Strait.

I do not trust the crew of the Phoenix or their captain. I fear that if they knew of the coordinates I recorded at Alert, they would have no qualms about leaving us behind and pursuing their "Eden" alone. In the captain's own words: the less bellies need be fed, the more miles covered instead…

*

'Iceberg!' Hard to port!'

Reece's cry rang out across the deck like a claxon in the otherwise deep silence as the Phoenix drifted near scattered pack ice along the coast, the channel entombed in a thick fog so cold it froze on the skin.

Cody looked up and saw the huge 'berg loom ahead as they rounded the narrow clear water channel alongside the coast south of Smith Sound. The fog enshrouded the coastline and the sheer mountains rising up from the ice sheets in walls of rugged grey and white, their soaring heights lost in the gloom.

Saunders span the wheel hard and the Phoenix began turning away from the sheer cliff of craggy white ice. Cody dashed for the starboard bow along with Denton, Taylor and Sauri as smaller chunks of ice began thumping against the hull.

Cody saw that the channel running toward Grise Fjord was packed with a solid mass of jagged white ice that stretched back into Jones Sound and blocked the way into Craig Harbour like an enormous glacier.

'We're cut off,' Saunders said as he moved to stand along the bulwark. 'We'll never reach Grise Fjord through that.'

His voice sounded dull and flat, distorted by the cold air and the fog. The Phoenix drifted slowly around the immense shelf of the iceberg, which had become lodged against the coastline several hundred metres away.

'Probably calved off the Jakeman Glacier,' Saunders said as he pointed out to the west, 'got turned around in the currents here. The rest of it is ice melt that's got packed up into the channel and frozen again.'

Hank Mears strode across and joined them at the bulwarks. He scanned the densely packed iced channel for a few moments and then made his decision.

'We can't make Grise Fjord,' he said finally. 'We'll have to push on south.'

Cody watched as the ship slowly rounded the iceberg and Jones Sound appeared before them. A broad stretch of water between Ellesmere Island's south coast and the north coast of Devon Island, the Sound was filled with rugged ice compressed into the channel. The dark, foreboding water gave way to the white pack ice which in turn gave way to the featureless grey fog.

'How come it wasn't like this further north?' Cody asked Jake. 'How did we get down out of Alert?'

'The currents drag icebergs around the tip of Ellesmere Island,' Saunders replied, 'packs 'em in here sometimes against the year-round ice. You can't get to Grise Fjord without an aeroplane when it's like this. It's sometimes the same at Alert, but you guys were lucky. The winds cleared the ice from the shore as we made our way up, gave us that clear water channel, and coming back down we just floated along with the current.' Saunders dragged deeply on a cigarette and then flicked the butt out into the pristine water below. 'But if the channel had frozen again, like here, it would have crushed the ship's hull and we'd all have been long dead.'

'What about Bobby?' Cody asked him.

'No way we're risking landfall up here now,' Saunders said, 'too dangerous. If we get boxed in we could be stuck for weeks, months even. Your boy will be buried at sea.'

'That's not what he would have wanted.'

'He didn't want to die either, did he?' Saunders replied. 'But it happened, and I'm sure he doesn't give a damn now bein' gone and all.'

Saunders turned away from the view and followed his captain back toward the wheelhouse. Hank directed Denton, Seth and Taylor to retrieve Bobby's body from the powder store below decks.

'They're just going to dump him here?' Bethany gasped.

Charlotte was behind Bethany and watched in silence as Denton and his crewmates hefted Bobby's body up through the main hatch. He was wrapped in old sheets, probably a sail that had torn during a storm, the canvas stitched closed around him with thick cordage.

'Hold her steady! Fly topsails!'

The captain's voice blasted like a shotgun across the decks, startling a pair of Arctic terns on the distant shore. Their flapping wings echoed eerily as they flew away and vanished into the fog as the Phoenix drifted listlessly in the current, Saunders holding her rudder full to port to prevent her from turning toward the densely packed ice in the channel to their right.

Four crewmen scrambled across the decks and hauled on the rigging lines, releasing triangular sails that rumbled as they fell from the uppermost yards. Cody watched as they braced the lines, bringing the canvas taut and then tying the rigging down.

'He's using the breeze to bring us out of the channel,' Jake said.

The Phoenix got underway, the barely noticeable wind producing just enough thrust to keep the ship moving away from the treacherous ice.

Hank Mears strode back to the bulwarks as Denton's men set Bobby's body down on the boarding ramp, which was normally lashed to the bulwarks but lay now on the deck. The captain looked at the body and then at Jake McDermott.

'You got anything you want to say?'

The crew gathered nearby in silence and watched as Jake stood forward. Cody could not bring himself to look at Bobby's body as Jake spoke. He could see Bethany look at him from time to time from the corner of his eye, but he refused to raise his head. Nearby, Reece stared at the corpse, a horrible sense of guilt etched like stone into his features. He occasionally looked back and forth between Cody to Jake.

Cody tried not to look at him as Jake spoke.

'This is not something that we ever thought we'd have to do, bury one of our own,' Jake said, his gravelly voice rattling out into the uncaring wilderness around them. 'Bobby Leary was a sociable man who sought to learn what he could from the world and from his companions in the Arctic. He was an orphan, and we never learned if he had extended family somewhere out there. Maybe losing his folks affected him more than he let on and he chose not to contact them. We'll never know. What we do know is that when the time came and we were all tested, Bobby stepped up and did not once shirk his responsibilities. That courage cost him his life so that ours might go on.' Jake exhaled noisily on the cold air, his breath billowing in thick clouds. 'We owe it to him that he not be forgotten, by any of us, for our every breath is thanks to his courage.'

Jake looked down at the body and then stepped back.

Hank nodded to Denton. The sailor stepped forward and with Seth and Muir lifted the ramp and rested the bottom end atop the bulwarks. Taylor, the tallest man in the crew, stepped to the back and lifted the ramp high in his chunky hands and tilted it toward the sea.

Bobby's body slid down the ramp and over the side. A moment later it slipped with barely a ripple into the bitter waters and vanished into the icy darkness.

The ship remained silent as though frozen in time for what felt to Cody like an eternity. He noticed Denton and Seth watching him with barely concealed satisfaction on their faces. Then, the captain bellowed an order.

'Brace the foretop!'

The crew scattered to tighten the canvas further and make headway as Hank span on his heel and headed back to the wheelhouse. Cody stared at the black water swirling like oil past the hull, unable to shift the image of its bitter depths from his mind and the distant sound of the grinding ice. The glaciers sounded forever as though they were alive, creeping with unstoppable force across the barren, rocky lands.

'C'mon.'

Cody turned and saw Bethany standing beside him. She slipped one arm through his and tugged him away from the bulwarks and the lonely, bleak vista that lay beyond.

'I don't want us to lose anybody else,' he whispered.

'We won't,' Bethany replied. 'We won't.'

'All hands, step lively!' the captain boomed. 'We're joining the floes again.'

The Phoenix was drifting out of the sound toward the coast of Devon Island somewhere far to the south. With pack ice behind and icebergs to her port side, there was only one way to go and no way to turn back. Cody headed for the port bulwarks, the sound of the grinding glaciers seeming to increase in volume behind him.

Cody slowed and turned as behind him the grinding and crunching noise became even louder. He dashed back to the starboard bulwarks as he spotted something moving on the shore far behind them.

'Bradley! Jesus Christ, it's Brad!'

Charlotte's frantic cry caused every head to turn as a pair of headlight beams sliced through the fog on the southern shore of Ellesmere Island. Cody felt his guts lurch as through the grey mist the blocky form of a yellow BV appeared, puffs of black smoke spilling from its exhaust stack as it headed for the shoreline.

Jake whirled to the captain and pointed back at the shore.

'We've got to go back for him!'

The captain stood on the quarterdeck, his gaze unblinking as he surveyed the shore and the thick icebergs spilling from the channel into the sound. Even as Cody watched he knew with an unbearable certainty that there was nothing they could do.

Hank Mears shook his head once.

'He's your man,' the captain said. 'We can't turn back now.'

Charlotte screamed something unintelligible and hurled herself at the captain. Jake leaped across and wrapped his arms about her waist to prevent her from scratching the big man's eyes out. Charlotte broke free and dashed to the bulwarks as the BV shuddered to a halt near the water's edge and the cab door swung open.

Even across the expanse of ice-flecked water Cody could see Bradley's haggard features as he staggered to the water's edge and flung his arms wide at them, shouting and hollering, his voice carrying faintly across the lonely sea.

Cody looked up at the Phoenix's mainmast and saw that the beacon was still shining there. He looked down to where Saunders manned the ship's wheel, saw the old man avert his eyes behind the wheelhouse windows.

'You can't leave him here!' Cody shouted at Hank.

The captain did not look at Cody as he replied. 'Yes, I can.'

Cody whirled away and glimpsed Denton smirking at him. The scrawny youth raised one pierced eyebrow. 'Less bellies to be fed….'

Denton didn't see Sauri coming. The Inuit span Denton around by the shoulder punched him hard enough that the crack echoed across the ship. Denton whirled and hit the deck just as Taylor reached Sauri and drove an elbow deep into his belly.

Sauri tumbled sideways into the bulwarks and doubled over at the waist as Taylor stepped in to bring his knee up into the Inuit's face. Jake dashed across to them and shoulder barged Taylor aside, knocking the big man off balance as Denton scrambled to his feet, a knife flickering in the pale light and his face shining with mindless malice.

Dean Crawford

19

Cody moved without thinking as the crew began swarming to the defence of their fellow seamen, spilling from the rigging lines and the quarterdeck. Cody stepped in front of Denton and blocked his path to Sauri as he raised a hand.

'That's one step too far,' Cody uttered as he looked at the blade. 'Back off.'

'Out of my way, freak,' Denton spat, 'or I'll gut you here and now.'

Cody stood his ground and glanced up to the quarterdeck. The captain was standing with his hands behind his back, watching but clearly not about to intervene. Denton, Taylor, Seth and several others were all wearing expressions of fervour, infected with a lust for blood.

'What the hell will that achieve?' Cody snapped at Denton with more gusto than he felt.

'Just like I said,' Denton replied, 'less bellies.'

'Gut him,' Seth sneered, his tattooed face pulsing with delight. 'Do him!'

The sailor hopped forward and swiped the knife at Cody's face. Cody leaped backwards in shock as the wicked blade flashed past an inch from his eyes. A moment later, a heavy chunk of rigging tackle swung past in the opposite direction and landed in Denton's belly with a dull thud that folded the sailor over and dropped him to his knees.

Cody turned to see Bethany haul the rigging up again, Jake moving alongside her.

The crew turned to face them when Charlotte's cry echoed across the deck.

'He's in the water!'

Every head turned to the shore, which had almost vanished through the fog. Cody gasped as he saw the BV's exhaust stack billow smoke as it charged to the shoreline and plunged into the black water, scattering chunks of ice before it.

'Christ, he's insane,' Taylor growled.

'The BV's amphibious,' Jake replied. 'But it won't take hits from icebergs for long. If he loses a window he's done for.'

'Let him sink!' Denton screamed as he sucked in a lungful of air, his hands clasped around his stomach as tears streamed down his face. 'Let the bastard sink!'

Charlotte looked up at the captain, who was watching the BV as it churned through a flotsam of ice in its desperate attempt to reach the ship before she cleared the headland.

'He's not moving fast enough!' Charlotte yelled at Hank. 'Do something! Lower a boat!'

The captain's voice boomed across the deck. 'Shorten sail!'

The crew remained silent and motionless. Cody felt alarm ripple through his body as he saw Seth's malicious grin spread like a disease across his features.

'To hell with them all!' he bellowed back at the captain, and glared at Jake. 'This ship is our priority, not your friend,' he snapped enough force to carry across the entire deck. 'It's not worth the risk.'

Cody looked up at the captain, who merely shrugged.

Charlotte took one look at the BV struggling through the thick ice and then whirled away, one hand across a face that streamed with tears as she dashed past Cody and the crew and into the fore deckhouse.

Denton looked up at Seth and grinned through his pain. 'Ten dollars says he doesn't make it.'

'I'm in,' Seth chuckled.

Cody span on his heel and saw the BV colliding with huge chunks of ice, careering in the water as it weaved left and right in an attempt to avoid the biggest obstacles.

'He's not going to make it,' Jake uttered.

The Phoenix was drifting out of the sound, where the deeper water moved faster. The BV could not keep pace and seemed encased in an undulating floe of ice that closed in around it. The engine laboured and belched thick diesel clouds onto the frigid air.

'Don't panic,' Cody whispered under his breath. 'Just keep moving.'

A voice called out. 'He's taking in water!'

Cody felt his guts plunge as the BV's Articulated rear began to drag in the water, the engine note changing as Bradley struggled to keep the vehicle moving. He was aiming for an intercept point some fifty yards ahead but almost certainly could not make it as water flooded in through a cracked window.

Denton chuckled in delight as he struggled to his feet. 'He's a goner, boys!'

Cody stared with macabre fascination into Denton's manic gaze, stunned by how a man could be so intensely callous. Cody whirled away and called across to the captain.

'Is this what you are? Is this what you've become?!'

Hank did not respond, his gaze fixed upon the struggling BV out amongst the ice.

'Why don't you swim out and fetch him?' Denton chuckled maniacally to Cody.

Before Cody could respond, Bethany dropped the rope and tackle she still held in her grasp and it thumped to the deck. 'He's sinking.'

Cody saw the BV's rear section swamped by the water as the front began to rise above the waves, the engine screaming. The cab door opened and Bradley hurled a large canvas sack out onto the roof before hauling himself out of the flooding cab and onto the roof.

The BV slowed in the water barely fifty yards from the Phoenix as Bradley raised his arms and shouted across to them.

'What the hell are you waiting for?!'

Cody stared as the BV sank further and bitter water sloshed across the cab ceiling and over Bradley's boots.

'Do something!' Bethany screamed at Hank.

Her cry was followed by a harsh rattling that crashed out from the fore deckhouse. Cody saw the bow anchor plunge from its mountings and crash into the water as Denton and the crew's macabre delight turned to panic.

'No!'

The Phoenix lurched as the anchor thumped into the seabed and the chain was yanked taut under the ship's enormous weight. The whole deck titled wildly as the hull began to rotate in the water around its anchor and the chain began thudding out link by link under the strain, threatening to foul the hull.

'Secure the capstan and get that anchor raised!' Hank bellowed as he hung on to the quarterdeck rail. 'Hard to starboard!'

Saunders heaved into the wheel to try to slow the Phoenix's wild gyration, Hank joining him. The crew scattered for the capstan and Charlotte staggered across to the port bulwarks as the Phoenix heaved in the water.

Cody ran to join her on the tilting deck, the canvas sails above thundering as the breeze spilled from them.

'What are you doing?!' Cody yelled.

Charlotte did not reply as she dashed across to the rigging. Coils of spare rope were lashed down near each of the masts, and she dragged one of them across to the bulwarks and tied one end to the railings.

'Fetch me a float!' she screamed.

Cody dashed to where a brightly coloured float sat in its mountings attached to the bulwarks. He yanked it out and handed it to Charlotte, who tied the other end of the rope to the float. Cody stared at her in amazement as she whirled and in one fluid motion hurled the float up at a high angle into the sky in the direction of the BV.

The float arced out toward the BV but the weight of the line hauled it quickly back down. It splashed into the icy some fifteen yards from the sinking vehicle.

Bradley didn't even wait for it to land. As the float flew through the air he hauled the sack onto his back and jumped headlong into the water.

Cody's heart almost stopped. Bradley had seconds to make it to the float before the brutally cold convection of the water literally sucked the heat from his body and prevented him from moving. Bradley's head popped up out of the water and he swam powerfully for several strokes, but already his face was blotchy with the severe shock of the cold and his limbs began gyrating wildly as he struggled to swim.

'Come on!' Charlotte yelled. 'Keep moving!'

Bradley splashed his way toward the ship, his head ducking beneath the black water and his legs vanishing. His hands groped blindly for the float as it bobbed on the water, and then both of his arms splashed down onto it and he hauled his head above the surface.

'Pull!'

Cody hauled with all of his strength on the line, dragging Bradley's body against the water and the ship's movement through it. On his third heave the line became suddenly lighter.

'He's off the line!'

'No he's not.'

Cody turned and saw Jake, Sauri, Reece and behind them Bethany pulling fiercely on the rope. From Cody's right, the captain leaped down off the quarterdeck and hurled a rope ladder over the side of the ship, securing it against the bulwarks.

Bradley's drenched body bumped against the Phoenix's hull and with trembling arms he managed to clamber up the ladder far enough for Cody and Hank to reach him. With a heave of effort they dragged the soldier's body over the bulwarks and he thumped down onto the deck in a splash of icy water.

Charlotte dashed to his side, dropping to her knees as she threw her hands around the soldier's neck.

Bradley's skin was pale white and his body was trembling and shuddering as though rolling with a live current, but through stuttering purple lips he managed to speak.

'Got…, medicine, ….Bobby.'

Cody felt something lodge painfully in his throat as Charlotte cupped the soldier's face in her hands in disbelief and amazement.

'Taylor, light the generator!' Hank snapped. 'Bethany, get something boiled up immediately. Soup, coffee, anything!'

As Bethany and Taylor dashed away a series of cries went up from the foredeck house.

'We need help here!'

The anchor chain rumbled and the hull creaked as the huge anchor dragged across the seabed below and strained the capstan, Denton, Seth, Ice and Muir struggling to hold the capstan in place and prevent the anchor from ripping it out of its housing.

'We're heading for the ice pack!' Saunders shouted from the wheelhouse.

Astern the Phoenix, dense ice floes as tall as houses loomed through the fog as the ship drifted backward toward them. Cody knew instantly that if the ship hit them stern first she could be damaged beyond repair, her rudder smashed.

'Get in there!' Hank bellowed and then ran past them toward the stern.

Cody ran for the fore deckhouse. The Phoenix was listing to port as she drifted backwards with the current, held by the anchor dragging along the seabed. Cody dashed inside to see the crew grimacing with effort as they tried to haul the anchor away from the seabed.

Cody plunged into one of the bars and heaved as Jake and Sauri both fell into other bars and dug in against the immense pressure. The capstan creaked and the sound of bolts, bearings and muscles under immense strain filled the deckhouse as they fought the seabed's savage grip.

'As one!' Jake yelled. 'Now!'

They heaved together and the capstan suddenly jolted and span viciously as the anchor was torn free of the sediment below. The bars whirled and Cody stumbled as the capstan turned easily beneath their grip.

'Anchor free!' Denton bellowed at the top of his lungs.

Cody staggered out onto the main deck to hear the stern anchor plunge into the water as the captain freed her. Saunders held the wheel hard to starboard as soon as the stern anchor chain caught the seabed below. The Phoenix silently and gracefully rotated in the current, and the sails above rumbled as the light wind flukes filled them once more.

Cody rushed into the aft deckhouse and joined Hank at the rear capstan.

'Stern away!' Saunders yelled.

In unison, Hank and Cody heaved on the smaller capstan at the rear and moments later the anchor lifted free of the seabed. They turned the capstan until the anchor was secured and Hank drove a belaying pin into the chain.

They dashed outside to see the ice floes drifting past twenty yards out on the starboard bow. Cody sighed in relief, rubbed his face with his hands as he looked at Hank.

'That was too close.'

The captain did not look at Cody as he replied. 'Far too close. Keep your people below decks from now on unless ordered otherwise.'

Cody stared at the captain. 'Why?'

Hank walked away as he replied. 'Because if any of you ever again endanger my ship or my crew I will kill you all.'

*

The generator bathed the interior of the ship in a rare blanket of warmth, the lights glowing as Cody walked to the for'ard sick bay. Charlotte and Bethany sat on the spare bed alongside Bradley, who lay beneath sheets with hot water bottles tucked around him.

The soldier looked up as Cody entered the bay.

'About time you came to pay your respects, Doctor.'

'You made it,' Cody replied. 'I never thought I'd say it to such an extraordinary asshole, but I'm glad you got through.'

The soldier's jaw twisted into a crooked grin, an effort at humour that belied what Bradley must by now already know. Bradley stuck a hand out from beneath the sheets and Cody shook it as the soldier replied.

'Touched, I'm sure. Wouldn't be here at all if Charlie hadn't thrown me a line. What's the beef with the crew?'

'They don't play well with others.'

'He didn't make it,' the soldier said. 'Bobby.'

'Buried him at sea just before you turned up,' Cody replied, and managed somehow to keep his face emotionless. 'But he succumbed to the infection three days ago.'

Bradley exhaled a long, slow breath. 'Well, we got plenty of antibiotics now and a few other choice goodies I found at Eureka.'

'Where's the bag?' Cody asked.

'Here,' Charlotte replied. 'I managed to keep it out of Denton's hands.'

'Just as well,' Bradley said, 'because there are six handguns in there. Sig Sauer P225's, good kit and two clips each. Probably personal defence against wolves for staff stationed at Eureka.'

'You find anybody there?'

Bradley shook his head. 'Empty. Tried to reach Grise Fjord but on the way I saw a light out to the east and figured somebody was out there.'

Cody felt a meagre crumb of redemption warm his belly.

'Saunders,' he replied. 'I asked him to attach a light to the topmast in case you were close by.'

'Then I owe you a great deal, Doctor,' Bradley said.

'Just get your head down and get recovered. We need you.'

Bradley nodded. Cody saw one of Charlotte's hands resting atop the soldier's. As Cody turned away, Bethany joined him and they walked aft down the corridor outside together.

'Bobby wouldn't have held on another three days,' she whispered to him. 'You know that, right?'

Cody didn't reply, unable to think of a response that would satisfy him. Bethany gripped his arm in one hand and slowed him down. 'He wouldn't,' she insisted. 'He was too far gone. I'd have been surprised if he had made it through that night.'

'It wasn't our place to decide,' Cody uttered.

'Nor was it our place to make him suffer further,' Bethany replied. 'We can't know the future, Cody. We did what we thought was right, for the best.'

'And next time?' he asked her. 'What would you do now, if it were Jake or Charlotte or me suffering?'

Bethany averted her eyes from his, sucked in a breath.

'Let's just hope that we never have to think about it, okay? We've got a long way to go and God knows what's waiting for us. One day at a time.'

Cody saw her look up at him in a way he had not really noticed before.

'One day at a time,' he agreed.

Bethany smiled and walked away.

TEMPERANCE

Dean Crawford

20

Week 30

Dearest Maria,

We are finally free of the Arctic and have covered some two hundred nautical miles since leaving Ellesmere Island. It is difficult to describe how wonderful it is to feel the sun's warmth on our faces as we traverse the Davis Strait, to see the decks free of ice and the sails straining to the sound of the winds that drive us ever farther south. Although we maintain a sharp lookout for icebergs which remain a hazard in these waters and the going is tough, spirits are a little higher now than they once were.

Bradley has recovered from his ordeal and already has made his mark on Denton, Seth and their cohorts, who are now reluctant to threaten us in any meaningful way. However, supplies are running woefully short and we have a long way to go before we raise home. Hunger is a real issue, and the captain informed us that due to our inflated numbers we only have a few meals remaining from the last polar bear shot by the crew.

Attempts at fishing and even whaling have so far proven ineffective.

I have set up the radios taken from Alert in the captain's cabin and he spends many hours searching the wavebands for some sign of human life. As yet, he has found none.

*

Hank Mears stood over the table in the wheelhouse and pored over the large map spread before them. Cody and the team stood on one side, the crew on the other, while Saunders manned the wheel and watched over the table and the ship beyond through the windows.

'So, ladies and gentlemen, whence and where to travel?'

The maps and nautical charts were the captain's prized possessions and kept hidden from the crew and Cody's team. Hank's reasoning was that mankind had mostly burned anything that could be ignited to ward off the bitter winters, so any remaining charts and maps were now worth more than any precious metal.

The Phoenix was heeled over before a blow blustering in from the north-east, her bow rising and falling as she shouldered her way into the slate grey waves churning across the endless ocean. Clouds scudded across the sullen sky above, squalls and spray filling the air.

Everybody aboard leaned and swayed with the rolling ship by unthinking reflex, fully acclimatised to the movement of the schooner beneath them.

'I say Tahiti,' announced Muir. 'Saw a documentary about it once. Hot women, hot beaches and nothing to do but breed.'

'Fiji,' said Seth. 'Same deal, less volcanoes.'

'Boston,' said Jake. 'Some of us have families there.'

The crew stared at the old man as though he had gone insane. 'Forget it,' Denton spat. 'You don't get to make choices here.'

'Like hell we'd go there anyway,' Taylor growled. 'We got the pick of the world and you want some two-bit city on the east coast?'

'I'm surprised at you, Taylor,' Jake said. 'Denton I can imagine being a bastard orphan who would sell his own grandmother, but you must have family too somewhere?'

Taylor shrugged his big round shoulders. 'Most of 'em died in the panic after the storm,' he replied, 'no point in me worrying 'bout any that might be left.'

'You're all heart,' Cody murmured, and looked at the captain. 'As long as we're heading south we've got to stay close to the shore for supplies, right? We're low on food and we need fresh water, so we pick locations all down the eastern seaboard. No reason Boston can't be one of them.'

'The Pacific is out of bounds for us right now,' Charlotte pointed out to Taylor. 'We can't support ourselves in deep water until we can store enough fresh provisions to make the journey. That also means we can't cross the Atlantic so right now we're pretty much tied to the seaboard.'

Hank Mears raised an eyebrow at her in surprise. 'I didn't realise you had a nautical bone in your body.'

'I used to sail with my father out of Cambridge Bay in his yacht,' she replied tartly.

'How far do we have to go to reach America?' Bethany asked. 'Maybe some communities have survived, are being rebuilt?'

Jake sighed.

'Given the harsh weather and all it has brought, I'd say Maine is our first best bet at finding other survivors. They might have pulled through there, but probably the further south we go the better chance people will have had.'

'Boston's not far south of Maine,' Cody pointed out to the captain.

'This is bullshit,' Denton uttered. 'We all saw what it was like when we left. There are no cities any more, no more communities, no more people. If anybody survived it'll be way down toward the panhandle. South Carolina, Georgia, Florida. There ain't shit up here.'

Hank nodded slowly in agreement.

'I haven't detected any radio signals so as far as I can tell there's no broadcasting technology anywhere within a few hundred miles of us. Can't be sure until we raise St John's in Newfoundland and see if there are any lights on.'

'Or we could head west,' Saunders suggested as he held the wheel, 'cut through the North West Passages into the Beaufort Sea, round Alaska and head south down the Pacific seaboard. Didn't California have a lot of green energy down there, solar panels and all that shit? Maybe they'll have had something to hang on to.'

'Doesn't matter much,' Reece replied through the lank hair dangling in front of his eyes, 'it's the circuitry in everything that got fried.'

Jake watched Reece but did not reply. Cody realised that the two hadn't spoken since Bobby's burial.

'I'd rather take the west coast than the east,' Seth said, scratching his tattooed neck.

'You'd rather sail across the entire north American coast?' Cody uttered. 'Then down the Pacific seaboard to what amount to desert states without water, instead of just heading directly south? You were happy to come up through Panama to come here.'

'We weren't heading to the Arctic,' Hank replied for his crew, 'when we sailed through the canal and turned north. Only your signals brought us here.'

'That may be so but you already abandoned the west coast. Why head back and a different way at that?'

'It's not about the distance,' Denton sneered. 'It's about what's there when we arrive. Every city we passed on the way here was a smoking ruin filled with people so hungry they chased us like zombies. I'm not setting foot back there as long as I live.'

'We're not asking you to,' Cody replied reasonably and looked at Hank. 'It's our families we want. It's where we want to go.'

The captain stood up and looked at Cody and his colleagues for a long moment.

'I'm sorry to put it so harshly but the chances of any of your families having survived a winter on our once great eastern seaboard, without heat, light, food or water is extremely unlikely.'

'But not impossible,' Charlotte snapped. 'We thought it was impossible for Brad to make it to Grise Fjord in the BV, but he did it.'

Hank's eyes flicked to the soldier, who was leaning against the wall with his muscular arms folded across his chest, watching the exchange. Cody noticed the tension between the two men, Bradley representing the only real threat to Hank's dominance aboard the ship. Although Taylor was physically huge he was hardly an intellectual. Bradley was a trained soldier, liable to speak his mind and to back his opinions with force.

The captain looked down at the map again as Saunders spoke.

'We need to head somewhere warm,' he reiterated, 'with fresh water, food, somewhere we can get ourselves sorted out. The ship needs repairs. We need to rest.' Saunders looked across at Cody. 'We're not going to find that in Boston.'

Cody thumped his fist down on the map table as a pinch of grief choked his throat.

'Fine, then just drop me off on the goddamned way,' he snapped. 'You may not give a damn about the families you left behind but I'm not moving an inch south of Charleston Harbour until I know, without a shadow of a doubt, that my wife and child are gone and that there's nothing I can do about it.'

Charlotte stepped up beside him. 'Me too, I'm not leaving without being sure that my father is truly gone.'

Denton's voice carried across the table to them as he turned for the door. 'Suits us.'

'We shouldn't split up,' Jake said from behind Cody as he moved to stand next to him. 'Remember, what we agreed? We stick together.'

Cody nodded. 'So do families, Jake. I can't leave them.'

Jake sighed and then glanced at the captain. 'Can you get us to the city, even if you don't come with us?'

Hank nodded. 'If that's what you want.'

'It's not what we want to do,' Cody replied. 'It's what we *need* to do.' A sudden thought occurred to Cody, and he added: 'And it's what you need to do.'

Hank looked up at Cody in confusion as Denton hesitated at the door.

'What do you mean?' the captain asked.

'Charlotte's father,' Cody explained. 'You say that you believe that politicians, people of power, would have fled somewhere. If anybody ever was likely to know where your Eden is, it's a powerful senator.'

Hank's gaze settled on Charlotte. 'He either died or he abandoned you. How would that kind of man be of use to us?'

'He may have had no time to warn anybody,' Bethany joined in. 'Imagine if you're in the senate and suddenly you're called up, like they used to do in alien invasion movies. You're flown somewhere, told that you cannot contact anybody because something classified is at risk. By the time you're there, you no longer have the ability to go back.'

Hank's eyes narrowed.

'There's something else,' Jake added. 'Right down from Boston is New York City. That's where the United Nations was headquartered. If these people did flee they wouldn't have had much time to organise their journey. There's bound to be some kind of a trail, something that could hint at where they went, and I'd bet the UN building is a good place to start.'

Denton stormed back to the table.

'This is bullshit. We've sailed thousands of miles through all kinds of crap chasing this Eden. It's not worth the risk, setting foot ashore for this. We'd be better off just listening for broadcasts.'

'Eden might not have the ability to broadcast,' Cody pointed out. 'There's nothing to say that where they travelled was free from the solar storm.'

'Funny,' Denton sneered. 'I thought that Eden was an idea but now you're talking as though it really exists.' The sailor turned to his captain. 'They're playing you Hank, trying to get a free escort through that hell hole of a city. What if they find their families? Are we going to invite them aboard too and starve ourselves a little more?'

Hank frowned as he looked at Cody.

'I've got nothing to lose by going back,' Cody said before the captain could speak, 'and everything to gain. We all do if we can find something to support this notion of a safe haven. It's all we've got. The alternative is to wander the oceans for the rest of your lives. The world's a big place, captain, and the longer any evidence of Eden is left to rot in what's left of our cities the less chance there is of you or anybody else finding it.'

'We don't know if there is any evidence of anything!' Denton screeched. 'You're chasing rainbows!'

'Absence of evidence,' Hank murmured in reply, 'is not evidence of absence. If there is the slightest chance that we can find something in Boston then we should take it.'

'At the risk of losing the ship?' Seth challenged. 'Or even our lives? Who knows what's waiting for us there?'

Hank sucked in a lungful of breath that seemed to Cody to empty the cabin of air as he waited for the captain to make his decision. Cody stopped breathing. Hank exhaled the air.

'Very well,' Hank said. 'We'll make for Boston.'

Cody let the breath go as Denton whirled away in disgust. 'Jesus, you'll kill us all.'

Hank glared across at the sailor. 'My ship and my rules Denton. You don't like it, take a swim.'

Denton shot the captain a dirty looked as he whipped the cabin door open and stormed out onto the deck with the crew following close behind. As the door slammed noisily shut, the captain turned to Cody.

'You got what you wanted,' he rumbled. 'Make sure I do too.'

*

The Phoenix sailed south past the entrance to the north-west passages that ran along the south coast of Devon Island. As the fog cleared and the barren, windswept coasts of jagged rock and permafrost slipped by, Cody felt the eyes of the crew upon him in the failing light.

Denton, Seth, Taylor and the others had laboured through the icy weather for weeks, perhaps months, to reach the northern tip of Ellesmere Island, only to be both disappointed and then burdened with more people with whom to share their meagre supplies. Exhausted and hungry, it didn't take a genius in psychology to figure out that they were directing their anger toward him.

'You watch your back,' Jake warned him as they hauled on rigging lines to square the yards away from the wind.

'It's not my fault,' Cody pointed out. 'And they won't achieve anything by taking out their frustration on me or anybody else.'

'You're thinking like a scientist, not an illiterate deckhand,' Jake replied. 'Right now Denton would probably burn the ship just to see the sparks it made going up. They're former convicts, Cody. They don't spend a whole lot of time thinking about consequences.'

Cody did not reply as they secured the rigging. The ship's masts were almost bare, the canvas stowed on all but the topmast yardarms as night fell. Even out across Baffin Bay the prevailing current and wind was still strong enough to carry the ship at a steady four to five knots through the darkness of the night. The captain maintained a rolling two-hour watch, four strong: one aft at the wheel, one amidships and two at the bow armed with a battery powered flashlight. If an iceberg loomed, there were enough hands available to steer the ship safely around it.

Cody followed Jake down into the ship as Bradley, Sauri, Muir and Ice took the first evening watch. The smell of cooking wafted from the mid-ships as they strode into the crew's quarters. Seth was hauling steel cooking bowls from the galley into place on the table, steam puffing from within them. With Bethany and Charlotte having been on watch duty and temporarily barred from the galley after Charlotte's reckless rescue of Bradley Trent, Seth had taken over cooking duties.

Bethany, Charlotte and Reece were already seated opposite Taylor as the meal was served.

Cody looked down at the plate of reddish-brown meat that Seth slopped onto the plate, dumping a meagre pair of potatoes boiled down to a barely recognisable pulp alongside it.

'Tuck in,' the sailor grinned with malevolent delight.

Cody sat down, picked up a fork and twirled it thoughtfully in his fingers. He was hungry but cautious of the sailor standing over him.

'What's wrong?' Seth uttered. 'You got a problem with my cooking?'

'That depends,' Cody uttered.

Seth laughed out loud, grabbed a fork and stabbed it into a small chunk of meat before shovelling it into his mouth. He chewed loudly as he tossed the fork to clatter onto Cody's plate and sat down to his own meal. Seth scooped chunks of meat into his square head and stared at the table top as he chewed.

Bethany and Charlotte ate in silence.

'Eating without your boyfriend?' Seth asked Charlotte around a mouthful of food.

Charlotte did not reply. Seth laughed, shaking his head as he shovelled more mush into it. 'Shame, it would have been so romantic.'

Jake stared down at his plate. 'What is this stuff?' he asked.

Seth looked up as he chewed. 'Last of the polar bear. It's getting a bit chewy ain't it?'

Cody hesitated as he held his fork in his hand. Something wasn't right but he couldn't put his finger on it.

Bethany stood up and grabbed the lid of the serving pan. She lifted it and scooped inside with her fork. Moments later she lifted out a small bone that was floating in the greasy sauce within.

'What's that?' Charlotte asked.

Bethany held the bone in her fingers for a few moments and then she dropped it onto the table as her face blanched.

'What is it?' Jake repeated Charlotte's question.

Bethany's hand flew to her face as she spoke. 'Proximal phalanx.'

'A what?'

'A human finger bone.'

Cody spat his mouthful of food out almost as quickly as Jake.

Charlotte coughed out a piece of meat and then covered her mouth as she dashed out of the cabin and through the hatch into the galley, slamming it shut behind her.

Dean Crawford

21

Charlotte staggered through the half-darkened galley to a large plastic container with a small tap attached to the bottom. She crouched down beneath it, opened the tap and swallowed a mouthful of water. She drank more, then swilled it around before spitting it out into a sink.

Charlotte rested her hands on the edge of the sink and hung her head, thick locks of red hair dangling either side of it as she tried to control her breathing and avoid vomiting.

Something scratched the floor behind her and she whirled to see Denton looming over her.

'Hush now, little missy,' he whispered.

Charlotte opened her mouth to scream just in time for Denton to shove a ball of canvas into it. She gagged as Denton leaped forward and his weight slammed into her, preventing her from getting her hands and nails into his skin as he buried his face into her neck. Her spine arched painfully backwards over the sink as her legs lifted off the deck. Denton pulled her against him and whirled, swinging her around and thumping her down on the worktop behind them.

Charlotte's legs were forced up into the air as Denton landed on top of her. He grabbed her wrists in his hands and slammed then down onto the table, tying them with another strip of canvas that he yanked tight. Denton leaned his weight fully down on her body as from his belt he produced a large blade that he rested against her throat. The touch of the cold steel froze her as she looked at Denton.

'Your friends next door are at gunpoint right now,' he sneered at her, 'so you be good and quiet or there'll be a bit of an accident, if you know what I mean?'

Charlotte felt sick again as Denton reached down and struggled to undo his jeans, his foul breath quickening as he loosened them. He chuckled maniacally. 'Believe me, this won't take a minute.'

*

Jake leaped out of his seat as he spat bits of flesh from his mouth and lunged across the table at Seth, who laughed in delight as he jumped backwards and out of the way.

'What's wrong?' the sailor sneered. 'A little gristle never hurt anybody!'

Taylor looked up questioningly at Seth, who screwed his tattooed face up at the big man. 'Chill out you asshole, yours is a bear.'

Jake tore around the table and reached out for Seth. The sailor whipped a knife from his belt and waved it at Jake.

'Easy now, old timer,' he chuckled maniacally. 'You don't want to be next on the menu, do you?'

'Who the hell was that?' Jake roared. 'A sailor who died? Who the hell was it?'

Seth's eyes shined with malicious euphoria. 'Well, I can't rightly remember but I think he was one leg short of a pair.'

Cody's blood ran cold through his veins as he stared at the sailor.

'We buried Bobby at sea,' he uttered.

Seth's cruel smile spread across his face, jagged teeth glinting in the light. 'You buried the polar bear's leftovers.'

Jake whirled for the cabin door. 'I'll have Hank string you up from the goddamned yards for this.'

Seth leaped across the cabin and slammed into the door, blocking Jake's way as he pressed the knife against the old man's belly.

'Don't think so,' Seth snapped. 'He knows.'

Cody shook his head. 'He wouldn't have.'

'Why not?' Seth grinned. 'This is survival, douchebag! Bobby didn't need his body anymore and it preserved real well in the powder store with the rest of the polar bear meat. The captain gets what you idiots don't: his crew have.., needs.'

Seth looked at Bethany and licked his lips.

'Hank's no animal,' Bethany shuddered as she retreated from the sailor's probing gaze. 'He'd string you up if you even thought about it.'

'Doesn't matter much,' Seth said as he shoved Jake away hard enough to make the old man stumble against the table, 'because if he doesn't like this I'll shoot the bastard myself. We're about done with him and all of you.' He looked at Bethany again. 'So how about you put out for me honey or I'll send your friends for a swim?'

Bethany stared at Seth in disgust.

'I'd rather freeze out there than let you get your stubby little dick near me.'

The sailor gritted his teeth in a tight smile as he moved toward Jake. 'Either you give me some of that sugar, or McDermott here loses a finger.'

'This is insane,' Cody snapped. 'Even Denton wouldn't do this.'

Seth smiled. 'Who says so?'

Cody stared at Seth for a long moment and then called out toward the galley. 'Charlotte?'

The silence said it all. Cody looked at Seth, who grinned at them. 'You girls have got to pay for your bed and board, don't y'think? Denton's probably humping her right now down in the galley and…'

Seth's knife tumbled from his grasp as Taylor lurched out of his seat and punched a huge fist straight into Seth's face. Seth flew like a rag doll into the wall of the cabin and slumped out cold onto the deck.

'This ain't right!' Taylor boomed.

Cody did not wait to see what happened. As Seth was hurled aside he leaped over his body and made for the galley door.

*

Charlotte twisted away from the blade and sought a weapon, but the table had been cleared and Denton was too heavy to hurl off her. He jabbed the tip of the blade into her flesh and she felt a sharp pain.

'Don't you move,' he hissed and then chuckled again. 'You only want one weapon inside you, right?'

Denton, one hand still gripping her bound wrists, brought the blade down with a thump. The weapon pinned the excess canvas to the table, fixing her wrists in place. Denton leaned forward further, his chest pressing against her breasts as he pulled her zip down and began yanking at her jeans. She felt his hands rasp against the soft skin of her thighs, and then he yanked her panties down.

Denton gasped as he unhitched his own jeans, his breath rasping in his throat and his heart thumping in his chest. Charlotte could feel it reverberating inside him as she tried to shut her mind off to what was coming.

Denton shuffled out of his pants and grabbed at his manhood with his free hand and shoved it against her. Charlotte winced as she felt the tip thrust painfully inside her body as the door to the galley burst open with a deafening crash and Cody charged inside with Jake right behind him.

Denton lurched away from her and yanked the knife from the table, the blade whipping around toward Cody.

Cody grabbed a heavy steel pan from a hook on the wall and swung it with all of his strength into Denton's hand. The heavy pan smashed into his wrist and Denton cried out in pain as the knife spun from his grasp.

Jake ploughed into him and swung a punch that knocked the sailor off his feet and sent him sprawling across the galley as pans and cutlery clattered down around him.

Denton scrambled backwards on his knees away from Jake as Charlotte pulled her panties up and saw the sailor grab his knife from where it had fallen and lunge at Jake. Cody hit Denton again with the pan, smashing the weapon aside. Cody slammed his boot down across Denton's wrist, pinning the knife against the deck as he raised the pan to bring it crashing down on the sailor's head.

Cody froze, unable to move as he stared down at Denton laying on his back with one arm desperately shielding his panicked face.

'What are you waiting for?' Charlotte snapped. 'Finish him!'

A gunshot burst out loud enough to hurt Cody's ears. Everybody whirled to see Hank Mears standing in the doorway of the galley with a heavy pistol in his hand. Wisps of blue smoke spilled from the barrel. Behind him stood Taylor, clearly out of breath after what Cody assumed was a mad dash for assistance.

'Drop the knife,' Hank growled at Denton.

The sailor dropped the blade, his flaccid penis still dangling from his open jeans. Hank took in the scene and glared at Cody. 'And you, drop it!'

Cody lowered the pan and lifted his boot off Denton's arm. The sailor scrambled to his feet and back away from Cody, pointing and shrieking.

'They're insane, all of them!'

'What the hell is going on?' Hank demanded.

'Rape,' Cody uttered.

'That's bullshit!' Denton screamed. 'They've had it in for me since they got here. They did this, were going to cut me up and say I attacked her!'

Cody stared at Denton in amazement. 'Seriously?' he uttered. 'You're going with that?'

Denton looked past the captain to where Seth stood, blood trickling from his nose. The seaman nodded slowly.

'Been talk of mutiny,' Seth said to the captain. 'They want to take the ship from us. McDermott hit me, tried to take my knife.'

Cody looked at the captain. 'We survived for six months in the high Arctic without attacking Bethany, Charlotte or anybody else, but now you believe that we'd suddenly turn against the very people who got us out of there?'

'They want to head for Boston,' Denton uttered, 'get us ashore and then take the ship.'

Hank's gaze skipped from Seth to Denton and Cody as if unsure of who to believe.

'You saw what happened,' Cody said, pointing at Taylor. 'You stopped it.'

Hank looked across at the big man, who remained immobile and impassive.

'I ain't no part of this,' he uttered.

'Is anybody going to ask *me* what goddamned happened?!' Charlotte snapped in disgust.

The captain considered her for a moment but then Bethany spoke up. 'Seth claimed that he was going to take the ship from you. He had a knife at Jake's belly until Taylor floored him.'

Hank looked at Saunders, who shrugged but remained silent. The captain lowered the pistol and looked at the first mate.

'Irons for two,' he murmured.

Cody did not understand what the captain meant until Saunders hurried off and returned with two sets of steel hand cuffs.

'Denton and Ryan,' the captain instructed him.

'What the hell are you doing?' Charlotte demanded. 'Cody protected me from Denton!'

'They attacked us!' Denton snapped in outrage.

The captain said nothing, watching as Saunders cuffed Cody and Denton. Cody noticed a change in the atmosphere in the galley, a hunger in the eyes of the rest of the crew as they stared at Cody.

Charlotte stepped up to the captain. 'Your goddamned crew are all enemies,' she hissed. 'They'll kill you and all of us if it suits them.'

Hank smiled at her without warmth.

'Then it's time to find out who I can really rely on.'

*

Cody was jostled out of the galley and through the 'tween decks to a large hatch, aft of where the mainmast descended through the ship and down through the hold to the keel.

The hatch was yanked open by the crew, who then stood back eagerly as Cody and Denton were shoved to the edge of the hatch. Jake, Charlotte, Bethany, Reece and Sauri followed just as Bradley burst into the deck.

'What the hell's going on?'

Cody had felt the Phoenix heave to in the darkness, the watch bustling down as word spread of whatever was about to happen. Denton stood on the opposite side of the hatch to Cody, his features twisted with a volatile fusion of excitement and rage.

Below, the hatch opened into the hold, which was largely empty but for some barrels and rope cordage. Most of the diesel taken from Alert was stored in the aft hold, beyond the bulkheads that sealed one section from the next. The abyss below was perhaps fifteen feet square and dimly illuminated.

The captain walked onto the deck, the crew parting for him as he passed through. In his hand he held a silver pistol that looked to Cody like some kind of ceremonial weapon. Into it, he loaded a single bullet as he stopped at the side of the hatch and looked at Cody and Denton.

'We no longer have the luxury of court martial, of due process or the Geneva Convention,' Hank announced. 'These are difficult times and though none of us chose to be here and none of us can be blamed for what has befallen us, we all must learn to work together. We cannot risk the lives of those around us in our own pursuit of power.'

The captain paused as he looked at each and every person on the deck.

'Our lives, our futures, will be judged by what we do in the here and now. I have no time to delve into what really happened tonight. Frankly, I don't care. All that matters to me is the survival of this ship and its company and for that I need the strongest, the fittest and the most honourable of human beings alongside me. Only Providence can judge us, for there is no greater power remaining.'

The captain nodded to Saunders, who moved behind Denton and unlocked his cuffs before shoving him forwards. Denton jumped and dropped into the hold below, landing like a cat in the dim light.

Bradley stood forward. 'Put me in there,' he ordered the captain.

'My beef ain't with you,' Denton shouted at the soldier with false bravado, 'so stay out of it, Canuck!'

'You stay here,' Hank replied to Bradley, and rested a hand on a pistol at his side. 'You interfere, I'll shoot you myself.'

Bradley glared at the captain but remained still as Saunders moved around the hatch and unlocked Cody's cuffs. Cody looked at the captain.

'I told you, it's cooperation that helped us survive, not conflict.'

'Then cooperate,' Hank replied.

'This is insane,' Cody said. 'This won't achieve anything but…'

Saunders shoved him hard in the back and Cody tumbled into the hold. He hit the deck hard, managed to roll a bit and came up on his knees to see Denton standing over him.

'You're a madman,' Cody heard Bethany whisper to the captain above.

'No,' Hank replied. 'It is insanity to bring war to this ship when mankind may now exist in such small numbers. And that insanity must be removed. Providence will save the righteous man.'

'That's not a higher power you're invoking,' Charlotte cried at him. 'That's avoiding responsibility for your own actions!'

The captain ignored her as he stood at the edge of the hatch and looked down at Cody and Denton.

'May the best man, win.'

The captain tossed the pistol out into the hold. Cody stared as the silver weapon spun in a graceful arc down toward the deck and Denton leaped across the hold for it.

Cody's legs felt as though they had been evacuated of life, rigid and unbending beneath him as he watched Denton catch the pistol in mid-air and swing it toward

Cody. He heard shouts from above and the crew roared with a sudden and deafening bloodlust that sounded like something out of a war movie, the hymn of mankind's hatred of himself.

Cody saw the pistol whip around and he finally found the strength to move. He ducked back and sideways and hid behind one of several thick stanchions that supported the deck above.

He saw Denton's shadow shift across the hull as he moved.

'Come out, come out, Doctor,' the sailor sneered. 'There's nowhere to hide.'

Cody tucked in behind the stanchion as he called out to the captain.

'This isn't the way to solve problems, Hank!'

Any reply that might have come from above was drowned out by the shouts and sneers of the crew as Cody sought desperately for a weapon in the hold. Barrels made of both wood and aluminium were stacked and braced against the hull walls, and he could see a pair of iron belaying pins sitting in racks on the opposite side of the hold. But he knew that Denton would shoot him long before he got to them.

Denton's shadow edged closer as Cody huddled out of sight.

'Where do you want the bullet, Doc'?' he asked, 'nice and quick in the head or slow and painful in the belly?'

Cody packed himself tighter against the pillar as he thought of Maria and tears filled his eyes as he realised that this may be the last moment of his life. That he would never see her again, never be able to hold her again, be unable to help her. He didn't deserve this.

Rage spilled from his heart into his belly.

'I don't deserve this!' he roared.

The crew above burst into laughter as they watched and Cody heard Denton's chuckles from just the other side of the pillar.

'Poor Doctor, are you afraid?'

Cody saw the shadow of the pistol on the deck before him as Denton tried to edge around the pillar for a clear shot while staying out of Cody's reach. The illumination from the dim light in the hold betrayed Denton's position. Cody turned and pressed his face against the stanchion.

'Come out, come out, wherever you are,' Denton chuckled as he shifted further around the pillar.

Cody swung his fist hard overarm, the belt that he had un-slipped from his waist flashing as the heavy buckle whipped down across Denton's face. The sailor flinched away from the unexpected blow as Cody burst from behind the pillar with a scream of something alien, a fearsome anger surging inside of him that felt like a brother he had rarely met.

Denton tried to aim at him but Cody lunged inside the weapon as he swung a wild right hook that shattered Denton's nasal bridge with a dull crunch. The crew roared as they saw blood and bayed for more. Denton staggered backwards and sideways, pivoting around the pistol that Cody had now clenched in his fist, twisting it over for all he was worth.

Denton fell across a small barrel that shattered beneath him into wooden splinters that plunged into the flesh of his thigh.

Denton cried out in pain as he struggled to hang on to the weapon and landed hard on his knees on the deck. Cody turned and with a grunt of effort slammed his knee into the sailor's face. Pain bolted down Cody's leg as his bones smashed across Denton's jaw. The crewman's head snapped sideways and he sprawled onto his back as his eyes rolled in their sockets.

Cody wrenched the pistol from Denton's grasp and staggered back, turning the weapon around and aiming it at the sailor.

'Kill him!' Bradley yelled above the shouts of the crew.

The raging, competing voices swirled in a maelstrom through Cody's mind as he watched Denton recover his senses. He crawled onto his hands and knees and looked up. The sailor saw the pistol pointed at him, saw the rage blazing in Cody's expression, and all at once Denton's bladder gave way and spilled onto the deck beneath him as he raised his hands.

Cody could not hear his voice above the roaring of the crew, but he could see Denton's lips move as tears spilled from his eyes.

'Please, no.'

Cody's anger changed shape, mutated within him. It seethed within its prison deep inside his chest, seeking an escape but finding none until he looked up out of the hatch and saw Hank Mears watching him with that uncaring, uncompromising gaze.

Cody pointed the pistol at Hank as the rage found its way out of him in a rush and a scream.

'We're not animals! Do you understand? We're not animals!'

'Cody!'

Bethany's scream rose above the hollering of the crew just as Cody saw a shadow flicker behind him.

The belaying pin hit him across the back of the neck. There was no pain, just a momentary loss of vision and sensation as he saw the hold tilt over sideways and then shudder as he landed on the deck. The sounds of the crew became distant and muted and he felt a tingling in his legs as the shocked nerve endings came back to life. He rolled onto his back as a deep, dull ache throbbed inside his skull.

The crew looked down upon him from the hatch above, pink mouths agape as they cheered, fingers pointing, eyes filled with malice. He saw Bethany's face, flushed with horror and tears.

Then Denton appeared to stand over him. He took the pistol from beside Cody's useless hand and pointed it at Cody. His lips moved again.

'Good bye, Doctor.'

Cody thought he heard Maria's little voice in his mind as sadness heavier than all of the world's many burdens weighed down upon him.

The gun fired a bright flash of flame and smoke. Cody felt his chest shudder as the world heaved beneath him, and then all was silent.

Dean Crawford

# HOMECOMING

Dean Crawford

22

Traffic.

Lights spilled across the Harvard Bridge like a river of bright white orbs flowing through the darkness. The lights of Boston's financial district shimmered on the black waters of the Charles River below as Cody drove his beloved Buick Riviera, a '66 he'd bought from a collector two years previously.

The late fall weather was warm enough for him to keep the window down as he drove, the brisk night air flushed with the saline scent of the nearby Atlantic. Horns blared, tail lights glowed and engines hummed as he crawled across the bridge toward home. Cody had worked late, as he often did: part and parcel of being at the prestigious Massachusetts Institute of Technology. Despite the workload he had managed to get out early enough to see Maria before Danielle put her to bed, only to hit the damned traffic.

Hazard lights ahead hinted at a wreck near the southern end of the bridge, and Cody passed a truck that had hit the barriers after a tyre had blown out. Nobody had been hurt as far as he could tell, just a few fenders bent as the traffic stream had come to an abrupt and unexpected halt. And yet cars crawled past the wreck, drivers straining for a glimpse of what was happening.

Cody felt something in his guts twist in disgust. There was no obstacle to the traffic, the truck having been already towed clear of the road. Yet still people slowed as they passed by, enslaved to a macabre fascination with the misfortune of others.

Cody glanced at the wreck but he did not slow. As the traffic began to move more freely he instead moved up closer to the car in front and hurried them along.

'Get out and take a damned photograph if you're that interested,' he muttered.

Cody turned west off the bridge and out toward the suburbs. Rows of trees lined colonial-style homes with good sized gardens, patriotic flags in most of them softly illuminated by street lights that glowed amongst the leaves.

Cody pulled into his drive and jumped out of the Buick. He hurried up to the front door and let himself in.

'Dadda!'

He heard Maria's voice before he saw her, heard her feet thump quickly from the lounge out back and into the hall. Bright smile. Blonde hair. To-die-for brown eyes. Arms outstretched toward him as she ran. 'Dadda!'

Cody scooped Maria up into his arms and hugged her closely as he walked through the house and into the kitchen. Danielle looked up and smiled as he wandered in, Maria clinging to his neck with one warm cheek pressed against his own. Pots and pans bubbled with aromatic odours as Cody crossed the kitchen to his wife's side.

'Just made it,' he said as he leaned in and kissed her on the cheek. 'Traffic's lousy. How's she been?'

'Okay,' Danielle said as she swept a strand of hair from her face. 'Busy as always and full of new words.'

'Much like being at work,' Cody said as he tugged at Maria's cheek.

'Hey, we're low on bread,' Danielle said. 'Could you get some from the store? I'll fix dinner once Her Ladyship's settled down for the night.'

'Sure,' Cody said. 'Wine?'

'Merlot, and don't skimp on it.'

Cody walked through into the lounge and kissed his daughter on the cheek with a whispered *be good* as he set her down inside a safe play-den. Maria busied herself with a collection of toys as Cody walked back out of the lounge and headed for the front door. He fished about in his wallet for cash and was about to open the door when he heard a faint tinkle of breaking glass.

Cody stopped in his tracks and turned, called out.

'You okay?'

He heard nothing in reply and turned back down the hall, his pace quickened by some unknown instinct that surged through him as he hurried into the kitchen and came up short.

Danielle was standing with her back to the kitchen counter.

Standing opposite her in the open door to their back yard was a man dressed in ragged, dirty clothes stained with what Cody guessed was a foul mixture of alcohol and vomit, his face weather beaten and his eyes infected with a radical glitter as they shifted focus to Cody.

'Don't move,' he snapped in a hoarse voice.

Cody did not know much about guns. The snub-nosed pistol in the vagrant's hands, pointed at his wife, could have come from any period and any country. Unlike many Americans, Cody just wasn't a firearms fan. He did not keep one in the house. Nor had his father, a man of nobler principles forged in a grander age.

'Pete?' Cody stared at the bedraggled form of his brother and tried to see the man he knew through the shell that remained. 'You can take anything you want,' Cody added automatically. 'Just keep the gun out of it.'

Peter Ryan shifted the pistol to point at Cody.

'Cash,' he demanded. 'All of it, or I'll turn your family into bullet art.'

'Jesus,' Danielle gasped as she stared in horror at Cody's brother. 'What the hell are you doing?'

Cody did not understand what separated him by such magnitude from his brother. They had been raised together in a close knit, loving family. Their father had worked hard to provide for them, as had their mother. They had both done well in school. Cody had gone on to college, Peter into the army, his great love of sports and the outdoors driving his ambition. Six years later he had been dishonourably discharged after being found guilty of possession of marijuana with intent to supply while serving in Guam.

From there, Peter's life had degenerated into years spent wandering from one half-way house to another, interspersed with spells in both jails and prison for a colourful array of misdemeanour felonies. Experiments with the very drugs he peddled to losers on Boston's meaner streets led to escalating addiction until he spent his every waking hour fixated on the destructive pleasures of methamphetamine.

Cody slowly retrieved his wallet and tossed it onto the counter within Peter's reach.

'Sixty dollars and change,' Cody said, 'only cash in the house. Now get out.'

Peter snatched the wallet up and then his eyes settled on Cody again.

'Jewellery,' he spat. 'I know it's in here, Cody. Fetch it me.'

Cody didn't move. Nor did Danielle. Peter's features twisted with fury as he screamed at her, his mouth a morass of blackened teeth. 'Get them now, bitch!'

To Cody's surprise Danielle stared at Peter for a moment before replying calmly.

'You don't need to do this, Peter.'

'Shut up,' Peter sneered. 'You run or try callin' the law and I'll put holes in my dear little brother here.'

Danielle turned and walked away. Cody looked Peter up and down, tried to swallow his revulsion as he spoke.

'Is this what you've come down to?' he uttered. 'You used to just ask for money.'

'I'm done askin' any of you for anythin',' Peter spat at him.

Peter had always gone to their parents for money, and they had given him what they could until there was no more they could give. It had been the last they'd seen of their eldest son. The man Cody had once looked up to, a soldier, a natural leader, was now a decrepit and shuffling wreck who could barely string a sentence together. He guessed it was a cruel kindness that their folks had gone to their graves without seeing what he had become.

'You can't do this forever, Pete,' Cody said. 'You're dying.'

Peter shot him a fearsome glare. 'Ain't nothing worth living for.'

'Not for you maybe,' Cody replied. 'But this is the last time you'll come here.'

Peter whirled and lunged at Cody, the pistol pushed hard into his temple as Peter shouted at him, his breath a foul stench of alcohol and decay.

'I'll come here for as long as I like, you understand?!' he bellowed.

Cody shot a glance at Danielle, who had returned and was standing by the kitchen door, her bottom lip quivering as she held a jewellery box in her hand.

Peter grinned as he saw her, yellowing stumps loosely anchored to blackened gums. 'Pretty little thing, ain't she Cody?'

'Take the box and get the hell out of here,' Danielle hissed.

'Bet young Maria is a heartbreaker too, eh little brother?'

'You leave my little girl alone,' Cody uttered, his voice choked.

'Don't you worry,' Peter sneered. 'I want her alive because even if you don't give a damn about me, she might of use to me one day,' Peter looked over his shoulder at Danielle, and then back at Cody, 'for all sorts of things.'

Cody's vision blurred and the world around him receded as a hot flush rushed up his spine and over his head. The fear infecting him was shouldered aside by something hot and dangerous that seared his veins and burst from his synapses with a scream that sounded as though it came from another universe.

Cody stepped in and dropped his forehead with a deep crack across Peter's nose. His brother gagged as he tumbled backwards and hit the kitchen units beneath the window, the pistol waving dangerously as Peter tried to draw aim on his brother.

Cody swung a boot at the weapon and it crashed into Peter's wrist with a sharp crack. The pistol flew from Peter's grasp and clattered down onto the tiles across the kitchen. Cody jumped backwards from his brother as the former soldier leaped to his feet, his bunched fists flying toward Cody.

The boiling water crashed into Peter's face in a cloud of steam as Danielle swung the pan at him. Peter's hands flew to his face as he collapsed to his knees with a broadside of agonised screams. Peter's agony warred with Danielle's rage as she rushed forward. The heavy metal pan landed with a deep thud of metal against bone. Peter's bloodshot eyes rolled up into his skull to expose yellowing conjunctivae as Danielle raised the pan again. The second blow landed beside the first and Cody heard the skull fracture, saw blood spill from the wound as flesh was scraped aside to expose white bone.

Cody froze on the spot as though he were watching events from afar.

Danielle slammed the pan again and again into Peter's head, her teeth gritted and her eyes ablaze with something that Cody had never witnessed before. Horror spurred him from his rictus of disbelief and he dashed forward and grabbed his wife's arms.

'Jesus, stop!'

Danielle stopped. Her chest heaved and he realised that she was sobbing, her body shaking as thick globules of blood drooped from the pan she held. Beneath them, Peter lay in a pool of thick blood that glistened in the glow of the kitchen lights. Cody staggered backward as he looked down at the body slumped beneath him. Peter's chest was still and the blood pooled beneath his head was no longer spreading.

Cody felt devoid of emotion, scoured of remorse for the terrible thing he had witnessed. He turned to see Danielle staring at him, her jaw agape and her eyes wide with emotions that for some reason he could not recognise.

'Oh God, what have we done?' he gasped.

'Where's Maria?' she asked.

Cody stared at her as though unable to formulate a reply. 'She's okay. We need to call nine-one-one, right now.'

Cody looked down at his brother's body as slowly his senses began to reconnect themselves, like a computer rebooting.

'I've killed him,' Danielle whispered.

'In self-defence,' Cody replied, taken aback by his inability to feel remorse for his own brother.

'What if they don't believe me? What if they think I murdered him in cold blood?'

'A biologist and climatologist, in their own home, kill a drug-addicted vagrant?' Cody tried to soothe her, moving closer. 'I don't think so. We need to stay calm here and do this right.'

Danielle stepped away from Cody. 'But they could claim I used excessive force,' she said, panic infecting her voice. 'They could argue for the death penalty. Jesus, I killed him, I killed your brother.'

'It won't come to that,' he reassured her, 'they'll believe us because he had a long history of violence and drug abuse and….'

'You don't know that!' she shrieked.

Maria called out to them, touched with alarm after the screams. Danielle's hand flew to her mouth as she tried to calm herself down. Tears spilled from her eyes.

'Cody, we can't do this. We can't go to the police.'

Cody looked down at his brother's inert corpse and he realised just how much he had come to hate his brother, a selfish, cruel shadow of his former self.

'This isn't worth it,' Cody uttered. 'I'm not going to let him destroy our lives.'

'He already has!'

Cody caught an accusing undercurrent in her voice. 'You're saying this is my fault?'

'He was your brother!'

'Christ, Danielle, don't make this worse than it already is.'

'It can't get any worse!'

'Not for him,' Cody snapped as he pointed at Peter's inert corpse.

'He threatened us, Cody,' she snapped. 'He threatened Maria.'

'Danielle, right now we're looking at self-defence against an armed intruder. You try to conceal this we'll be looking at perverting the course of justice, culpable manslaughter, maybe even premeditated homicide. Peter was a war veteran, something that could be used against us. We have to be honest and maintain every bit of integrity that we have or everything could fall apart.'

'And if I don't?' she uttered. 'If it goes against us? Will you still be here in twenty years' time when I get parole?' Her voice cracked as tears formed in her eyes. 'Will Maria?'

'And how do you think that you're going to hide this from her?' Cody uttered, 'or from the police?'

She looked down at the body and then her gaze lifted to his, stricken with a paralysis of fear.

'Don't let them take Maria away from me,' she sobbed. 'I can't do this.'

Cody felt a surge of empathy and he crossed the kitchen and threw his arms around her shoulders as she buried her face into his chest.

Over her shoulder he stared down at his brother's ruined body, every fibre of his being alive with hate for what Peter had done to them, for all that he had done to them over the years. How his parents worried for Peter's wellbeing and how he had taken from them so many times, giving nothing back. Cody tightened his hold on his wife's shoulders.

'I'll find a way,' he said. 'Nobody will ever know he was ever here. He was a drug addict and a loser. Nobody will ever miss him.'

Danielle looked up at him and nodded. Maria called out again from the lounge. Danielle wiped her face with her sleeve and stood back from Cody as between them a gulf emerged that somehow he knew could never be bridged. Danielle backed away from the kitchen, her eyes fixed upon his brother's corpse.

'I want you to get rid of it,' she whispered. 'Take it away, please. I don't want to think about this ever again.'

Danielle turned and hurried toward the lounge and their daughter. Cody stared after her, and then looked down at the body in their kitchen.

*

It was about a ten mile drive east out of the district to Sudbury Reservoir, but to Cody it felt like the longest journey of his life.

Never, in all of his years, would he have envisaged what had happened that night or what he was about to do. His brother's body lay in the trunk, wrapped in plastic sheets Cody had grabbed from the garage. Beside it lay a sack containing every tile in the kitchen. It was almost hilarious that a diet of intense and realistic police dramas on television could arm an innocent citizen with the knowledge to effectively conceal a crime, even one like homicide.

Blood splatter on the kitchen units would disappear when Cody replaced the doors. The bloodied tiles would soon vanish into a municipal waste dump in town to be buried in landfill. Peter's pistol was already sinking into the abyssal depths of the Charleston River, hurled from Cody's car on a long, dark stretch of road far from watching traffic cameras.

There had been no noise to alert the neighbours during the fight. His brother had carried no identification and no possessions but for a well-used crack pipe in one pocket. He had been utterly alone and unknown except maybe to other vagrants haunting Boston's lonely city streets.

Cody drove out to a remote beauty spot near a small airfield beside the reservoir's northern shore, and there he stopped. At 2am in the morning there were no vehicles on the narrow, pitch black road to witness Cody lift the body out of the trunk. Cody hefted the corpse onto his shoulder and staggered into the woods with it. Then he returned to the vehicle and lifted out a steel storage box and a set of tools.

He walked back into the woods where the body lay well out of sight and let his eyes adjust to the darkness of the night. Then he un-wrapped the body. To his relief it was dark enough that he could only just make out the form of the corpse and could not see his brother's face.

Cody lifted up a large hack saw and examined it for a few moments. His stomach felt empty and cold, his mind filled with strange and conflicting emotions, none of which felt good. Images of his brother as a young man tried to infiltrate his thoughts as he worked but he forced them away, bludgeoned them out of existence with each angry thrust of the saw. The darkened forest echoed to the sound of ripping flesh and splintering bone as though wild dogs were feasting on carrion in the night.

He knew that he must leave as little as possible to identify his brother's remains.

His grim task took half an hour. Sweat drenched his skin. Each chunk of flesh and bone was discarded into the storage box. When he was finished, Cody turned away and walked several paces in the darkness before he lurched forward and vomited into the foliage, choking back sobs as he did so.

A long time passed as he sat alone in the darkness, engulfed by an unspeakable emotional turmoil. Cody finally dragged himself back to the body and grabbed a shovel. He dug down for an hour before he dumped his brother's remains into the ragged grave and filled it in. He stamped the ground down and brushed leaves over the grave until it was entirely concealed.

Cody slipped out of his clothes and gloves then placed them carefully in a plastic bag and sealed it. He put fresh, clean clothes on and then sealed the storage box. The soiled clothes would be trashed the following morning. The tools would be cleaned and disposed of in his local recycling plant. His brother's head and hands, his identifiable remains, would have to be taken somewhere far away and buried.

Then he drove out onto the old post road and across to Arlington, staying away from as many street cameras as he could before driving back into Boston from the north-east.

Maria was still asleep when he returned but Danielle was awake, her features haunted as she sat in bed staring at the wall. She did not look at him when he walked into the bedroom, did not speak to him.

Cody slipped into bed, turned his back to his wife and stared at the opposite wall.

He hoped that somehow in the eyes of God, if not the law, he had done his best to protect his wife and daughter. That he had committed no crime and neither had Danielle. Yet despite all of his prayers he knew that somehow they would never be able to leave this night behind.

Cody began to think of ways to get away for a while until things settled down again. Somewhere to hide the remains.

Maybe some kind of research trip, somewhere distant.

23

Jake McDermott strode onto the Phoenix's bridge, a mug of coffee steaming in each hand as he crossed to the wheel and handed the mugs to Saunders and Hank.

The deck outside was being lashed by horizontal streaks of snow flecked rain that streamed down the windows and billowed in gusts between the masts. The grey and white surface of the water off the port bow stretched away into the boundless ocean beyond. To starboard, the coast of Newfoundland crouched against the cruel gales.

'Moment of truth,' Jake murmured as the ship heeled against the blow, the deck steeply inclined.

'If we don't see any evidence of habitation at St John,' Hank agreed, 'we'll sail on by and keep heading south.'

'Don't reckon there'll be anybody home,' Saunders said as he held the ship's wheel against the winds buffeting the hull and the magnificent sails, 'too bleak up here.'

Hank watched the figures of his crew huddled against the bitter wind, their hoods of their waterproofs up as they worked the ship's rigging to keep the yards and sails angled correctly, loosening them with the wilder blows.

'We're making good time,' Saunders added. 'We could go ashore and hunt for food as soon as the weather eases.'

'How are your people holding up?' Hank asked Jake.

Jake did not look at the captain as he replied.

'As well as can be expected after what happened. Right now I don't think that they know who to trust or turn to.

You fed us a member of our team for Christ's sake, and then made another fight to the death.'

The captain kept his eye on the crew outside.

'Not my job to worry about that. They need only stay in line and they'll be fine.'

'They were doing just fine until Denton's attack,' Jake pointed out. 'Look, I get it okay? You've got to dominate your crew. They're tough and dangerous and without discipline they'd probably kill us all. But my team aren't criminals. They don't work under the same code and they don't understand it.'

'They've nothing to be afraid of.'

'They're afraid of your crew,' Jake snapped, 'and they're afraid of you.'

'Is that so?'

Jake said nothing more, but Saunders spoke quietly as he guided the ship through the never ending waves that thundered across the bows in cascades of white water.

'Would I still be standing here if the captain couldn't be trusted?'

Jake regarded the old helmsman for a while.

'That depends,' Jake replied, 'on who's doing the trusting.'

Hank turned to Saunders and gestured to the coast. 'Take us in. We'll anchor off the quays, just in case.'

Charlotte hurried into the wheelhouse, her coat drenched in rain as she threw her hood back.

'He's awake,' she said.

*

The room came into view slowly. Breaths were hard to take, pain swelling and receding with each breath as though pulsing in rhythm to the dip and sway of the ship.

Cody blinked up at the light above him, confused.

'Maria?' he cried out. 'Danielle?'

A softly lit face appeared above him and came into focus. Bethany rested a hand on Cody's forearm.

'You're okay, Cody, you're aboard the Phoenix.'

Cody tried to sit up but pain throbbed through his chest. He slumped back down as he looked at Bethany and realised where he lay. In the sick bay, in Bobby's bed. He tried again to move and this time Bethany helped him up into a sitting position.

Cody looked down and saw that his chest was stained with a large and ugly purple bruise ringed with pale yellow skin.

'What happened?'

Bethany arranged his pillows to make him more comfortable. 'I don't know. I think that the gun was loaded with blanks. Some sort of test by the captain.'

Cody frowned. 'Test? I got shot.'

Bethany nodded. 'Yeah, but Denton's the one who's been placed in irons. He's chained up in the hold.'

Cody struggled to understand, and was relieved when Charlotte and Jake walked in through the doorway. Jake smiled as he saw recognition in Cody's eyes.

'Welcome back.'

Charlotte looked at Cody's chest and winced. 'At least it wasn't a real bullet.'

'How long was I out?'

'Just less than twenty-four hours,' Bethany said, 'likely owing to exhaustion as much as your injury.'

Jake eased himself down onto the end of the bed as he spoke.

'The captain felt he had no choice but to test what he calls our humanity, if you can believe that. I think he must have had religion at some point in his life or something.

The gun he tossed you and Denton was loaded with a blank round to see if either of you would refuse to shoot the other. Denton failed the test.'

Cody rubbed his head. 'What's going to happen to Denton?'

Jake shrugged. 'The hell do we care? That asshole's had it in for us since they first showed up at Alert.'

'It's not as simple as that,' Charlotte pointed out. 'The crew, especially Seth, sees it that Denton was duped by the captain and they're not happy about it. Hank's taken to wearing a pistol at all times now, which tells us all we need to know.'

Cody sighed and let his head sink back onto the pillow. 'Jesus, we're in as much danger here as we were in the Arctic.'

'The crew could turn at any time,' Bethany agreed. 'It's all they can do to look us in the eye. Hank sent a hunting party ashore yesterday and they came back with a lot of seals and ice that they melted. We've got enough supplies to get us down to Boston without having to eat....'

Bethany cut herself off.

'St John?' Cody asked Jake, changing the subject.

'You'll get to see it for yourself,' Jake replied. 'Captain wants you on deck for some reason once you're up to it, before we leave.'

'We're at anchor?' Cody asked.

'Off the Narrows,' Jake replied. 'Captain's just waiting for you,'

Cody struggled to get out of the bed. 'I'll be okay. Let's see what he wants.'

Bethany helped Cody dress and fetched him a weak cup of coffee from the galley. He gingerly shrugged on a thick coat, which Bethany zipped up for him. He watched as she worked, suddenly aware of her closeness.

'You said you've got family back in Boston?' he said.

Bethany slowed as she sealed his jacket. 'A little brother, Ben,' she said, 'my mom and dad too, but I don't want anything to do with my folks. They were into drugs.'

'I'm sorry,' he said.

Bethany shrugged and finished pushing the Velcro seals into place. 'It is what it is. You're good to go.'

Cody turned and walked out of the bay and down the corridor that led to the 'tween decks, Bethany following. Cody glanced down at the hatch to the hold as he passed through and on into the stern quarters. He clambered up the steps into the wheelhouse to see Hank Mears, Saunders and Jake manning the deck.

The captain glanced at Cody and then turned back to survey the view from the wheelhouse windows.

A broad coastline, a natural bay of steep cliffs peppered with small houses that led toward something that Cody felt as though he had not seen in a lifetime. A skyline of low buildings crouched against the bitter firmament. The masts of countless boats lined the shore. To the left, a stonewall harbour contained smaller vessels sheltered against the bitter winds gusting in from the bleak ocean.

The whole scene was cast in shades of grey, as though the veils of rain falling from the scudding clouds had rinsed the town of colour. Squalls spilled against ancient granite cliffs that towered over the harbour entrance.

'Why don't we dock?' Cody asked.

Jake replied as he gestured at the town.

'We've been ashore,' he said. 'That's when we shot the seals we found. They were in a pack a few miles down from here. Too busy eating the remains of townsfolk to pay us any mind.'

Cody looked across at Jake as the captain finally spoke.

'If there's anybody left alive here, there's nothing that we can do for them,' he said.

Cody stared at the town and suddenly details resolved themselves that he had not at first noticed. Many of the boats in the harbour were sunk, their masts jumbled at odd angles. Others were mere shells of blackened wood like the skeletons of bizarre sea creatures beached on a lonely shore.

Buildings were stained with black soot where they had burned. Litter and debris filled the streets and the choppy waves of the harbour in a grim flotsam. It was then that Cody saw the bodies floating amid the waves and wreckage or laying in the streets. Flocks of birds wheeled overhead and pecked at them, hovering in flocks above the carrion in the gusting winds.

'The town is dead,' Bethany whispered for Cody. 'Nothing and nobody left. No food, no water, not much fuel. Any boat that was functional when the storm hit has either been destroyed or has fled.'

'They burned their own boats?' Cody asked.

'Survival,' the captain said. 'They were seeking warmth, things to burn.'

'We found a library in the smaller town,' Jake said. 'Not a single book left inside. These people became so desperate they burned the very things that might have helped them survive.'

The captain turned to Cody.

'This is what we truly are, Doctor,' he said. 'When it comes down to the last meal or the last drink of water; when it comes to protecting our families or our own lives, we all show our true colours. We are not loving, kind and humane creatures. That's just the kind of bullshit we could convince ourselves of when we had heat and light and warm meals and cinemas and music concerts and all that stuff we loved. Take it all away and we're exposed for what we truly are: animals, just like every other animal on our planet, and we'll fight like animals until there's nobody left.'

Cody shook his head.

'That doesn't mean we should act like animals, no matter what. If we lose who we are, we'll lose everything that goes with it.'

'Tell that to a starving population of ten thousand people, all of whom would give their own lives to protect their families. You've got family, a daughter. You tell me: would you let Denton live in place of your little girl?'

'That's not the same thing. Denton's already proven himself a threat. My daughter is only three years old.'

'Doesn't matter,' the captain replied. 'You'd choose between one and the other, and that's what all of these people did.'

'That's my point,' Cody nodded. 'They fought, and look what happened to them. They're all dead because they didn't cooperate.'

'You think they'd all be alive if they'd held hands and sung happy songs?' Hank uttered.

'No,' Cody admitted, 'but they'd have stood a better chance together than alone.'

The captain shook his head.

'Now you're awake, we can leave. I wanted you to witness this before we sailed.'

'Witness what?'

Hank didn't reply as he buttoned up his jacket and marched out onto the main deck. Cody followed with Bethany and Jake. The cold wind whistled through the rigging high above and whipped the surface of the bay into choppy waves like a vast sheet of beaten iron flecked with white rollers.

The crew mustered beside the mainmast at Saunders' command. Cody saw Bradley nearby, and the soldier nodded at him in silent greeting. Sauri stood beside his comrade, watching quietly as the captain addressed the crew.

'You've all sailed under me these months passed,' he boomed. 'You all know how I work and how I expect you to work. This ship is all that we have left. Unless we can find a safe haven where we can build a new life, we will be doomed to ever sail the oceans. I know that you do not want that any more than I do.' The captain glanced at Cody. 'But unless we cooperate, we will all die aboard this ship. I cannot afford the time, the effort or the risk that any man among you may try to take this vessel or harm its occupants. We have a duty not just to ourselves but to each other, because together we are greater than the sum of our parts.'

The captain nodded to Saunders, who turned and yanked off the canvas sheets covering one of the ship's life boats. Cody was surprised to see Denton's shivering form hauled from the boat's hull, his wrists and ankles bound and a canvas sack roughly tied over his head. He wore only jeans, sneakers and a thick pullover.

Saunders yanked Denton from the lifeboat and prodded him to the ship's port bulwarks as the captain went on.

'We are all in this together. Any of you who refuse to work as part of a team, who prefer to act alone, will see that wish granted.'

Saunders yanked the hood off Denton's face. The sailor's skin was mottled with the cold, his limbs quivering as Saunders used a stubby knife to slice through the thick tape binding Denton's ankles. Cody looked at the rest of the crew and saw Seth glaring at him in silence.

The sailor tried to plead but his lips trembled so violently that he could not form words. Spittle dribbled from his mouth and as he tried to take a step forward his legs gave way beneath him and he thumped to his knees on the deck.

'What are you going to do to him? Bethany asked.

'Nothing,' the captain replied.

Hank nodded at Saunders, who reached out for one of several inflatable life-rafts that were flat-packed into cases around the deck. Saunders pulled the raft free of its container and hurled it overboard as he pulled the inflation cord. The raft landed beside the Phoenix and inflated until it bobbed about on the choppy grey water.

Cody felt his guts plunge. 'You're marooning him. Is this really necessary?'

The captain's reply came on the wind.

'It is, if you really believe that cooperation is the key to our survival. Denton is not capable of it.'

Denton struggled against the first mate but Bradley Trent grabbed the sailor's weakened frame and hoisted him clear off his feet and hurled Denton over the side. The sailor crashed down into the freezing water alongside the bright yellow raft and somehow managed to haul himself aboard before the cold stiffened his limbs entirely.

'I heard you made bet on my survival not so long ago,' Bradley called down to Denton. 'I'd put ten bucks down that you're dead by tomorrow, but nobody took my odds.'

The soldier smiled grimly and then turned away from the bulwarks.

'All hands!' Hank thundered. 'Weigh anchor and make sail! Start the engine to break us free of the bay!'

The crew ambled to their duty, casting dark glances at Cody as they moved off. Seth brushed past him. 'This isn't over, Ryan,' he spat.

Hank Mears turned for the wheelhouse.

'You're turning your own men against you,' Cody uttered as the captain passed by.

Hank did not reply.

Ever so slowly, the Phoenix made headway against the current as Saunders and Taylor got the diesel engine running. The crew labouring on the decks cast long glances back as the ship drew out of the lonely bay, at the tiny yellow speck of the life raft as it vanished into the distance.

Denton sat in the raft with his hands raised in the air as he waved and pleaded and begged, his cries whipped away by the bitter wind snapping through the bay.

Cody watched until the Phoenix turned out of the narrows and the town of St John's vanished far behind them.

24

Week 34

My beloved Maria,

This morning we rounded the southern headlands of Nova Scotia. The captain has assured us that with a fair wind we should raise Boston by tomorrow morning. Such hopes and fears as I have never felt fill me now with a wonderful excitement and a terrible dread at what we might find, and whether I might find you.

The city of Halifax, past which we recently sailed, was a burning cinder devoid of life. We found no surviving human inhabitants. The population appears to have succumbed to the winter and to each other. Bethany found evidence of diseases such as cholera when she studied the remains of several victims. The terrible fate of Halifax's citizens was repeated again at Yarmouth. Bethany's assessment matches the description of events after the storm related by the captain and crew of the Phoenix, and seems to follow the same pattern wherever we sail: after the storm there is at first confusion, then the spread of panic as law enforcement collapses. Conflict follows as food and water dwindle and families defend their right to survive. The cities empty as survivors flood into the wilderness in search of fresh water and live game, but without the basic ability to endure a winter in such harsh climes they quickly succumb to starvation, exposure, dehydration or predation by both animals and other humans.

In Halifax, Bethany found evidence of cannibalism. The sombre remains of hastily erected fires and charred human skulls haunt us all as we sail ever further south, but those terrible sights seem to have thawed the hostility of the Phoenix's crew toward us despite their own despicable acts. Perhaps, somehow, they are beginning to realise that it *truly is just us against the world and that if we do not stick together, we can only fall apart.*

Maria, in the next few days I know that I shall learn of what has become of you and your mother. I pray that I have the strength to accept what I find and that whatever has happened you have not suffered, for I do not believe I could live the rest of my days knowing that I have failed you so terribly. I fear that the choices I have made in life mean that I do not deserve to find you.

Regardless, know that I will not stop until I do.

I love you very much,

Dad

*

The dawn was a brilliant scythe of fearsome sunlight that stretched across the horizon through tattered ribbons of cloud strewn across a powder blue sky. Sharp black shadows struck across the deck of the Phoenix as she sailed on eerily calm waters under full sail, her canvas rumbling and thumping in the fluke winds.

Cody stood beside the foremast and managed a quiet smile as they sailed past Long Island and he saw the familiar skyline of Boston hove into view. Towering skyscrapers dominated the city headland, an iconic monolith of mankind's dominance, and to the right of the Charles River estuary he could see Logan International Airport and the specks of its control tower and low terminals.

Bethany stood beside him, one arm looped through his as they watched the city grow slowly before them. Sauri, Reece and Bradley stood with Charlotte nearby, while Jake stood with the captain and crew further back.

The captain had ordered the crew to sail past Spectacle Island, a kilometre off Boston's eastern shoreline. The island had been a recreational facility with walks, tourist cafes and a small harbour back before the storm but no permanent residents. A quick stop there had yielded no useful supplies.

The Phoenix sailed on by and headed for Castle Island, where the stoic walls of Fort Independence stood. As the ship passed by Cody could clearly see a ragged Star Spangled Banner still flying from its pole. The fort looked exactly as it had done when he had last seen it but for the detritus gusting across its lawns, a mass of old leaves and trash rolling with the wind, some piling up against the walls of the fort or spilling into the water.

The ship sailed onward, ever closer to the city, past the Maritime Park and the big piers and the state Court House until they reached the entrance to Fort Point Channel and Rowes Wharf. As the ship moved into the shelter of the city so the wind that had buffeted her for so many long weeks died down to a flurry of light flukes, and Cody felt the warmth of the morning sun beat down upon his skin.

'Shorten sail!'

Hank's voice thundered across the decks in the sunlit silence as the small harbour came into view a couple of hundred yards away. There were no boats moored there.

Under Hank's guidance the crew swarmed over the rigging and hauled in the ship's sails as the engine was started and Saunders began the delicate task of turning the schooner about.

'We'll anchor off shore and facing out of the harbour,' Hank said as he joined Cody near the bow. 'I'm not taking any chances that survivors might try to board us. At least we'll get some warning from out here.'

Cody frowned as he glanced at the wharf. 'We'll be lucky to find anybody.'

'True, but we've also been lucky to get this far at all,' Hank replied. 'We'll use the launch to get ashore.'

Cody nodded. There was little point in risking the ship by mooring her directly alongside the city. 'What about the crew?'

'What about them?'

'Who's going ashore?'

Hank thought for a moment. 'I'll leave Saunders in charge. The men won't cross him, he's too well liked.'

'They out number him,' Bethany pointed out.

'Not when he's armed.' The captain looked at Charlotte. 'Are you sure your father would have left you something here?'

Charlotte nodded. 'There's no way he would have taken off without trying to warn me. Since my mom died he's always been there for me.'

Hank turned to help lower the ship's launch as Cody scanned the city.

Although with the pristine sunrise glinting on the tower blocks and the calm water it seemed at first glance that everything was normal, it was obvious to Cody that the city was dead. The silence, for one thing. The roar of airliners landing at the airport, the whisper of distant traffic in the city streets and the flashes of sunlight glinting off car windows as they cruised by were all gone. The windows of many larger buildings were vacant black holes where glass had been shattered, their walls stained with black smudges of fire damage. The masts of boats in the harbours were jumbled just like those at St John's, and a column of grey smoke rose slowly up from somewhere in the city to mar the perfect sky.

'If we're lucky,' Bradley said, 'there's nobody left alive.'

'Speak for yourself,' Bethany snapped back at him.

'We have no idea what's waiting for us,' Hank silenced them all. 'So we go in armed, we move quietly, and if I say we're leaving then we're leaving. Too slow and you'll become permanent residents here again, understood?'

Cody nodded as the captain turned away and strode across to the wheelhouse.

The warmth in the air meant that the deckhouse windows were open, Saunders manning the wheel as the crew hollered commands at him. The diesel engine chugged into life as the Phoenix began a slow and careful rotation in the water, her rudder at full port lock as she swung gently around until her stern faced the city.

'Rudder amidships! Anchors away!'

Saunders spun the wheel back as the crew dropped both bow and stern anchors into the rippling grey water. The chains rattled and crashed as the anchors sank deep into the harbour, and then suddenly the noise faded and echoed away into nothingness.

'Secure!'

The diesel engine cut out a few moments later and the ship fell eerily silent. Only the sound of water lapping against the hull and the occasional call of a seabird wheeling above them broke the silence. Cody looked out across the immense city looming over them as though silently beckoning them toward the doom suffered by so many countless souls.

'It's like a giant graveyard,' Bethany whispered beside him.

Saunders' voice cut through the silence. 'Stand by the winch!'

The Phoenix had a single launch lashed to the forward deckhouse roof. Cody and Jake worked the manual winch, which lifted the launch off the ship and lowered it into the water alongside.

The captain and Bradley appeared from below decks, each armed with a rifle and carrying several small-arms between them. Cody was surprised when the captain shoved a 9mm pistol into his hand.

'You ever fired one of these before?' Hank asked.

'No,' Cody replied, seeing a sudden vision of his late brother's pistol.

The captain explained the weapon and finished with a warning. 'Fifteen rounds plus a spare clip. If, God forbid, you have to shoot then count down your rounds in your head. You don't want to get caught out with no bullets and your back to a wall, okay?'

'Got it,' Cody replied with less confidence than he felt.

The captain led the way down into the launch, followed by Jake, Bethany, Charlotte, Bradley and Sauri. Reece remained on board, but both Taylor and Seth climbed down the rope ladder into the launch alongside them. Cody noted that both men were armed with pistols much like his own, but figured that the captain wanted both men close by so that he could keep a watch on them.

Taylor pushed the launch clear of the Phoenix's hull and Seth yanked on the oars, his arms coated in a purple haze of tattoos that blended into each other in a demonic mess of knives, blood and skulls. The launch pulled away from the ship and turned for the shore.

Cody sat at the prow and watched as the city loomed over them as they crossed the bay. The sun was up above the skyline now, the broken cirrus clouds above scattered across the pearlescent blue.

Seth rowed the launch up to a triangular beach of golden sand nestled between the causeway and Harbour Walk. Cody saw Taylor nervously fingering the trigger of his pistol, his eyes searching the silent city for any sign of an impending attack.

The launch eased in and slid onto the sandy beach as Cody jumped out. Bethany and Bradley leaped out with him and together they hauled the launch up onto the beach. A detritus of discarded plastic cups and bags, old bits of cardboard and other junk littered the beach and floated near the water's edge.

'We'll have to cross the city to get to the state house,' Charlotte said, her voice sounding oddly loud. 'That's where my father's offices were.'

'What about the family home?' Cody asked her.

'St Elizabeth's.'

'Good,' Cody replied. 'That's less than a mile from Oak Square. Two birds, one stone.'

'What's in Oak Square?' Taylor asked.

'My daughter,' Cody replied and turned to face the sailor. 'Got a problem with that?'

The big man appeared momentarily surprised by Cody's attitude and blinked slowly. 'No.'

'What's the plan?' Cody asked Hank.

The captain checked his rifle and set the safety catch.

'We stay together as a group,' he replied. 'I don't want to risk us losing each other out here or coming under attack from who knows what. We find the senator's home and office, check them out. If we have time, you get to visit home too. Then we're gone, understood?'

Cody turned and led the way up the beach. There was no way in hell he was leaving without checking out his home.

The beach opened up onto a boulevard and residential streets lined with apartments. In the warm spring sunlight everything again seemed normal at first glance, but Cody was struck by the change that had occurred so rapidly in the nine months since he had last set foot in the city.

The once pristine asphalt roads were already smothered with a thin network of mosses that had taken hold. A winter of fearsome nor'-easters, the storms that frequently battered the eastern seaboard, plus frosts, snow and a lack of use had cracked the road surfaces and nature had taken its course, roots and weeds thriving.

'The city's already being reclaimed,' Bethany said as they walked, 'seems fast though.'

Cody realised why when he smelled a foul odour staining the air, drifting out of the myriad streets as though the city were exhaling its last rotten breaths.

Sewage lined the sidewalks. With pumping stations out of commission and unchecked storm surges flooding the city, raw human effluent had spilled through the streets and amassed near blocked drains. Now, with the spring thaw, the streets had been effectively filled with biological nutrients in which foliage was already taking hold.

Cody looked up and saw that many of the apartment buildings and stores lining the boulevard were without windows, exposing the interiors to the brutal elements and hastening their inevitable decay. Thick beds of rotting leaves lined the sidewalks, litter gusting along the roads in the breeze as they walked. Cody experienced a deep sense of loss as he strode through the silence, at what once had been and what he saw now. All of the innovation, all of the technology, all of the hopes and dreams and futures of countless souls eradicated in a single and unstoppable act of nature on one terrible night. The silence clung to them and enveloped the city in its lonely embrace. Cody realised that he could hear no songbirds, and the shore was far enough behind them that he could not hear the water. He felt as though he were walking through a gigantic, abandoned model.

The team behind him were likewise silent, eyes scanning the vacant buildings and abandoned homes. Some were capped with roofs burned to cinders, jagged strakes of blackened timber striking up into the flawless blue sky, towers of soot-stained brick and peeling paintwork.

'It's like we've been gone for years,' Bethany said.

'Weather's gotten into many of the buildings,' Jake confirmed. 'Nothing much is going to survive a few Boston winters.'

They walked through the residential area and out into south Boston's Broadway. Cody saw an American flag hanging limp from a pole outside a large bank. It had been left at half-mast, perhaps by the staff who had once worked inside. The portico frontage still stood proud but the entrance doors were smashed, glass still littering the steps.

'There's nobody here,' Bradley said. 'This was a big city.'

The captain replied as they walked, his rifle carried at port-arms and ready for the slightest hint of danger.

'It happened real fast,' he said. 'Here in Boston it was real cloudy when the Great Darkness came so unless people heard about the solar storm on the television they wouldn't have known much about it. They'd have gone to bed believing all to be well, and woken up in the morning to the beginning of the end. I'd bet that some people died never knowing what caused all of this in the first place.'

Cody had never before considered how abrupt and complete the end had been when it had finally arrived. He thought of all the Hollywood movies he had seen as a child, with their huge asteroids, deadly plagues and warmongering aliens. Yet when the real end had come it had been silent and even beautiful. He recalled the vibrant, bright aurora above the Arctic Circle, a shimmering veil of colour that had concealed the deadly particles of energy raining down through the atmosphere to swamp electrical grids around the world.

A sudden line entered his mind as he walked.

'Blessed are the meek, for they shall inherit the Earth,' he said.

'What's that now?' Bradley murmured.

'Matthew, five-five,' Hank replied. 'What's your point?'

'The storm took out technology,' Cody said. 'But there are millions of people around the world who don't own even a kettle. They may have been unaffected by what's happened, may not even know that the rest of the world has fallen.'

'Those with nothing will have had nothing to lose,' the captain agreed.

'The hell with that,' Bradley uttered. 'You all want to go back to living in huts made of dried dung and eating bugs for a living, that's your call. I want MTV and my goddamned car back. Speaking of which, why the hell are we walking? Couldn't we grab a working vehicle or just sail the launch round into the Charleston?'

'They don't work, dumbass, that's the whole point and anyway we don't know who's watching,' Hank replied. 'It's easier to keep a low profile if we stay on foot.'

'Harder to get away, too.'

The streets were littered with vehicles, abandoned when they had run out of gas or their circuits had fried during the solar storm. Massachusetts Avenue was packed with silent, empty cars left nose to tail with their doors open. Cody could envisage the mass exodus from the city, the jammed streets and panicked citizens seeking to flee the looting and the starvation. He blinked away images of screaming, hungry children and deadly conflict between warring families, unable to bear the hollow fear deep in his guts as he thought of Maria.

As he turned north onto a street dominated by a large cathedral, Cody slowed as he saw bodies strewn across the road ahead amid the debris. Flocks of birds fluttered as they swarmed across the bodies and a couple of feral dogs looked up as Cody appeared, their jaws drooling with meat.

The team stopped behind Cody.

'They're all dead, guys,' Bradley uttered. 'What are we waiting for?'

'Disease,' Bethany said, and looked at Cody. 'Will you help me? We need to check them out, see what happened.'

'Seriously?' Cody asked. 'Can't we just go around?'

'We need to know what we're dealing with here,' Bethany insisted. 'If we're hunting around for supplies we may pick up illnesses ourselves. The more I know, the better I can treat us if we get infected.'

Dean Crawford

25

'Wait here,' Bethany said.

The team obeyed as Bethany donned gloves and a mask, handing an identical set for Cody to wear before they strode toward the nearest corpse, an African-American woman lying on her back.

'The dogs,' Cody cautioned her. 'They've been eating the dead bodies.'

Bethany hesitated as she looked at the animals. Both were mangy, their fur matted and their eyes glowing with the strange light of true wild animals. Both were also large, powerful animals. Cody recalled that all so-called toy-dogs were the result of mankind influencing evolution, selective breeding creating novel forms of animal that had no ability to survive in a natural environment. All dogs had ultimately evolved from wolves, and only those with the size and strength to dominate like a wolf could live in a world devoid of humans. He knew that all small dogs would have died of starvation or predation shortly after the Great Darkness and that in a similar time frame all other dogs would have become feral and developed pack structures, completely eradicating thousands of years of domestication in a matter of weeks.

Bethany stepped back as the two dogs growled, saliva drooling from their jaws as they bared their fangs, their heads lowering as they turned to face the intruders.

'They see us as prey,' Cody whispered. 'Back up, real slow.'

Before anybody could stop him, Bradley aimed his pistol and fired a single shot.

The report cracked out like thunder and echoed away across the city. One of the dogs shuddered and dropped as though its legs had been whipped from beneath it as the other whirled and fled down the street. The birds took off in an enormous clatter of wing beats as they climbed up into the blue sky above.

'You idiot!' Charlotte slapped Bradley hard across the shoulder. 'You want everybody to know where we are?'

'There's nobody here,' Bradley replied without concern.

Hank turned and glared at the soldier. 'You screw up like that again I'll put the next bullet between your eyes. Understood?'

Bradley held the captain's gaze without fear, but he did not retaliate.

Cody turned back to the dozens of bodies before them, strewn across the street like discarded dolls. Bethany approached the woman's corpse.

Even from ten yards away Cody could see that her eyes had been pecked out by birds and that her belly, once swollen with internal gases, had ripped open as cleanly as though sliced with a surgical knife. The decayed innards swarmed with maggots, a cloud of flies buzzing like smoke on the air above her, but the woman's skin was slack and her bones protruded through some parts of her limbs and chest. Cody stayed a few yards back from the corpse.

'Any ideas?' he asked.

Bethany briefly examined the corpse and then stood up. 'Cholera again,' she said, 'probably been here a few months. The cold of winter slowed the decay.'

'Lovely,' Cody replied, looking further up the street and keeping thoughts of Maria out of his mind. 'Same for the rest of them?'

'Hard to be absolutely sure,' Bethany admitted as she moved from body to body, 'but they all have a classic symptom called washer-woman's hands, caused by massive dehydration. My guess is that the cathedral was used as a hostel, infected water was drunk and the pandemic spread.' She looked at Cody. 'Which means that they had no useful medicines or antibiotics here.'

'The area's already stripped clean,' Cody replied, 'probably right after the storm.'

'This is why things deteriorated so fast,' Bethany said as she gestured to the corpses behind her. 'People didn't know the simple basics of water treatment when they couldn't get it out of a tap or bottle. All they had to do was boil their water for ten minutes and it would have been fine.'

'Maybe they couldn't,' Cody said. 'Plenty of trees lining the streets but none have been stripped of their branches.'

'Which means people were already too far gone when supplies ran out,' Bethany said. 'Too much panic, not enough thought.'

Cody looked at another body near the cathedral steps. The corpse seemed fresher than the others. He walked across to it and looked down.

A man who had died somewhere in his twenties. Painfully emaciated, wearing several jumpers, two pairs of pants and a hat, presumably to keep warm. Despite the rigours he had endured Cody could tell that he had not lain long outside the cathedral. One of his eyes was still in its socket, not yet attacked by the birds.

'Shot,' Bethany said, 'back of the head.'

Cody saw the bloody exit wound of shattered bone and blood soaked hair.

'He can't have been here long,' Cody pointed out. 'The body's in too good a shape.'

'Less than a week,' Bethany agreed. 'Somebody was here, and they were armed.'

Cody hurried back to the group as he tore off his gloves and mask and filled Hank in on what they had learned.

'What about the others?' the captain asked. 'Any others shot?'

'Much older remains of cholera victims,' Bethany informed him. 'There's not much left of any of them.'

Hank was about to reply when Bradley's voice cut across him. 'I see movement.'

Bradley's comment caused everybody to duck down and move into the shelter of the cathedral's steps, keeping clear of the bodies nearby.

'Where away?' Hank demanded.

'Far side of the intersection,' Bradley replied.

The broad streets ahead were bathed in sunlight, and as he watched Cody saw a bedraggled figure shuffle into view with a slow, awkward gait. Moments later more followed, their heads hanging low.

'They look like zombies,' Jake uttered.

Cody frowned as he watched the shabby looking crowd slowly wander across the intersection. Their faces were dark with dirt, their hair falling past their shoulders and their ragged clothes hanging from their emaciated frames.

'Must have heard the gunshot,' Hank uttered as he cast a dirty look at Bradley. 'We saw people like this in Baltimore, driven insane by sickness and thirst.'

'Best we go around them,' Jake said, 'just in case.'

'Just in case of what?' Bradley asked, 'just in case they're flesh-eating monsters? Jesus Christ.'

The soldier stood up and strode out into the street, put two fingers in his mouth and whistled loudly.

'Brad, no!' Charlotte hissed.

The crowd of people stopped and slowly turned to look at Bradley. Then, they began shuffling toward him.

'Hey,' Bradley shouted at the crowd. 'Any of you tell me where the nearest Dunkin' Donuts is?'

The crowd continued toward him, began stumbling as they attempted to run. Cody saw faces blank with exposure, shock and terminal illnesses. Eyes were sunken into bruised orbs, skeletal jaws and cheekbones protruded through paper-thin skin, tongues hung limp from cracked lips.

Bradley's jaunty expression slipped as the crowd began to rush him.

'Get into cover!' Jake shouted at the soldier.

Bradley started to back up and raised his pistol. 'You all back off now, y'hear!?'

The crowd kept coming, a mournful wail swelling from their ranks as they rushed in a tumbling wave of pitiful desperation toward Bradley. Cody realised that in their extreme famine and sickness, the once ordinary citizens had deteriorated into a mindless mass of humanity blindly wandering the city streets.

'Take them down!' Hank yelled as he burst from cover.

Bradley fired at the nearest of the onrushing crowd, a man whose beard reached to his chest and whose face was infected with deep lesions that weeped thin yellow pus down his cheeks. The shot hit him in the chest and propelled him backward into the crowd behind him, his collapsing body trampled in the rush. Others fell over him, tumbling to their knees, but the crowd kept coming as though poured from a bottle, flowing over the obstacles with blind instinct. Cody saw mouths devoid of teeth, infected lesions bloodied and decaying, greying skin and thin, straggly hair advancing in one awful mass of suffering humanity.

The crowd let out a wail of anguish and fear at the sound of the gunshot, primeval reactions to danger, but like some unstoppable machine bent on self-destruction they continued toward Bradley even as Hank and Sauri opened fire, cutting them down one by one.

Bradley fired twice again, and then the crowd were upon him and too close to shoot. Cody saw the soldier swing his pistol into a man's face and send him flying onto the cracked, moss covered asphalt. A man grabbed the soldier, trying to cling to him as he screamed in a tearful rage. Bradley shook the man off and turned as he fell to his knees, drove a heavy boot into the man's face that flicked his head back with a sound like a snapping twig.

Cody dashed forward and grabbed Bradley, pulled him back by his shoulder as he yelled at him.

'They're not harming you! They just want help!'

Hank's voice shouted out above the commotion of gunfire and screams.

'Cease fire!'

Sauri and Hank fell back from the onrushing horde as Cody and Bradley joined them. Together with Bethany, Taylor and the rest they began jogging away from the feebly pursuing crowd.

'We go around, cut through to the next block!' Hank snapped. 'Let's avoid any more confrontations, understood Brad?!'

The soldier nodded as they ran and cut right through a service alley filled with litter and decomposing bodies. Cody leapt over them as he ran, then burst out into the adjoining street and cut right again. They kept running until they could no longer see the shuffling masses pursuing them. Cody slowed as they reached Brookline and waited for the others to catch up.

Jake laboured in last, his chest heaving as he waved his hand up and down.

'Let's not do that again,' he gasped, 'or you'll have another damned corpse on your hands.'

Charlotte took the lead and they walked in silence for a further hour, skirting bodies lying in the streets in their hundreds. Many had decomposed sufficiently that they were more bone than flesh, pale white scalps flecked with ugly clumps of wiry hair, skeletal arms poking out of tattered clothes still attached to bodies picked clean by countless marauding rodents.

They reached St Elizabeth's shortly before noon, the sun warm and the day surprisingly bright. The clement weather contrasted sharply with the silent city and the macabre remains haunting the lonely suburbs.

As they climbed a hill that looked out to the south, Hank waved his hand for them to slow. Since leaving south Boston they had seen no further wandering tribes of crazed survivors, nor indeed any signs of life other than birds and the occasional packs of dogs that showed their heckles and fangs in defiance before fleeing. Now it became obvious why.

'We can't go much further,' he said.

Cody looked ahead and felt his guts twinge as he saw the bright green woods and mossy roads give way to an ashen wilderness of skeletally dead trees and odd, patchy lawns and fields. Houses had been stripped of their paintwork and the bodies of both humans and animals lay strewn across the roads.

'What the hell happened here?' Bradley uttered.

'Plymouth nuclear storage facility would be my guess,' Hank replied. 'This is the fallout from the cooling station. Acid rain, radiation, you name it.'

'Christ, should we even be here?' Seth asked. 'What about radiation poisoning?'

'Most of it will have been washed away into the soil over the winter,' Jake replied. 'But that explains the state of those people we saw wandering Boston. They were suffering from radiation poisoning.'

'Where's your house?' Bethany asked Charlotte.

'It's along here,' Charlotte replied, gesturing to a leafy side street that narrowly skirted the dead zone ahead of them.

Charlotte led them to a once handsome Colonial style house that overlooked Chestnut Hill Reservoir. Multiple bedrooms, triple garage out back, surrounded by chestnut trees and with broad lawns that were now becoming overgrown with tall weeds. She stopped and a hand flew to her mouth as she surveyed the shattered windows, the busted front door, signs of small fires peppering the window ledges.

Bethany put her arm across Charlotte's shoulders. 'I'm sure he's not in there,' she whispered. 'He would have got out.'

'You want me to check it out first?' Bradley asked her, moving close by her side.

Charlotte shook her head, gathered herself. 'No, we go together.'

Bradley followed Charlotte inside, his pistol at the ready in case anybody leaped out at them. Cody followed with the rest of the team.

The interior of the house felt cold, long since devoid of the warmth and light of human occupation. The once deep carpets were filthy and littered with the debris of old leaves that had blown in, scraps of fallen wallpaper and peeled paint from the front door.

Charlotte walked into the living room and Cody saw a large canvas of a Revolution-era sea battle dominating a modern looking fireplace. Pictures lined the walls, some of them of Charlotte, her father and a good looking woman in her fifties. Charlotte pulled one of them from the wall and shoved it into her rucksack.

'People were here,' Bradley said as he gestured to the fireplace. Thick ash filled its base. 'They burned stuff to keep warm.'

'Make this quick,' Hank said to Charlotte, scanning through the broad windows for any sign of people outside.

Charlotte hurried through the house from room to room but found nobody in the building. Cody wasn't sure if she was relieved or upset not to have found her father, but Charlotte turned instead to a small office and stepped inside.

Redundant computers dominated a study. Cody saw a fax machine now splattered with bird droppings and leaves piled up against the base of a book cabinet, the books long gone.

'That's what they burned,' he realised, 'the people that were here.'

'Dad's books,' Charlotte said sadly as she looked at the cabinet. 'He would have been appalled.'

Charlotte turned to the back wall. A smaller cabinet stood before it, filled with small pieces of china and glass trinkets. She squatted down and heaved against it. The cabinet shifted easily and exposed a wall safe. Charlotte reached up and spun the locking mechanism back and forth, clearly knowing the code by heart.

The safe opened and she reached inside as a flash of delight filled her expression.

She retrieved an envelope and showed it to Cody.

The envelope was adorned with her name, written in a hasty script.

26

Charlotte tore open the letter, her hands shaking as she unfolded the single page within.

Her eyes began flicking across the page as she read, and a slow creeping horror filled her features with dismay as the rest of the team gathered in the doorway to the study.

'What does it say?' Bethany asked softly.

Charlotte's shoulders slumped and she handed the letter to Cody as she turned away and stared out of the office window. Cody read the letter to the rest of the group.

Dear Charlie,

I can only hope that someday you find this letter. I have so little time to write. I am being recalled to the city. A car is already here with a Secret Service escort and I have been prevented from contacting anybody. I have asked to gather some belongings in order to leave this note for you.

I know nothing of what has happened but whatever it is, it must be of monumental importance. In my experience, such panicked demands are rarely born of good news. Whatever happens I hope that you are safe and well and that you might read this upon your return. I dearly hope that we shall speak again soon.

I shall try to contact you at Alert as soon as I know more and am able to do so.

Lots of love,
Dad

'They were pulled out,' Bradley said. 'Same time as the Canadian forces at Alert most likely.'

'And the politicians,' Hank noted, 'all of them heading for that foreign conference, the location of which was never revealed.'

Cody lowered the letter and looked across at the captain.

'You were right,' he conceded. 'They knew. They knew what was coming and they tried to evade it without telling us, without telling anybody.'

'Maybe they didn't know,' Charlotte said in a weak voice. 'For sure, I mean.'

'I doubt that,' Jake said from the doorway.

Cody let the letter fall to the office floor as he stared out of the window past Charlotte to the sunny, silent streets outside. The people charged with the service of the citizens of their country had deliberately abandoned those people to their fate and fled to an unknown haven to wait out the fall of mankind. Cody thought of all the children, men and women: the young and the old and the infirm left without food, water or warmth, left to the uncaring brutality of those stronger than themselves. People like Maria. Hot rage simmered like a disease deep in the pit of his belly, poison running through his veins as he turned and barged his way out of the office.

'Where the hell are you going?' Bradley demanded.

Cody did not reply as he walked out of the house and struck out along the road that circled the reservoir, heading toward Oak Square. Bethany hurried out of the house after him.

'Cody, wait.'

Cody did not stop walking. Bethany jogged alongside him. 'We need to stick together and wait for…'

'I've been waiting nine months,' Cody shot back. 'I'm not waiting another second. I need to know, Beth, that's all there is to it.'

'So do I!' Bethany shouted. Cody stopped as she grabbed his arm. 'I have a brother too, remember? I have family. I've waited all this time but now I don't know what I'll find and that scares the hell out of me.'

Cody rubbed his temples. 'I'd rather know than not.'

'Then let's do it together,' Bethany replied. 'Storming off on your own won't help anybody, least of all your wife and daughter.'

Cody saw Hank and the others walk slowly out of the senator's home and across the unkempt lawns.

'Make it quick, Ryan,' the captain said. 'Sooner we're done here, the better.'

Cody looked at Charlotte. Her face was stricken, like shell-shock, her eyes vacant. Cody thought of the radio transmission that he'd picked up at Alert and the coded coordinates within it. The urge to tell her about it was overwhelming but he refrained once more. Hank Mears and the Phoenix were too important to them all now. Without the ship they could never reach Eden even if they knew where it was.

Cody turned and started walking. He waited until Bethany joined him, and let their path drift away from the others until he felt sure that nobody could hear them. He kept his voice quiet as they walked.

'I need you to do something for me,' he said.

'What?'

'I need you to memorise something, in case anything happens to me.'

Bethany looked up at him as they walked, her eyes filled with caution. 'Okay.'

Cody took a deep breath.

'There were coordinates in the message I intercepted at Alert.'

Bethany did an admirable job of keeping her features impassive as they walked, looking straight ahead. Cody kept his voice low as he went on.

'They were sent using Morse Code, presumably because of the weak signal. I managed to decipher them using a code book at Polaris Hall.'

'Why haven't you told anybody about this?' she whispered.

'You think we'd have got this far if I had?' Cody challenged. 'Hank and his men would have sailed directly for their mysterious Eden and left us behind. I didn't want anybody to know until we'd had the chance to come back here, if only once.'

Bethany did not reply.

'This is our only chance to find our families,' Cody added. 'Keeping this quiet is the right thing to do, for now. Are you good with this?'

Bethany was silent for a long time before she replied.

'I'll do it,' she said finally. 'What do you need me to memorise?'

'42N70W,' Cody said.

Bethany recited the coordinates as they walked until she could recall them at will.

The group rounded the reservoir and crossed into Oak Square. The bright sunshine and gentle breeze seemed docile and comforting yet the residential suburbs were haunted by the chill of abandonment, the houses like hollow caves, the streets strewn with litter and the rustle of leaves whispering of a past never to be revisited.

Cody saw in his mind's eye Maria in the back seat of the family car, or taking her first steps in the park near their house, or erratically throwing pieces of bread to ducks and pigeons and laughing as they gobbled the morsels up.

Patchwork weeds laced the asphalt as Cody turned onto Perthshire and hesitated. The road stretched away from him and with a pulse of anxiety in his belly he spotted the front of his house. Neat white clapperboard, two storeys, an unkempt lawn.

Maria's voice whispered to him amid the leaves drifting across the street as he bolted forwards and ran to the front of the home that had filled his mind and thoughts for so many long months. Raw grief ripped at his heart as he saw the shattered windows, the scorched woodwork and the front door hanging from its hinges. The once neatly trimmed hedgerows were tattered and in disarray as he vaulted over them and rushed up to the front door.

The faint smell of wood smoke filled the house as he stepped inside.

'Maria!?'

He heard the guttural distress in his own voice as it echoed through the lonely house, a tremor of grim realisation of his worst fears. Cody dashed from room to room, each filled with upturned furniture and debris blown in from outside on the winter storms.

It took him only minutes to ascertain that the house was empty, but he kept searching manically for some evidence of where they had gone. He emptied cupboards. He overturned tables and chairs. He rifled through drawers in the kitchen and then stood and stared down at the new tiles on the kitchen floor, lost beneath a scattering of rodent droppings and crumbling leaves blown in through the wrecked kitchen door.

Cody stumbled into the lounge and saw Maria's play-pen standing empty in the centre of the room. He turned away and thumped his fist against the unyielding walls over and over and over again until somebody grabbed hold of him and their arms wrapped around his neck. Cody crumbled into the embrace as his legs quivered and gave way beneath him. He dropped slowly to his knees as his life bled from his eyes into the soft hair crushed against his face as Bethany held him tight against her.

*

'It's getting late.'

Hank stood outside Cody's house and squinted up at the sun in the sky above, its path now crossed by rippling blankets of diaphanous cloud drifting in from the north.

'We can make the city before sundown,' Jake guessed, 'then get back to the beach before dark. It'll be a push though.'

'You two seen any bodies laying about recently?' Hank asked Taylor and Seth.

Taylor shook his head. 'Residents must have cleared out before the looting or the disease hit here.'

'Might have got more warning,' Jake said as he sipped water from a bottle. 'If they saw the city go up in smoke they could have pulled out for the country. They could even have gone south before the nuclear station went bust.'

Charlotte looked out to the south-west and finally spoke.

'You get out much past Worcester and there's nothing but wilderness and small towns all the way down to Connecticut. Out west it's the Big Indian Wilderness, New York state and Pennsylvania. Plenty of big country to hide in.'

'If you know how,' Hank pointed out.

'They gonna be much longer in there?' Bradley asked.

'They'll be as long as they need,' Jake cautioned.

'He'll be okay,' Charlotte said. 'Takes a while to process what's happened and pick yourself up, is all.'

'I'm sure your father didn't abandon you,' Jake said. 'It sounded like he had no choice but to leave right there and then.'

'But to where?' Charlotte asked. 'With whom? And how? If they didn't get out before the storm arrived then how could they have travelled anywhere?'

'The politicians quit several hours before the storm,' Jake said. 'Likely they knew it was too big to handle. Air Force One could reach anywhere on the globe.'

'Yeah,' Bradley agreed, 'but only within the time frame allowed. If they had, say, six hours' warning then the farthest they could go would be six hours' flying time away, right? That's probably about three thousand miles in any direction, assuming they took off immediately.'

Hank looked at Charlotte's letter, which he had picked up off the floor where Cody had dropped it.

'The senator did not e-mail or call his daughter,' he mused out loud. 'He could have made a call easily enough without hindering his travels, or sent an e-mail via his cell phone. But he does nothing. Why?'

'That suggests to me that he was prevented from doing so,' Jake replied, 'maybe to keep word from getting out.'

'Exactly,' Hank said. 'They kept this whole thing airtight so that they could get out before the panic or the storm set in. Complete media blackout followed by a literal global blackout.'

'Organised exodus,' Bradley agreed. 'Fits with your little theory of a safe haven but it doesn't tell us where the haven is or how to get there.'

'No,' Sauri said from nearby. 'But it does tell us something important.'

'What?' Jake asked.

Sauri guzzled from his water bottle and then spoke. 'The storm hit after sundown here in the USA, east coast time, right? The news reports on the Internet said that the politicians had flown for their overseas conference in the early afternoon. At that time of year, it means about five hours' of time to flee before the storm hit.'

Hank clicked his fingers.

'Good work. Five hours. Assume an hour to pull in all the officials that the president would want to take with him, close political allies, military heads, plus experts like engineers and doctors that any haven would need. He could get maybe four hundred aboard Air Force One and have select aircraft from around the military do something similar.'

Jake nodded, seeing the direction the captain was taking.

'They could have saved thousands of lives,' he agreed, 'especially the kind of people who agreed with them politically and militarily. They set up a temporary base somewhere within range of all participating aircraft and wait out the storm.'

'And then they come back?' Sauri asked.

Hank looked around them and shook his head.

'Maybe, but I don't reckon they'll ever be able to get this all going again.' He gestured at the houses around them. 'We had nearly four hundred million people in this country before the storm. God only knows how many are left but I'd wager there won't be enough of them with the skills or manpower to rebuild and replace everything before it all rots.'

Charlotte clicked her fingers, still thinking about her father.

'They'd need a rally point, somewhere to gather quickly. Probably Logan airport, but my father would have gone via the senate building or the state house in the city. There might be something there, a trail of evidence we could follow.'

'It's a long shot,' Jake replied, 'but it beats heading down to New York. At least here we know there's one senator who definitely had a chance of getting out.'

Hank nodded. 'We'll do it and then head back to the ship.'

Jake turned as he saw Cody walk out of the house, Bethany alongside him.

'Any sign?' he asked.

Cody shook his head in silence.

'House is empty,' Bethany answered for Cody. 'We grabbed a couple of items.'

'Hank reckons that most people would have pulled out before the riots and looting reached here from the city,' Jake said to Cody. 'No dead bodies lying about here and with big country to the west they could have disappeared before things got too rough. I'm sure they made it out.'

Cody nodded but said nothing.

'We're heading for the city,' Jake said. 'You both good with that?'

Cody turned and looked out to the west. Bethany tugged his arm.

'What if they're out there, somewhere?' he asked, his voice sounding small in his own ears.

'Then they're alive and we can find them later,' Bethany replied. 'Let's get going. I want to check my apartment in the city before it gets dark.'

Cody sighed and turned with Bethany as they set off. Hank watched them leave, the rest of the team following. A gentle breeze tossed old bits of paper across the sidewalk as he turned to follow them, and as he did so one of them caught his eye.

Hank shifted his boot and pinned the aged newspaper against the sidewalk. He crouched down and picked it up, scanned the page in silence for a moment. Then he folded the page up tightly and shoved it into his pocket.

The city was little more than a mile away, the glittering metal and glass of the financial district's towering skyscrapers grey-blue through the spring haze as they turned onto Beacon Street. Cody walked with Bethany, the once crowded arterial route into Boston now devoid of life. Abandoned red-brick apartment buildings and colonial halls lined one side of the street, the tree lined expanses of Boston Common ahead on the other. American flags hung limp over the sidewalks, the fabric stained and torn, and vehicles sat on deflated tyres in the centre of the street, some of them scorched shells of bare metal.

Ahead, the street crossed an intersection and climbed up toward Beacon Hill and the state house. The intersection was a wide pool of stagnant water, probably run-off from the hill that had flooded when untended drainage systems had clogged with debris.

Bradley and Sauri started to circle the pool of water to the left, seeking the cover of the houses as Seth and Taylor went right toward the treeline of Boston Common. Cody smelled the sewage staining the pool, saw clouds of small bugs hovering over it in the sunlight.

He was almost across the intersection when a gunshot shattered the silence with the force of a thunderclap. The bullet smacked into the house behind them as Bradley bellowed a warning across the street.

'Cover! Enemy east!'

Cody threw himself behind an abandoned Lincoln as a hail of gunfire swept past him, smacking into tree trunks and the Lincoln and cracking off the weed infested asphalt.

27

Cody ducked down flat behind the wrecked Lincoln as bullets stitched across the other side of the vehicle in a spray of sparks and chips of asphalt. Bethany covered her head as the rounds snapped and cracked across nearby brickwork to echo down the street behind them.

'How many?!' Hank yelled from where he crouched nearby.

'Too many!' Bradley shouted back. 'We need to fall back and get the hell out of here!'

Cody peered around the Lincoln's hood and saw that Seth and Taylor were crouched behind trees to the east on Boston Common. On the opposite side of the intersection, Bradley and Sauri sheltered behind houses, both men returning fire with single round bursts, conserving their ammunition. Charlotte, Jake and Hank were just behind the two soldiers. The sheer volume of the gunfire shocked Cody, each round deafeningly loud and causing his vision to blur. Raw fear twisted his guts as he realised that gunfights weren't like they were in the movies. They were loud, frightening and immobilising in their ferocity.

Another salvo of rounds pounded the street and the cars, bullets zipping off the bodywork or clanging into the chassis.

'Move, now!' Bradley yelled.

Hank and Jake leapt from cover as Bradley and Sauri returned fire down the street, peppering the side of a grey house further up the block and a series of trees opposite on the common. Cody saw figures there, ducking out and firing wild bursts from the flaming muzzles of automatic weapons.

'Cody!' Bradley yelled. 'Get over here!'

'No way!' Cody shouted back. 'Only takes one bullet to bring us down!'

Bradley cursed and then yelled across to Seth and Taylor.

'You two! Advance forward, cut them off before they flank us!'

Seth and Taylor looked at each other. Cody could not tell what they were saying but almost immediately he realised that they were ignoring Bradley.

'Seth!' Hank bellowed. 'Do as he says!'

Seth looked at his captain for a long beat, and then he turned and fired a quick burst up into the common ahead. Then, with Taylor firing alongside him, they began retreating down the street away from the rest of the group, toward the docks.

'Seth!' Hank bellowed. 'Get back here or I'll gut you from bow to stern!'

Seth flashed Hank a cruel grin, and moments later they turned and fled from the gunfight.

Bradley and Sauri opened fire again on the figures advancing from cover to cover through the trees. Cody flinched and reeled away from the noise and impacts of the bullets shuddering through the Lincoln behind which he hid. He looked desperately across the street at the rest of the group, but there was no way he and Bethany could cross the intersection without being cut down.

'We're pinned down!' Bethany shouted above the gunfire.

Hank's voice called back. 'Cody, that heavy thing in your hand! Try using it!'

Cody looked down at the ugly black pistol. He turned, carefully switching the weapon's safety catch to "off" as he peered around the Lincoln's hood once more.

Two figures nipped forward from the tree line to hide behind large stone pillars that flanked the entrance to the common. Cody rose up and rested his arms on the hood of the vehicle and aimed at the point where one of the men had vanished. He realised that his hands were shaking, each breath fluttering through his chest as though afraid to leave his body.

The figure popped his head around the pillar. Cody fired.

The single shot almost ripped the pistol from his grasp and pain jolted through his wrists as the weapon recoiled violently and a deafening crack rang through his ears. He glimpsed the figure flinch and hide as chunks of stone sprayed off the pillar shielding him.

'Well done!' Hank shouted. 'Now do that fourteen more times!'

Bradley and Sauri were still firing controlled bursts up Beacon Hill, but Cody could see dozens of figures rushing down through the trees to meet them.

'Fall back!' Bradley yelled.

Cody looked to make a break for it when rounds rattled off the Lincoln's bodywork and forced him down onto his knees for cover.

Suddenly, the gunfire ceased. A ringing silence filled the warm air as Cody crouched with Bethany, the pistol in his grasp woefully inadequate against the automatic weapons ranged against them.

He looked across at Bradley and Hank, who crouched in the stairwells of two brownstones opposite, dangerously exposed to gunfire from the common and with only a single route of egress behind them, the flooded exit off the intersection.

Cody peered over the hood of the Lincoln again and saw faces looking back at him.

'You're surrounded!' came a shout from the common. 'You fall back from there we'll just keep coming until we finish you off! Drop your weapons and come out with your hands in the air!'

Cody looked at Bethany, who shook her head.

'They attacked us!' she whispered harshly.

Cody shouted back without even thinking about it. 'You fired at us first! We can't trust you!'

A long silence followed before a more reasonable sounding voice replied.

'We're not too keen on asking questions first on account of all the militia in the city! Who are you?'

Cody glanced across at Hank and Jake, both of whom shook their heads.

'Out of towners,' Cody yelled back, 'just passing through!'

'Passing through what? There's nothin' left!'

Cody thought fast. 'The docks,' he called. 'We thought there might be boats or something, some way to head south quicker than walking.'

Another long pause. 'Where you headed to?'

'Anywhere but here!'

Cody peered across the street and glimpsed figures crouching behind trees and watching him. He figured about six gunmen, but could not tell how many more might have been coming in behind to support them. Suddenly he realised why: behind the trees in the common he could see that the ground had been cleared and crops were growing, rows of them stretching away toward the city. The gunmen were defending their land.

'They'll circle us,' Bethany whispered. 'We can't trust anybody.'

Cody knew that she was right. He looked across at Bradley and Hank. The captain drew a flat hand across his throat. Cody nodded in response, and pointed down the flooded street as he mimed firing his gun into Boston Common.

Hank mouthed the words *on three* back at him.

'We're leaving,' Cody said to Bethany. 'Ready?'

Bethany revolved on her heel as she crouched, aiming for the opposite side of the intersection.

Cody saw Hank and Bradley take aim, and then they fired a barrage across the intersection as Cody leaned out over the Lincoln and fired four shots at their assailants before he dashed for the cover of the street.

Bradley, Jake, Sauri and Hank all fired as they retreated back around the corner of the street, firing past Cody as he ran with Bethany into cover.

'Let's move, now!' Bradley shouted.

As one they ran down the street, their boots splashing through foul water as they cleared the flood and searched desperately for somewhere to hide.

A crackle of gunfire echoed down the street, rounds zipping off streetlights and walls as Cody changed direction and crouched down behind a row of parked vehicles. He saw Bradley duck into a service alley with Hank and Charlotte as Sauri threw himself over a fence into an abandoned garden.

'We can't keep this up!' Bradley yelled. 'They'll run us down eventually!'

Sauri fired a brief burst back up the street at the figures moving down toward them. Cody got a glimpse of shaven heads and muscular arms cradling assault rifles that spat clouds of lethal bullets all around them. Chips of sidewalk and even branches from roadside trees flew through the air around them.

Then the street fell deathly silent again. Cody waited, but no calls came this time. He was about to look to Hank for inspiration when he realised that they were one short.

'Where's Jake?' he asked.

Hank looked about them, and as if in reply to Cody's question a voice yelled down the street at them.

'Y' all come out now, or the old fella gets it!'

Cody cursed under his breath and peered around the edge of a Taurus to see Jake being held by a huge guy in black jeans and a leather jacket, the muzzle of a pistol jammed up under his throat.

'Don't listen to them!' Jake shouted breathlessly back.

Cody turned away and looked across at Hank and Bradley. Both of them wore uncompromising expressions. Cody heard Jake's words from months before on the lonely ice plains of Ellesmere Island. *We stick together.*

'We should shoot him ourselves,' Bradley said. 'Remove him from the equation.'

'We're done anyway,' Cody snapped in reply. 'Why waste another life?'

'They'll kill us all,' Bradley said. 'Better one dead than six.'

Bethany stood up and walked out into the street before anybody could stop her, her hands in the air as she shouted back at their assailants.

'We're coming out!' she yelled. 'Leave him be!'

Cody pressed the butt of his pistol to his head as he closed his eyes. Bradley sighed and locked his rifle off.

'We should never have brought women with us.'

Cody slowly stood up and walked out into the street to see a small army of heavily armed men stalking toward them, their eyes filled with hate.

'Drop your weapons and get on the ground!'

Cody set his pistol down and lowered himself onto his knees as the rest of the team did the same. The armed gang quickly surrounded them and picked up the discarded weapons before producing steel hand cuffs and binding Cody and his companions' hands behind their backs.

The biggest and oldest of their captors looked down at them all and smiled, showing two front teeth of solid gold that glinted in the sunlight.

'Welcome to Boston.'

Dean Crawford

28

The sun glinted off the glassy surface of tower blocks in the financial district, the glittering mirrored towers reflecting the glorious skies behind Cody and the team but marred by ugly black smoke-stained holes where fires had burned within. Long shadows swept across the asphalt ahead of them, cast by the abandoned vehicles and hollow buildings lining the street.

Cody shuffled along with his wrists bound behind his back, Jake behind him and attached to his cuffs by a length of tough cordage. Each member of the team was likewise bound and joined as they walked miserably through the darkening city streets, their footfalls echoing off the sombre buildings soaring up into the deep blue.

Their captors guided them between the ranks of abandoned and burned out vehicles. The winter's rain had already exposed patches of rust on once pristine bodywork, windows shattered and the weed speckled asphalt crunching beneath their feet as they trod on glittering broken glass. Bird droppings splattered everything with splotches of white and bats wheeled and clicked through the evening sky above their heads.

They walked alongside Boston Common onto Beacon Hill, the fields of crops visible between the trees on the common. The grass and trees blended with the weeds in the sidewalk and road, the evening gloom making the chill in the air seem harsher than it was. Cody caught sight of barricades in side-streets where cars had been upturned to form barriers where families had fought for their lives against looters and murderers, the vehicles scorched by long silenced flames.

Ahead, Cody could see the Bulfinch Front of the Massachusetts State House. Red brick walls, white colonnades and a vast golden dome glinted in the sunlight as the militia prodded and shoved them toward it.

A stale, rancid odour of decaying flesh wafted on the breeze as Cody reached the entrance to the building. A curved white wall topped with a black iron fence stood in front of the state house, and from the fence hung dozens of corpses.

Cody coughed as the stench coated the back of his throat, heard others behind him doing the same. Cruel black ravens balanced on pillars and on bodies, pecking and clawing at flesh exposed red and raw or foraging with beaks into ragged eye sockets. Flies buzzed in lazy clouds around other bodies hanging in tatters from the railings.

As Cody walked closer he heard a muted chorus of agonised groans and with a shock of loathing he realised that many of the people hanging from the railings were not yet dead. Strapped by their wrists, ankles and waists, they hung in agonisingly contorted positions, their heads dangling and saliva drooling from their parched lips. Blood oozed slowly from open wounds, some already infected with legions of maggots or ripped at by the birds that the victims were too weak to fend off.

The stench of death and decay became almost overwhelming as Cody fought the urge to vomit.

Two guards, both wearing kerchiefs pulled tight over their mouths and noses, opened the main gates as Cody's miserable team trudged toward them. Cody and his companions were forced between the gruesome ranks of dead and dying and up the steps toward the main entrance. Two huge doors awaited them. The two guards jogged up the remainder of the steps and pounded on the doors three times with the butts of their rifles. The sound of heavy locks rumbled through the doors and they creaked open as Cody was shoved through.

He recalled something about the first hall he encountered being called the Doric Hall.

Two rows of columns supported a high ceiling. Statues guarded the hall, George Washington among them, and canvases adorned the walls. Opposite Cody was a full length portrait of Abraham Lincoln. Two cannons and a bronze bust of John Hancock stood beneath Lincoln's sombre gaze.

Remarkably, none of the artefacts appeared to have been looted or damaged, and for a brief instant Cody hoped that somehow they had found a refuge of the sane within Boston's crumbling streets. His hopes were dashed as he saw more armed militia standing inside, smoking and watching as Cody and his companions were shoved through the hall and up the steps at the far end.

Flames flickered and crackled in alcoves where once light bulbs had burned, casting moving shadows and wisps of oily smoke that coiled up toward the ceiling like demons flitting from one shadowy refuge to the next. The guards led them through the Nurse's Hall and the Hall of Flags, icons of American independence and Bostonian heritage, until they were led into the great hall.

The hall was long and thin, its once pristine marble floors dusty and scratched. The high walls gave way to an ornate but grubby glass ceiling far above through which the last light of evening glowed. Flames snapped and snarled from trash cans set into deep alcoves in the walls, casting little warmth and illuminating the grim faces of armed militia who watched them as they were led to the far end of the hall.

There, in a throne-like seat that had no doubt been pilfered from one of the other halls, lounged a man who could have been in his twenties or his forties. In the dim and flickering light it was hard to tell. He watched Cody approach with a stern gaze, like a hawk scanning the ground below for hapless rodents caught in the open.

Cody felt his wrists yanked as the line was brought up short a few feet from where the man watched them. Cody wondered if the man had crowned himself King of what was left of Boston.

The man's head was shaved, but one side of his scalp was rippled with scar tissue like cold suet that made his left eyelid droop. He wore a long leather coat and a grubby white shirt, jeans and black boots. If he was trying to convey a piratical appearance it was working but for the delicate spectacles he wore.

The man stood up from his ornate seat and walked across. Two inches shorter, he had to look up into Cody's eyes but Cody felt no comfort in his greater size. The man was enveloped in a potent aura of psychosis, a glitter of radicalism flickering in his eyes like a distant, volatile star. The man briefly looked at Cody's mouth and then back into his eyes. Cody caught sight of a large, curved sabre stuffed into his belt, the polished blade flashing in the firelight.

'Welcome,' he said.

His voice was soft but all the more chilling for it. Cody made a stab at confidence.

'Who are you?' he demanded.

The man smiled brightly, white teeth flashing.

'Didn't you know?' He leaned closer. 'I'm the president.'

A ripple of guttural laughs echoed through the hall from the surrounding militia. Cody glanced at the muscular, heavily armed men. Bikers, convicts, every kind of bad-ass imaginable all crammed into the hall with a group of captive scientists. It was like being the captain of the chess team facing off against the local chapter of the Hell's Angels.

Cody swallowed thickly and tried to maintain his composure.

'We're looking for someone.'

'That so?' the man uttered, his humour draining away. 'Well, you've found somebody now, haven't you sunshine?'

Cody held his ground before the smaller man, who turned away briefly and then spun back. A tightly balled fist ploughed into Cody's belly like a cannonball. Cody's eyes bulged and the breath blasted from his lungs as he dropped like a stone onto his knees on the marble floor, heard his own strained gagging echo up through the hall.

'Get your hands off him!'

Bethany struggled out from behind Cody as he fell. The man looked at her without interest.

'Get back in line,' he suggested quietly. 'Or I'll kill you.'

The man pulled the blade from his belt. Bethany stood her ground, ignoring the weapon.

'Even on his knees he's twice the man you are,' she shot back.

A flicker of surprise skittered across the man's features and he burst out laughing. Cody, still on his knees, heard the man walk by and stand in front of Bethany.

'How poetic!' he uttered. 'Sawyer is my name. And yours?'

Bethany remained silent. Sawyer smiled and then turned. Cody felt a surprisingly strong hand haul him upright and he managed to stagger to his feet. Sawyer set him straight, dusted off his jacket and then nodded in apparent satisfaction.

'There, good as new,' he chortled. 'Now, what's your name?'

Sawyer's bizarre mood swings unnerved Cody. It was an unfortunate truth that people were less scared of giant, muscular meatheads than they were of small, unpredictable weirdoes who had no apparent care for consequences. Sawyer looked every inch the kind of man who would welcome you with smiles and hugs one moment and without warning or reason bury his knife into you the next.

'Cody Ryan.'

Sawyer's eyes narrowed as he looked Cody up and down. 'I feel like I know you. You from Boston?'

Cody swiftly changed the subject. 'These are my friends. They're not any threat to you.'

Sawyer's jaw fractured into a thin smile.

'Everybody is a threat,' he replied. 'Where are you from? We saw your ship arrive in the bay.'

Cody thought hard before replying. He did not want to let Sawyer know that the captain of the Phoenix was among them.

'The Arctic,' he replied. 'We're all members of a survey team that got stranded up there. We couldn't get out until the summer thaw. Soon as we could we sailed here.'

Sawyer whistled, his eyes glittering with delight.

'Well, you've all had one hell of a ride then haven't you? An Arctic winter and now this?' He spread his hands wide to encompass the room. 'I don't know about you, but I'd like to think that we're not the only Bostonians in this town. We've got something in common now, Cody, you and your friends and I. We're all from this great city. We're on the same team.'

Cody glanced at the knuckleheads lingering nearby and forced a grin onto his face.

'Sure we are.'

Sawyer clapped a hand onto Cody's shoulder and looked deep into his eyes. 'We both know that you're smarter than that, don't we?' Cody didn't reply as Sawyer squeezed his shoulder. 'We've about as much in common as my henchmen have with Albert Einstein.'

Cody gritted his teeth as he let the thin veil of concord he'd tried to create slip away.

'I think that you're a lunatic surrounded by lots of other lunatics.'

Sawyer nodded and clapped Cody's shoulder again. 'That's the spirit. Now, I've got something to show you.'

Sawyer drew back from them and waved his men over. 'To the senate chamber!'

The militia hustled Cody and his companions out of the great hall and down a corridor that led to a grand staircase. They climbed upward onto what Cody guessed was the second storey and through an open doorway that led into a large amphitheatre, panelled in mahogany. Cody recognised it as the Senate Chamber. Rows of desks and seats had been removed, probably smashed up for firewood, leaving the chamber floor empty. A raised podium with an elevated seat that had once belonged to the Speaker of the House faced them as they descended into the hall.

Above, an upper gallery contained more seats and armed militia who looked down upon them as they were shoved into the centre of the chamber. Bizarrely, the Sacred Cod, a symbol of the early importance of the fishing industry to Boston, still hung over the public gallery.

Around the edge of the amphitheatre were large cages, wire meshed affairs that might once have contained large and dangerous zoo animals. Inside each cage were dozens of people, crammed together in the darkness. In the few moments Cody had to look at them, he guessed that maybe a couple of hundred prisoners languished inside the chamber.

Sawyer took the Speaker's seat and gestured to his men. Cody felt the lines connecting him to Bethany and the rest loosened and removed, but his wrists remained cuffed behind his back. They were shuffled into a line before Sawyer, and Cody saw the galleries above fill with more interested militia. He guessed that Sawyer had maybe thirty men under his control. The entire amphitheatre crackled to the sound of flames and flickered with an unearthly light that shimmered off the ornate but crumbling paintwork around them.

'Ladies and gentlemen,' Sawyer said grandly. 'Welcome home. You may have noticed some changes but we hope you like what we've done with the place. You may also be aware that there is an extreme shortage of basic necessities. We have water but little food. Therefore, our capacity to support newcomers is, I'm afraid, greatly diminished. To that end we must select carefully who we choose to join our great revival and who we choose to reject.'

Cody frowned and glanced sideways at Jake.

'He's lost it,' Jake whispered from the corner of his mouth.

Sawyer stood up and gestured to the cages circling the amphitheatre.

'Regrettably, not all citizens are able to join our ranks and instead are forced to become what they probably were all of their miserable lives. Cattle.'

Cody glanced over his shoulder at the cages. The people inside were emaciated, weakened and slumped against the walls of their cages. Soft moans and shuffles permeated the silence until Sawyer's voice echoed through the amphitheatre once more.

'Some things never change,' he uttered in a mock-sombre voice. 'But, alas, in their final act they give us a greater gift, that of sustenance for the stronger few.'

Cody felt his guts plunge as he realised what Sawyer was saying.

'They're food?' Charlotte shrieked in horror.

Sawyer smiled and patted his belly. 'Needs must, and what good are they dead? If they're going to expire we might as well make use of them.' He reached in beneath his leather coat and pulled out a pistol. 'Now, which ones of you would be best cooked?'

Cody shook his head. 'You've got it all the wrong way around. You've got a workforce here, manpower. You put them to work growing food then you wouldn't have shortages.'

Sawyer grinned. 'One step ahead of you, my friend. Our workforce tends fields inside Boston Common. Unfortunately for us many of Boston's less civilised citizens often try to steal and plunder our hard-earned sustenance, so we have to shoot them. Then, some bright spark asked whether we shouldn't eat them too? Who'd have thought it? So we ended up shooting them and then eating them. Two birds, one stone.'

'And what happens when there's nobody left?' Jake challenged Sawyer. 'You gonna eat yourself?'

Sawyer stepped up close to Jake. 'No,' he whispered. Cody saw Sawyer glance at Jake's mouth. 'We'll just follow the herd, like lions on the African plains. There are millions of people out there, scattered and wandering, too damned stupid to look after themselves.' Sawyer looked at the rest of the group. 'What you see here is an emergency reserve. We're not animals or barbarians. We fish and we grow what we can, though that's not been much what with the winter and all. But when times get hard, what else are we to do?'

Sawyer returned to Cody.

'Now, you're a smart man Mister Ryan, I can tell that. You're a scientist, right?'

'MIT,' Cody replied.

'Good,' Sawyer murmured. 'So, Mister MIT scientist, you can tell me where your safe haven is and why you've come from there to here in your ship.'

Cody swallowed thickly. 'We didn't come from a safe haven.'

'Really?' Sawyer sneered. 'All of you, well fed and fit, leaping around in Boston having come here in a big pretty ship? You want me to believe that you're not hiding something from me? You mean you can't even tell me and my boys here where the hell the big suits went before anarchy kicked off?'

Cody blinked. 'Big suits?'

'The politicians!' Sawyer shouted in praise as he lifted his arms up toward the senate ceiling, his voice echoing. 'Our beloved leaders who fled just hours before our wonderful world came tumbling down. Those hallowed men who left us to face the Great Darkness alone.'

'We don't know,' Cody replied.

Sawyer looked at him pityingly. 'You don't know?'

Hank Mears spoke for the first time.

'We had the same idea,' he said. 'But so far we've not found anything to suggest where they might have gone.'

Sawyer looked at the big man with interest. 'How would you have known, if you were stuck up in the Arctic?'

'We had the Internet,' Jake replied, 'and a military airfield close by. The troops ducked out a few hours before the storm hit, left us there much like the politicians left the rest of the world behind.'

Sawyer appeared to lose his psychotic aura for a moment. 'What storm?'

'You didn't know?' Cody asked in amazement.

'Do I sound like I know?!' Sawyer raged, the pistol thumping up against Cody's head.

Bethany stepped forward. 'A solar storm,' she said, 'the biggest in recorded history. It shorted the power grids of every industrialised nation, stopped the power. Everything fell apart after that because the damage was so widespread there was no way to fix everything fast enough to prevent total collapse.'

Sawyer lowered the pistol, stared at Bethany. 'Every nation? You mean the whole world?'

'There's nothing left, anywhere,' Bethany confirmed. 'Apart from this supposed safe haven that people keep talking about, if you believe in it. Eden.'

Cody saw something flicker like a lost shadow behind Sawyer's eyes, a hint of regret and dismay at the scale of mankind's downfall. For a brief moment the psychotic leader was gone and was replaced by a small and broken man.

'The military left before the storm?' Sawyer echoed her comment as he turned away thoughtfully. 'So they must have known.'

'They knew,' Hank Mears nodded. 'Question is: what did they do about it, and where?'

'There were no warnings here in Boston?' Charlotte asked Sawyer. 'No attempt to let the people know?'

Sawyer shook his head. 'We just woke up in the morning and there was nothing. Only thing I remember is seeing news reports about bright aurora over Mexico. Boston was covered by heavy cloud, so we didn't see much of anything.'

Cody stepped forward. 'We're all in the same boat here, and our country had emancipation for a reason. Starting anew with slaves isn't going to work because it didn't work before.'

Sawyer peered sideways at Cody as he paced up and down. 'Really, doctor? And what would you, the great and the wise scientist, have me do?'

'Work with people, not against them,' Cody urged. 'Oppression has always led to discontent and rebellion. Your prisoners will rise up against you sooner or later.'

'Let them,' Sawyer shrugged. 'They'll be replaced.'

'You're not that kind of man.'

'And how, exactly, would you know that?' Sawyer asked.

'You're no killer. You've got this little army around you but you're as human as the rest of us.'

'You doubt my motivation?' Sawyer asked.

Cody swallowed thickly. 'This isn't about doubt, motivation or anything else. If we don't all cooperate then no matter how much power you have right now all of it will be for nothing. History shows us that oppressed people will always fight back and will eventually always overcome their oppressors.'

'Is that so?' Sawyer uttered.

'There's a saying,' Cody replied. 'Those who fail to learn the lessons of history are forced to relive them.'

Sawyer inclined his head and nodded as he raised an eyebrow.

'Then I hope that you'll learn this lesson of history.'

Sawyer turned and fired a single shot that thundered out across the amphitheatre.

Blood spilled from Bradley Trent's chest and a fine spray of blood and tissue burst from his back as the bullet passed through and he collapsed.

'No!'

Charlotte's shriek was almost as loud as the gunshot as she threw herself down beside Bradley. It took only a single glance at the soldier's blank expression to know that he had died instantly.

29

Charlotte wrapped her arms around Bradley's body and buried her face against his neck as Cody gaped at Sawyer in disbelief. Sauri stood immobile, his dark eyes fixed upon their psychotic gaoler. Sawyer reached across and yanked Cody forward, jammed the pistol up against his jaw as he raged into Cody's face.

'You think I can't tell the difference between scientists and soldiers, Mister Genius? You think me a fool? Now, about this Eden you mentioned?'

Cody swivelled his eyes to look down at Bradley's body, still unable to process the fact that the soldier was gone. In a blink of an eye the man who had featured so heavily in their lives had been extinguished like a candle flame pinched between the fingers of an uncaring psychopath.

Cody turned back to Sawyer, flushed with an unexpected zeal of his own. 'Bite me.'

Sawyer grinned. 'Not today, but soon.'

Sawyer gestured to his men as he shoved Cody away. 'Put them in the cages. They're on work detail for the morning.'

The guards grabbed them and shoved them towards the nearest of the cages. Bethany struggled to keep up with Cody as he walked, shrugging off the big hands of the militia guiding them. Behind, he heard Charlotte sobbing as she was dragged off Bradley's body.

The guard in front of Cody reached up and unlocked a heavy padlock that sealed the handle of a cage shut. The ragged prisoners incarcerated within barely looked up as the cage door was rolled open to the sound of metal on metal. Cody was pushed inside along with Bethany and Jake and the door slammed shut behind them. Sauri was shoved into a cage to their right.

Cody turned and saw Hank and Charlotte propelled into a cage further down the line, the heavy door slamming shut and echoing around the amphitheatre as the guards stalked away. Charlotte collapsed onto her knees on the metal floor of the cage, bowing her head and shielding her face with her hands. Hank looked down at her in silence and then turned away to survey their surroundings.

The prisoners in the cages made no effort to communicate with the new arrivals, instead avoiding eye contact as they recoiled away from them and huddled against the bars of the cage.

'This is what I was afraid of,' Hank Mears uttered across to them. 'Now we're stuck here.'

'Sawyer's a psychopath,' Jake said to Cody. 'I don't think he's kidding when he says they'll eat us.'

'Jesus,' Cody uttered, rubbing his temples with his finger and thumb as he whispered out to Hank. 'Any chance that Taylor and the crew will attempt a rescue?'

Hank shook his head. 'They'll run at the first chance they get if Saunders can't hold them. Nothing here for them and with me cooped up there's not much to stop them from taking the ship wherever they want to go.'

Cody nodded, unwilling to think about how quickly their plan to leave Boston had been scuppered by Sawyer's militia. He caught the gaze of other prisoners trapped in the cages, watching him with defeated eyes. Many slept, presumably exhausted from their labours out on Boston Common. Each prisoner had a bowl alongside them, picked clean of whatever had been within. From the smell, Cody guessed some kind of potatoes and maybe small amounts of chicken. Sawyer's men might have managed to capture a few domesticated fowl before they became extinct in the wake of mankind's fall.

'We shouldn't have come here,' Sauri said softly. 'We've gained nothing and lost much.'

'Sawyer thinks that Eden exists too,' Cody replied. 'We've got to figure out a way of getting him onside long enough to get out of here.'

Hank Mears called across. 'That radio message you intercepted would be a damned good start.'

Cody nodded and saw Charlotte look up at him, her cheeks smeared with tears as she launched herself across the cage to bang against the bars.

'You bastard!' she screamed. 'You killed Brad! You killed him!'

'Sawyer killed Brad,' Jake snapped at her. 'Not us. Not any of us.'

'The message,' Hank snapped at Cody. 'What did it say?'

'There was a code.'

'What kind of code?' Jake asked. His expression was crestfallen, as though the one person he could trust had let him down. Which, Cody realised, he kind of had.

'Morse,' Cody said, still unable to bring himself to reveal everything, 'maybe a cypher code or something.'

A cypher code was a simple means of concealing a message by using alternative figures to represent established alphabetical letters. Done two or three times, even the most complex computers could struggle with the cypher, especially if the cypher-key was based on something truly random. Cody had once based a cypher code for his credit card PIN on the number of birds that flew within fifty yards of his house in a ten minute period.

'You didn't hear anybody speaking?' Sauri asked.

Cody exhaled. 'Briefly,' he admitted, 'a man.'

Charlotte's rage faltered as she digested what he had said. 'An old man?'

'I don't know,' Cody said. 'It was a weak transmission.'

Charlotte's expression collapsed into something between regret and disgust.

'My father might have sent me a message and you knew about it!' she raged. 'You knew about it and you never said a word. We could have sailed past Boston! This never needed to happen!'

'I didn't know that your father might have the means to be looking for you any more than you did,' Cody shot back at her. 'It meant nothing at the time, except that maybe somewhere there were people who had survived.'

'Why hide it at all?' Jake asked.

'We couldn't trust Hank's crew with the knowledge,' Cody replied. 'We'd have never got this far. And you wanted to find your father just as much as I wanted to find my family.'

'If I'd known about the damned message I wouldn't have come here!' Charlotte snapped. 'None of us would have come here!'

'Bethany would,' Cody said in reply. 'Her brother's here.'

Bethany's head dropped at the mention of her younger brother.

'Whatever the purpose of the message,' Hank said, 'the person who sent it must have had electrical power to do so.'

'That's right,' Cody agreed as he glanced at the other prisoners, 'and we need to keep this to ourselves. It could be our only leverage.'

'Not entirely,' Sauri said. 'Charlotte's father might have sent the message, and she's here. If Sawyer knows about it then she's safe.'

'Not necessarily,' Cody replied. 'And it means nothing if we're all dead. We need to find a way to use the information to get us all the hell out of here. We need to stick together.'

'This your idea of sticking together?' Sauri uttered. 'You got Bradley killed.'

'No he didn't,' Jake snapped. 'Sawyer killed Bradley because he was the most likely threat, a trained soldier. It removed the potential for rebellion, or so Sawyer probably believes. The rest of us he thinks are just scientists.'

'Regardless,' Hank replied. 'I'll do the damned talking from now on, unless anybody's got any complaints?'

Nobody spoke.

'Jesus,' Cody uttered in exasperation. 'We need to work together. What's to stop you from negotiating your own release?'

'Nothing,' Hank replied. 'Except that Sawyer will believe what I say because he'll assume I'm loyal to all of you. You're his leverage over me, and we'll let him keep thinking that.'

Cody shook his head and looked away from the captain. He cast his gaze out of the side of the cage to the one alongside it. Faces looked back at him, scoured of emotion, eyes glazed with the haze of the defeated.

The shambling, bedraggled mass of prisoners shifted slightly as something moved amongst them. Cody's gaze drifted down between them as a small hand shoved bodies aside and a pair of big brown eyes peered cautiously between pairs of dirty jeans and grubby sleeves.

Cody experienced a transient blurring of his vision as he saw the small face look out at him. Soft skin was marred by dirt, the eyes haunted by confusion and fear, but the blonde hair curling down to the shoulders sent a pulse of disbelief racing like a freight train through Cody's heart. He felt the earth shift beneath his feet, felt his balance fail him as the child pushed through the crowd and a tiny smile flickered in recognition.

His breath fell from his lips as though torn from within him as the little girl reached out and touched the bars of the cage, her gaze fixed upon his from just a few feet away. Cody fell into the bars of his cage as tears spilled from his eyes and he slid down onto his knees.

'Maria.'

Suddenly every moment of his suffering was lost into a maelstrom of joy that felt like grief as Cody saw his little girl standing before him, too far to reach and yet now so close. Her voice was tiny as she spoke.

'Dadda?'

Cody pressed his face against the bars of the cell as though he could push through them by sheer force of will as he cried openly, not caring who witnessed it. He reached out, stretched his hand as far as he could toward Maria, but she was too far away.

Hands grabbed his shoulders and yanked Cody away from the bars. Cody shouted out, but a hand clamped over his mouth as Jake whispered into his ear.

'Don't let them see you! They'll use her against us!'

Maria's face collapsed into confusion and grief. Jake released him immediately as Cody gathered his wildly flying emotions and saw the faces of the other prisoners in the cage with Maria looking at them both.

'It's okay,' Cody whispered across to Maria, forcing a smile through his tears. 'It's okay, everything's okay.'

'Daddy?' she asked. 'Where's mom?'

Cody felt his throat constrict and his hands were shaking as he replied. 'I don't know.'

Maria watched him with interest as Sauri moved protectively alongside her. Cody stared at them both for a long moment and then turned to whisper to Hank in his cage.

'You sure you can get Sawyer on-side, with us?'

Hank nodded. 'Only way we're getting out of here is with his blessing. We need to convince him that we're too valuable to let go. We get back to the Phoenix, sail, and then toss Sawyer overboard.'

'What about my brother?' Bethany asked. 'He might be here in Boston too.'

'That's a long shot,' Jake said to her. 'Cody finding Maria was probably a one in a thousand chance.'

'But he did,' Bethany said. 'I can't just leave without trying.'

'He could be in the country by now,' Hank insisted. 'Cody's daughter's probably here because she was too young to run far. Lucky she's still alive, got people caring for her.'

'My brother's seven years old,' Bethany said.

'Sawyer's men don't appear to have eaten any children,' Charlotte pointed out, 'or women. Maybe Beth's right.'

Hank shook his head.

'You've all got to make a choice,' he warned Bethany. 'You're either leaving or staying because we can't do this piecemeal. One way or the other, my ship is going to sail out of this hellhole and it's not coming back. I intend to be aboard, and anybody who isn't there when we weigh anchor is stuck here for good. Make your choice.'

Hank turned away from them and walked to the bars of his cage. He thumped them with one hand and caught the attention of one of the guards.

'I need to speak to Sawyer,' he said. 'He'll be real interested in what I have to say to him.'

The guard looked at Hank for a moment as though considering whether to ignore him, but then thought better of it and stalked away.

Dean Crawford

30

'Something's gone wrong.'

Saunders stood by the Phoenix's stern rail and looked out across the channel to the city skyline. The deserted skyscrapers and city blocks were cast in sharp silhouette against the fiery sunset washing across the horizon, mankind's harsh and angular architecture clashing with the elegant freehand strokes of creation that spanned the skies.

'Maybe they decided to stay overnight in the city,' Reece suggested.

'I doubt it,' Saunders said as he lowered his binoculars and packed them away. 'It's likely cold, dark and uncomfortable wherever they go. They'd have signalled if there was a change of plan.'

'So what do we do?' Reece asked.

Saunders turned from the rail. 'We wait, and we keep a permanent watch up just in case.'

As they turned they saw the crew watching them silently from the main deck, shadows amongst the shadows, dark expressions haunting their features. Muir, Ice and the others hovered like vultures near a kill.

'I don't like this,' Reece whispered. 'We're outnumbered.'

Saunders grinned. 'Only by hands. We've got the bullets, remember?'

Reece looked down at the crew, who refused to meet his eye as they lingered in the lengthening shadows.

'Who keeps watch when we're sleeping?' Reece asked him as he swiped his black hair away from his eyes.

Saunders' grin slipped a little. 'I'll skip sleep for tonight, until the captain gets back. 'Kay?'

The first mate made his way over to the wheelhouse, Reece staying close by as Saunders kicked a chair into position behind the wheel and eased himself into it. He hefted his shotgun into place, resting it between the handles of the wheel to point down the ship.

'Believe me, son, there ain't nobody coming at us from here. Now, go into the wheelhouse and get everything ready, just like I said. If the men decide they're going to try to leave port we need control of the wheel to stop them.'

Reece nodded. 'Barricade, right?'

'Damned right,' Saunders nodded. 'That's where we'll stand until the captain comes back, okay?'

Reece nodded and walked back into the wheelhouse, shutting the door behind him as he began dragging heavy boxes alongside the door and on top of the hatch to the 'tween decks before it got dark, praying with every step that they would not have to defend them.

*

Taylor rowed the launch silently through the silky black water, Seth matching his smooth pulls and watching over his shoulder as the Phoenix loomed large before them. In the darkness, Seth could only pick the ship out when her masts eclipsed the stars in the night sky.

The skyline of Boston was as black as the sky above. Even now it seemed odd to know that the vast city lay so close by in utter silence and desolation. Once, bright street lights would have flickered in reflection across the waters of the channel, thousands of office buildings glowing like a galaxy across the shoreline. To see it so dark unnerved Seth, as though he were floating alone in an immense and unpopulated universe.

He had led Taylor out of the city as soon as he'd realised that Hank, Cody and the rest of the idiots they'd picked up in the Arctic were pinned down. Seth knew an opportunity when he saw it, just like he knew a lost cause. Chasing around for some mythical damned city would get them about as far as looking for goddamned Atlantis, and with Boston now the domain of the insanely dangerous or terminally infected he saw nothing useful to hang around for.

The launch had been where they'd left it. Sure, they had been forced to wait out the sunset before rowing to the Phoenix, but in total darkness and silence their approach had gone unnoticed.

'We're almost there,' Taylor said between heaves.

'Keep your voice down,' Seth whispered. 'Sound travels further at night, especially across water.'

The Phoenix was illuminated by a pair of faint lanterns hung from the stern, their dim light only visible from close proximity to the ship. Seth guessed that Saunders would not want to advertise the ship's presence to anybody on shore in Boston after dark, a wise move as they had found out to their cost.

The city was just as brutal a haven for thuggery and violence as Seth had feared, filled with sick citizens wandering in infected crowds and dangerous gangs preying upon them. The sooner they got out of here the better and to hell with Hank and his goddamned Eden.

Taylor eased up as they approached the ship in silence, the boat slipping through the water without a sound as it drifted to the Phoenix's bow. Taylor knew that the Phoenix was large enough that boarding her at the stern would be impossible, but beneath the schooner's bowsprit was a series of looped rigging lines that provided a way up onto the deck.

With the launch hidden beneath the ship's bow, Taylor stood up and balanced in the boat as he reached up and gripped one of the lines. With a heave of effort he hauled himself up and swung his legs around the rope, crawling up to the bowsprit in the darkness and then easing his way down onto the deck.

Seth followed Taylor up onto the Phoenix's deck, and they crouched in the darkness as Taylor slipped his rifle from his shoulder and checked the mechanism.

'I don't see anybody,' Taylor whispered.

'Probably at the wheel house,' Seth guessed. 'Saunders won't let anybody else in there as long as the captain's away.'

'So what do we do?'

Seth crept away across the deck in silence, and Taylor gripped his pistol tighter as he followed.

*

Reece leaned against the bulwarks, the deck bathed in a faint but comforting glow from the pair of lights hanging from the stern rail. Beyond, the inky blackness of the water merged seamlessly with the darkened decks.

There, near the mainmast, several of the crew lingered. An occasional flare from a cigarette glowed against their faces, making them look like demons lingering at the gates of Hades.

Reece was not fooled by Saunders' confidence in the captain. The crew were regularly swapping watch, catching some sleep as others watched. They knew that it was only a matter of time before exhaustion got the better of Saunders, and without him there was no way that Reece could hold off the entire remaining crew on his own.

He looked down at the heavy pistol in his hand, and wondered not for the first time just how the hell he had gone from a career in biochemistry to a sailor on an antiquated ship holding off a mutinous crew with a handgun he'd never fired before.

None of this had been their fault, and yet since the storm he had seen Bobby Leary cover for him only to be mauled to death by a polar bear, and then seen his remains eaten by the crew of the Phoenix. God only knew what had happened to the captain and his friends ashore, but after everything else Reece guessed that it was not good.

He looked up at Saunders. The old man was sitting with his eyes closed, his chin resting on his chest. Reece looked at the crew. They remained in place, watching, waiting and biding their time. It would not last much longer, a few hours maybe? Then Reece and Saunders would be overrun, and then…

He shivered as he thought of what might become of them and forced the thought from his mind.

A movement to his right caught his attention and he looked across the decks to see the crew vanish into the darkness. Reece squinted, trying to see where they were going, but only silence and blackness loomed. He turned and gave Saunders a nudge with his boot.

Saunders blinked awake, looking up as Reece indicated the deck.

'Where have they gone?' he whispered.

'Just walked off,' Reece replied. 'Maybe they got bored of waiting.'

Saunders's finger touched the safety catch of the shotgun as he shook his head. 'Not likely. Stay here.'

Saunders eased himself out of his chair and crept forward to the edge of the light, peering into the darkness near the mainmast.

'Careful,' Reece whispered, his grip on his pistol fierce.

Saunders edged further into the darkness, careful to keep his back to the stern and cover any retreat he might be forced to make. He took another step and then a sharp crack rolled out over the deck. For a moment Reece thought that one of the rigging lines had snapped, but then Saunders cried out as his leg buckled beneath him and he crashed down onto the hard deck.

Reece leapt forward to help the old man, but froze as Taylor and Seth loomed out of the darkness amidships, Seth's pistol aimed at Saunders.

'Don't move!' Taylor growled.

Saunders rolled on the deck, one hand clasping his wounded leg as the other swung the shotgun around to point at Taylor.

'Don't even think about it!' Seth yelled as he changed position. 'You shoot and I'll put a bullet in Reece's brain!'

Saunders glanced up at Reece. Reece stared back in horror as the rest of the crew swarmed in behind Taylor and Seth. Muir nipped forward and stamped the shotgun down against the deck before Saunders could respond, then yanked it from the old man's grasp.

'Give up the pistol,' Seth snapped.

Reece stared at Seth's tattooed visage, half in shadow from the stern lights, his eyes glinting like evil points of light and his tattoos looking like dark veins lacing his skin.

'Man the wheel!' Saunders managed to shout above his pain. 'Don't quit, Reece!'

'Shut up!' Muir roared as he stamped a foot down on the old man's knee.

Saunders screamed in pain and Reece felt rage and fear flush through his veins as he stared at Seth.

'Drop the pistol!' Seth shouted.

Reece raised a placating hand at Seth and crouched down, pointing the pistol at the deck. His shadow across the crew vanished as he ducked below the lights from the stern and into darkness. Seth's features squinted as he tried to watch Reece.

Reece whipped the pistol up to point at Muir and then he pulled the trigger.

Time seemed to grind into a slow-motion blur of silent movement as the gunshot rang in Reece's ears. The recoil snapped Reece's wrist back, a flash of muzzle flame spurting from the weapon to illuminate Muir's face as Reece's vision momentarily blurred from the bullet's shockwave.

Muir's head snapped back as the bullet smashed through his forehead and exited the back of his skull to smack into the mainmast. A fine haze of black blood splattered the deck and his legs quivered as they collapsed beneath him.

The crew scattered in surprise as Taylor whirled to aim the shotgun at Reece. Muir dropped like a stone onto the deck as the pistol dropped from his grasp. Saunders grabbed for the weapon as Taylor backed up and fired the shotgun.

Reece hurled himself to one side and hit the wheelhouse door as the shotgun's blast peppered the panelled wall beside him. Reece aimed the pistol at Taylor just in time to see Saunders fire at the big man.

Taylor folded over as the bullet impacted low in his belly and he collapsed on top of the shotgun. Saunders fired twice more, Taylor's huge bulk shuddering with each impact of the bullets before he fell silent and still.

Reece aimed the pistol out across the decks but he could see nothing of the rest of the crew. Saunders groaned and sucked in painful breaths of air as Reece hurried across to him.

The old man's knee was a bloodied mess that soaked his jeans and had spilled onto the deck.

'Stay at the wheel,' Saunders gasped. 'Get the guns and get back in there!'

Reece tried to grab the old man by the arm to haul him to a safer spot but Saunders shook him off angrily. 'Man the goddamned wheel!'

Reece staggered backwards. He turned and managed to pull the shotgun from beneath Taylor's inert body and retreated up the steps to the wheelhouse, back into the glow of the stern lanterns. He realised that he was shaking, his face damp. He touched his hand to his face and his fingers came away wet with tears.

'Lock the door!' Saunders yelled.

Reece reached out for the door and slammed it shut, then pushed down hard on the door brace until it slid into position. He turned the key in the lock and backed away until he bumped into the wheel.

In the darkness he glimpsed through the windows the faintest hint of light across the eastern sky. Maybe a couple more hours and then he would be able to see everything again.

He was about to let hope creep through his veins when a voice called to him from outside.

'Now, Reece, we're going to make this just as easy as we can for y'all!'

Reece lurched to the wheelhouse windows and saw Seth standing over Saunders. Seth had Saunders' pistol in one hand and a belaying pin in the other.

'How 'bout you open that door for us?' Seth yelled.

Reece gave his best shot at a confident answer. 'No can do!' he shouted. He sounded like a five year old cornered by the high school football team.

Seth cackled a laugh. 'That's a shame, boy. Don't want to get all medieval on your asses!'

Moments later he felt sick as he saw Seth drive the belaying pin into Saunders' wound. The old man writhed and screamed in agony as metal grated against bone.

31

Cody leaned back against the thick bars of his cage as he waited for Sawyer's henchman to return for Hank. The vast amphitheatre echoed with soft shuffles and the murmurs of other prisoners, and in the cage to Cody's left he could see Charlotte asleep and Hank sitting with his chained crucifix in his hand, fingering the icon in thoughtful silence.

Cody fixed his gaze back upon Maria.

She lay asleep on a pile of old jackets in the cage to his right, covered in a shawl and watched over by a young girl of maybe twenty years old called Lena who seemed to have taken Maria under her wing. Her protector's face was stained with grime and her cheeks hollow with starvation but she lay alongside Maria as the little girl slept, unwilling to leave her side.

Sauri watched over the both of them.

Cody had learned much from the young girl in the past hour. Lena Harris had been a downtown bank clerk, she had told him, before the storm hit. Two brothers, both parents, a nice home just outside the city. The perfect suburban image of the American Dream realised. Both her parents had been killed in the riots in Boston as they tried to find food for their family: her mother had been gang raped and shot, her father beaten to death. Her brothers had died attempting to protect Lena from more rapists weeks later. Lena had been caught but had escaped without molestation soon after, only to land in the hands of Sawyer's men a few months later as she scavenged the city for morsels in the bitter snows of winter. She had made little attempt to escape, barely able to walk let alone run.

Lena had found Maria in the cages and instinctively protected the tiny girl. Half of the people in her cage had suffered likewise, seen families murdered or die from exposure or disease, and they too were protective of the young in their company no matter whose child they might have been.

Such humanity in the wake of unspeakable barbarism, like small flowers blossoming amid smouldering plains of ash, tugged hard at Cody's heart.

'How long has she been here?' Cody whispered across to her as he looked at Maria.

Both Charlotte and Bethany were watching them in the darkness, Jake standing opposite Cody to block the view of the guards lingering near the exits.

'Two months, give or take,' Lena whispered back. 'I don't know about other militia in the city but I've never seen Sawyer kill or harm children.'

'Wow,' Jake murmured, 'he's all heart.'

'Anybody ever escaped?' Cody asked her.

'Sure,' Lena replied. 'The guards often brawl among themselves and people slip away when their backs are turned, but not for a long time now.'

'How come?'

Lena cast him a foreboding look through the bars of her cage. 'You see the walls outside when you came here, the bodies?'

When Cody nodded, Lena sighed and gently stroked Maria's hair.

'If Sawyer's men capture an escapee, they bring them here and throw them back into the cages. Then, they take the closest friend or family of that escapee and strap them to the fences outside to die.' Lena looked down at Maria.

'That's how they guarantee obedience. They punish the innocent.'

Cody swallowed thickly as he looked at Maria.

'And the rest of the prisoners?' he asked her. 'Sawyer said that they're food.'

Lena nodded. 'If things get hard, yes,' she replied. 'They'll take the oldest or weakest and kill them to eat. It was worst in the winter, but nobody's been taken for a while now.'

It was said with such a frank expression that Cody wondered briefly if Lena's mind had gone, that she was no longer capable of being emotionally moved by the horrors that she had witnessed. Then he watched her hand stroking Maria's hair and realised that he did not fear for his daughter, that his instincts and her actions assured him that Maria's protector was still sound of mind. Only her soul had been scoured of its emotion, as though she were somehow hollow like a ghost, a shadowy reflection of the young girl she had once been.

'I don't understand how Maria got here,' Cody said. 'How did she survive the Great Darkness?'

'She was with a group,' Lena replied. 'A bunch of scientists from MIT so I was told, stuck together after the storm. Wives, friends, family or whatever, they tried to make a go of it and get out of the city.'

Cody sighed in relief as he realised that his colleagues at the famous institute must have guessed what was happening before the rest of the population. They would have gathered together, made calls, got wives and parents and children alongside them, stockpiled and prepared for the onrushing collapse of civilisation.

Maybe Danielle made it out with them too, with Maria, but got separated somehow.

'You hear anything of her mother from the people at MIT?' he asked. 'Her name was Danielle.'

Lena's eyes flicked to Cody's at the mention of the name, and he saw within them a grief that seemed to have become a constant companion in all of their lives as she whispered in reply.

'She died.'

Cody swallowed as silent tears flooded his eyes once more. 'How?'

Lena's reply seemed to come from far away. 'They were attacked, by looters searching for food. The children were sent south with younger survivors to flee while the parents stayed to hold back the looters. I guess they failed.'

Cody buried his head into his arm, tried to hold back the disbelief and the shame that he felt. He had not been there. He should have been there. He had fled when his family needed him the most and now his wife was dead, nothing but a memory.

'The group held out for a few months before they were attacked,' Lena whispered in the darkness. 'They looked after the children, kept them safe. I guess Sawyer's men picked them up soon after and brought them here. Maria's never been alone, Cody. There was always somebody looking out for her.'

Cody felt fresh grief sweep across him as he heard the young girl trying to console him, after all that she had endured. He felt Bethany's hand rest on his shoulder but he could not bring himself to look at either of the women.

'I heard you all talking earlier,' Lena said, 'something about signals, from outside the city?'

Cody, relieved at the change of subject, managed to master his grief. For reasons he did not want to think about it was getting easier each time to swallow his pain, like a bitter pill or a noxious fume endured so many times the brain becomes immune to it.

'There may be other survivors, organised people,' he said. 'But we don't know where they are.'

'You called it Eden,' Lena replied. 'People talk about it from time to time, a safe haven.'

'Just like I said,' Hank whispered from somewhere behind them.

'What have you heard?' Cody asked her.

Lena shrugged and her shoulders slumped slightly as though fatigue was slowly wearing her down.

'Rumours mostly,' she replied. 'A lot of survivors believe in it, and that somehow people will come back with working machines again and everything will be restored to the way it once was.' She looked up at Cody. 'You think that it's true?'

Cody stared at her for a long moment. The temptation to lie and to tell her that everything was going to be all right was almost overwhelming, but when he looked at his daughter, alive and well, he knew that he owed Lena more than that.

'No, it's not true,' he said. 'Things will never be the same again.' Lena nodded to herself in silence as though she had known all along as Cody went on. 'Silicon chips have been burnt, cables will have frayed, power-stations are crumbling, materials and pipelines decaying. It's already too late, Lena. The world we knew is gone and it won't come back in our lifetimes.'

A silence descended in the cages around him and Cody realised belatedly that every pair of eyes were watching him. A lone voice spoke up, tremulous with age.

'You sure about that, son?'

'I used to work at MIT,' Cody replied into the darkness. 'If there was any chance humanity could recover from this, believe me I'd champion it. But there isn't. All we have is each other.'

Heavy footfalls alerted Cody and he turned away from the cage bars as a muscular man stepped up and shoved a key into the locking mechanism of Hank's cage.

'You,' he snapped as he pointed at the captain, 'with me, now.'

Hank stepped away from the bars as the door was hauled open and stepped outside. Another of Sawyer's thugs snapped a pair of handcuffs around the captain's wrists and shoved him in the general direction of the exit.

Nobody said anything until Hank and his escort were out of sight.

'You think he'll do us right?' Jake whispered, almost to himself.

'We don't have much choice but to trust him,' Charlotte uttered as she glared across at Cody. 'Can't trust anybody else.'

Cody did not reply but Bethany shook her head. 'We should trust in ourselves. Hank will sail out of here if he gets the chance. He owes us nothing.'

'Better than being stuck with Cody,' Charlotte snapped.

Cody ignored her as he turned back to Lena.

'Do you know who Sawyer was, before the storm? How did he come to lead these people?'

Lena shook her head, her eyes heavy with sleep. 'I don't know. I don't want to know.'

Cody sighed as he looked about the vast hall and listened to the moans of the sick and the weak, a hymn of mankind's suffering echoing around what had once represented the power of government and the security of democracy. All gone now. Mankind had lost far more than just the ability to light and heat buildings or power vehicles: he had lost the will to succeed, the spark of resilience and innovation that had driven him to excel and overcome. Mankind had given up, and only those born of more brutal minds held sway over the beleaguered remains of a once great nation.

'We've got to get out of here,' Cody whispered, 'even if Hank doesn't manage to turn Sawyer.'

A man with lank, greasy black hair and dull eyes shook his head as he squatted nearby.

'Ain't gonna happen, boy,' he murmured. 'You heard what the lady said. You run, we die. You won't get out of this cage because we won't let you.'

Cody looked up and saw that the other thirty or so people in the cage were still watching him in silence, but the air in the cage had become charged as though a live current seethed through the air between them.

'They'll *eat* you,' Cody said. 'Is that what you want?'

The old man shrugged his emaciated shoulders, a bitter smile fracturing his jaw.

'Ain't much left to live for is there? Why worry about it?'

*

Hank Mears was prodded by a chunky guard into an office one storey above the great hall, where a long mahogany table was surrounded by chairs. At the head of the table sat Sawyer. He leaned on the table with one arm as the other shovelled steaming chunks of meat and roasted potatoes and vegetables into his mouth. He looked up briefly as he ate and gestured with his fork to a seat opposite.

Hank walked to the seat before Sawyer's goon could shove him there and sat down, watching the meat that Sawyer ate. Sawyer noticed the direction of his gaze.

'Dog,' he reassured the captain between mouthfuls.

'That's all right then.'

Sawyer popped the last morsel of what had once been a man's best friend into his mouth and dabbed at his lips with a napkin. He sipped a pale brown liquid from a glass and frowned at it.

'We haven't quite got this stuff right yet,' he said. 'Alcohol brewed from potatoes. It's called *potch*, from the Irish drink. Some of my crew learned to make it in prison.'

'I'm shocked,' Hank uttered as he glanced at the guard standing nearby. 'They seem such nice boys.'

Sawyer watched Hank from the corner of his eye as he drained his glass and dabbed again at his lips.

'You're no scientist,' he said. 'What's your story?'

'Navy,' Hank replied. 'I was at sea when the storm hit.'

'Safest place to be,' Sawyer said. 'You should have stayed out there. Why come to Boston?'

Hank eased himself back in his chair. 'Eden.'

'You won't find it here.'

'I'm not looking for it here,' Hank reasoned. 'My idea was that most people would have died in harsher climes in the north due to the hard winters there, so we'd be safer. The cold oceans are as abundant with life as the land is empty, so we could sail and fish on the move, only coming ashore for fresh water. It was working well enough when we detected a radio signal, very weak, coming from the far north.'

Sawyer's expression changed, his gaze fixed on Hank.

'You've got a working radio set?'

'Partially,' Hank admitted, 'a spare that we had in the ship's hold, packed in a powder store below the sea-line. It must have protected the circuits from the solar storm.'

Sawyer absent-mindedly dabbed at his lips with his napkin as he went on. 'So you're the captain of that ship, correct? And this signal you detected?'

'I'd hoped we'd found Eden,' Hank explained. 'We sailed north and found those scientists stranded up on Ellesmere Island. The signal we detected was their distress beacons. We picked them up and sailed south.'

Sawyer scowled and tossed the napkin onto the table. 'Then you're of no use to me.' He looked up at the guard. 'Get this asshole out of here.'

The escort moved behind Hank and reached out for him. Hank jerked up and backwards out of his seat, the back of his skull thumping into the man's nasal bridge with an audible crunch. The man grunted as his eyes rolled up into his head and he slumped backwards against the wall. Hank turned and drove a heavy boot into the guard's face, his jaw crunching under the blow.

Sawyer bolted out of his seat, one hand reaching for a pistol at his side, but Hank turned toward him and simply stood still.

'I haven't finished yet,' the captain said.

Sawyer looked at his fallen henchman, one hand fingering the butt of his pistol as he looked back at Hank.

'Make it worthwhile,' he replied, 'or you won't leave this room alive.'

Hank smiled, deflecting Sawyer's bravado. 'The scientists detected another signal at their base, before I got there. The coordinates of that signal are encoded. To have been detected so far north they must either have been emitted by a powerful source or relayed by a satellite that is still functional in orbit.'

Hank watched as Sawyer's mind digested what he had said.

'Military?' the man hazarded.

Hank nodded. In truth he had no idea, but he didn't give a damn as long as Sawyer played along.

'Can you find it?' Sawyer asked, 'the source?'

'I have five scientists with me,' Hank replied. 'I can find the source.'

Sawyer's eyes flickered with delight as though sunlight had broken through within, but almost instantly clouds of suspicion drifted in. He glanced at the thug still lying unconscious behind Hank.

'You'd have to leave your men behind,' Hank said, keeping his voice low. 'My ship can't take many people.'

'Who has these coordinates?' Sawyer demanded.

'Cody Ryan, the man you recognised and who tried to argue with you earlier.'

Sawyer's hand moved from his pistol to the handle of the long blade dangling from his belt.

'Good,' he murmured. 'This shouldn't take long.'

'You try that and you'll get nothing from him,' Hank warned. 'He's a stubborn son of a bitch and will cheerfully go to his grave knowing he's denied you what you want. He kept the existence of the signal from his own team for months.'

Sawyer glanced at Hank testily. 'Then he'll die and we'll find another way, agreed?'

Hank smiled again. 'I already have another way.'

Hank shuffled his hips and managed to get one of his cuffed hands into his jeans. From a pocket he produced a folded piece of newspaper that he tossed awkwardly onto the table in front of Sawyer.

Sawyer unfolded the paper and stared down at it for a long moment, then back up at Hank as a brutal smile creased his face.

32

Reece winced as he heard Saunders scream again, a grinding, drawn out sob of agony that rolled out across the lonely bay as Seth ground the belaying pin into the old man's leg.

'You comin' out yet Mister Reece?' Seth called.

Hatred seethed like acid through Reece's veins as he saw Seth's manic face in the feeble light of dawn now leaking across the decks. The sky above was laden with heavy clouds, slate grey and menacing as they drifted down from the north. Beyond the relative sanctuary of the harbour Reece could see that the water in the channel was rough and choppy.

The crew were standing back from Seth, watching as he waited for a response from Reece.

'Put him in a boat!' Reece yelled through the barricaded door. 'The same one you came here in! And dress his wound!'

'What the hell for?' Seth bellowed back.

'Do it!'

Seth stared at his companions and they nodded as one. Reece heard a soft, whispered conversation pass between them. Seth lifted the belaying pin away from Saunders as two of the crew gathered around the old man and began tending to him. Reece saw another man hurry away to fetch a medical kit.

'This don't change nothin'!' Seth yelled at Reece. 'We're coming in there, one way or th'other!'

'You want the ship or not?!' Reece shouted back. 'You do as I say or I'll burn her down right here in the harbour!'

Seth did not reply. Reece staggered back from the door and bumped against the wheel. He turned and looked at it for a long moment. As long as he remained barricaded inside the wheelhouse and the wheel was locked down, there was no way for the crew to steer the ship.

He knew that Seth would abandon them as soon as they took control of the Phoenix. They hated Saunders for his unyielding support of the captain, they hated their captain's ruthlessness and his pursuit of Eden and they hated Reece and the team from Alert. Reece guessed they'd probably be happier looting, plundering and raping like modern day pirates. That they would probably bring about their own downfall without Hank Mears' guiding hand was an irony that Reece doubted they would understand or even care about.

He looked at the wheel again.

The wheel was connected to a shaft in the hold that turned the ship's rudder. Thick metal chains ensured a link secure enough to take the battering of the open ocean's wildest weather. Reece glanced again out of the windows at the severe seas building out on the ocean, and on an impulse he moved around to the wheel stand and prised off the steerage panel's cover.

The steel steerage chain looped through links in the wheel and disappeared down into the depths of the ship. Reece ran his hand up the heavily greased chains and quickly found what he was looking for: a collapsible link, used to remove the steerage chain for cleaning and replacement.

Reece stood up and looked around the cabin until his eyes settled on some frayed para-cord lying coiled on the map table nearby. He picked it up and examined it. Probably five-hundred pound cord, no more. Not thick enough to take the immense strain of high seas. He turned and crouched behind the steerage chain again, and tied the cord to the links either side of the collapsible link, knotting them until they were secure. He then took a steel ruler from the map table and thrust it between the cords, twisting it until they began to draw together and take some of the strain off the collapsible link.

Reece grabbed his pistol with his free hand and turned it around, using the butt to push the collapsible edge of the chain-link in. With a heave of effort the link opened and he pulled it out of the chain.

Reece lifted the chain link out and then gently let the cord take the strain. With the ship in harbour it only had to bear the weight of the chain. He heard the cord creak under the strain but it held.

Reece slipped the spare link into his pocket and replaced the steerage panel. The wheel would hold in the calm waters of the harbour, but out on the ocean the huge stresses on the rudder would snap that para-cord long before the Phoenix made it to deeper water. Getting below decks and re-linking the chain would be near impossible before she was smashed to pieces on the shore. If Seth wanted the damned ship, he could take it with him to his grave.

'Come on out, Reece!'

Reece walked to the wheelhouse door and saw Seth standing alone on the deck, a pistol still in his hand.

'Where's the boat?' Reece yelled.

'Starboard hull,' Seth replied, gesturing to the ship's bulwarks. 'Saunders's aboard.'

'Where did you last see Saunders and the team?' Reece demanded.

'Beacon Street, under fire!' Seth yelled. 'How about you get off while you still can?'

'Get out of sight!' Reece ordered. 'We'll be gone soon enough!'

Seth stalked away toward the ship's bow, disappearing into the grim shadows cast by the weak dawn as though the world had been rinsed of colour. Reece unlocked the wheel house door and slid the heavy braces out of their holders, then pulled the assortment of boxes aside. He pulled the collar of his jacket up against the wind as he opened the door, his pistol held before him.

The wind was bitter as it snapped and whistled through the rigging above. He hurried across the deck to the starboard bulwarks. He peeked down into the water below and saw a small launch rolling on the waves, secured by a single line. Saunders lay on his back at one end and looked up at Reece.

'Come on,' the old man said. 'Get us the hell out of here!'

Reece looked down the Phoenix's deck and saw Seth watching him with the remaining crew from the bow. The sailor waved with a grim smile. Reece turned away, stuffed his pistol into his belt and clambered over the side, slipping down the rope ladder as fast as he could. He thumped down into the boat and unfastened the line, then grabbed the oars and pushed away from the Phoenix's hull.

He tossed Saunders his pistol, the old man catching it and aiming it back at the ship.

Reece cranked the oars into their clasps and pulled away from the Phoenix like a mad-man as he saw Seth and the rest of the crew appear at the bulwarks and aim their weapons at the boat. Saunders fired instantly, the shots hitting the bulwarks. Seth and his companions ducked down out of sight.

Reece heaved back on the oars for all he was worth as Saunders fired a few more warning shots at the Phoenix.

'How many rounds do we have?' Saunders asked, his gaze fixed back at the ship.

'Twelve,' Reece said, 'minus the four you just shot.'

Saunders nodded as he saw Seth appear again. This time, the sailor waved at them.

'Give my regards to the captain!' he bellowed.

A chorus of laughter drifted across the water between the boat and the ship as Saunders lowered the pistol. Seth and his companions disappeared but Reece kept rowing hard anyway.

'That's it then,' Saunders said. 'We've lost the ship.'

Reece hauled back on the oars. 'We've all lost the ship,' he said.

When Saunders frowned, Reece eased his grip on the oars and fished the chain link from his pocket. The old man's eyes widened as he realised what he was looking at.

'Para cord,' Reece explained, 'won't last them long.'

A smile crept across Saunders's features.

'They'll have to try to sail her back into the harbour once they lose the rudder,' Saunders said. 'Use the topsails or something.'

'Maybe,' Reece replied. 'Either way, they're not going far.'

Dean Crawford

MAN KIND

Dean Crawford

33

The hall was filled with endless murmurs and groans as hundreds of people slept on the bare floors of the cages, exhausted and in the throes of deep and nightmare-filled slumber.

Cody sat with his back against the bars of the cage and stared at Maria. Despite his own exhaustion sleep would not come. Having waited so long to see her again he could not bring himself to break his gaze. Alternating waves of joy, rage, anguish and anxiety flushed through his nervous system in an intoxicating elixir that buzzed through his veins. He could not tell what horrors she had witnessed but he raged against himself for ever fleeing her side.

'She's okay.'

Cody looked up to see Bethany watching him from the darkness. Cody managed a brief smile. Charlotte was asleep now in the next cage and he felt a pinch of regret as he thought about her. He struggled to find in himself any hint of doubt that his course of action had been the right one, but he could find none. Maria had been his priority and he could not have known who the mysterious caller on the radio at Alert had been. Charlotte had said it herself: she would have petitioned the captain to sail on past Boston without a care for Cody's daughter, Bethany's brother or anybody else but herself.

To hell with her.

'She'll get over it,' Bethany said clairvoyantly as she watched him.

Cody nodded but did not reply, his eyes fixed again on Maria. He kept his gaze guarded, one eye always on the handful of Sawyer's henchmen posted near the entrance to the amphitheatre. He had learned that most all times they simply sat around smoking, bored with their lot. That Sawyer was able to hold them together as a group of enforcers was a source of some amazement to Cody, driven as it was by the human need for inclusion and interaction.

It didn't matter whether one was considering children in school clubs, young hoodlums joining gangs, members of the military or even those of government, the desire to be a part of something bigger was an overwhelming feature in the human psyche. Human beings did not generally like being alone. Sawyer's thugs followed their insane leader not because they feared or even liked him, but simply because his was currently the best game in town: the biggest gang, the coolest club. To not be a member was to be excluded, to be controlled and to be prey.

Cody remembered stories of Nazi soldiers during the Second World War, carrying out extermination orders on innocent Jews or hideous experiments on little children so cruel that it beggared belief any human being could conduct them. And yet to have not done so, to have refused, would have seen those same soldiers themselves become victims, tarred as enemy sympathisers and shot at dawn. Or worse. Experiments had repeatedly proven that people were more than capable of inflicting terrible pain on their fellow human beings if that pain represented a requirement of some higher and adulated power or leader, or that the threat of not fulfilling that leader's wishes was to suffer a like treatment.

However, rebellion and discord were only a step away. Those same inflictors of appalling suffering abruptly regained their sanity and humanity when the need to perform their murderous acts was removed. Indeed, many suffered themselves for the rest of their lives as the regret, grief and disgust at their own actions haunted their every moment.

Cody looked around at the cages lining the hall and felt certain that with sufficient motivation the people could stand again, could rally against their incarcerators or perhaps even turn the henchmen against their leader. If, and only if, something better could be offered in return.

'Hank's been gone too long,' Cody said.

'You think he's in trouble?' Bethany asked.

'I don't trust him.'

'And we don't trust you.'

Charlotte had not moved but her eyes were now open, watching Cody from where she lay in the next cage.

'Sawyer will kill us all,' Cody insisted. 'He'd burn this whole place down if it got him what he wanted, and Hank owes us nothing'

'You had your chance,' Charlotte shot back. 'Let Hank get back before we cut him loose, or is betrayal your new currency Cody?'

Cody flinched at the accusation and felt a sudden sense of shame as he glanced at his sleeping daughter. How would she see him in years to come? How would she feel about the things that he had done? Would she be proud? Would she speak his name with conviction or whisper it in shame? Cody felt a renewed vigour surge through his veins as he turned back to Charlotte.

'Sawyer believes in Eden,' Cody insisted, letting his voice rise up loud enough to be heard by other prisoners around them. 'That's what he wants. He'd dump these assholes in a flash if he thought he had a way out of here.'

Cody gestured to the henchmen at the nearby door. Brooding, shaved heads turned in his direction. Cody let his instincts do the talking, shielding his anxiety with a thin veneer of bravado.

'Yeah, all of you,' he said out loud as he looked at them. 'We're talking about you. You think that asshole Sawyer's got your best interests at heart? Like hell. He's out for himself just like all of you. You don't follow him because you like him, it's because he's the only game in town, right?'

Heads rose up inside the other cages as Cody got to his feet. Some of the other prisoners hissed at Cody to *shut up* but he ignored them.

'Be quiet, or I'll twist your head off,' rumbled one of the guards.

'Sure,' Cody sniped, 'cause that'll fix everything. We may be the ones in the cages but it's all of you who are the real prisoners. We're locked in but you're free to choose your lives and yet you're still acting like little sheep following an insane shepherd.'

The heavies lumbered toward him in a tight knot. Cigarette butts were flicked away, triggers fingered as the leader, a man with a pot belly and a thick Mexican moustache jabbed a thick finger at Cody's chest through the bars.

'Any more from you and you'll be tomorrow's lunch, you scrawny little shit.'

Cody stood his ground at the bars.

'And if you slip up?' he challenged. 'You think you'll be dinner? Got any family?'

'None of your business.'

But the man's hard expression faltered, a tremor of suppressed grief in his eyes.

'If they turned up in one of these cages,' Cody asked, 'would you still kill and eat them?'

A huge fist snapped out and grabbed Cody's shirt, yanking him against the cold bars as the thug's face screwed up in hatred.

'Fuck you.'

Cody breathed his reply. 'Would you tell them that too?'

The thug glared at Cody but seemed suddenly unable to formulate a reply. Cody spoke more to his companions than to his assailant.

'You're doing this because you think it's the only thing you've got left. It isn't.'

'What are you talking about?' the thug growled, pulling even harder.

'You think that it's power and fear that control people,' Cody gasped in reply, refusing to reveal any intimidation. 'It isn't. Every time that's been used it causes people to rebel and they overthrow their leaders. Sawyer doesn't own you - he's too small and weak. He uses your own fears to control you just like he does to keep these people working. You're all prisoners here, every one of you, just like us. Even Sawyer is, because if he shows a weakness then he'll be overthrown so he acts just as crazy as he can to keep you all in line. You can't escape because you think you'll end up in cages just like us.'

The thug's nose touched Cody's, his eyes blazing with fury.

'You callin' me a coward?'

'No, I'm calling you a human being. We all are and we're all stuck in this goddamned hell hole together. We can either keep it like this, a pit of misery and despair, or we can toss Sawyer out and change it for the better.'

A voice came from behind the leader. 'Like how? There ain't nothing left for any of us.'

'Not like this there isn't,' Cody replied. 'Any of you enjoy living in here like medieval peasants, having to be cannibals when it suits Sawyer's mood? Any of you think that you're not better than that psychotic dwarf?'

The other prisoners, in his and other cages, were awake now and watching Cody as he faced down the guards.

Hands were wrapped around bars, eyes peering out from the shadows, feet shuffling and the whisper of hundreds of breaths rising with each passing exchange.

'I'd rather follow him than you,' the thug muttered as he looked Cody up and down.

Cody managed a slight chuckle.

'Great,' he said, 'a big guy like you is happy to take orders from a psychotic dentist.'

A silence descended over the watching prisoners as the guard scrutinised Cody. 'What the hell are you talking about?'

'I think Sawyer was a dentist,' Cody replied. 'You ever noticed how often he looks at your mouths when he talks to you? The habit of a lifetime while working on people's teeth, he probably can't help himself. And his teeth are perfect, professionally cared for. Sawyer pretends to be Mad Max on speed but he's nothing more than a dentist and probably led a privileged life before all of this. Don't believe me? Let me ask him when he turns up, see what he says?'

The thug examined Cody for a moment longer, then slowly relinquished his grip and took a step back from the cage. He turned his bulky head to look at his companions. They returned curious but non-committal gazes back at him.

'He's talking out of his ass,' one of them said and looked at Cody. 'There's nothing else left out there but the Great Darkness.'

'Isn't there?' Cody challenged. 'We lost power, we lost technology and most people lost their minds, but look at the Amish. They'll have survived the Great Darkness in their communities because they shun technology. Did they go insane or start eating each other because they didn't have cell phones? No, they focused on growing crops and living in peace. Our world, what's left of it, doesn't have to be like *this*.'

Cody gestured to the misery surrounding them.

'We heard your talk about the signals,' the lead thug murmured as he looked at Cody. 'What do you know about this Eden everybody's talking about?'

'What's your name?' Cody countered, eager to establish familiarity. It was harder to kill a man you had formed a bond with, however slim. 'All of you, and none of those slang or gang names. What are your real names?'

'Why?' demanded the thug.

'Because Sawyer has dehumanised you all,' Cody replied. 'No names, minimal contact with prisoners, all that prison camp stuff. You're nothing but a number. Drive it into people and they forget that they're human beings with a right to their own decisions. What's your name?'

The thug seemed almost to have to think for a moment.

'Cyrus,' he said finally.

'That's a good name,' Cody replied, 'from the Persian.' He looked at the men behind Cyrus. 'And yours?'

Reluctantly, the three men behind revealed their names as Patrick, Gus and Scott, and as though a wall had been broken they spilled their histories for all to hear. All three had been members of a biker gang, but none were criminals. Patrick worked construction, Gus and Scott both in a hardware store down south Boston way. Cyrus built custom choppers for a local firm. All had children they hadn't seen for months, all were divorced from equally absent wives.

'You're all *people*,' Cody insisted. 'You don't need to follow Sawyer's orders and you sure as hell don't need to treat other people like this.' He gestured to the other cages. 'Ask yourselves: if you found your children being treated like this, what would you do?'

Their features darkened as one. Cyrus clenched his fists at his sides.

'I'd kill each and every man I found.'

Cody nodded. 'These cages are filled with somebody else's sons, daughters, brothers and sisters. If their families find them, what do you think they'll do to you?'

The four men exchanged glances but then Cyrus looked back at Cody.

'What the hell difference does it make to you anyway? You just want out of here.'

'Damned right I do,' Cody agreed. 'But I'm not sure where we'd go afterward. Alone, we're all nothing. The whole world's been hurled back into medieval times and only the smartest are going to survive. The more we work together the better we'll do. That's what America was, a democracy, people working together. This isn't America, it's a dictatorship. It's China. It's North Korea. You want a chance to find your own families, then we all need to get out of here because you're not going to find them sitting on your ass or running around after Sawyer like whipped dogs.'

The guards glared at him but Cody turned and looked up at the crowded cages surrounding them, let his voice carry and echo around the gloomy hall. He saw Bethany, Jake, Sauri and Charlotte watching him as he spoke.

'We are nothing as long as we sit here begging for mercy from psychopaths! Sawyer thinks that it is brutality and strength, the domination of man over other species that brought humankind to greatness. It was not. It was our ability to cooperate, to work together as groups and to protect both ourselves and our families that took us from living in caves to sending men to the Moon.' Cody rapped the wall of his cage with one hand. 'This is not who we are! This is what will bring our last remaining survivors down until not a single human being remains alive in this city!'

Cody turned back to Cyrus and the other guards.

'Sawyer is not the saviour of mankind,' he said finally. 'He's the last nail in all of our coffins. We bring him down, we save ourselves.'

Gus, Scott and Patrick both looked at Cyrus, who was scrutinising the surrounding cages as his mind struggled to overcome months of denial and conditioning by Sawyer. Cody saw something shift in Cyrus's gaze and he nodded.

'And if we do this?' he asked. 'What's in it for us?'

Cody felt relief sweep like a wave of warmth across his shoulders as the knotted muscles in his belly relaxed.

'Freedom to determine for ourselves, *together*, what happens tomorrow,' he said, 'because we can survive in this world without putting innocent people in cages. And you'll have the gratitude of every single person watching you right now in this hall. They'll follow you if you set them free. I would.'

Cyrus stared at Cody for a long moment longer and then his big hand shifted to the keys dangling from his belt.

'Stand back from the door,' he rumbled.

Cody stood back as Cyrus reached out for the door, and then the crash of a gunshot shattered the darkness and Cyrus's big head flicked to one side as hot blood splattered Cody's face.

34

Sawyer stood at the entrance to the hall, his big silver pistol smouldering as he lowered it.

A half dozen shaven-headed freaks brandishing assault rifles flanked him and moved out through the amphitheatre, their weapons pointed at Gus, Patrick and Scott. Cyrus lay on his back near the cage door, his eyes staring lifelessly up at the ceiling.

'Drop your weapons, boys!' Sawyer flashed his brilliant smile up at them. 'Daddy's back!'

The guards kept their weapons trained on Sawyer, but Cody saw their faces pinched with anxiety. Outnumbered and cornered, they could not possibly win.

'Now don't be like that boys,' Sawyer said as he regarded the three nervous guards aiming their weapons at him. 'You won't feel so offended when you hear what I have to say about our friend Cody Ryan.'

Cody felt a twinge of anxiety at Sawyer's jovial demeanour. The three guards all hesitated but kept their weapons up, and Sawyer shrugged.

'All righty then,' he chirped. 'You keep your weapons and I'll let the evidence do the talking shall I?'

They made their way toward the cages and stopped as Cody, Jake, Sauri, Charlotte and Bethany stared blankly out through the bars at them.

'A rousing speech,' Sawyer said to Cody as he glanced around at the watching prisoners. 'I nearly joined you myself!'

Sawyer gestured to the cage gate and one of his thugs unlocked it. The door swung open with a high-pitched squeal that echoed through the room. Sawyer gestured to Cody.

'Out here, now.'

Cody glanced across at Maria in the next cage. She was awake and watching in silence as Cody stepped over Cyrus's corpse and out into the midst of Sawyer's most trusted enforcers. The cage door was slammed behind him and locked. The thug then turned and walked across to the next cage, unlocked it and stepped inside.

Cody's guts turned to slime within him as he saw the thug make for Maria.

'No!'

Sauri got to his feet and stood protectively over the little girl and Lena, then swung a hard right at the man's big head. The thug blocked it with a huge forearm and swung his free fist into Sauri's temple. The Inuit crashed into the wall of the cage as the other prisoners shrank away.

Lena leapt to her feet in the cage and launched herself at the thug. Her nails gouged into his face and he roared as he threw her off and into the cage bars with a clang of bone against metal. Cody saw the thick-set man's shoulders swing as he batted the other prisoners aside with callous swipes of his forearm. They stumbled backwards and away from him as Lena lurched unsteadily forward again and swung a tiny fist at the man's face.

The thug did not even attempt to block the blow as it cracked across his cheek, his big square head barely registering the impact as he stepped in and swung a stubby baton across Lena's knee. She screamed and collapsed sideways as the thug picked Maria up under one thick arm, carried her out of the cage and dumped her outside. She sat on the cold floor and turned her dark eyes toward Cody as she raised her arms toward him.

Cody reacted without conscious thought and rushed forward, swept Maria up into his arms as though she were the only thing on Earth that could keep him alive. He felt her arms wrap tightly around his neck and squeeze him as his heart melted inside his chest and he dropped to his knees, hot tears trickling down his cheeks against her hair.

Maria released her grip on him and stared into his eyes, a smile melting through her grimy features. Cody felt as though he could kneel there enveloped in joy for the rest of his life.

'Are you okay, daddy?' she asked him.

Cody nodded, almost laughed as he squeezed her tightly against him again. Sawyer's brittle voice shattered the warmth of the moment like a bullet through glass.

'Cody Ryan.'

Cody, still holding his daughter, climbed to his feet and turned to face Sawyer. The insane militiaman spoke softly but his voice carried to the farthest reaches of the hall.

'I knew that I recognised your name,' he said. 'It took me a while, sure enough, but then it all came back to me.'

Sawyer was holding his sabre and examined the bright edge of the polished blade as he spoke.

'Why don't you show him, Jimmy?'

One of the thugs stepped forward, and in his hand he held what looked like a page pulled from one of Boston's broadsheets. Aged and torn, Cody watched as the man unfolded it and held it before him. There, on what had once been the front page of the *Boston Globe*, was a picture of his brother's face and a broad headline.

REMAINS OF WAR VETERAN FOUND NEAR RESERVOIR

BOSTONIAN SOUGHT FOR FIRST DEGREE MURDER

Cody swallowed as he briefly scanned the article beneath, words flashing through his mind: climatologist, break and enter, distraught wife confesses all to police and triggers a manhunt, DNA evidence in lonely woods.

Cody looked at the top corner of the page and saw that it was dated the day after the storm. The paper had reached circulation, but by then the population of the entire planet had bigger problems on its mind. Within days most newspapers would have been burned for fuel amid the freezing temperatures, erasing all evidence of the crime. All but scraps, one of which Sawyer had evidently found.

Sawyer stepped forward and tapped the wicked tip of the sabre at the article.

'Who's been a naughty boy then?' he asked.

Cody remained silent as Sawyer turned away and spoke loudly, hundreds of prisoners watching him from the surrounding cages.

'What a wonderful story Doctor Ryan has woven! The great, the good, the all-knowing and reasonable Doctor Ryan, wanted for the cold-blooded murder of a vagrant. Bludgeoned him to death, so he did!' Sawyer cast a glance at Cody, a wicked twinkle in his eye. 'And there was I, believing him to be such a gentle soul. There were you all, believing him to be a man of virtue and humanity long lost to the rest of us, your new saviour.' Sawyer's gaze turned cruel. 'But no. Instead, we find him to be as murderous as the very worst of us, because the victim was none other than his own brother!'

Jake, Charlotte, Sauri and Bethany all stared at Cody, eyes wide with disbelief.

'The Internet, back at Alert,' Bethany whispered. 'You were always watching the news, waiting to hear what had happened?'

Cody held Maria as he replied, her face buried in his shoulder.

'We were being robbed. He was armed and a drug addict.'

Gus, Patrick and Scott all lowered their weapons. Cody knew without a doubt that Sawyer was giving them the excuse they needed to extricate themselves from their mutiny without fear of punishment. They had made a mistake, been misled. Without Cyrus to lead them, their courage had deserted them.

Cody saw Jake staring at him from within the cage, a strange kind of betrayal shadowing his gaze as he spoke.

'The body,' he whispered.

'What body?' Bethany gasped as she looked at the old man.

Cody felt his guts plunge and he held Maria tightly as Jake spoke.

'I found a head and hands buried in the snow behind the observatory,' he said, 'looked like it had been dead a while. The polar bear must have smelled the remains and dug them up. Then Bobby must have attracted its attention, and….'

Cody squeezed his eyes shut as pain seared them, kept his face buried beside his daughter's as he slowly rocked her from side to side.

'…. the bear attacked Bobby afterward,' Jake finished his sentence. 'Those remains you buried, of your brother, caused Bobby's death.'

Cody could feel the eyes of countless people upon him; the judge, the jury. The executioner.

'You're a murderer,' Charlotte uttered from her cage.

'He was a drug addict!' Cody gasped. 'He threatened my wife and my daughter. I had no choice.'

'No choice!' Sawyer snapped. 'Yet you parade your high-and-mighty crap to all about how they should preserve our humanity, work together, clap our hands and sing happy songs?' He jabbed the sabre up toward Cody's face. 'We had no choice either, Ryan! None of us had a goddamned choice!'

Cody stared at Sawyer for a long moment, saw the same anguish in his eyes that coursed through Cody's body, a laborious pain and regret that ached through the veins and throbbed inside the heart.

'What happened to you, Sawyer?' he asked.

Sawyer gestured to his men with his pistol. 'Get him out of here,' he snapped.

'What about the rest of them?' Patrick asked, eager to please Sawyer.

Sawyer glanced at the nearby cages. 'Take the women from them and keep them apart, and that woman there, the young one. Put her on the fences.'

Cody turned in horror as Patrick lumbered into the cage and dragged Lena to her knees.

'No,' Cody gasped. 'Don't do it!'

Maria cried out as Lena was dragged away through the amphitheatre. Cody, with Maria held in his arms, was prodded out of the amphitheatre as he heard Bethany and Charlotte being yanked forcibly from their cages.

'You're a killer, Cody!' Charlotte screamed after him as they were led away. 'You're a goddamned psychopath!'

Her voice echoed up into the hall around them, chasing Cody as he walked. He heard Maria's voice in his ear.

'Did you hurt somebody, daddy?'

Cody squeezed her tight, unable to meet her gaze as they walked. 'Somebody who was going to hurt you, honey,' he whispered.

Sawyer led them up the grand staircase and along the hall to what Cody figured were the senate executive offices, grandly decorated rooms with broad windows looking out over the darkened city. Sawyer led them into one such room and fell rather than sat into a large leather chair in front of a polished mahogany desk.

He gestured loosely to a seat opposite as two guards stood by the office entrance. Cody sat down, Maria on his lap but still clutching to his jacket as she stared silently at Sawyer.

'What do you want?' Cody asked.

Sawyer looked at Cody and a small smile curled from one corner of his lips as he studied him. 'You fascinate me, Ryan,' he said finally. 'A family man, an academic, and yet you killed your own brother, smuggled bits of him up into the Arctic and buried them in a snow drift. You know, according to the article the police only found the torso and limbs after a dog-walker's pet stumbled on blood and bone chips in the woods. The cops got DNA from them, identified your brother from his army records and would have sent you down for twenty to life on your wife's testimony.'

Cody swallowed. 'It didn't go down like that.'

'I'm sure it didn't,' Sawyer agreed, 'but that doesn't matter much to me. See, to have left that much mess and to have gotten his hands and head or whatever out of the country you must have sawed him up, no?'

Cody tried to remain silent and still but his expression betrayed him.

'You did,' Sawyer grinned as though admonishing a wayward schoolboy. 'Why? Why did you do that?'

Months of anguish, of sleepless nights poisoned with regret coursing through his veins seemed to swell up like an un-lanced abscess in Cody's chest. For reasons he could not adequately explain to himself, he started talking.

'To protect my wife and I from prison,' Cody replied. The tension wracking his chest fell away as he spoke. 'My brother was once a hero, my hero, but drugs turned him into something horrible, a leech, a poison that kept our folks awake at night with worry. When he tried to raid our house, he threatened my family.' Cody breathed easily as his anxiety spilled from his lungs like a noxious gas and vanished into thin air. 'Like I said, we had no choice.'

'No choice,' Sawyer echoed again. 'We always have a choice, Ryan, and you made yours.'

Cody knew that he could deflect the accusation, tell him that his wife had struck the blows, but he didn't feel like giving Sawyer the satisfaction of watching him try to wriggle his way out of complicity to homicide.

'Your wife sold out,' Sawyer said. 'Couldn't live with the knowledge of what you had done. You got lucky, Ryan.'

'You call this lucky?' Cody flicked his head back briefly to indicate the two guards by the door. 'These people follow you, Sawyer. They have the right to know who they're following don't they? The right to know that you'll keep them alive?'

The thug's innate human nature made them curious and they glanced at Sawyer.

'They know who I am,' Sawyer spat back. 'They all know that I keep them alive, every day.'

'Because they couldn't save themselves? Do you think they're idiots or something?'

'Don't even bother,' Sawyer smirked at him. 'They're not going to suddenly get all turn-coat because of anything you say.'

'It's not what I say that matters,' Cody replied, keeping his voice even. 'It's what you do that counts.'

'And what the hell is that supposed to mean?' Sawyer snapped back.

'You murdered one of your best men,' Cody replied. 'You call me a murderer but I killed in self-defence. You killed Cyrus in cold blood, shot him in the back. That's who you are, Sawyer. You really think that any of these people, whether inside cages or outside of them, is going to watch that and think they can trust you as far as they could throw you?'

'I provide them with everything they want.'

Cody nodded. 'But nothing that they *need*. Where is Captain Mears?'

'Otherwise indisposed,' Sawyer muttered as he reached up and touched the crucifix now dangling from his throat. 'We had a disagreement.'

'You act like human life has no meaning,' Cody said, 'and it's your downfall. Hank was the only person with the skills to sail us out of here and the charts to find Eden.'

'I said he was otherwise indisposed,' Sawyer snapped, 'not dead. You think me an idiot?'

'What happened to your face, Sawyer?'

Sawyer turned away and fiddled with the handle of his sabre. 'I understand that you have something for us, Doctor Ryan. Coordinates, I believe,' Sawyer added. 'You'll share them with us, now.'

'Was it your family?' Cody asked.

Sawyer slid the bright metal sabre from its sheath and casually levelled it across the table at Cody and Maria, who flinched away from the wicked blade.

'Coordinates,' he repeated, 'but I'll give you a sweetener. You tell me and I'll make sure you come with us, you and your daughter here.'

Cody's heart skipped a beat. A mental image of his companions back in the cages flashed through his mind. Sawyer clairvoyantly sensed his conflicted emotions.

'They hate you, Ryan, just like they hate me,' he said. 'They'd abandon you in a heartbeat and your daughter too, just to get revenge. You caused the death of one of your own, hiding your crimes. You're like me, Ryan, we're the same. Horrible things have happened to us and we've had to adapt, survive and evolve to stay alive in this world of ours. It's not pretty, is it? And it's not pleasant, but we're alive and others are not because they could not do what we have done. Have you ever read Homer's *Iliad*?'

Cody nodded vacantly, unable to meet Sawyer's eye as he spoke.

'A most revealing insight into the human condition,' Sawyer went on, 'of love, of hate, of betrayal and revenge. My favourite line is that of Achilles' lament to King Priam: "We men are wretched things, and the gods, who have no cares themselves, have woven sorrow into the very pattern of our lives.".'

Cody stared into the distance, but then his eyes focused back on Sawyer once more as the mythical warrior's later words flickered into existence in his mind.

'"You must endure and not be broken hearted, lamenting for your son will do no good at all."'

Sawyer's expression slipped and he swallowed.

'See, you wouldn't have got those wounds from an accident I don't think,' Cody said quietly. 'The scar tissue is on the side of your head but also on the front of your chest, so you must have been burned and turned your head away from the heat. Your hands are also scarred but I'm guessing your legs are not. I figure you weren't trapped, Sawyer. You were trying to reach somebody, weren't you, through flames?'

Sawyer glared catatonically at Cody, the sabre quivering as he held it.

'Family,' Cody whispered. 'You lost them, in a fire, couldn't reach them. Got burned trying. Your son, perhaps? Is it that which really makes you think of King Priam?'

Sawyer edged the sabre toward Maria, who turned her head away and buried it in Cody's neck. 'Coordinates, or I'll take your little girl and hang her from the fences outside.'

Cody felt anguish surge through his veins, unable to choose between rage and grief.

'She's a child,' he snapped. 'Is that who you are? A child killer?'

'I'll have her working the land when she's old enough,' Sawyer replied. 'You should thank me for looking after her. That can change.'

'You're no psychopath Sawyer,' Cody rasped. 'You've just lost the will to trust people, to believe that there's a decent reason for living, for carrying on. It allows you to threaten little children but only if there's a pair of thugs in the room to back you up.'

Sawyer's thin lips creased into a tight grin, a thin veil to whatever storms were raging inside his mind.

'Last chance, Ryan.'

Cody let the new anguish go, resigned to the fact that he could not change the man sitting before him.

'The coordinates are in my diary,' he said, 'aboard the Phoenix. They're tucked inside.'

Sawyer held the blade in place for a moment longer before slowly withdrawing it and sliding it into its sheath. He clapped his hands, the sound echoing around the room.

'There, see? That wasn't so tough.'

Cody held his daughter close to him and closed his eyes, not willing to let Sawyer's joy contaminate his own at holding her again. Sawyer gestured to the guards, who lumbered over.

'Take Ryan back to his cage,' Sawyer said. 'The girl goes downstairs. Keep her under guard.'

Cody looked up at Sawyer. 'What the hell for?'

'Insurance,' Sawyer snapped. 'I don't want you running around in your cage like a demented chimp rallying my workers into rebellion. So you'll be nice and quiet, like a good boy, understood?'

Cody held Maria tightly.

'Don't you harm her,' he hissed. 'Don't let happen to her whatever happened to your family.'

Sheet lightning danced behind Sawyer's eyes as he clicked his fingers at the guards.

Something heavy clubbed into the back of Cody's neck and his vision starred as he slumped forward in the chair. He heard Maria's cries as she was snatched from his grasp, felt himself dragged off the chair, but his limbs would not respond as his mind filled with darkness.

35

The boat bumped up against the quay as Reece guided it in and leaped up onto the boardwalk to tie it off.

Saunders managed to haul himself upright, a thick dressing tied around the wound in his leg and his jeans soaked with blood. Reece watched anxiously as the old sailor dragged himself up onto the quay, sweat beading on his skin.

'Take it easy,' Reece said, gripping Saunders' hand to help him up.

'Now you tell me.'

Reece glanced up at the soaring city skyline, the skyscrapers looming dark against the ominous clouds. He had rowed them across the mouth of Fort Point Channel to a mooring on Harbour Walk, right on the edge of the city where the team had gone ashore. Boston Common was barely a mile away across town but he could see already that some of the streets were flooded and the thick odour of raw sewage spilled from the silent depths of the city.

'Beacon Street's not that far,' Reece said, 'but you'd best stay here.'

Saunders chuckled as he turned a twinkling eye in Reece's direction. 'Ain't no way that's happening kid.'

'You'll slow me down,' Reece insisted. 'If we have to leave in a hurry how the hell are you going to run with your leg in that state?'

Saunders bit his lip as he looked down at his jeans. The dressing was holding for now but blood soaked his thigh.

Exhausted and hungry, Reece knew damned well that any exertion would be enough to put Saunders out like a light.

'Stay here,' he ordered the old man, 'be ready to cast the lines if we show up.'

Saunders sat on the quay and looked Reece up and down for a brief moment.

'You've sure come on a ways since we picked you up,' he said.

'A lot's happened.'

Saunders reached around to his belt, pulled his pistol from it and handed it to Reece. 'I get into trouble I can row myself out of range. You'll need the ammunition.'

Reece hefted the pistol in his hand for a moment and realised that there was no good reason not to take it with him.

'You know where Long Wharf is?' Saunders asked. Reece shook his head and the old man gestured over his shoulder. 'Maybe three hundred yards north, around the headland. If I have to move, that's where I'll head.'

Reece nodded and stuffed the pistol into his jeans.

'Good luck,' Saunders said.

Reece turned and hurried off the quay. He crossed Atlantic Avenue, the broad asphalt visible beneath a haze of green shoots and mosses. An occasional abandoned vehicle showing the first signs of rust blocked his way, but within a couple of minutes he was walking down what had once been Pearl Street, soaring buildings either side of him as he dodged pools of filthy, stagnant water.

It took him twenty minutes to cross the city's financial district and reach the edge of Boston Common. The eerie silence and darkened buildings seemed to pursue him as he walked. He looked over his shoulder frequently, as though hordes of zombies might suddenly pour from the abandoned buildings, hungry for his flesh.

The silence and the desolation was at once both intoxicating and frightening. The bizarre elation at being alone and utterly free in the huge city began to fade as Reece realised the true extent of mankind's suffering and loss. It wasn't just the bodies he saw rotting in doorways or the abandoned and blood-stained vehicles in the streets, but the pervasive silence. Reece began to realise that the city had become a monument to what mankind had once achieved but would never manage again. The cities would never again be filled with light and life, the hustle and bustle of mankind flowing like blood through its arterial streets.

Reece slowed and for a few moments stood at the corner of Hamilton Place and just listened. There was almost no noise but for the small sounds of birds nested in the trees of the common across the street, calling for the dawn. Reece felt new fear inside of him as the last of his excitement at coming ashore vanished like the last voices from these very streets. Mankind had fallen.

It was truly over.

'Jesus,' he uttered.

Visions of family, of friends from school and clubs, the countless faces from his life known both well and briefly flashed through his mind in a rush of realisation and dread as he realised that they were all gone. Long dead. He had spent much of his life shunning human contact, and now there was nobody left. Reece leaned against a street lamp and rubbed his face, as though he were dreaming and would suddenly wake up and see cars and people and trucks and hear the city's noise all around him.

Instead, he heard only the birds. Above, clouds blustered by above the buildings, bruised dark grey as though pummelled by the blows from winds that had not yet penetrated the dense city streets.

Movement caught his eye and in the pale light he saw somebody walking up near the State House. Reece ducked across the street and into the shelter of trees at the edge of the common. He hurried forward until he could see the State House before him on Beacon Hill.

The stench of decaying bodies hit him quickly, as did the feeble murmuring of men and women chained to the fences outside. A pair of guards patrolled with bored steps just inside the fence, one of them leaving a trail of blue cigarette smoke as he puffed away.

Trees lined either side of the main gardens, which were flanked by secondary entrances. The light was still low, the gloomy dawn still holding shadows as though reluctant to shed light on the sombre scene below. Reece moved west through the shelter of the common's trees and crossed Beacon Street further down and out of sight of the state house before moving back up the street and clambering over a fence into the state house's west grounds.

He crept up a long flight of broad steps that led toward the west wing, staying low enough to avoid being spotted by the gate guards to his right, and then moved along past a mounted statue to a smaller set of doors set back into the west wing of the house. He tested the handle as quietly as he could, but the doors were firmly locked. Reece quickly pulled off his jacket and bundled it across the surface of the window. Then, he clicked his pistol's safety catch off and fired a single shot into the jacket. The muffled crack of the gunshot was mostly swallowed by the jacket, but the noise was amplified by the surrounding walls of the wing.

Reece heard a voice coming from the direction of the main gate, questions followed by a brisk response. He pulled his jacket away from the window and ran in a crouch along the wall of the main gardens to peek through the decorative foliage across the lawns toward the gate.

One of the guards was crossing the lawn toward him, a rifle held ready.

Reece whirled and dashed back to the doors to examine the window. The bullet had passed through the jacket, leaving a small splintered hole in the glass. Reece carefully eased his index finger through the hole and pulled. A chunk of glass broke away and fell at his feet. Reece worked away a few more chunks of glass until he could reach inside the window.

He reached down and grabbed the door handle, turned it.

Still locked.

He pushed his arm further in and the glass sliced painfully into his skin as his fingers rested on the handle of a key inside. He grabbed at it, turned it. The locking mechanism clicked and he quickly reached up and grabbed the handle.

The door swung open and Reece retrieved his arm. He reached down and picked up the shards of glass and tossed them into nearby foliage before he stepped inside and shut the door behind him, then ducked out of sight behind the nearest wall.

The guard's head appeared at the top of the steps and scanned the wing of the house for several seconds. Reece held his breath as the man waited for what felt like an age, and then turned and strolled back down the steps and out of sight.

Reece breathed a deep sigh of relief and turned, looking down the corridor that led toward the main state house from the wing. The glass windows of the house were still intact, an oddity considering how most ground level windows in the city had been smashed by looters during the riots that had raged in the aftermath of the storm. Reece figured that maybe troops or police had held sway here for longer than elsewhere in the city, and managed to preserve the building until they too had abandoned their posts. Or that somehow the imposing building had represented something stronger than the people and that they had left it alone for fear of reprisals if government ever regained control. By the time they knew that such a feat was impossible, there were no longer enough people left in the city with the means or the will to do much damage.

Reece eased his way down the corridor. The weak light through the windows outside was not sufficient to illuminate the interior of the building beyond. Dark shadows awaited.

He moved silently into the main corridor of the Doric Hall. He could faintly see the large main entrance doors to his right. The smell of wood smoke was thick on the air, the white walls either side of the doors scorched with pillars of black soot. Reece turned left and crept through the Nurse's Hall and on toward the Great Hall. He slowed as he saw flickering plumes of firelight shimmering off towering walls.

Reece squatted in the shadows and let his eyes adjust properly to the darkness around him. Slowly, he was able to pick out the form of several guards asleep against the wall on one side of the entrance. Reece eased his way past and climbed the grand staircase to the upper floor, making his way toward what had once been the Senate Chamber.

Reece edged his way to the entrance and saw the large amphitheatre, windows to either side through which filtered the dull morning light. Two flaming torches rested in iron clasps against the far wall. As Reece focused on the hall, he realised that he was looking at rows of cages, and that the cages were filled with people.

All at once, he knew he was in the right place and he ducked into a shadowy alcove.

He could see the keys to the cages within a few yards of where he crouched, dangling from then belt of one of a pair of sleeping guards. He was judging his chances of grabbing the keys without being spotted by the two awake guards when a fifth guard strode quietly up and whispered to his two companions.

In silence, the three men slipped away and abandoned their sleeping companions.

*

Sawyer sat in his chair and looked at the two women before him.

Despite the fearsome anarchy that had raged throughout the city of Boston in the wake of the Great Darkness, Sawyer had never thought of violating a woman. During those bleakest of days and weeks as humanity sank into deprivation and despair he had seen so many terrible things that he no longer felt as though he existed in the real world. He had seen entire families beaten and raped by gangs of drunken thugs, seen others imprisoned to serve biker gangs marauding through the city like harbingers of death until there was nobody left to prey upon.

Sawyer was not a particularly religious man, but through the drifting smoke, writhing flames and echoing screams haunting Boston in those dark days he had truly believed that he was witnessing the end of days. The final judgement on mankind's excesses seemed somehow appropriate in all of its gruesome glory until his own family, huddling in his apartment in the suburbs, had been smoked out by a gang.

By that time, food was scarce and drunken debauchery had metamorphosed into a genuine fight for survival. The stakes were high, millions facing starvation and disease, and although the dark spectre of cannibalism had not yet reared its macabre head, the killing of the weak for their resources to feed the strong was well under way.

His family's meagre remaining supplies were worth more to the gang than all the gold in the world. As Sawyer had tried to reason with the murderous gang they had tossed Molotov cocktails in through the windows, setting the apartment aflame while manning the fire escape. The only way out was through the windows to a three storey drop, or for Sawyer to fight to protect his children.

Sawyer had fought on the fire escape, his wife alongside him.

They had battered their way out and opened fire on the thugs with a .38 that Sawyer kept for self-defence, just as the Constitution allowed him to. Then they had fought with a crow bar and a baseball bat when the bullets had run out.

His wife died beside him from a blow to the head that had stove her skull in.

Sawyer managed to kill the remaining members of the gang, driven by a force of nature seething through his veins the likes of which he had never known before. Yet despite the sacrifice and the courage, the flames had spread too far. Sawyer had charged back into his apartment, into that hellish inferno, only to find his two young sons long dead from the smoke and the flames.

The memory of them seared his brain just as the fire had once seared his skin.

'What do you want from us?'

Charlotte, the feisty one, glared at him. Sawyer blinked his memories away.

'Very little,' he replied, 'but your cooperation.'

'Why the hell should we cooperate with you?' Charlotte challenged him. 'You're nothing but a killer.'

There were no guards in the room this time, both women instead bound with cuffs.

'Yes I am,' Sawyer replied. 'But that doesn't mean I wish to remain one.'

'What do you mean?'

It was the quieter one this time, Bethany, who had spoken. Sawyer found himself curiously drawn to her. Despite the horrors infecting the lives of every human being around them she seemed strangely unaffected, her gaze clear as though she were not judging but merely observing.

'I want to leave this place just as much as you all do,' he replied finally. 'The question is: whom do I take with me?'

'You won't make it aboard the ship,' Charlotte snorted. 'They'll cut you and your merry band to pieces without Hank.'

Sawyer smiled at her. 'Possibly. Right now, however, I would like to offer one of you a place. For the right price, of course.'

Sawyer let his gaze wander over their bodies.

Charlotte baulked. 'I'd rather be eaten alive.'

'I can arrange that,' Sawyer pointed out. Bethany remained silent and Sawyer looked at her instead.

'Don't you dare,' Charlotte uttered at Bethany.

Bethany sighed. 'I'm tired and I want out of here.'

Charlotte did not rebuke her friend, but instead shot Sawyer a dirty look. Sawyer looked Bethany over one more time and then made his decision.

'You may leave,' he said to Charlotte and rapped his knuckles on his desk loudly. The office door opened and two guards stalked in. 'Take her back to her cage,' he ordered.

The guards lifted Charlotte out of the chair and guided her away from the office. The door closed behind them, leaving Bethany alone with Sawyer. The two looked at each other for a long moment before Sawyer spoke.

'I have no intention of harming you,' he said.

'And I have no intention of letting you rape me,' Bethany replied.

'You think that you can stop me?'

'No,' Bethany replied, 'but I have something far more valuable to you, and you're going to do something for me.'

Sawyer looked at her curiously for a moment and then leaned forward across the desk.

'And what might that be?'

Bethany spoke quietly, and as she did so Sawyer realised that he would indeed be looking after her and that they would be leaving immediately.

36

Cody sat in the cage and stared into the darkness.

Jake sat in the next cage, likewise alone with his thoughts.

Cody knew that Sawyer would gather his men and make an attempt to board the Phoenix, probably by dawn. That Maria was being held against her will and beyond his reach infected him with fresh anguish that felt almost like a constant companion. It throbbed through his bones as one fear was replaced with another, clogging his arteries and aching in his labouring heart.

'Why didn't you tell me?'

Jake's voice reached out for Cody in the darkness. There was no accusation in the tone, only a plea for understanding.

'Don't say that you'd have understood,' Cody replied. 'You wouldn't have.'

'I'd have listened,' Jake said. 'I know you didn't mean for it to happen, Cody, but you caused Bobby's death.'

Cody swallowed. 'I put him out with the morphine too. Beth' couldn't bring herself to do it.'

He heard a muffled *Jesus* from the darkness.

'I can't change the past,' Cody said.

'No,' Jake agreed. 'You can't.'

Cody could not think of anything to say. He sat in silence.

A movement caught his eye. Two of the nearby guards were sleeping as two kept watch. A fifth approached silently from behind them and whispered something. Moments later, the three guards slipped away from the hall and left their sleeping companions behind.

Cody stared curiously at the exit for several long minutes, awaiting the guards' return and wondering if Sawyer was making his move already. He spotted fresh movement and was about to look away when something caused him to sit up and take notice.

A shadow against shadows at the entrance to the hall. Cody squinted as he searched for the source of the movement and his heart leapt against the wall of his chest as he saw Reece emerge into the flickering firelight and creep toward the sleeping guards.

Cody silently got to his feet and moved to the bars of the cage. Reece had sneaked up alongside the sleeping guards and had reached out for the keys dangling from one of their belts. Cody felt himself tense up as Reece carefully unhooked the keys off the belt and backed away.

Cody watched in fearful amazement, his fingernails digging into his palms as Reece slipped away and then turned to face the cages. Cody waved his arms in silence and Reece hurried silently across to the cage as other prisoners began to wake up and realise what was happening in a rush of whispers.

Reece reached the cage door and fumbled through the keys.

'How did you get here?' Cody asked in a whisper.

Reece replied as he shoved a key into the lock. 'Shot through a window on the west wing.'

The key didn't fit and he immediately tried another.

'I wouldn't do that, if I were you,' Jake said from the next cage.

Reece froze, looking at the old man. 'What, you don't want to get out?'

Jake looked at Cody. 'I don't know that I want him out of there.'

The prisoners in Cody's cage gasped and began reaching out of the cage for Reece's keys as their wary eyes watched the guards sleeping nearby.

'Why the hell not?' Reece whispered.

Cody looked at Jake and shook his head, but the old man spoke softly. His words carried softly to Reece, who lowered his hand from the lock as he stared in horror at Cody and began backing away.

'*You* killed Bobby?' he uttered. 'And somebody else too?'

'It wasn't like that,' Cody pleaded.

'Unlock this cage,' Jake ordered Reece. 'We need to get out of here.'

Reece nodded vacantly, his eyes still fixed on Cody.

'They've got my daughter,' Cody said to Reece. 'They've got Maria.'

Reece turned for the next cage, hurrying across and testing keys in the lock.

'Where's Saunders?' Jake asked.

'Injured,' Reece explained. 'Back at the boat.'

'The crew are all here?' Cody asked, his spirits rising.

Reece answered, but he looked at Jake as he did so. 'They mutinied. Saunders and I were lucky to get away.'

'The ship's gone?' Jake uttered.

'No,' Reece grinned, and Cody watched as he pulled a metal link from his shirt pocket. 'Rudder's out, unless they can replace this.'

The key in the door clicked into place and Reece turned it with a smile as he pocketed the rudder link and drew his pistol.

'Looks like I'm the hero,' he grinned.

Something flickered through the darkness from behind Reece. Cody shouted a warning but it was too late. A blur of bright light thumped into Reece's back between his shoulder blades.

Reece slammed against the cage as the huge knife quivered in his back, the grin snatched from his face as he stared wide-eyed at Jake, his fingers gripping the bars. Jake reached out for Reece as he slipped, caught his weight and pinned Reece's pistol between them as a voice thundered out from across the amphitheatre.

'Get away from the cage!'

Cody saw the two guards lumbering toward them, awake now and both aiming pistols.

He turned and saw Jake look down at Reece, who glanced down at the pistol between them.

'Do it,' Reece rasped, tears filling his eyes as his legs quivered beneath him, 'before I let go.'

His voice rattled as blood leaked furiously into his lungs and spluttered from his lips as his aorta ruptured somewhere deep within him. Jake reached down and grabbed the pistol as Reece held onto his shirt, his legs bowing as the strength went out of them. Jake turned the pistol, flicked off the safety catch.

'You're a hero all right,' Jake whispered to Reece.

Reece smiled.

Jake whipped the pistol up and aimed it through the bars of the cell at the two hulking men bearing down on them. Patrick and Gus halted as they recognised the old man.

'Wait,' Gus said, raised a hand. 'We're not…'

Cody felt a pulse of alarm as he saw the grin determination on Jake's face and he shouted. 'No! We need them!'

Jake ignored him and fired the pistol.

Cody watched Gus fall, his pistol clattering to the ground and his hands clasped to his chest as blood spilled from his fractured heart. Jake turned and aimed at Patrick, who had realised that with Reece's inert body blocking his view he could not hit Jake and was turning to run for cover.

The shot hit Patrick in the back and sent him tumbling to his knees. The guard kept scrambling for cover, his legs kicking as he tried to drag himself out of sight. Jake let go of Reece and aimed double handed before firing twice.

Both shots slammed into Patrick's body just below his neck and he slumped on the marble floor. Jake lowered the smouldering pistol and stared at the two dead men as Reece collapsed to his knees and toppled onto his back at the foot of the cage door.

'Open your cage!' Cody yelled at Jake, who was staring at his victims. 'Quickly!'

'Open *our* cage!'

The voice came from behind Cody as an emaciated man staggered toward the door.

Jake reached out through the bars and grabbed the keys, fumbling with them as shouts echoed down the corridors outside the amphitheatre, bellicose roars of alarm that became louder with every passing second.

'They heard the shots!' another prisoner yelled. 'You'll get us all killed!'

Jake fumbled with the keys until suddenly the mechanism clicked and the heavy door swung open. Cody yelled at him.

'Get the other guns, but don't shoot!'

Jake burst from the cage and ran at the dead bodies of the guards as from behind him in the cage a flood of prisoners burst shrieking from their incarceration and flooded toward the main exit.

Jake grabbed Gus's fallen pistol and turned to look at Cody. For a long moment they stared at each other.

'Throw the keys!' Cody yelled.

Jake hefted the keys in his hand for a long moment, and then tossed them across to the cage alongside Cody's. The keys rattled down through the bars as the prisoners within pounced on them, Sauri among them.

'Find Maria!' Cody pleaded as Jake fled for the exit.

37

Hank heard the commotion and turned to Sawyer as the leader of the militia tossed him back his crucifix, the golden chain sparkling in the dawn light from the windows.

'They're out,' Sawyer said clairvoyantly. 'We go now.'

Hank caught the crucifix and fastened it about his thick neck as he looked at Bethany. She stood with a child held close to her hip, an anxious expression painted across her features.

Sawyer stuffed a pair of pistols into his belt and lifted an AR-15 assault rifle to his shoulder. His pockets bulged with ammunition clips. To Hank he looked like some kind of school child festooned with plastic toys. The horror was that the weapons were real.

Sawyer reached into what looked like some kind of military chest and lifted out what Hank recognised as a handful of distress flares.

'They'll tear us apart if they find us,' Bethany urged.

'We're going,' Sawyer replied. 'I'll lead the way.'

Sawyer stepped out of the governor's office and into the hallway outside. They turned right as Sawyer jogged down the thickly carpeted hall. Light from outside now illuminated the corridors, which remained virtually pristine in condition. Only thick dust on ornaments and picture frames betrayed the lack of human attention.

Sawyer slowed at the end of the corridor and peeked around to the left. The main hall led to the grand staircase. Sporadic screams and the sound of gunfire echoed up from the senate chamber as though from the gates of hell itself.

'The guards will be overrun,' Hank pointed out.

'They'll hold them for as long as they can near the great hall,' Sawyer replied. 'We'll move past behind them and make for the main doors and out of here. We'll lock them behind us if we can, buy some time.'

Sawyer crossed to the galleries that overlooked the senate chamber, where the sound of screaming prisoners and guards filled the air. Sawyer yanked the caps off two of the distress flares, the brilliant flares blazing into life amid a cloud of sparks and blue smoke as Sawyer tossed them down into the amphitheatre below.

From his vantage point, Hank saw the flares catch on the ornate furniture and velvet fittings, flames and smoke billowing into the air to a fresh cacophony of alarmed screams.

Sawyer turned away and led the way to the grand staircase. They jogged down them two at a time, circling around to the second floor. The sound of fighting leaped in volume, amplified by the confined corridors into deafening staccato gunshots and the shrieks and cries of human beings locked in mortal combat.

Hank saw two of Sawyer's men retreating down the hall, firing bursts as they went.

'Hold them off!' Sawyer yelled. 'I've got your backs!'

Sawyer brandished his assault rifle as he ran down the steps. The two guards, both of them injured, saw him coming and held their positions. Sawyer leaped to the bottom of the staircase and retreated away from the Great Hall.

Hank ducked as gunfire shattered chips of marble and stone from the walls and floor around him.

'The prisoners are armed!' he yelled in surprise.

Hank grabbed Bethany and the child and pushed them behind him, shielding them with his body as they retreated toward the Doric Hall and the main doors. The prisoners were firing wild bursts at the guards in their way and forcing Hank and Sawyer to duck into cover behind the rows of columns lining the route.

'Open the doors!' one of the guards bellowed to Sawyer above the din.

Sawyer was already there. He yanked a large table out of the way of the doors, presumably some kind of barricade in case the locks failed. Hank watched from behind a pillar as Sawyer shoved a key into each of the three locks on the door and turned them before reaching down to release the catch and throwing the doors open.

Light burst into the building and illuminated the seething mass of prisoners at the far end of the Nurse's Hall. They saw the light as one and a great scream filled the hall as they suddenly broke cover beneath the weight of those pushing from behind and thundered toward the main doors.

'Go, now!' Sawyer yelled.

Hank pushed Bethany in the direction of the doors and then ran behind her and hurled himself through as Sawyer let three of his men through the doors and then whirled to fire a prolonged burst of automatic rounds into the building. Hank turned to see bullets tear into the charging crowd. Sawyer kept his finger on the trigger, the chattering assault rifle spitting flame and smoke as the lethal hail scythed into the mass of humanity. Bodies twitched and jerked as they were hit, those behind tumbling over the falling corpses as though the crowd were some massive, dirty brown wave crashing through the hall.

'Fall back!' Hank yelled.

Hank saw Bethany shielding the child from the carnage as Sawyer kept his grip on the rifle until suddenly it stopped firing, the clip emptied in a matter of seconds.

Sawyer dropped the rifle and heaved against the doors. Hank leaped up and pushed with him as the huge doors closed on the charging mass of humanity, a flood of gaping mouths and flying limbs. Hank heaved harder and the doors slammed with a great boom that echoed through the building within.

Sawyer turned one key in one lock, fumbled for the next and got the lock turned as the prisoners plunged en masse into the other side, the heavy doors shuddering.

'That's enough,' Hank breathed. 'But they'll use the windows to get out, let's move.'

Sawyer jumped back from the rattling door, his features flushed with blood and his eyes jerking back and forth between the rifle at his feet and the door.

'Man, you see that shit?' he cackled, joy creasing his features.

Hank stared at Sawyer for a long moment, saw the crazed look on his face slither away as Sawyer turned and jack-knifed to vomit a thin stream of bile onto the lawn. Hank turned as two guards rushed up the steps toward them, their rifles held ready.

'What's going on?' one of them demanded, looking back and forth between Sawyer and Hank.

'Prisoners have escaped,' Hank replied. 'They're running riot in there, killed all the other men.'

Sawyer spat bile from his mouth and turned to glare at the two guards.

'Somebody freed them,' he snarled. 'How did anybody get in here?'

'We didn't see anybody,' the guards uttered, both fingering the triggers of their rifles as they stared at Sawyer. 'Nobody got in.'

Sawyer raged in silence for a moment, then his shoulders sagged slightly and he nodded.

'Fine,' he replied. 'Cover the main gates while we figure out a way to get the prisoners back under control.'

The two guards nodded and turned away.

Sawyer pulled one of the pistols from his belt and fired two shots. Both hit the guards square in the middle of their backs and they fell onto the steps with a sickening crunch of bone and flesh against stone. Sawyer stepped down to their groaning, twitching bodies and fired two more shots into the backs of their heads.

Bethany shot Hank a serious look of concern as Sawyer murdered his own men. Hank watched as Sawyer took a deep breath on the morning air and then turned to him.

'Time to find your ship, captain.'

*

Cody saw the flares spiral down into the amphitheatre from above from within his cage, brilliant arcs of light that showered fearsome sparks into dry, dusty velvet cushions and curtains and across old wooden plinths. Smoke and flame added to the hellish chaos around him.

A blast of gunfire crashed out above the screaming prisoners as they crashed into the guards somewhere outside the amphitheatre. Cody turned and watched as the prisoners in the next cage struggled to unlock their door, screaming for release. Sauri fought his way to the keys and then to the door. Suddenly the cage door burst open and the spilled out like a dirty flood.

'The keys!' one of the trapped prisoners yelled from the side of Cody's cage.

Sauri yanked the keys from the open door and tossed them toward Cody's cage. Hands reached for them in desperation and the prisoners leaped as one to catch them. Cody smashed the weaker prisoners aside as he grasped the keys and rushed for the cage door.

A young man grabbed Cody's arm in desperation, his eyes filled with fear. 'Hide the keys or we'll all be hung on the fences outside! They're coming!'

Cody could hear the rattle of gunfire and the hellish screams of the dead and the dying coming from beyond the hall. Others protested, shouting at Cody to open the door. Cody whirled and shoved the young man away. Another, older guy made a reach for the keys. Cody turned and smashed an elbow into his face. The man's nose crunched flat against his grimacing features as he tumbled back and away from the door.

Cody reached out again, tried another key, and this time the key turned in the lock and the heavy door swung open with his weight. Cody leaped out as shrieking humanity pursued him, legs and arms tumbling in a dirty mass as the prisoners rushed out of the cage and through the amphitheatre.

Cody hurried to Reece's inert form knelt down alongside him. Reece's face was slack, his eyes devoid of life. Blood was no longer flowing from his wounds and Cody knew that his heart had stopped. He reached into Reece's pocket and retrieved the chain link stolen from the Phoenix. Another death filled Cody's chest with an aching vacuum of remorse, but before he could dwell on the loss any further he heard his name being called above the commotion.

'Cody!'

Sauri's voice jerked him from his grief just as he turned and saw half a dozen guards burst into the amphitheatre. The thirty or so prisoners from Cody's cage plunged into them as a rattle of wild gunfire sent bullets ricocheting around the hall. Cody ducked the random bullets zipping through the air, looked up to see prisoners huddling in deep mounds in their cages, cries of fear and alarm as bullets thumped into defenceless bodies as the guards fought for their lives just yards away.

The amphitheatre filled with the screams of mankind at war, the fearful and the enraged competing for dominance.

'Open the damned cages!' Sauri yelled. 'The guards are coming from everywhere!'

Cody leaped to his feet and dashed to the next cage along, shoved a key into the lock and turned it. The door mercifully clicked open on his first attempt and he hurled himself clear as the prisoners exploded from the cage in a flood of screams that joined the Hadean scene behind him.

'No, wait!' Cody yelled.

The prisoners plunged into the mass of bodies and Cody saw Sauri topple as they ploughed into him, trampled by countless panicked feet as the prisoners stampeded toward the exit.

Cody hurried to the next cage in the line and unlocked the door. More prisoners tumbled out toward the exits.

'Where's Maria?!' Cody demanded of them as they ran past him.

Nobody answered or even looked at him as they fled for the exit.

Cody dashed up through the amphitheatre as the prisoners overwhelmed the guards and ripped them to shreds like a pack of wild animals. Cody saw them biting into the still conscious men like zombies from a horror movie, others stamping down on heads that crunched and fractured beneath the frenzied blows.

The mass of prisoners blocked the exit like a singular, ugly organism of writhing limbs and shouting faces. Cody picked up a guard's discarded assault rifle, not even sure of how to work it as the crowd finally burst through the bottlenecked exit and spilled toward the grand staircase.

Cody hesitated as he saw Sauri's body laying among others, trampled and broken. The Inuit stared sightlessly up at the amphitheatre ceiling, his jaw smashed and his chest deformed where his ribs had broken, some poking out against the fabric of his shirt, others no doubt impaling his internal organs.

Cody leaped over the Inuit's body and turned in the opposite direction to the vanishing prisoners. He dashed along the corridor toward the Governor's office, bursting in.

'Maria?!'

Each room was as empty as the last, and in a brief moment he recalled the guards disappearing from the corridors outside the senate chamber. Cody whirled and dashed down the hall as prisoners rushed past him like a pack of wolves down toward the second floor.

Cody leaped down the steps and then looked out through a window at the lawns in front of the senate house. There, he saw Hank Mears running down the steps outside behind Sawyer and three of his militia. Bethany ran close behind them, a child cradled in her arms, dressed in a hooded top against the blustering rain squalls spilling from the turbulent skies. A rush of gratitude and relief swept through Cody, warring with rage that seethed deep inside.

'Maria,' he whispered.

Hank had betrayed them all, but Bethany had stood by him and protected his daughter. Cody gripped the rifle in his hands tighter as he watched Hank flee from the state house.

Thundering footsteps echoed down the corridor from the Great Hall as the prisoners rushed down, and Cody turned and aimed as two guards burst out into the corridor from his right at the bottom of the staircase. Without conscious thought, Cody pulled the rifle into his shoulder and fired twice at the first man, both rounds hitting him hard and knocking him to the ground.

In the commotion Cody saw Charlotte, her hands cuffed before her, break free from the second guard's grasp as he struggled to bring his rifle to bear on Cody. He recognised Scott.

'Don't shoot man!' the guard yelled up at Cody. 'I'm with you! I'm with…'

Cody lowered his rifle but the guard quivered as a bullet struck him high in the chest and he collapsed, his rifle falling from his grasp. Cody turned and saw Charlotte with the dead guard's pistol in her hands and revenge etched into her features.

More footfalls echoed in thunderous rhythm toward them as prisoners poured from the staircase toward the Nurse's Hall, where dozens of armed guards stood in a line with their weapons raised. Cody ducked back out of sight, the rifle pulled close to his chest.

Before Cody could react dozens of prisoners rushed toward the hall and into the line of fire.

'Wait!' Cody yelled. 'Stay here!'

Cody's words were lost in the tumult as the citizens plunged down through the hall and straight into the incoming guards. Cody heard a rattle of panicked gunfire, screams of pain competing with the charging prisoners and then more screams as they plunged en masse into the guards. The body weight of dozens of men, women and children ploughed through the guards and drove them into the floor as hundreds of feet trampled the bodies into the unforgiving marble.

Cody looked at Charlotte.

'We need to find another way,' he said.

Cody led the way down to the Nurse's Corridor, where a frenzied mass of prisoners were smashing the butts of rifles or the soles of boots and shoes into the comatose bodies of the guards laying in their way. Cody could see the bodies rolling with the blows, could see limbs bent at impossible angles and blood pooling like a scarlet lake across the flags.

Dean Crawford

38

Cody looked past the violent scenes to see the Doric Hall filled with a bloodied, writhing mass of groaning and wounded humanity.

'Oh my God,' Charlotte uttered as her hand flew to her mouth.

Large numbers of escaped prisoners were hammering their fists against the main doors, the heavy doors reverberating with the blows. But nearby many were on their knees or slumped against the walls, transfixed by the terrible carnage wrought by Sawyer and his men as they fled the building. Men, women and children lay sprawled on the thick lake of blood seeping across the tiles.

Cody stared at the horrific slaughter, unable to move as he swallowed down a bolus of vomit. He saw several of Sawyer's guards lying dead near the doors, prisoners picking up their rifles and looking at each other. Some of them looked back up the Doric Hall at Cody, who stood with a rifle clasped to his chest.

Cody looked across at Charlotte, who was already backing away.

'You!' shouted one of the armed prisoners. 'Where's that ship of yours?!'

'Come on,' Cody said to Charlotte as he turned. 'Reece said he got in through the east wing.'

'Reece?' Charlotte asked.

'He freed us,' Cody replied, 'but he's gone now.'

'Charlotte!'

The voice came from among the prisoners. Cody looked over his shoulder and saw Jake aiming a rifle at them.

'Don't stop,' Cody urged her. 'Jake left me for dead back there.'

Charlotte hesitated, her features wracked with indecision.

'Charlotte!' Jake yelled. 'He's a murderer!'

Charlotte turned to look at Cody, still holding the pistol in her hand. She looked at him and he returned her gaze.

'They've got Maria,' he said. 'I've got to go.'

Charlotte stared at him. She raised the pistol. Cody snapped the rifle up to point at her before she could take proper aim.

'Drop it,' he snapped.

The sound of the prisoners charged toward them through the Doric Hall. Cody turned and fired a burst of rounds from the rifle. The bullets hit the ceiling amid a spray of marble chips as the running prisoners scattered for cover. Cody turned the rifle back on Charlotte, who dropped the pistol.

What felt like an age passed by, and then Cody turned and ran for the East Wing and prayed that Charlotte would not shoot him in the back.

He ran through the Doric Hall and turned left toward the East Wing.

'Give us your guns!' bellowed the prisoners as they began to pursue him.

Cody ran to the corridor adjoining the hall to the east wing and did not take long to find the shattered window. He knew that it would only take a few moments for one of the other prisoners to break a window or two themselves, and then every one of them would flood out of the state house toward the docks.

Cody opened the door and slipped out. He dashed down the steps toward Beacon Street, leaping over the corpses of two guards sprawled across the steps that he assumed had been shot by Sawyer. One of them had a thick bladed knife attached to his belt and Cody paused and yanked it free. Beside the man he saw a handful of discarded distress flares. On an impulse he grabbed two of them and shoved them in his pockets before he ran on.

He stopped instinctively at the main gates and hesitated there, looked left and right at the bodies strapped to the railings.

'Cody?'

The small voice reached him from the railings and he turned to see Lena strapped to the iron, her long hair lank and her eyes weary with fatigue. Cody dashed across to her and sliced through her bonds, her waif like frame toppling down onto him.

'Jesus,' he whispered in dismay as he held her. 'Are you going to be okay?'

Lena whimpered as he set her gently down, her leg injured where Sawyer's thug had hit her. He sat her down with her back against the wall. 'Where's Maria?' she asked.

'Sawyer's got her, with Bethany,' Cody replied. 'I'm going after her. You're coming too.'

Lena smiled weakly and shook her head.

'Go,' she whispered. 'My leg won't let me run anywhere. Just promise you'll come back for me?'

Cody bit his lip, felt tears form in his eyes once more.

'I don't know if I can promise that,' he replied. 'But if I can, I will.'

She smiled, Cody guessed, at his honesty. 'I know you will. Now go.'

The wind was gusting from the north east, low clouds spilling a fine drizzle that had dampened the sidewalk and street. Bundles of paper and debris tumbled before the wind along the edge of Boston Common. Cody looked up from Lena to see thick clouds of billowing black smoke spilling from the state house's upper floors as the senate chamber burned.

A distant crack of broken glass reached them on the wind. Cody saw two figures emerge on the steps outside the state house's west wing. Jake and Charlotte searched and pointed. Moments later, the main doors thundered as the prisoners within began ramming their way out, the heavy wood splintering under the blows and shouting voices from within echoing out onto the streets.

'Go!' Lena snapped with sudden force.

Cody fled across the street as he heard the main doors split with a deafening crack, the prisoners spilling from within with a ragged cheer behind one of the statues from the Doric Hall as Cody ducked out of sight into a service alley, Jake and Charlotte shouting as they ran in pursuit. Gunshots rang out as Cody sprinted down the alley and out onto an adjoining street. A pair of feral dogs leaped out of Cody's path, growling with their tails between their legs as they loped away.

Cody turned right, heading south east and blinking the fine misty rain out of his eyes as he ran. He heard Charlotte shouting at him from far behind.

'This is insane, Cody! Wait for us!'

Cody kept moving, Maria's image filling his mind as he raced toward the docks. His legs pounded the moss covered asphalt, his heart thundered in his ears and raw fury drove the blood through his veins.

'Cody, wait!'

He looked over his shoulder to see Charlotte falling behind and Jake even further back, his gait faltering as he gave up the chase. Cody cried out in desperation as he saw the prisoners flooding the city street behind Jake, but thoughts of Maria filled his mind and his legs kept pumping of their own accord.

A gunshot cracked the air and Cody saw Jake stagger sideways and collapse against a vehicle as he clutched his shoulder and cried out in pain. Charlotte dodged sideways and hauled him out of the line of fire, tucking in behind a scorched vehicle slumped across the sidewalk as they huddled together, unable to flee any more. Their words flickered accusingly through Cody's mind. *We stick together. Is betrayal your currency now?*

Cody dashed and dodged and fled through the debris and the abandoned cars, hoping that the wind in his ears would deafen him to the terrible screams and cries that echoed in pursuit down the abandoned streets around him.

Ahead, he saw figures moving down by the harbour, running at a slow jog. Cody squinted into the fine drizzle and saw Hank's form towering over Sawyer's, and Bethany between them, Maria in her arms as they followed Sawyer's henchmen toward the docks. Cody slowed as elation flooded his body. He whirled, looking back toward where Charlotte and Jake were crouched. He raised his rifle at the oncoming mass of prisoners and fired three rounds, sending them scattering for cover.

Cody ran back up the street toward Charlotte and Jake.

'Jesus,' Charlotte raged at him as he rushed down alongside them. 'Could you have left it any goddamned later?'

Blood stained Jake's jacket as Charlotte tried to stem the bleeding. Cody peered over the top of the vehicle's hood and saw a man approaching them with a rifle.

Cody aimed and fired at the man, who immediately fled back into cover.

'Stay back!' Cody yelled.

'We just want the guns!' a voice called back.

'Get us out of here on your ship!' shouted another.

Cody shook his head. 'You'd kill us as soon as help us!'

'Why?!' the man yelled. 'You're the only ones who know how to find Eden!'

'Then why are you shooting?'

'To stop you from leaving without us!'

Cody looked down at Jake, who managed a grim smile at him. 'Hurts like hell but no real harm done. Get out of here, both of you.'

Cody sighed and shook his head. 'No, we stick together, right? We get back to the ship, we'll be okay.'

Jake coughed and chuckled. 'No, we don't Cody. This is the end of the line for me. You need to protect your daughter. I'll be fine.'

'They'll kill you!' Cody hissed.

'No, they won't' Charlotte insisted. 'I'm staying here too. It's time to end this and bring back something that people recognise. You were right, Cody. The only way to survive this is to start working together. If the Amish can do it then so can we. Maybe we could even find them. You get aboard the ship with Maria and come back for us if you can convince Hank it's worth it. We'll try to hold the prisoners back, convince them that there's a better way. You go do what you have to do.'

Cody stared at her for a long beat. 'Why?'

Charlotte looked down at Jake again and sighed.

'I don't have anybody else. If the voice you heard was my father's then I know that he's safe. If he abandoned these people then I'll stay in his place and do what he should have done. If it wasn't him in the message you heard then he's probably dead. You have Maria, and she needs you as much as I know you need her. Find her, Cody.' She gripped his jacket and glared up at him. 'Make this worth it and come back for us.'

Cody was unable to find words before Charlotte stood up in plain view of their pursuers and walked out into the street amid the debris tumbling on the wind.

'I'm coming out!' she yelled. 'I just want to talk!'

Jake tugged at Cody's arm. 'Get moving!'

Cody turned to run, but then turned back and reached into his jacket. He pulled out the two flares he had found outside the state house and handed them to Jake along with his pistol.

'One flare for distress, two for success,' Cody said. 'Try to signal the ship. I'll come back for you if I can.'

Cody turned and ran low between the abandoned vehicles until he found another service alley and ducked down it. He listened as he ran but could hear no gunfire from behind him as he sprinted through puddles of slimy water and vaulted over discarded store karts and the carcasses of dogs.

It took him a full ten minutes to reach the shore, where Boston's harbour walk rounded the city's financial district. He ran out onto the quay, searching for a boat as he squinted across the channel.

There, in the distance, he could see the Phoenix at anchor in the choppy waters of the bay. She had been cast off and then the crew must have realised that she was rudderless. Anchoring her again was the only way to prevent a catastrophe.

Cody shielded his eyes with his hands against the fine drizzle and saw a small launch making its way to the Phoenix. Sawyer, Hank and Bethany occupied the launch, Maria huddled in her arms.

Cody turned and ran along the quay, looking for a boat.

He found the body moments later, sprawled on the quay with a pool of blood glistening beneath it. Cody slowed until he stood over the corpse, felt his guts squirm with disbelief.

Saunders stared unblinkingly up into the cold sky. Droplets of rain fell onto his face as though the universe were spitting at him even in death. The asphalt beneath his leg was covered in a sea of blood that had leaked from a deep wound in his thigh. Cody knelt down alongside the old man and closed his eyes for the last time with one hand. He looked up along the quay and saw a small boat rocking on the swells.

Cosy sprinted to the boat and unmoored her, then jumped inside and grabbed the pair of oars lying along her keel. He pushed away from the quay and hoped that he could reach the Phoenix before they jury rigged the rudder.

Behind him, a rush of cries and shouts filled the quay as people ran in pursuit of him and saw for the first time the ship anchored nearby on the choppy water. They flooded the quay and some leapt directly into the cold grey water as others took aim and fired shots at Cody.

Cody ducked and flinched as shots hit the water around him and smacked into the hull of his boat. Cold water seeped in around his feet.

Cody began pulling harder on the oars as some of the escaped prisoners began running toward other parts of the harbour and hauling boats toward the water.

39

Hank rowed most of the way through the choppy water, Sawyer watching him with a pistol aimed lazily at the captain's belly. Sawyer's three men sat between them with Beth. But as they neared the ship Hank knew that he would have to take control of negotiations with his crew.

'Your turn,' he said abruptly and relinquished the oars.

Sawyer smiled faintly and cocked his pistol, aimed it at Hank's head. 'I insist, you row.'

'I'll need to do the talking,' Hank went on. 'They see you holding a gun to me they'll shoot you on sight.'

'Maybe,' Sawyer murmured, 'maybe not. You don't appear to be much of a captain if your crew has mutinied.'

'They haven't sailed away, have they?'

'Shut up!'

The two men stopped talking as Bethany stared at them, her face twisted with restrained fury as she sheltered the child from the rain with her arms. 'Just get us aboard and then get us out of here! You can have your cock fight once we're all safe!'

Sawyer watched Hank for a long moment and then looked at the ship looming nearby. Heads were already appearing over the bulwarks to watch the approaching boat and Hank figured that they were holding weapons. Whichever side Sawyer chose he was outgunned and outnumbered.

Sawyer shoved his pistol down by his side and grabbed the oars from Hank. Hank glanced at Bethany and the child that she held close to her, then stood up in the boat and turned to face the *Phoenix* as they drew alongside.

Several of the watching faces stared down the barrel of rifles at the captain. At their head was the tattooed killer, Seth.

'What the hell do you want?' Seth shouted from the deck.

Hank bellowed back loudly enough to make Bethany flinch beside him.

'I want your ass on a stake, Seth! I'll get me a look at your spine before we sail from here!'

'That so?' Seth yelled. 'Seems to me that this ship no longer wants you as its captain!'

Hank smiled, balancing easily in the boat despite the squalls and choppy waves.

'I think that it's you that doesn't want me as a captain, Seth,' he replied. 'But the ship needs me, and I can see right now that she's going nowhere! You're still anchored against the current, which means something's wrong with the ship.'

The other crew members looked at their new leader. Seth's face twisted with rage.

'Nothin' we can't handle,' he shouted back, and then looked at Hank's companions in the boat. 'Who are these assholes? What happened to Ryan and the others?'

'They ran into some bother,' Hank said, and then turned his attention to the rest of the crew. 'Right now I've got with me the coordinates of Eden and I can have this ship sailing within the hour. Right behind us are several hundred raging lunatics who will burn this ship as soon as they board it. What's it going to be, gentlemen? Your lives in Seth's barely capable hands? Or in mine?'

'Don't listen to him!' Seth yelled at his men. 'We're done chasing his goddamned Eden, it doesn't exist! Almost got all of us killed, chasing his fantasies.'

The crew watched Seth silently, some looking at Hank and then back at their mutinous shipmate. Hank grinned at them.

'You think Seth here's going to do any better? Last I saw, he couldn't walk and talk at the same time.'

Seth raised the rifle in his grasp to point at Hank. Several of the crew whirled and levelled their weapons at Seth. Hank saw the crewman's features twist into implacable fury, and suddenly Seth hurled his unfired weapon across the decks and flung an arm to point at Hank.

'You'd better get us out of this!'

Hank did not dignify him with a reply as Sawyer guided the boat alongside the Phoenix's hull. The crew tossed a rope ladder down, and Hank lifted the child from Bethany as he guided her up the ladder. Hank followed her up, Sawyer behind with his three henchmen.

Hank handed the child back to Bethany and directed her to the wheelhouse for shelter as he turned back to his crew. Seth stood in silence alongside them. Hank decided that he would be best served by dealing with mutinous crewman later. Right now, he needed numbers on his side to protect against Sawyer's henchmen.

'Get the launch up and stowed!' he ordered.

A gunshot froze the crew in motion on the deck as Sawyer fired his pistol into the air. He looked at the crew of the Phoenix. 'New boss in town, boys. You won't be needing your guns!'

Sawyer's three henchmen levelled their shotguns at the crewmen. They crew all looked instinctively at Hank, who nodded once. Slowly, the crew lowered their weapons and stood back. Sawyer's men scooped up the rifles and pistols.

Sawyer jabbed his heavy pistol into Hank's side and sneered up at him.

'How about you find those coordinates and get us out of here?'

Hank did not look down at Sawyer and instead turned to Seth. Give the mutinous crewman responsibility and he might serve once more.

'Why is the ship still at anchor?'

'Rudder's out!' Seth snapped. 'The sea's too rough to send somebody over the side to check it out.'

Hank shook his head. 'If somebody disabled the rudder, don't you think they might also have been unable to do so underwater?'

Seth frowned as Hank turned and strode toward the wheelhouse. He heard Sawyer bellowing orders of his own to his men as he walked.

'Take up positions, stay alert!'

He heard Sawyer following him as he burst into the wheelhouse. Bethany shielded the child from both himself and Sawyer as they hurried in.

Hank looked at the wheel, knelt down and yanked off the steerage cover. In a moment he saw the frayed cable, barely holding up the steerage chain. Hank got to his feet and rushed over to a cabinet, throwing the doors open and grabbing a bunch of plastic cable ties. He hurried back and secured the chain before the weakened cordage failed.

'Will that hold?' Sawyer asked.

Hank shook his head. 'Not a chance against rough seas,' he said. 'Somebody sabotaged this and took the main link and I know we don't have a spare steerage-chain aboard.'

'Then you'd better think fast.'

Hank stood up straight and towered over Sawyer. He saw a flicker of apprehension in the smaller man's eyes as he growled down at him.

'You may have the weapons but aboard this ship I give the orders, because without me nobody's going anywhere. Is that clear?'

Sawyer stood his ground and smirked as he gestured to the broken wheel chain. 'Chop chop, captain.'

Hank turned to Bethany. 'Do you remember the coordinates clearly?'

Bethany nodded, still clutching the child to her.

'Write them down in the log for me then get below to your cabin,' Hank told her.

Bethany crossed the wheelhouse and picked up a pen from the map table. Sawyer moved closer to her, watching as she scribbled a line of figures and then eased her way past, giving him as much space as possible as she climbed down the steps into the 'tween decks. Hank turned to the wheel and gripped the handles.

'We'll need to strip the rudder chain out and lower the position of the wheel to compensate for the missing link,' he said. 'Quicker and safer to do that than to risk going to sea in a blow like this.'

'How long will that take?' Sawyer demanded.

'An hour or two.'

'We don't have that much time. Those prisoners will reach us long before that.'

Hank looked down at him. 'Then *you'd* better think fast because they're your problem. I can't fix this and defend the ship at the same time.'

Sawyer scowled at Hank and cocked the pistol.

'We sail now,' he snapped. 'Stick to the coast and get clear of Boston. We can do the repairs later.'

Hank shook his head. 'We'll beach within minutes, you idiot,' he replied. 'The tides here are already turning against us. The crew missed their chance.'

'You've got engines, right?' Sawyer challenged. 'Use them.'

'They're not powerful enough to fight currents or these winds,' Hank snapped. 'You're not a sailor and you don't know shit about this ship, Sawyer. Get over it and start making yourself useful because if you don't, we'll never leave this city!'

Sawyer was about to reply when Seth burst into the wheelhouse.

'There are boats coming!'

*

Cody rowed like a man possessed, the little boat heaving and plunging on the rolling waves as the wind whipped them up into a frenzy of churning dark water and flying spray. Salt water tainted his lips and a buffeting wind chilled his bones but he hauled on the oars with long, powerful strokes. All the while, dull green water swilled through the belly of his boat as it seeped through the damaged hull.

He was aware of a buzzing in his brain and a dull ache in his belly. He had not slept in forty-eight hours and not eaten for at least eighteen. He forced the weakness from his mind as he pulled on the oars, checking over his shoulder every couple of minutes to ensure he was heading toward the ship.

As he rowed he could see following him on the rolling waves a flotilla of tiny boats, their oars crashing in pursuit. Cries and shouts reached out to be snatched away by the wind that buffeted them, a mutating chorus of anger and desperation, pleas warring with threats. A gunshot snapped on the wind. Cody heard the shot whistle by somewhere out to his right, hopelessly off target.

He glanced over his shoulder again and saw the Phoenix looming large, saw heads appearing at the bulwarks as he heaved and strained on the oars against the rolling waves and the current that now seemed to be trying to pull him away from the ship. His shoulders burned and his thighs ached with each and every stroke, and at the first opportunity he dredged a cry from his laboured lungs.

'I've got the rudder link!'

His cry sounded feeble and pathetic as it was snapped away by the brisk wind and the effort broke the rhythm of his oars. He struggled to get moving again, the boat wallowing on the waves as he dragged the oars through the churning water.

'I can fix the rudder!'

He saw Hank appear at the bulwarks, saw Seth and several of Sawyer's henchmen aiming rifles at him as he screamed at the top of his lungs.

'I've got the rudder link!'

He looked over his shoulder and saw Hank push the muzzles of the weapons down and start frantically waving Cody on. Cody almost burst into tears of relief as he saw the rope ladder hurled from the side of the ship. Waves crashed around him as he brought the boat alongside and heard Hank's voice yelling down at him.

'Let me see it! Let me see the link!'

Exhausted, Cody reached into his jacket pocket and retrieved the steel coupling, held it aloft as he squinted up into the rain at Hank and shouted.

'Is she aboard?'

Hank nodded at him.

Cody struggled to his feet on legs that felt rubbery and weak, ankle deep in cold sea water. He took hold of the ladder and dragged himself up. Hank reached down for him and grabbed him as soon as he was within reach,

Sawyer also taking hold of his drenched shirt as they hauled him over the bulwarks and onto the sodden deck.

Cody handed the link to Hank, who dashed away as Sawyer looked down at Cody, his features almost silhouetted against the bright but cloudy sky above.

'Is she aboard?' Cody asked again, his chest heaving.

'She's aboard,' Sawyer replied, and then walked away.

Cody rolled onto his side and up onto his knees in time to hear a crashing crescendo of gunshots that shuddered through him. Laughter rolled and echoed across the ship's deck as Sawyer's henchmen stood at the side of the ship and fired upon the flotilla of boats trying to reach the Phoenix.

Cody saw bodies topple into the water, saw boats desperately try to turn back against the swells only to be swamped and overwhelmed as the exhausted occupants were swallowed by the waves. Cody sat in silence, oblivious to the salt water spilling down his face as he watched the prisoners drown in the bleak waters.

He stared down at the deck, at his own hands, the palms rubbed raw and spilling blood into the rain that ran in rivulets between the deck planks. He stared transfixed, barely hearing Hank's bellowed order echoing across the deck as he emerged from the wheelhouse.

'Fly topsails and bow anchor away! Set her free!'

Seth and another crewman were already there, and moments later the ship began to drift as the stern anchor was freed and the Phoenix moved slowly in the water. The crew swarmed up the ratlines and freed the top-mast sails, the yards twisted to pick up the force of the nor-easter and allow the Phoenix to tack out of the bay.

'Bow anchor away!'

Seth and a companion sprinted down the damp, slippery decks and hauled on the bow capstan until she came free, the ship's slow forward motion helping to drag the anchor from the seabed.

Cody turned and saw the remaining boats fleeing or upturned and bobbing on the relentless waves as the Phoenix began slowly carving her way out of Boston harbour.

Cody somehow found the strength to stagger across the pitching, rolling deck and into the wheelhouse. He almost fell through the door and slammed it shut behind him against the wind and the rain.

Sawyer and Hank both looked at him.

'Where?' Cody demanded.

'Below decks,' Hank replied.

Cody staggered down into the 'tween deck, the ship's darkness blinding him as he headed for a dull light glowing from one of the cabins. He stumbled and bounced off the walls as he made his weary way to the light and turned into the doorway.

A single lamp burned, casting a warm glow through the tiny berth.

Bethany sat on the bed, the child hugged close to her body and tears falling from her face to drench her shirt as she looked up at Cody. Cody's eyes settled on the small child curled in her lap, a mop of damp brown hair above a pair of fearful blue eyes that stared back at him.

A boy.

Cody felt nothing. Numbness enveloped his body, a strange, alien sensation as he looked at Bethany and the small boy she held close to her shoulder. Her voice reached him from afar, as though from another universe.

'I'm so sorry,' she sobbed. 'There was no time. I had to save my brother. I'm so sorry.'

Cody sagged against the doorframe and then he turned.

He ran, through the darkened corridor and up the steps into the wheelhouse. Past Sawyer and Hank who watched him as he burst out of the wheelhouse and onto the rain sodden deck.

He dashed to the bulwarks at the stern, saw the city skyline looming through the rain squalls, saw the fires raging deep within the city and the black smoke staining the sullen sky as the state house burned in a hellish inferno.

'Maria!'

Cody's scream was snatched away by the wind as he collapsed to his knees, the rain spilling down his face as his heart fluttered dangerously inside his chest. He grabbed the bulwarks and pulled as he prepared for the embrace of the icy water below.

Hands grabbed him and hauled him back from the bulwarks. Cody writhed and screamed, hurled fists and boots at the men trying to pin him down. Spittle flew from his lips and blood from his palms as he saw Hank's big head appear above him.

'It's over, Cody!' Hank bellowed. 'There's nothing else you can do!'

'Go back for her!' Cody screamed. 'Turn the ship around!'

Hank's features registered no apparent emotion. Cody barely saw the blow coming and then his vision starred as the world tilted crazily and he slumped against the bulwarks. Another blow and everything went black.

*

The noise was horrible. So was the smell.

But the warmth was nice.

The huge grey building burned with fearsome flames that snapped and snarled from shattering glass windows and climbed up toward the turbulent grey sky above, coiling up into fascinating towers of oily black smoke.

She watched as they spiralled up in patterns to be snatched away by the blustering winds.

People staggered from the burning building, their clothes aflame in bright colours as they collapsed onto the lawns. The sharp odours made her curl up her nose in disgust and she coughed as a swirling cloud of smoke billowed around her.

Instinctively she turned away from the raging inferno, and with small and uncertain steps she walked down between the main gates of the building and looked at the vast city before her. Huge buildings stood stoically against the surging storm as litter and debris gusted across empty streets.

Voices whispered to her and she turned to see the odd figures hanging from the fences nearby, haggard and limp.

She didn't like the smell or their skull-like faces.

She turned, and across the city she heard distant bangs, like popping noises that attracted her curiosity.

'Daddy?'

Maria Ryan stepped out alone onto the street and walked unsteadily away into the city.

Dean Crawford

40

The wheelhouse was dimly illuminated by a pair of lamps and grey daylight as Hank held the wheel steady against the currents and the wind driving across the endlessly marching waves. The Phoenix was heeling before the wind and the bow rose and fell as she shouldered her way through the crashing seas.

Sawyer steadied himself against one wall, his features drained of colour as he swallowed thickly and wiped sweat from his forehead.

'You should lay down somewhere,' Hank observed.

Sawyer did not reply.

Behind them sat Bethany, her brother sitting next to her on a sea chest strapped to the cabin wall. The child remained silent, apparently in awe of the ship and the men surrounding them.

Sawyer swallowed again, coughed, and then turned to Hank.

'Time to figure out where we're going, don't you think?'

Hank's gaze swivelled sideways to peer at Sawyer. 'There's no rush.'

Sawyer managed a smirk above his discomfort. 'The charts, captain. Don't make a fuss and I won't shoot you both and make a mess.'

Hank glanced at Bethany and the child. 'Get back below decks,' he told them.

Bethany looked at the two men for a moment and then turned and took her brother's hand and led him down into the 'tween decks.

As soon as they had vanished, Hank secured the wheel against the forces acting on the hull and then turned to a cabinet that lined one wall of the wheelhouse. But instead of reaching into the cabinet, he reached up to the panelled ceiling above it and pushed his hands against one of the panels.

The panel rotated upward and inward on concealed hinges, exposing a narrow storage compartment. Hank lifted out a series of bound volumes, each marked with latitudes and longitudes.

'Most impressive,' Sawyer said with a raised eyebrow. 'You haven't trusted your own crew for some time.'

Hank laid the volumes down on the map table and replied as he opened one of them.

'This ship was a training vessel for young sailors, all of them former convicts. The crew kept any weapons aboard ship in that panel, to ensure the kids never knew where they were. The seas are a dangerous place, Sawyer, and you can never be too sure of what you'll encounter.'

Hank laid out the volume he'd selected and glanced at the coordinates Bethany had scribbled onto the log book. He carefully traced the lines on the map as Sawyer stepped alongside him and watched.

42N70W

Hank's finger's drew together from the top and the side of the map and met on a point that clearly matched the coordinates.

Hank stared at the map for a long, silent moment and then looked up at Sawyer.

*

Pain.

It came slowly through the darkness.

Cody opened his eyes as a dull ache throbbed behind them, blinked as he struggled to focus on his surroundings. His mind was empty, devoid of thought. The faint glow from a lantern illuminated the hold around him, pillars and racks and barrels, and a deep rhythmic thump like a giant heartbeat reverberated through the hull as the ship shouldered through the waves.

For a few blissful moments he felt nothing, recalled nothing and was strangely at peace. And then he remembered the hold. The fight with the crewman that had almost cost him his life. A rush of recollections raced through his mind as he sat in the dim light. The observatory at Alert. Bobby Leary's injuries, the rescue. The voyage. Boston. Sawyer. The betrayal.

Maria.

Cody lurched to stand but he was bound to the mainmast by coarse ropes that bit into his skin. He struggled frantically against them.

'They think you're dangerous.'

The voice was small, reaching out for him from somewhere in the shadows. He recognised the voice, felt his chest ache.

'Bethany?'

She stepped into view, balancing against the lethargic roll of the deck that caused the light from the lantern to shift back and forth as though the shadows themselves were swaying with the rolls.

The small boy stood beside her, his hand clasping hers and his eyes watching Cody as though he were something to be feared. No words came to Cody, his mind an empty void through which Bethany's voice echoed, lonely and afraid.

'This is Ben,' she whispered. 'He was in the cage next to Hank and Charlotte's. You couldn't have known, nor could they. I was too scared for him to say anything to anybody, after what happened to you and Maria.'

Cody stared at the deck as every emotion he had ever felt spilled from his body and drained away from him. Memories flashed through his mind: Bethany falling oddly silent after their capture and imprisonment by Sawyer's men, her concern at Hank's possible betrayal.

As soon as she saw Ben she would have known that she must protect her little brother, just as Cody so needed to protect Maria from the brutal world that now surrounded them. But here, at the very last and most dangerous hurdle, Bethany had failed him.

'Why?' he whispered, barely able to speak. 'You could have said something to me. Why?'

Bethany's face was a tear-stained visage of regret and self-loathing.

'I had to make sure Ben was okay first,' she gasped between sobs, her words coming in staccato bursts punctuated by sharp intakes of breath. 'But the prisoners escaped and we got cut off and there was no time for us to reach Maria. There was nothing that I could do.'

Cody stared at her in silence for a long moment. He had fled the building believing Maria to be safe, when in fact in his haste he had abandoned her to her fate yet again. If he had only waited. Searing regret churned like poison through his veins.

'Where did you last see her?'

Bethany managed to choke out the last few words.

'The State House. I think Sawyer put her under guard in one of the ground floor rooms.'

Cody stared down at the deck rolling around them. 'How long have we been at sea?'

'Twenty minutes, maybe a little more.'

Cody shifted position against the mainmast and looked away from her. 'I'm glad you found your brother.'

He let the silence build in the darkness.

'I had no choice,' Bethany said. 'You would have done the same.'

Cody drew back against the mast, away from the light. 'We all had a choice.'

'You would have done the same,' Bethany repeated.

'I doubt that,' came another voice from nearby.

Seth stood at the entrance to the hold, a journal of some kind in his hands and delight on his face. He chuckled as he leafed through the pages, his features demonic in the dim light.

'It seems dear old Jake was keeping a journal about all of you,' Seth said. 'He recorded every little thing that you did, right up until you went ashore.'

Cody stared at the journal. 'What for?'

'Who the hell knows?' Seth chortled. 'But he sure as hell didn't get his sums right, Mister Ryan. It says here that Bethany Rogers was a steadfast and loyal member of the team who could be relied upon and represented the voice of reason.' Seth looked up at her. 'A little off the mark now, don't you think, Miss Rogers?'

'Get out of here,' Cody uttered.

'What?' Seth pleaded. 'You don't want to hear what he wrote about you, Cody?'

'I'm amazed you can read at all,' Bethany said.

Seth flipped through a few pages and stopped at one. 'Ah, listen to this: Doctor Ryan is the one member of the team who seems out of his depth. I suspect that he is more at home in a laboratory surrounding, as his nervous disposition and thinly veiled anxiety make his assignment here an unusual choice, especially for a family man.' Seth grinned at Cody. 'But we all know why now don't we, Doctor Ryan? Sawyer told us about your brother. Tragic.'

Seth snapped the pages of the journal closed and stepped down into the hold until he stood over Cody.

'Not the kind of family man that Jake had in mind, eh?' Seth challenged.

'Because you're an icon of virtue, right?' Bethany spat.

Cody kept his head turned away from her, unable any longer to bear the sound of her voice. Bethany stood in silence for a long moment and then the hatch above them was hauled back. The light from the deck above spilled into the hold as Cody saw Hank and Sawyer glaring down at him.

'You lied!' Sawyer screamed, pointing at Bethany. 'The coordinates point to nothing but empty ocean!'

Cody looked across at Bethany as it all became clear. She had shared the coordinates with Sawyer in order to get away from Boston. He saw the flare of guilt in her eyes as she averted them from his.

Sawyer's voice reached him from the hatch above. 'Where are the coordinates?! Where's your diary?'

Cody felt a curious warmth spread through his body, hot rather than satisfying as he looked up at Sawyer and saw the tremendous rage etched into the psychopath's features. In an instant Cody realised why: Sawyer had just lost everything too. He had lost his fortress, his control, his men and his chances of survival, not to mention his status.

Cody's face twisted of its own accord into a brittle smile.

Sawyer screamed something unintelligible and leaped down into the hold. He landed with a deep thud alongside Cody, the broad sabre he kept at his side shimmering in the light as he drew it and placed it alongside Cody's throat.

'Tell me the real coordinates, now!'

Cody felt the cold steel touch his skin, felt his own pulse threading its way past the blade. The smile spread further across his features and he began to laugh. He couldn't help himself. Mirth wracked his body as he laughed out loud, his own booming chuckles echoing through his mind as he felt himself let go of the grief, of the regret, of the unspeakable fear for Maria that scalded through his veins.

Sawyer stood back from him and looked up at Hank. The captain said nothing, watching as Cody's macabre delight finally subsided. Sawyer turned and the blade flashed up to Bethany's face. Sawyer caught the weapon a bare inch from her neck, his eyes fixed on Cody.

'The coordinates,' he snarled.

Cody did not look at Bethany as he spoke.

'She just killed my little girl,' he managed to rasp, his throat dry. 'I don't care what you do to her. I don't care what any of you do any more. I hope to hell that you sail this ship into a hurricane and spend your last moments listening to each other drowning and being eaten alive by sharks.'

Bethany flinched visibly at his words. Sawyer snarled and raised the sabre high to bring it down upon Bethany. The sound of a pistol being cocked caused him to hesitate and look up at Hank. The captain aimed the pistol at Sawyer and shook his head.

'Not just charts in that compartment, Sawyer,' he snarled. 'Bethany, get out of the hold.'

Bethany cast one last look at Cody and then turned and fled. Cody looked at Sawyer, who stared down at him in a paralysis of volatile emotions, rage alternating with disbelief for space on his features.

'I'll get it out of you, Ryan,' he spat.

'Turn the ship around,' Cody replied, 'and you'll get what you want.'

The captain watched Cody for what felt like an eternity before he spoke.

'We can't go back now and there's no longer any good reason to. By nightfall we'll be well clear of Boston.'

'Then throw me over the side!' Cody yelled. 'Let me go back!'

Sawyer moved to stand over him, the demonic grin plastered across his face.

'Not a chance, my young friend,' he chortled. 'You're staying right there, just for the goddamned hell of it. Unless you tell us where Eden really is.'

'I don't know!' Cody raged. 'Those were the coordinates I wrote down, the ones sent to Alert! I don't know why they're in the goddamned ocean and I don't care anymore! Just cut me loose and let me go back to Boston!'

Sawyer's expression slipped into despair as he realised that Cody was telling the truth.

'If I did all of this for nothing,' he growled, 'then so did you.'

Sawyer stood up and turned his back on Cody.

Cody squirmed against the bonds tying him to the mainmast. Sawyer chuckled in delight as he climbed the steps out of the hold. Cody looked up and saw Hank staring down at him. There was no pity on the captain's features. His voice carried down to Cody softly as the crew closed the hatch.

'She's gone, Cody,' he said.

Cody did not reply. He kept his gaze fixed upon the captain's until the hatch slammed shut above him and only the weak light from the lantern illuminated his world.

Cody sat alone in the darkness for several minutes as he stared blindly into the shadows. Maria's image hovered in his mind's eye, watching him in silence. But for the first time in all of the long months that he had sought her there was no longer any emotion. He laughed, his lonely chuckles echoing through the hold. He had been a fool, such a fool to think that he or Maria could survive in this horrible world, a world stalked by men who were no longer men at all. It would have been better if she had died in the storm, if he had died, or even if his deranged brother had killed them all when he'd had the chance all those months before. Maybe that was what had driven Peter Ryan to the heartless excesses he had achieved, to threaten the weak and the helpless. Maybe the old guy in the cage at the state house had been right: that there was just no sense in caring anymore, because there was nothing left to care for.

He felt as though he had been bled by medieval hardship of his ability to feel anything.

In the darkness he felt the fragments of his remaining compassion and love slip away like phantoms into the night. The pressure on his chest lifted, the seething grief and overpowering helplessness faded like fluke winds as the gentle rolling of the Phoenix through the rough seas outside rocked him in a lullaby.

For a moment his mind remained empty of thought and then he realised that he finally understood. After all these years, he finally realised how it was that people like Sawyer and Hank could be the way that they were. Something inside, something powerful and ancient and harboured by all men had simply vanished, disappeared, become extinct. Their empathy, their tendency to rage when witness to injustice and suffering had simply been switched off. No concerns, no fears, no consequences to their actions.

Life was simply a series of events, flowing one after the other, and as each passed and another presented itself so they forged ahead, uncaring of each other and of themselves.

Cody smiled in the brutal shadows. It did not require rage. It did not require injustice. It did not require loss or pain or hatred. It required nothing, the loss of all that it was to be human and humane. Cody felt a cold ball form somewhere deep inside him.

There was really only one thing left to fight for.

Cody turned his head and saw in the faint light shards of the barrel that had shattered when he had last been in the hold, fighting for his life with Denton. They were scattered near the main mast. Cody shuffled around the mast and used his boot to pin a splinter and drag it across the deck. He then kicked it backwards with his heel into the mast behind him.

He grabbed it in his fingers and turned it, began to work the edge against the rope binding his wrists. He knew that the ropes would have been tied well but he diligently kept the edge of the wood rubbing against them. There was no rush. There was nothing to fear.

There was nothing to care for any longer.

It took twenty minutes, but he felt the rope part and the pressure on his wrists ease as the splinter frayed and then separated the rope. Another five minutes of working his wrists and easing them between the ropes and he finally yanked them free as the cords fell away.

Cody rubbed his sore wrists and looked quietly about the hold, his mind clear and devoid of hubris or doubt. He saw the fragments of the shattered barrel cast into the corner of the hold nearby. A belaying pin in its mount on the wall of the hold. The ropes he had just freed himself from.

The lantern, flickering nearby under the weak power from its battery.

Cody walked across to the barrel and gathered the pieces of wood, then stacked them in the centre of the hold. He turned to the ropes and used wood splinters to shred the rope into fine fibres that he bundled up into a ball and set beside the stack of wood.

He turned and walked across to the lantern and lifted it off the hull. He knelt back down alongside the ball of rope fibres and took off his belt and shirt. Then, carefully, he turned the lantern upside down and plucked the small battery from its base. The hold was plunged into near total darkness but for a sliver of light peeking through gaps in the hatch above him.

Working by touch alone, Cody used the metal edge of the lantern to slice off the battery's plastic sleeve on the negative side, careful to leave half of the sleeve remaining. A strip of paper insulator covered the cap of the battery beneath the sleeve.

He put the battery in his lap, and then reached into the base of the lantern. He fumbled for a few seconds before he felt a wire. Cody yanked the wire out and then used the lantern's metal base to strip the wire back to the copper.

Cody picked up the stripped battery and slipped one end of the wire under the insulator. Then he grabbed a small piece of the shredded rope fibres and wrapped them around the other end of the wire before pressing them against the battery's negative contact.

The battery immediately sent current flowing through the thin wire and Cody saw it glow red hot in the darkness. The small bundle of fibres smouldered with smoke moments later as he touched the hot copper to them. Cody blew gently on the fibres and saw bright embers flare as they burned, and then a flickering flame burst into life within the bundle.

Cody lowered the burning kindling into the stack of wood, then grabbed his discarded shirt and tore off one sleeve. Slowly, he lowered the sleeve into the flames. Steam puffed off the shirt as the dampness boiled off, and then it caught with writhing flames that began to coil their way slowly up the sleeve.

Cody held onto the shirt for as long as he could bear and then draped it across the inside of the stack of wood. Burning from within, the wood began to char as a flickering red light filled the hold and thick smoke boiled upward toward the hatch.

He stood back as the fire began to crackle and spit, then crouched down as the smoke began to fill the hold. He wrapped the remaining strips of shirt around his face, and gripped the belaying pin in his fist as he watched the flames writhe up toward the hatch.

41

Hank stood in the wheelhouse and watched squalls of rain spilling from the turbulent sky above. The sun was peeking through ethereal veils of falling rain, the pale orb hovering motionless as translucent clouds scudded before it.

Bethany sat nearby, her brother on her lap. Hank guessed the kid as maybe seven or eight years old. Bethany held the boy as though he were her own, staring out to sea through the windows and watching the crew toiling out on the rain swept decks.

'He lied,' Sawyer seethed from behind the captain. 'He's hiding something.'

'Not necessarily,' Hank replied. 'He could have written the coordinates down wrong.'

'We'll never be able to figure out where this Eden of yours is now,' Sawyer uttered and smacked his hand down on the map table. 'That idiot just cost us everything.'

Sawyer stormed out of the wheelhouse and slammed the door behind him. Hank watched him stagger unsteadily across the Phoenix's heaving deck to talk to one of his henchmen, who were keeping watch on the crew and struggling to stand upright.

'Do you think Cody's telling the truth?' Bethany asked.

Hank nodded slowly in reply. Fact was, Cody had nothing left to trade and wanted only to return to his daughter, presumably now his only remaining family. He had no reason to lie about the coordinates. That meant that they represented something else. Hank looked down at the map, at the patch of ocean some ten miles off the coast Massachusetts. Not far from Boston. He thought of Charlotte Dennis, of her father's senate career and began to wonder whether the coordinates Cody had recorded might not represent Eden but something entirely different.

The distress beacons they had recovered from the Arctic were still broadcasting as they had been during the entire voyage down from Alert. If somehow Senator Dennis had tried to contact his daughter at Alert, then he would not have wanted her to attempt to get into Boston. He would have known how dangerous the city had become. Thus, he might have sent her coordinates that she would have understood.

Hank glanced over his shoulder to starboard. The city skyline of Boston dominated the horizon beyond the nearby docks. He could still see a haze of black smoke staining the sky above the city, the immense fire being fuelled by the nor-easter howling through the lonely streets.

He turned back to the ship. Drifting veils of sunlight beamed down onto the glittering surface of the ocean, turning the clouds ahead an even darker shade of blue grey. A white gull swooped across the ocean surface, brightly lit by the brief flare of sunlight. Their path looked ominous and threatening, the white gull free to escape it. Hank touched the crucifix at his neck.

'Are you satisfied now?'

Bethany's voice was small but filled with venom that stung Hank with unexpected force.

'I have done nothing more, or less, than you have,' he replied without looking at her.

Bethany's smile was cold, empty. 'Providence, isn't that what you call it? Leaving the fate of others in the hands of a higher power?'

Hank gripped the wheel tighter, but his gaze was drawn to the child sitting just yards from where he guided the

Phoenix away from Boston. Young, defenceless, dependent on adults for his own survival. We were all like that once, Hank realised. Where would he have been without his own parents? Could he have survived alone in this world, as it was now, as a child?

'I can't save everybody,' Hank insisted. 'Any more than you can.'

Bethany might have shaken her head, or maybe it was just rolling with the sway of the deck as the Phoenix heeled gamely into the waves. He couldn't tell, but her voice reached him as though from afar.

'I notice you didn't take the chance of leaving your own escape to providence,' she said. 'Any more than I did.'

Hank's guts twisted and he felt waves of anguish spill over him just as the waves outside crashed over the schooner's bows. An image of a tiny five year-old girl wandering through the streets of Boston, followed by hungry dogs, filled his mind and sent a bolus of puke surging up into his throat.

And then he realised. Senator Dennis would not have left his daughter's survival to Providence any more than Cody had. He would have arranged something. A single word flickered through his mind. *Rendezvous*. Charlotte Dennis's words from months before echoed through his thoughts: *I used to sail with my father out of Cambridge Bay in his yacht.*

Charlotte Dennis knew how to sail. The coordinates were a place to meet.

He saw Sawyer shouting at his men to keep their weapons trained on the crew, and as hate for the psychopath filled his veins he finally made his decision.

'Bethany,' he said. She looked up at him. 'We're going back. Hang on to something.'

Bethany grabbed the side of her seat and her brother as Hank braced himself against the wheel and then drove all of his weight against it as he hurled it to starboard.

The Phoenix heeled over as though she had been struck by a tsunami, the deck pitching and the topsails flagging and cracking like thunder as the wind spilled from them. The entire hull shuddered as though alive and a wall of white spray burst over the bows as she took the full force of the ocean across her hull.

Hank leaped out from behind the wheel and charged the wheelhouse door as the ship pitched wildly over. He burst through it onto the heaving deck as he saw Sawyer and his henchmen tumble like skittles across the sodden planking toward the port bulwarks.

Hank's voice thundered out to his crew, who had balanced instinctively against the wild gyration of the deck.

'Take the ship back!'

Seth turned first, leaning easily into the ship's steeply inclined deck as he turned and drove his forehead into the nearest of Sawyer's henchmen. The man staggered as Seth grabbed his jacket and spun him around to hurl him down the deck toward the ocean.

Hank saw the man fly through the air and smack into the bulwarks with a dull thump, his eyes rolling up into their sockets.

Hank rushed upon another of the shaven-headed freaks as he struggled to his knees and swung his boot fully under the man's jaw. The thug's head snapped back as his neck broke and his teeth flew in a spray of blood across the deck. Hank grabbed at the man's assault rifle and searched for Sawyer.

The psychopath was scrambling across the Phoenix's deck, his pistol in one hand as he aimed at Hank.

A gunshot burst out as Hank dove to his right into the cover of the mainmast, Sawyer's shot splintering wood from the giant mast as it narrowly missed Hank's shoulder. The Phoenix surged in the rolling waves as she pitched back in the opposite direction, searching for her natural point of balance on the tumultuous seas.

Hank stretched out and fired at another of Sawyer's men, hitting him square in the back as he fought with one of the crew. The thug fell to his knees in time for the crewman to swing a fire-axe into his skull and cleave off a huge chunk of bone and brain that skittered like a bloodied crab down the ship's deck.

'Hold your fire!'

Hank heard the screamed command from Seth coming from the bow, and saw the sailor pointing frantically at the mid-ships. For a moment Hank didn't get it, and then suddenly a raw fear surged through his body as he realised what Seth was pointing at.

Smoke was billowing from the main hatch.

'We're on fire!' Seth yelled.

Hank leaped to his feet in horror as he stared at the thick grey smoke boiling from inside the ship. In an instant the fight turned to an uneasy alliance as the new threat presented itself and Sawyer broke from cover with his eyes fixed on the smoke. Hank whirled and pointed at Seth.

'Get on the pumps!' he bellowed. 'Get a line down there, now!'

Hank turned and dashed for the wheelhouse, desperate to regain then wheel before the Phoenix was overcome by the towering seas. He was almost there when he saw Bethany standing behind the wheel, holding the ship steady and turning the bow back into the rolling waves as Sawyer's voice rang out across the decks.

'Kill the bastard! Kill Ryan!'

Hank turned as Sawyer's remaining henchman staggered to his feet from where Seth had hurled him and plunged unsteadily down the main hatch toward the hold.

'No!' Hank yelled. 'Don't open the hatch!'

The henchman ignored him and vanished from sight. Seth staggered to the hoses as the ship's deck levelled out again.

'Get the lines down there!' Hank yelled at Seth. 'Flood that compartment right now!'

Hank shielded his eyes against the stinging smoke that spilled out from the 'tween decks and began enshrouding the ship in a choking fog as Seth dragged the hoses toward the hatch.

*

Cody crouched in the darkness, his face pressed against the deck planking as smoke boiled and writhed in dense banks above his head. His eyes watered and stung, his breath rasping as the thick smoke penetrated his thin veil and poisoned his lungs as though somebody were forcing a heavy, hot blanket into them.

The writhing fire in the centre of the hold had spread, glowing through the thick smoke like a demonic lighthouse. Flames climbed the pillars and crawled like a living creature across the deck, reaching out to scorch anything in its path.

Cody breathed softly, struggling not to cough and fill his lungs further with the lethal black smoke. He was almost certain that he would pass out before Hank's men rushed to contain the blaze when the main hatch suddenly burst open and one of Sawyer's henchmen loomed in the light.

A rush of air swept into the hold and almost instantly the flames soared as though somebody had poured gasoline onto them. The blast of heat and flame sent the thug reeling backwards from the hatch. Cody burst upright from where he crouched and rushed forward, jumped up to grip the edge of the hatch and hauled himself up into the 'tween decks.

Cody leaped to his feet, the belaying pin heavy in his hand as he swung it at the militiaman's face with cold blooded rage.

The heavy iron pin punched through the thug's eye socket and burst his eyeball like a water balloon. The thug screamed in agony and fell to his knees as Cody swung the pin again, this time down on top of the man's exposed skull. The blow shuddered through Cody's arm as the pin stove the skull in with a muted crunch. The thug slumped onto his back, his body twitching as though a live current were surging through his limbs.

Cody dropped the belaying pin and grabbed the dead thug's assault rifle. He turned amid the thick smoke and flames that leapt out of the hold and scorched the ship's timbers around him.

Figures appeared in the light shafting down into the 'tween decks from the main hatch, obscured by the smoke filling the deck. Cody swung the rifle around and aimed at them as he saw Seth and another crewman pulling a thick hose and what looked like a hand pump.

Seth cried out as he saw Cody through the swirling smoke, the killer's tattoos stretched taut across his panicked face.

'Wait up Ryan! The ship's on fire and we're going to...'

Cody squeezed the trigger and saw the muzzle of the rifle spit flames that flickered in the half-light shimmering through the deck. Seth screamed as bullets thumped into his chest. A round smashed into his tattooed face and hurled him backwards into the hull.

Cody held the muzzle of the rifle down and turned even as Seth's shipmate dropped the hose and ran for his life. Bullets hammered into the man's back and sent him sprawling onto his belly on the steps, crying out in pain and fear as his life blood spilled from his body.

Cody screamed as he charged the main hatch and ran up the dying man's back.

*

'Clear the hose!'

Hank yelled orders at his remaining two crewmen as they dropped the other end of the hose into the water alongside the ship and began pumping with all of their might. The hose bulged as it sucked seawater up from the ocean toward the blaze inside the ship.

A rattle of muted gunfire hammered the air from below decks and Sawyer turned to face the smoke billowing out into the blustery air.

'Pump harder!' Hank yelled.

He rushed to the pump to help his men as Sawyer dashed for the main hatch.

'Leave it!' Hank yelled at Sawyer. 'Get on the pump!'

Sawyer ignored Hank as he ran at the hatch and down into the smoky gloom within.

Flames licked and spat all around him, and in an instant Sawyer saw the bodies of Seth and another member of the crew writhing in bullet-ridden agony at the bottom of the steps. Sawyer raised his pistol in the darkness, but was too slow to bring it to bear as from the thick smoke and writhing flames a hideous image rushed toward him.

Stripped to his waist and with his face splattered with blood, Cody Ryan screamed as he ran straight at Sawyer, an assault rifle pulled into his hip. Sawyer swung his pistol around at the muzzle of the rifle as he leaped to one side.

Both weapons discharged, bright muzzle flash illuminating the writhing banks of smoke around them. Cody's shot went wide as Sawyer's pistol smacked into the rifle's muzzle, his own shot going down into the deck as

Cody ploughed into him and sent them both sprawling off the side of the steps to crash down onto the deck.

Sawyer landed hard and the back of his head cracked against the unforgiving planks as his vision starred. He saw Cody land next to him and then spring upon him like a wounded animal, the scientist's features twisted with something so primal that it sent a pulse of terror through Sawyer's guts and for one terrible moment he froze, unable to move.

In that awful moment, he knew that he would die.

Cody landed upon Sawyer's chest and the blows from his bloodied fists crashed against Sawyer's face like cannonballs, his nose collapsing and blood filling his mouth and eyes as Ryan pounded him as though he were trying to bludgeon him through the ship itself and into the ocean beyond. Flames roared and felt hot against his skin, blood spilled around his face and felt wet beneath his hair.

Sawyer reached blindly down to his belt, hauled out his sabre and swung it at Ryan.

The blade sliced into Ryan's flank and wedged against his ribs, but to Sawyer's horror Ryan's screams did not cease and he simply grabbed the silvery blade and wrenched it from Sawyer's weakened grip, blood from his fingers spilling down the bright steel. Sawyer, short of breath, numb and barely able to see, saw the ship vanish as it was replaced with a flash of bright metal and then a pair of eyes that glared down into his with a fearsome, incomparable fury.

Sawyer felt his bowels spill beneath him as he bore witness to something he had never seen before in the eyes of a man, and then white pain ripped across his throat as his own blade scythed into his flesh, hot fluid spilling across his chest and neck.

Sawyer gagged and squirmed as he felt the life drain from his body, saw Ryan laughing amid the smoke and flames as he sawed the wicked blade back and forth across Sawyer's neck.

Then the blackness overtook him.

*

'It's not working!'

Hank pounded down on the pump with all of his might as the smoke poured from the hold but he could already tell it was useless. The entire hold was aflame, smoke appearing now from the stern as it spread aft.

Hank leaped up from the pump.

'Lower a boat!' he shouted, barely able to believe what he was ordering.

The Phoenix was lost.

His two remaining crewmen dashed to the side of the ship and began frantically working the winch. Hank watched as the winch lifted the launch once more from the decks and swung it out over the side, the whole ship now enshrouded in smoke as the entire world took on shades of grey, the sun above a glowing orb as the thick smoke competed with the scudding clouds to blot out the rest of a lonely, abandoned world.

Hank dashed to the wheelhouse and grabbed Bethany and the child, hurrying them down to the boat as it crashed into the water below.

'Jump!' he yelled at her as he snatched the boy from her arms.

Bethany clambered over the side and jumped into the boat below as the crew held the boat on the winch just above the waves. Hank grabbed the child by the wrists and swung him over the bulwarks. Bethany reached up as Hank let her brother go and she caught him, tumbling backwards into the swaying boat. Hank tossed his pistol down to Bethany, then he reached up and yanked hard on the winch release lever. The boat crashed down into the churning water.

'Get out of here!' he yelled. 'We'll follow!'

Hank turned to his men.

'Grab the weapons and then get the other boat into the water! I'll get the charts.'

The two men whirled and dashed across the deck. Hank turned to follow them, but then froze as something arced out of the ship's hold amid the flames and smoke and landed with a thud in the centre of the deck.

Both crewmen stopped in their tracks as they looked down. The face of Sawyer stared back up at them, his features locked in a grim rictus of agony and his neck ending in a ragged mess of blood and bone.

A hellish scream came from the 'tween decks. Hank saw Ryan burst from the ship's interior as flames snapped and snarled from the edges of the main hatch. His torso was bare and splattered with blood and dirt as he ran up onto the deck and opened fire. The hail of bullets sliced the remaining two crewmen down as they screamed for mercy, their bodies twitching as they fell onto the deck.

As if in slow motion Hank saw Cody turn to look at him. Every inch of the man he had known seemed gone, replaced by something cruel and feral that looked upon Hank as though he were prey. Hank reached for his gun and then realised that he had just tossed it to Bethany.

He stared at Cody as the ship burned around them. Flames crawled up the mainmast from the hatch where the ship's interior was now an inferno of heat as pillars of smoke billowed up the outside of the hull. The buffeting winds fanned the flames, gusting down through the hatch as the schooner was consumed from the inside out.

Cody stalked closer, his chest heaving and the assault rifle held ready as he glared at the captain.

'We were going back, Cody!' Hank yelled above the wind and the roaring flames. 'We were turning back for you! That's why she heeled over!'

Cody did not reply, stopping just out of Hank's reach. Hank looked into Cody's eyes and saw nothing there, no recognition, no remorse. Nothing.

'This isn't you, Cody!' Hank said. 'This isn't you!'

A smile that looked more like a snarl curled from Cody's lip as he replied.

'No, it's you,' he said. 'It's you, captain.'

Hank swallowed thickly. 'You were right. I turned back for your daughter. I couldn't leave without trying. Drop the gun Cody, we're going back! You said that we survive best if we cooperate, right? Then cooperate now, and we can put this all right!'

Cody seemed to consider the captain's words for a moment before he replied.

'I am putting it right.'

The rifle seemed to fire in slow motion, a spurt of flame from its muzzle. Hank felt the impacts of the bullets as they slammed into his belly, chest and shoulder but there was no pain. He saw the world flip as he was hurled backwards over the bulwarks and plunged into the ocean below as everything turned black and silent.

42

Cody let the rifle fall from his grasp to clatter to the deck at his feet.

He staggered to the bulwarks and looked out over the ocean as smoke spilled around him to choke the air.

The Phoenix had turned about, unguided and wallowing at the mercy of the waves as she faced back toward the shore and the city skyline. Cody rested his hands against the bulwarks, utterly exhausted as he squinted through the smoke and saw a lone boat struggling through the waves.

He could make out Bethany and her brother in the boat. Bethany was rowing slowly away from the stricken schooner, but she was still close enough for him to see the horror on her face as she looked at him. The city behind her was bathed in alternate patches of shadow and light from the sunbeams sweeping down from the turbulent skies, the buildings at once crouched in darkness and shimmering in the light.

The boat churned across the bay, dipping and vanishing behind one wave only to appear over the next as Bethany rowed away from the Phoenix and Cody.

Cody turned away and looked at the ship around him. Flames seared along the bulwarks and had climbed the rigging. The sails were burning, trailing curtains of rippling black smoke. Flames burst from the wheelhouse windows as glass shattered, whorls of fire spiralling out into the wind like flaming dust devils, and a howling reverberated through the ship as though she were screaming in her death throes as the winds soared through her hold.

The ship was his, and like him, she was doomed.

Cody staggered to the centre of the deck, close to where snakes of flame embraced the main mast. Tears spilled down his cheeks as he thought of his beloved Maria and bore the burden of the cruel and uncaring hand of fate that had taken so much from him and from every human being who had ever lived.

A dull rending sound grew in intensity as the ship's keel began to fail somewhere deep in the hold. The heat seared Cody's skin, seemed to crackle through his hair as the smoke obscured his vision and enveloped the ship in a deadly, choking embrace.

Cody closed his eyes and tried to let the flames and the smoke consume him, but he could not. The heat and the pain and the danger were too great to ignore and he cried out in frustration as he turned and ran at the bulwarks. His hands touched flame and he saw his skin burn and slough away from his palms. Just like Sawyer's, he realised absent-mindedly, as he vaulted over the side of the burning ship and plunged into the cold water below.

The heat vanished, bitter cold scalding his skin instead as he sank beneath the tumultuous waves. Cody struggled for the surface, broke through amid spray and choking salt water as he turned and saw the ship looming over him like an immense funeral pyre, black smoke churning up to stain the sky above.

A chunk of yard arm crashed down into the ocean close by and Cody struck out for it, wrapping his arms around the charred wood that singed the hairs on his skin. He wrapped one leg over the broad beamed yard and lay his head down against it, watched as the current pulled him away from the stricken schooner's fearsome demise.

The waves crashed over the Phoenix as her stern began to sink into the water, great clouds of smoke and steam billowing up into the gusting skies as she was consumed by the ocean. The once proud, beautiful ship finally vanished into a swirling maelstrom of water and smouldering debris.

Exhaustion overwhelmed Cody, his every limb as heavy as all the earth and dragging in the cold water as he watched the bowsprit of the schooner descend almost gracefully into the darkness of the deep. Blood spilled from the deep wound in his side but there was no pain, only a creeping lethargy as his life began to slowly drain away into the ocean.

Cody felt himself rising and falling on the waves as the powerful currents dragged him out of the bay and into deeper water. The smoke from the Phoenix's burning hull was broken and smeared away by the powerful winds, and as it cleared from Cody's vision he saw something out on the docks beyond the flotsam of debris surrounding him.

He tried to lift his head off the yard arm, but it was too heavy. He blinked seawater from his eyes as he tried to focus on the distant glow that competed with the glinting of windows across Boston's skyline.

The crest of a wave lifted him briefly higher and he finally focused on a pair of lights shimmering out on the edge of the docks. He could see Bethany's boat heading toward the lights, almost there now, far away across the endlessly rolling waves.

The two lights drifted back and forth, thin trails of blue smoke whipped away from them as they moved, and he remembered his own command from what felt like hours before: *one light for distress and two for success.* Cody somehow found the strength to lift his head and for a brief moment he knew he was looking at Jake McDermott, his arms frantically waving the flares. Charlotte Dennis stood next to him, and next to her was a girl with long locks standing with a child held at her hip, a mop of blonde hair fluttering in the wind as she clung to Lena's side.

A rush of delight swamped Cody's body and tears flooded from his eyes once again as he saw Maria. He heard his own ragged cry of unbridled joy snatched away by the buffeting gale. There seemed to be other people standing on the dock, maybe prisoners who had not tried to reach the Phoenix. Charlotte and Jake had come through, one last time.

Cody's joy briefly warmed him, but the cold and the exhaustion soon made it feel muted and distant. He tried to turn the yard arm about and aim for the docks, but already the rolling waves blocked his view of them and he could no longer feel his arms. His exhaustion was complete, his limbs leaden and even his eyes felt as heavy as all the earth.

His lips briefly formed his daughter's name as he saw the distant crowd of survivors turn away from the Phoenix's fiery demise and walk slowly away until he could see them no more.

The wind buffeted his naked torso, splashed cold water across his back until he could not feel his skin and his eyes drooped wearily. Salty ocean water splashed his face and ran in rivulets through his hair and he felt his teeth chattering and his lips trembling, but he had not the strength to even shiver.

Slowly, inexorably, he watched the skyline of Boston shrink away from him, haunted by a bitter sweet melancholy for all that he had done and all that he had lost.

The buffeting winds turned to blue skies wreathed in tattered ribbons of high white cloud. Cody felt his senses slipping away as he drifted. Immeasurable chunks of time passed in silence, awareness of his existence interspersed with darkness and oblivion. His eyes opened sometimes to see the distant, perfectly straight horizon of endless ocean surrounding him. He heard the water lapping against the yard on which he slumped, too weak to climb off it and end his suffering.

The empty ocean, devoid of life, was as lonely as the abandoned cities left smouldering across the world. The surface of the ocean was as smooth as glass, reflecting the scattered clouds above. Cody welcomed the surcease of death. Whatever he had been before, whoever he had been before, was long gone.

Somewhere, at some time upon the open ocean, Cody became aware of the waves swelling beneath him as though the ocean was opening up to receive him at last. The horizon tilted as waves crashed over him and tossed the yard arm about and through bleary eyes he glimpsed what appeared to be a gigantic black whale surfacing directly beneath him. He slid from the yard arm into the bleak water and felt something hard and cold thump into his battered body as his consciousness began to slip away.

Cody Ryan closed his eyes, for there was no more left to do.

Dean Crawford

EDEN

It will never be measured, how many have fallen.

I feel a deep regret beyond mere words to even wonder at how many died to protect their children, their wives, their husbands or their parents. Our best estimates suggest that at least five billion people have died since the Great Darkness that so irrevocably altered our lives and ended those of so many whose names will forever be lost to history. If only I had possessed the strength, inside, to do more for them.

We chose to abandon them, to abandon our own. We fled, believing that there was nothing that we could, or should, do. In the moment, in those terrible few hours before western civilisation ceased to exist, we made many decisions that now haunt our days and our nights. Our cowardice has been laid bare for all to see, grovelling in the shadow of countless acts of great courage for which no survivors bear witness.

But we are not alone. There are survivors out there, and as long as there is strength in my body and blood in my veins I shall lead us out into the world and put right what has been left so very wrong. I shall not rest until we have made every endeavour to redeem ourselves, until I too have redeemed myself. And this lone man we have found, floating barely alive in a vast ocean, shall be the first. He cannot have come to be here alone. There may be others whom he cares for.

We will find them.

Senator Larry Dennis, USS Louisiana.

ABOUT THE AUTHOR

Dean Crawford is the best-selling author of the *Ethan Warner* series of thrillers and many independent novels. Published internationally, his books have sold hundreds of thousands of copies and earned the interest of major Hollywood production studios.

www.deancrawfordbooks.com

Printed in Great Britain
by Amazon.co.uk, Ltd
Marston Gate.